C000146758

CRUISE SHIP ART THEFT

STUART ST PAUL

EDITION updated 23 Apr 2121
Copyright © 2020 Stuart St Paul
All rights reserved.
DORIS CRUISE BOOKS
Northwood, England.

ISBN: 9798630583253

This is book four in the CSCI (Cruise Ship Crime Investigators) series, although they can all be read as stand-alone books. With the improved ending, this is the second draft. The improvement came from editors Laura Aikman's as always honest notes, and she felt the female agents were a little lost in the old ending. That was certainly an error and the all the script loops are resolved in this version.

****

All ships are totally multicultural, with a wide mix of nationalities and various languages as well as varied versions of English spoken below decks. The narrative of these books and the colloquialisms used are probably equally as confused. Most ships are filled with art.

This is totally a work of fiction. Any references to ships, locations and characters are invented with one exception, Manuel Martinez, a magician and a great friend. He gave us permission to use his character name, and a magician is tracked in Laundry Wars the novel before this and also in this book, where he positively aids the plot. Also there maybe references to Doris Visits, but we are part of that.

Other characters and places may take snapshots from reality in order to create and give the book an authentic sense of cruising, albeit a side of cruising rarely seen by the guest. The crimes are exaggerated and dramatized. All names, references, characters, ships and incidents are a product of the author's wild imagination.

Almost nothing is real. But just because it never happened, it doesn't mean to say it isn't true.

Stuart St Paul

1 – DEAD CITY

The Cruise Ship Crime Investigators' office, next to Wild Mary's Diner in Charlotte City, has contributed no beneficial effect to the complex. They are the only active unit in the otherwise dead, ex-commercial hub. Upturned shopping trolleys have replaced parked cars. If it were a disguise they were after, they have it. The days of Charlotte 'dead' City attempting to entice vendors in any shape or form are over. The blacked-out windows of their unit, with the initials CSCI in a different shade of charcoal is very artistic and they can thank Macey for that. The US Letter sheet stuck to their door saying 'go next door' is not the work of the artist Macey. That is the work of Wild Mary.

Wild Mary's is the all-day diner next door, where Wild Mary, a forceful African American woman, calls the shots and Stan does the cooking in his lazy-jazzed style. The trilby hat he always wears looks as old as him. His laughter is infectious, her's is not. Though technically a part of Charlotte City, Wild Mary's can deny association because it is on the corner facing out to the main road. Its rear wall, cupboards and toilets may adjoin the sidewall of the CSCI unit, but they have their own parking out front. Wild Mary's could use either, but never gets that busy.

Macey, like the other two students whom Mary has quasi adopted, not only works there, eats there, and studies there, but is also kept in line and on the straight and narrow by Wild Mary, a force to be reckoned with.

Cruise Ship Crime Investigators moving next door has changed each one of their lives in a major way. It started when one of the two CSCI team put a nail into the adjoining wall and burst a pipe, unknowingly flooding Mary's store cupboard and adjacent toilets. Mary took a large hammer and demolished the wall until she found the pipe and could fix it. The wall has never been put back. The door to her cupboard goes through to the major control centre which now has state-of-the-art computer power run by Dwight. He is a large African American man who lost his legs and shortly after, his wife, Ruby. An ex-military man, he is now a very good, though self-taught, computer data analyst and researcher. He works with the IT student Croc from Wild Mary's next door. Young Croc was a top hacker until Mary had to bail him out of police custody then get him a lawyer. Stan's assistant burger-flipper is now an important member of an advanced investigators' unit which deals with international cruise crime. Croc can get into anything, from phones to company systems and he loves the unofficial job at CSCI.

The cupboard door between the restaurant and the Crime Investigation centre is always closed unless something is going on, and for days the intercom between the two units has been silent. Dwight has been chasing money billed as extras for what they call the 'laundry wars' job. That certainly was not as trivial as it sounds, and it would have got nasty and maybe closed them down if it hadn't been for their new female investigators saving the day. Bedriška a firmly spoken Russian, and Prisha a small and polite Indian, were both key players in the eventual outcome. Today, the same as yesterday, the only two in CSCI HQ are Dwight and 'Croc the tech'. Stan is cleaning his grill following the breakfast rush, after which, he does his own brunch. The few customers who have long since finished their meals would sit there all day if Wild Mary let them.

Macey, a local from down town Miami, is in her painting-dungarees, hair in a bun, brushes pushed into it at every angle possible. She sits at her easel, making beauty out of the deep decaying urban car park. Balloons are sketched as foreground earpieces. Macey's paintings have to say something, she is harsh, political, and she sees things others don't. Her painted images of the Wild Mary's Diner have adorned the walls for years. But despite it being her own private gallery, she has only sold one.

Mary is taking 'happy birthday' balloons down from all over the restaurant.

"I went to all this trouble and none of you seemed impressed," Mary mutters, though everyone can hear.

"We're not kids anymore, birthdays ain't important," Macey explains. Her accent can wander from adapting to Stan and Mary's southern drawl, to the faster Miami slang the Cubans use. Or she can normal and college like if she has too; it depends who she is with.

"Let me tell you, birthdays are good for you," Stan says, breaking his quiet. Stan was born in Muscogee with a lineage harking back to the dark days of chattel slavery. While his brothers and sisters remained there to fight for their rights to be recognised as descendants of Black tribes from the Creek, he decided to leave Oklahoma. With little more than his ability to sing and shuffle his shoes, he joined a show in Pensacola, which is where he met Mary.

"Why would that be, Stan?" Mary demands.

"The more you have, the longer you live."

Macey laughs, Mary is not impressed. She has more than a handful of balloons.

"You gonna help, or just paint them, girl," Wild Mary barks at her.

Macey ignores her. Her attempt to paint a happy birthday scene of balloons against the backdrop of upturned trolleys is laid on a table next to her and she drops another sheet down and sits back waiting for inspiration.

For her, CSCI has stretched her artistic horizons and given her the confidence to show Mary her nastier images. The balloons seem too nice for her current mindset. She has always enjoyed painting images that play with light, and her incredible portrait of Dwight has her thinking of portraits. He is very well captured, deep in thought and lit by the computer. His face is full of different emotions and concerns. It is her current prized work, and it hangs above the jukebox. That painting is sold. Dwight bought it and as he has no time to enjoy it in his apartment, he has loaned it back to Wild Mary's 'Gallery'.

"Maybe a drifter at the window looking in and the grill foreground," Macey suggests.

"That mean I'm in it, Mace?" Stan asks.

"You ain't in nothing, Stan," Mary barks.

The military banter sometimes spars with the dry humour of Downtown Miami when the investigators are in.

"You ain't in nothing but trouble," Mary adds privately to him.

"What?" Stan whispers.

"You never worried?"

"'Bout what, Mary?"

"We now got an investigator business next door. One day they gonna find out way too much about us. Things long forgotten."

"What's them, Mary?"

"You ain't funny, Stan. Ain't funny."

Stan is left, genuinely puzzled.

Mary studies her order book, determined not to look up. Stan has annoyed her.

"Someone order a takeaway?" Macey shouts.

"Ain't no one ever ordered no 'take-away' from here. We don't sell food-to-go, never have done, never will do. Someone want a takeaway, they can just eat their food at their own home!" Mary blurts out.

"That's kind of how it works," Macey says with sarcasm.

"You been learning that English subtext stuff from Mr Commander Kieron, 'I'm British' Philips?"

"Definitely ain't one of them 'Deliver-to-you vans' pulled up outside. And it sure ain't come to collect no takeaway."

"They got lost," Mary says, refusing to take an interest. Mary pops a sinking balloon. Stan jumps.

"Me thought he was shooting."

"Only one ever gonna shoot you is me. Now get rid of the rubbish," she says, pushing him the limp balloons.

"Someone has to do the ordering; someone needs to work in this place." Mary bends further, head hidden over her order book.

"We need tomatoes, Mary," he says.

"Stan, I'm concentrating," Mary says not wanting his input. Working out her vegetable order is the only time she wears her glasses. It is the time her anger is focussed on suppliers who, far too often seem unable to find green tomatoes. Fried green tomatoes is her signature dish. Stan flips a steak on the clean grill.

Mary looks up and sees the long, stretched, classy limousine outside and looks down again trying hard not be impressed.

"They sure got lost," Macey suggests, walking to the window. "That limo ain't the kind that gets hired for a posh kid's ball. That's super classy. Spells money."

"They come in here, I'll serve them the same seven-dollar breakfast," Wild Mary says.

"Don't think you'll need to worry. No suited-up man ever eaten in here," Macey jokes.

"What you implying girl? More English subtext?"

"Looks like they is developers. 'bout time someone knocked this place down and built something useful."

"What's more useful than a diner serving good food?"

"Let me see, shopping mall, bowling, and a movie theatre. They'd have to re-locate us," Macey says, turning to Wild Mary. "You want me to carry on?"

"They ain't knocking my diner down, are they Stan?" Mary asks, refusing to look up.

"Whatever you say, Mary, but not every dude gonna do what you tell 'em," Stan says with his usual rhythm and head nodding. He looks out of the window and frowns. "Reckon he's mafia, and he's packing."

"He ain't got a gun under that suit, look at the cut," Macey says.

"Well the driver be packing," Stan says. "They mean business, girl."

2 - STRANGER

Miami-1035hrs

"He ain't demolition man. They be turning over the bank on the other corner. They want them safe deposit boxes with who knows what inside," Mary says, still taking no interest.

Macey watches the driver get out next and walk around the car. He walks like a ballroom dancer; toes straight, heels planted.

"Drivers got one smart suit, and look at the man's shoes," Macey says excitedly.

"I seen shoes, don't need no reminder what they look like. If I do, I'll look at Stan's," Mary says, head down.

Macey looks for the passenger's shoes.

"Well bend me and spank me."

"What was that girl? You go and wash your mouth out," Mary fires curtly.

"The main guy is a million dollars, suit's crisp as five of them 'Michelin Stars' you ain't got."

"Stars and stripes are only stars I need."

"They're Louis Vuitton Manhattan Richelieu shoes."

"Shoes is shoes."

"No, Mary, they are way over ten-thousand dollars, pure alligator skin."

"Why he call them Manhattan? Crocodile skin should be Miami."

"He mafia all right," Stan says.

"He want the bank," Mary confirms, picking up her counter-phone still bent over her order.

"Nope, he coming here."

"He must make a lot of money delivering takeout food, but he ain't getting my business, eh Stan?" she says, phone to ear waiting for an answer.

Stan looks back at the griddle. He flips his steak.

"Oh hi, it be Wild Mary," she says into her phone. "You got me any firm-ripe green tomatoes yet?" She waits for an answer. "No! Then you ain't getting the rest of my order!" Mary hangs up.

"That's my prince. I knew he'd come for me," Macey swoons.

Mary looks up for the first time. The three of them are statue-like watching the man and his driver eye-check from the CSCI office next door then look around the horseshoe of dead units.

"I reckon it's one of them, fancy food critics," Stan says. A smoke cloud rises behind him. He flips the meat and waves the air with his spatula.

The man outside walks back towards the diner.

"Told you, Mary, I had a vision this morning. A vision I was gonna be saved."

"You save that vision and paint it later girl, coz he's heard about my famous tomatoes," Mary says, straightening her clothes.

"You got enough left, Stan?"

"Yes, boss, and he about to meet the man dat cooks 'em," Stan says, beaming the way he often does.

"Pair of you, zip it."

All three look at the spring above the door, rocking the bell back and forth. They must have seen it a thousand times before, but not when time stood still. The man glides in and they are spellbound.

"Good afternoon, ladies," the man in the sharp suit and million-dollar shoes says.

Macey spins her easel around and starts to sketch the man's shoes. Just his shoes; there is less than an inch of his pants.

Stan shuffles, almost squaring up to dance. He doffs the old hat that is rarely off his head and throws it down like a busker. Realising what he has done, he nervously lifts his hand to say hi, even though the man only addressed the ladies.

"Sir," the man says, addressing Stan.

The man looks around at the diner and the jukebox catches his eye.

"Still takes nickels, dimes or quarters," Mary says.

Macey and Stan both dress her down with their eyes and she knows she said the wrong thing. She wafts her pinafore and visually suggests they not worry. Macey moves past a few tables nearer the small dance floor, carrying her pad. She pencils in the reflection of the jukebox in the shine of the desaturated floor and on his shoes.

"It's a Wurlitzer-Twelve-Fifty," Macey says.

"I collect old jukeboxes. But love to see them in classic working environments," he says.

He is not looking at the jukebox. Mary realises he has never looked at the jukebox, which worries her. He is looking at the painting above it and he doesn't move from his long, hard study. It is Macey's oil painting of Dwight, the land-boss of CSCI.

"There he is, the man I've been searching for," the stranger says.

Dwight has had a shady past, of which he has revealed little. The two ex-military types that complete the male side of CSCI are the same. This could be one of his skeletons come out of his closet. Mary hits the intercom, then silences her speaker.

"Are you gonna order, or just look at that great painting above my environmental jukebox?" Mary says, to give Dwight a heads-up next door.

The man turns slowly.

"I'll have the house speciality. What is it, chef?"

"Ain't no one ever called me a chef before," Stan chuckles, looking to the rest of his team who fail to respond to his joy.

"Fried green tomatoes," Mary is quick to add.

"That sounds great as I prefer not to eat meat."

"It comes with egg, bacon, sausage and hash browns."

"Let's jump the bacon and sausage. What's your name?"

"Costs the same," Mary is fast to add.

"That's fine. What's your name, chef?"

"Stan, sir. Chef Stan," he replies, having a great time with the title.

"Wild Mary they call me, same as above the door," she butts in.

"You have a great gallery, Mary?"

"Yeah, you wanna look at the menu? That's the art they all comes to look at."

The man stays by the painting.

"I'll take coffee too."

Dwight wheels in through the black partition door attracting everyone's attention. Croc is a few paces behind him.

Mary leans and mouths a question to Dwight. 'Do you know him'?

Dwight shakes his head; he has no idea.

"Is the painting for sale?"

"Sure is," Mary replies.

"No, it ain't," Dwight adds quickly. "That's mine. And I'll have coffee too, Mary. It's break-time," Dwight says, with a power-grin.

"The man in the painting," the stranger says pointedly at Dwight. He has a huge smile as if he has found a man that owes him money. "How about ten thousand dollars, cash, today," the man says.

"That'll do just fine," Mary says, holding her hand out.

"No, I like that painting. Macey did it for me," Dwight says.

"What if I simply took the painting?" the stranger asks.

Croc raises a long automatic gun that he was hiding down behind Dwight's chair.

"I'd shoot your ass," he says.

"What if I took it and you never knew I'd got it?"

"You one of them magicians, like Generator?" Mary asks. "Throw a few cards at the window and try and impress me."

"What if, I'd already taken the painting and you didn't know?"

"I still shoot your ass," Croc says.

3 – THE PRICE OF ART

Miami-1040hrs

Macey is annoyed that everyone is trying to trade the work she painted, even wanting to steal it, and she has not been asked. She stomps up, completely fearless, and stands next to the man. She only needs to glance at the painting.

"That my painting and it's still there."

"What if I swapped it for a forgery? You'd never know?"

Macey gets close and studies her work.

"I know. I know my paintings."

"But do you?" the stranger asks.

"Don't need no fine art degree to tell my own painting."

"Mace, stand yourself back. I ain't a good shot; so I got this tool on spray," Croc says.

Macey backs off and Mary gets involved again.

"You watch my decor, Croc! And my windows!"

Dwight takes the gun and switches it to single shot. Macey puts her hands on her hips, her head tilts in a cocky street stance. She has nothing to lose and she knows how to go head to head, even if she is the shyest of the three students Mary 'employs'.

"Twenty-five-grand."

"Done," the man says.

"No," Dwight says, holding the gun.

"What you mean, no? I painted it to sell," Macey is quick to add indignantly.

"And I already bought it!"

"But not for that much," Macey says.

"Look, it's in my gallery!" Mary says.

The man looks at Macey's painting of the 'Parking Area with Balloons'.

"Your birthday?"

"It all our birthday," Croc says.

"Would you like to sit at a table, sir? Stan asks. "Or you gonna keep me company here at the counter?"

"How could I resist such an offer? 'Chef's Table' is a privilege that normally costs a lot of money."

The man walks forward, sits at the counter, and tastes his breakfast tomatoes.

"I didn't mean to start an argument," he says.

"You like them? They a piece of real art," Mary says. "You want to make me an offer?"

"Thirty thousand dollars."

Dwight is both puzzled and confused.

"Mary, Stan's fried green tomatoes are excellent, I will discuss your menu with you later. But, now, what we have here is an art auction. Macey, you officially have a piece of art in an auction, at a gallery," the man glees at her.

Macey stands up and walks over to join them.

"Does that mean I gonna be rich?"

"From this? Sadly, I think not," the man says. "You already sold the painting."

"Plus, it's in my gallery," Mary insists.

"Diner!" Macey says.

"Let me try and deal with this. I would like the painting, and luckily, I have enough money to solve any argument. But, technically Macey, if you are the artist, once you sell, that is all you get. Even if the work eventually sells for millions."

"That's not fair!"

"But you have the same fee even if the painting is worthless, and the price goes down. What is fair is: your value as an artist goes up. You will sell more paintings for a much higher fee. I can help you."

"So how about my gallery?"

"Wild Mary, or can I call you Mary?"

Mary raises eyebrows at him.

"If you are selling new paintings from your artist, you get the share you agree with the artist."

"How much is that share I get?"

"It can be as low as 5% if the artist is famous and much more if they are not."

"So, the money is all mine," Dwight says.

"Unless Mary takes a sales commission as it was sold while hanging in her gallery."

'Mary does," she adds.

"But," Dwight starts, "sorry I don't know your name. We don't need money. Money won't change any of our lives. It won't give me my legs back."

"Not your original legs."

"They were the ones I liked, so, why should I sell it?"

"My name is Yonan Schmeichel, but please call me Yonan. I would like the painting; how can we resolve this?"

"I have the answer. I painted three, two were rehearsals, then I did this one. You can have one of the others."

"I already have the first rehearsal. I would also like the one that is exploding with life," he says, turning to indicate the one above the jukebox. They are all puzzled.

"I don't want to sell, so, do you mind if I get back to work?" Dwight asks him, twisting the chair.

"You have no work You're not working on any crime," Yonan says.

"You sure confident 'bout that," is Dwight's retort.

"I know everything that is going on in the cruise industry, and you're only working on a debt. I can also help with that."

"Is that so?" Dwight asks, simply to grab time while he computes. The painting and Yonan's knowledge of CSCI's work together means 'pay attention'.

"Can I finish sketching your shoes, and take a 'shoefi' so I can paint them when you gone?" Macey asks, bending down with her phone.

"You will have lots of time to paint these shoes. I would like to take you with me."

"We stop human trafficking, we don't sell women," Dwight says firmly, in case that's what the guy meant.

"Sorry, I left out that I would want to take you all to a long lunch so we can discuss something," Yonan says, smiling.

Dwight digests every detail of the styled silver haired man who speaks very well. Possibly third generation Balkan immigrant. His suit, reserved but deliberate mannerisms, right down to the shoes he twists on. He moves well.

'Discuss something?' Dwight thinks. 'He knows all about the cruise industry. He must need us for something pretty dam special'.

Dwight notices a second limousine pulls up outside and a very well-dressed woman slide out. Her moves are also deliberate, but more robotic. She is not military, more a senior office executive attending to the man's every need, but she travelled in a second stretch limousine.

"Me going too?" Stan asks.

"Chef. You sit next to me."

"How about me?" Croc asks. He has been taking every detail in.

"I mean all of you, as my family. Dwight, please call Commander Philips and Hunter Witowski for me. I'm sorry, but I don't know Mr Witowski's grade or title."

"No one does," Mary says. "Family?" She asks.

"Let's say I've been doing some ancestral research."

"Well you've been getting a few things wrong," Macey suggests. She stands next to him and shows the skin on her wrist against his.

"I'm gonna need a new dress, Stan. Look out there at Miss 'I ain't from round here'. It's gonna be some fancy restaurant," Mary says, as the lady comes in looking a million dollars.

"It's lunch, Mary, and you have style. My Executive Assistant will help with all the arrangements. Now Macey, would you like to travel with me?" He turns to Stan. "And you chef?"

Stan shuffles out as if he needs both his old hips replaced. His steak is left on a plate.

"Stan," Mary shouts. "You know you gonna be the cabaret."

"No worries Mary. I can still shuffle a shoe."

"You couldn't do it back then, I'm damn sure you can't do it now," she says, under her breath so only Dwight can hear.

"Mr Ritter, I would take you too, but my guess is you need to call the others and do some research on me."

"I can't close the restaurant," Mary says.

As Stan goes with the driver to the limo, his executive assistant has the door of the diner held open. Six uniformed chefs march in.

Macey holds back to whisper a few chosen sentences of pure information to Dwight.

"Clément, an art dealer. One name on his card. He bought the first draft I painted of you. On the cruise ship before that nutty conference, you pranked. Five hundred dollars. I told Clément I had another, much better; the finished piece. Showed him the picture on my phone."

Dwight nods. He not only appreciates the knowledge, but how accurate and determined Macey was to deliver all the information before she left. Like a natural investigator.

"Croc!" Dwight says. "Go with them."

Croc runs out.

The bell above the door rings as it hits the round spring closing.

4 – BRIGHT RED

Miami-1215hrs

Hunter's bright red drop-top pulls up outside an apartment block. The car looks too small for him at 6ft 3" with shoulders as wide as the seat. The graffitied door of the old apartment block slams behind Commander Kieron Philips. He crosses the sidewalk, rounding an attractive young lady.

"Good morning," he ventures to her, in his charming British way. The accent always gets him attention in Florida. She turns and smiles as she continues to walk away.

"Get in the car," Hunter Witowski shouts, leaning over and flipping the passenger door open. Kieron gets in and now there are two big men in a small car.

"Lost your razor?"

"Stubble's in vogue around here," Kieron replies.

"It's about time you relocated," Hunter continues, as he checks traffic and pulls out.

"It's about time you bought a bigger car?"

"I'm never here, and Elaine loves it."

"I'm never here, and I'm enjoying the local culture," Kieron says.

"Is there any of your British sub-text in that?"

"No. I could move upmarket to a place where neighbours never talk to each other, but first, this is my education into America."

"Americans are friendly; even when you move upmarket."

"Have you met your neighbours in Coral Gables?"

"No, but I intend to."

Kieron smiles at Hunter's reply.

"So," Kieron starts. "We're going to a real posh lunch. I packed a few clothes, as whenever something like this happens you have a mission planned."

"Nope. The whole of Wild Mary's Diner's going," Hunter says.

"Hmm. With respect, it can't be that posh."

"With respect, we don't have a class system in the States."

"I think you do; it's based on money, not lineage."

Kieron knows they are heading to a bridge that means only one thing.

"Where is this restaurant?" Kieron asks.

"The Port of Miami."

"Don't you call it Dodge?"

"Not when it's a posh lunch. We got valet parking; someone'll meet us."

"Why?"

"They love Macey and it's about art. That's all I know."

"I'm so glad I packed a bag. But unless yours is in the boot..."

"Trunk," Hunter intercepts.

"Unless yours is in the trunk, any efforts to suggest I go solo again will sadly fall on rocky ground," Kieron points out. "Art?" He asks.

"A rich guy wants to buy one of Macey's paintings. And before you say anything, I know, it sounds stupid."

"I don't think it does. She has fantastic vision, her use of colour to find light is extraordinary, and the way she lays paint down is also amazing."

"Since when did you know about painting?" Hunter asks as they go over the bridge. At the peak, it rises to reveal eight ships berthed in a line with little space between them.

"I'm English. Our 'posh' comes from birth; we know art. Sadly my family had none, in fact, no money. So, I joined the army."

"As an officer, right?" Dwight mocks.

"Yes. Sandhurst, then army officer."

The car pulls in as directed by Hunter's GPS. Two suited valets attend, one each side. Kieron leans towards Hunter before they disembark.

"Expensive suits for car-jockeys."

"I noticed. We recognise money, right?"

The two crime investigators get out. One valet gets in to drive, the other takes Kieron's bag.

"Don't I get a ticket?"

The car pulls away gently and the remaining valet answers.

"No, Sir. A receipt for your car won't be necessary."

Hunter and Kieron follow him.

"He means your car is small and worth nothing," Kieron mocks and it becomes obvious they are being led towards the ships.

"What the fuck's going on?" Hunter asks quietly.

"You never seem to know."

Hunter's phone rings as they approach one of the smaller ships.

"This is money," Hunter says, looking up at it. He attends his cell-phone, then repeats to Kieron. "The French guy who bought Macey's picture is Clement."

"Probably pronounced Klee-mawn, if he's French," Kieron corrects him.

"And the guy throwing lunch is Yonan Schmeichel."

"…meaning?"

"The richest cruise owner on the seas," Hunter says.

"It should be a nice lunch." Kieron reads a text on his watch. "…and a big fee, because he wants us for something. Dwight's beat us there. He says it smells of money."

The valet leaves them at the gangway where an officer greets them. They receive a visitor's cruise card each; a card that allows them on and off the ship.

"Your other guests have arrived, gentlemen," the officer says.

They both nod.

"Please comply with the security request for a photograph at the top of the gangway," the officer says.

"I've never seen inside a ship like this," Hunter says, as cool as he can be but super interested.

"How can it be different?" Kieron asks.

"With suites at ten thousand dollars a night and a helipad, I guess we're gonna find out. But, it ain't gonna have a waterslide."

"No worries, I never use the slide."

"I remember; you prefer the laundry chute!"

5 – THE SILVER ROOM

Miami-1245hrs

Kieron and Hunter are taken directly to an elevator, then a short distance down the most ornate corridor, with exquisite decoration and paintings on the walls. Large flower sprays adorn almost every small side-table.

The last door is the entrance to the owner's suite, which has a butler. Inside, it is all gold leaf mirrors, art, and two magnificent Czechoslovakian crystal chandeliers hanging, one above each end of a giant table. The silver platters on the long serving table against the wall are highly polished and sit on a white tablecloth. Perfectly uniformed waiters with white gloves stand ready to serve.

The twelve-place table is covered with an impeccably ironed tablecloth fringed with lace. Kieron has not seen table covers ironed on any of the ships he has been on thus far. As an army officer, ironed tablecloths are expected. Dwight nods to them from the other end of the room.

Macey moves from painting to painting, thoroughly enjoying herself. Yonan Schmeichel is behind her, using the odd phrase to guide her eye. But she needs little guiding; she is studious. Her fine art degree is the bones of her huge knowledge. Having nothing else in her life, her massive outside study was done at Wild Mary's where she almost lives. There she keeps several books that Mary has bought her. The student's quasi mother follows behind the two and it annoys her that she finds herself nodding with them but having no idea why. She slaps herself. Macey and Yonan both turn.

"A fly."

"I hope not. If it was, my sincere apologies."

Mary shakes her head; she has caused another minor crisis.

"My new ship will have six pieces of art in each suite, and there are six-hundred suites," he says.

Izzy is taking notes, ever the would-be reporter. She is the third of the post graduate students who work at Wild Mary's Diner, she was about to start work when the limousine arrived for the others. This is not the afternoon she was expecting and it is interesting.

Mary knows it is a big number, but she can have no idea of what art costs. She has no idea what this kind of ship costs.

"You booked this restaurant just for us?" Mary asks, impressed.

"This is my private restaurant, in my apartment," he indicates. "No one else lives here."

"All this?" Mary asks shocked. She looks squarely at Macey, "I said I'd buy you three an apartment but not like this."

"Mary, I'll show you around after lunch. You'll love the bedroom."

"I hope you ain't making no suggestive remark. My man Stan is here."

Yonan laughs lightly, expecting that to have been a joke, though with Mary you can never tell.

"Mary, what a wonderful dress you are wearing," Philips says, approaching her but focussing on the man who owns all this.

He offers his right hand, but Yonan's left hand rises to stop him speaking, then he shakes with his right hand.

"…My cousin, it's been too long. I'm so glad you could come. But, cousins, we are missing your partners,

Prisha and Bedriška. I find Bedi a puzzle I would like to get to the bottom of."

"Are you sure about that?" Dwight asks, offering his hand. 'Cousins? That was too pointed.' He computes. There is a play being made. Like a poker player, Dwight ups-the-stakes and throws a greeting back to see what response he gets.

"Hi cuz, mum said to say hi. Both young women are on their way. They were a bit shy, not being close family and all," Dwight announces, mainly for Kieron and Hunter to translate.

They are new to the room but are watching and taking in the language. Looks to each other confirms each is alert.

"Fashionably late," Yonan says with a huge smile. "Do you want to eat now or wait for them?"

"I suggest we don't wait," Dwight says, which both Kieron and Hunter compute as them not having been summoned. Dwight will be texting them.

They are all helped to their seats by the waiters, who remove their gloves to touch the chairs. Stan, as promised sits next to Yonan in the middle of the long table. The waiters put their gloves back on to serve.

"I hope your people looking after my restaurant are doing all this dandy stuff," Mary says.

"I'm sure they are having the time of their lives," Yonan says.

The waiters hand out menus.

-

Prisha and Bedriška both know almost every ship on the oceans by name and reputation. They were cruise crew for years. They may have seen this one, MS Overlord, berthed at a few ports but never been onboard. The women had communicated with each other on what to wear and shared a cab. They arrive about ninety minutes late.

Once inside, they avoid the pressure to be taken straight to the elevator. They admire the most astonishing atrium with chandeliers that are infinity light balls. An endless vision from any angle. Every wall and supporting pillar are marble and gold. The officer follows them as they are continually amazed.

"I will find place to stowaway," Bedriška says.

The officer escorting them is not sure how to take her stoic Russian humour. Seeing he is embarrassed, she starts to play with him.

"What drink guests offered when board wonderful ship?" she asks him.

"A glass of Dom Pérignon 2008, madame," he says.

Bedriška stops in her tracks, looks shocked, and gestures with her empty hands. She is asking for her glass. Prisha holds back a laugh, unable to compute the wealth. Their escort waves for something to happen and the three women continue to view their surroundings. Much of what they see is familiar to Bedi and Prisha, but it is another world of opulence, style, and service to all three. Glasses of champagne arrive, and the women enjoy their walk.

"We should join the others," Prisha says, having a little more guilt than Bedi.

"Really?" Bedi says, flatly.

6 – FAMILY

Miami-1430

The female investigators enter the plush dining area like a whirlwind. Yonan is instantly taken by Bedriška. She can guess who he is and makes him work for the greeting; cheek kisses, one on each side. Seeing he went one way; she is quick enough to match him so they almost bump. She passes her glass to Prisha.

"Three," she says. "I Russian."

Yonan goes to kiss her cheek again, and she allows it but draws back.

"No, you must start again. Three together."

Yonan is only too pleased to comply but on completion, he is shocked as she hugs him; a long and tight bear hug.

Kieron and Hunter both restrain their amusement. They know how hard and playful she can be.

"Three kisses, then hug, perfect Russian etiquette," she says, without any hint of a smile.

Yonan likes her even more. Mary, who is sitting next to Kieron on the opposite side of the table is watching.

"He's got that look in his eyes."

"What look is that?" Kieron asks.

"Same look as at Dwight's painting, he ain't gonna give up on her," she whispers to him.

Kieron smiles, watching Prisha accept a gentle handshake. Then Yonan presses his hands together close to the chest, palms touching and fingers pointing upward. He offers a slight bow.

"Namaste," Yonan says. "I hope I did that correctly and it wasn't an insult.

"It was a perfect Añjali Mudrā," Prisha smiles.

"I hope to have you smiling later," he says to Bedriška.

"Me also," she replies.

Waiters begin to show the ladies to their chairs. They are not persuaded to sit as easily as the others were, because they are distracted by the amazing apartment. Yonan walks around and encourages them. Waiters assist by offering menus to study but Bedriška is still entranced by the suite.

"It run around front of ship, like bridge," she whispers to Prisha, taking the champagne glass and expecting it to be filled. "Window, amazing view and deck for party."

"I have more windows than the bridge below me," Yonan says. "We will have a drink on the sun-deck after dinner."

It could hardly be referred to as a balcony because it is the width of the front of the ship.

"We have found each other and can be one big family now. Each one of you can play an important part here if you wish to join my little empire," Yonan says.

"So, you want me to do a little soft shoe shuffle, Mr Yonan, Sir?" Stan says.

"Call me Yonan, Stan. I would rather you told me what you thought of the food," he says, keeping them all confused but making everyone feel at home.

"He's about as good with food as he is at shuffling," Mary says.

Yonan appreciates their basic humour, which he hears too little. The women are given their food and he has everyone's attention except Bedriška whom he assumes is playing a game and that he shouldn't wait.

"Macey, you are a very special talent. Your study of Dwight is as good as I was led to believe by other top buyers. Incredible presence, confidence, and natural ability. You will be one of the American greats. I would love to have the first option on all your paintings, but your agent is tough. Take a cruise, stay on the ship. It goes to Key West and New Orleans, ideal for inspiration. Paint on board ship," Yonan says. He turns and addresses the room. "Ladies, anyone, would you like to order something else before I dismiss the staff?"

Bedriška holds up her champagne glass and it is filled. She takes the bottle and tells the waiter he can go.

"I love vodka, but this is special," she says.

Yonan waves all the waiters to leave and dismisses his junior officer in-waiting by the door and his butler.

Hunter and Kieron look at Dwight for clues, but he has none to offer. All three know a play is on. Each of the team looks around. Mary's head turns wide arcs of the table. Dwight's doesn't move he is watching Kieron and Hunter. Croc flicks between watching Yonan and the chemistry being worked with Hunter and Kieron. Those two investigators are moving their eyes rather than their heads and each has taken one side of the space. Neither tries to scan the whole room. Izzy and Macey are both confused, but as Izzy was the journalist major at college, she is listening to everything and wishing she could take notes. Prisha watches Bedi fill her glass again so she holds her glass out.

"Don't try to stay with me, dangerous game," Bedi whispers to Prisha. "I in control and watching."

Yonan rises for a toast but puts his glass down.

"Now, it's nice to be alone," there is a pause, "as a family. And to find there is such a talent in the family tree. The most talented young artist I have ever seen is a relative of mine." He raises his glass. "To Macey."

He toasts, they are all still puzzled. Kieron is about to ask a question when Yonan signals him not to. He has not finished.

"I am so glad I found you, all of you. It is my new hobby, searching…"

Yonan hits the word 'searching' both vocally and with an arm action pointing at the walls. They get that he is delivering a message. Yonan doesn't stop gesture and searches the whole room saying nothing. Finally, he cups his ear.

Kieron and Hunter both get up quietly and gently start a search for listening bugs. Dwight wheels around the table encouraging each person to feel under the table, and he checks each lump and bump found. Bedi picks up very quickly on what is going on. She climbs on her chair. Prisha takes Bedi's hand as she wobbles about to step on the table. Yonan crinkles his face and waves at her shoes. Bedi gives a huge smile, hiccups then flips her shoes at him. He catches them and she steps onto the table and walks to one end and starts to search the chandelier. The three investigators are now the cabaret. Yonan narrates.

"…searching my ancestral chain. Let me tell you all, I am amazed at the results. Results going back so far, with tickets on shipping lines and immigration papers. So many relatives I never knew."

Hunter levers every frame forward struggling to do it silently. Worried about the value of the paintings, Macey rushes to help him. Izzy copies going to assist Kieron.

Stan is talking to Yonan about food.

"Like I said, I would normally give fries, maybe too many, but fries work. Try fries as a side."

"Stan, there is a reason for the small portions."

Stan stops and thinks while he mumbles to himself. Finding an answer, he points a finger.

"They drink more, Mr Yonan."

"Stan, you are smarter than you think."

"Oh, I know I smart, Mr Yonan. I know. It just Mary who have no idea."

They watch Bedi twisting the chandelier round and around carefully until she finds something. Reaching inside using the lightest touch, she pulls it out. She holds it up for both men to see, a tiny radio receiver with its aerial dangling. Bedi negotiates the full length of the table, stepping in and out of the silverware. Her moves are always intoxicating.

"Stan, get your eyes down, you an old man, act like it."

"Mary, I think Stan is acting all man," Yonan defends.

"If I knew table dancers were like that, I would have gone years ago," Stan glees.

"Sadly, Stan. They're not," Yonan says. But seeing the sharp look he is getting from Mary. "So I am told."

"Someone told you damn right, so no need to go researching, Stan."

At the other end of the table, Bedi knows where to look and she easily removes a second device.

The two men have come up with nothing. They gently help her down. Bedi shouts into the devices.

"Oh no! Help. Help."

Bedi drops the two transmitting microphones into a glass of water and casually walks the glass to the windowsill at the far end of the room. On any call for help all staff should attend, but only those listening to the bugs will have heard the call. She knows what is going to happen behind her, so she does not turn.

The two investigators go, one to each door. Two waiters burst in at Hunter's door. He immediately immobilises one, throwing him away towards Kieron. He claims the second man, bending his arm way too far behind his back. Kieron has the first waiter, arm uncomfortably behind his back. They hold the two men face to face, then crash their heads together.

"Easy guys," Kieron says blaming them. "Watch where you're going."

"Where you listening from?" Hunter asks gently but physically nearly popping one of the waiter's arms out of his shoulder. The man refuses to answer. His legs are swept from under him and he is dumped on the floor with Hunter falling on top of him. It is a move designed to break ribs if Hunter dropped on him with his whole weight. The man is winded and shocked.

"You work for me now, I own your ass," Hunter tells him.

Izzy is shocked. She has only ever seen street violence, which is more shouting and untrained attacks. This was so fast and accurate it is obvious Hunter and Kieron are trained killers. These two have worked behind enemy lines doing something more demanding for many years. Her hands drop from her face, not that she had ever stopped looking.

Macey studies the moves and bent mass of arms and legs as if human modern art. Her cell-phone comes up and captures it. She sees the reflection in the silver platter at the end of the table and she photographs that.

"Those pictures ain't going anywhere, Macey," Dwight says to her firmly

7 - NOW YOU LISTEN

Miami-1530

Dwight wheels out and stops, automatically taking a point position to stop other waiters entering. Yonan plays a wise forward move by going ahead of his new team and peering into the main kitchen.

"Once again, fantastic service. Do you mind if I close you in for a moment longer?"

It wasn't a question; he closes the door behind him.

"Let's go," Dwight says, and the detainee waiters are forced to lead them. They pass the kitchen and show Hunter and Kieron into the small anteroom behind it, which is the clearance area for the Silver Room. Prisha follows them in and closes the door behind her. Dwight nods to thank Yonan for his cooperation and to release him from diversion duties.

"Good food guys," Dwight says, re-opening the kitchen door.

The small anteroom is full of plates and cutlery that are being stacked ready for washing. Between the dishwasher and a large brown food bin a receiver with two small ariels is coupled to a small laptop computer with headphones to the side. There is a lot of waste food on a cruise ship, which is pulped and processed. The biodegradable liquid is released into the sea when the vessel is at least three miles from shore. It is not food for fish, though sea life can ingest it.

"Death's an option for you," Hunter starts, "into the industrial food pulper and dissolved three miles into the ocean."

"Crew cards," Philips demands.

They both offer up their crew cruise cards in fear. Prisha takes them both and steps back, re-taking her assisting position against the door. She is keen to learn everything about CSCI, but all her natural instincts are correct.

"Who do you work for?" Hunter demands.

"We don't know; we listen in on Mr Yonan. He always have meetings in Silver Room, we clean waste."

"Cabin number?" Philips demands.

"3126; we share," one says, very frightened.

"Prisha, clear their room out. Make it look like they jumped ship," Kieron says. "Find yourself a couple of hoodies, use their crew cruise cards and check yourself off the ship. Needs two of you; take Izzy, she needs the experience."

"I know, I saw her reaction," Prisha says.

"It's what we do," Hunter says.

Prisha leaves.

"What do you do with the conversations?" Hunter bullies the prisoners.

"Upload."

Hunter throws them back against the appliances and rushes out leaving Philips alone. Kieron Philips rips their shirts off and tears them into shreds. He gags both men, then ties their hands. He unplugs the power cables from the machines but not the power. Those live cables are used to tie them to the solid steel table, which is fixed down in case of a storm.

"Don't struggle. Look, cables, electric. If the table cuts into the cables; electric. Dead."

"Croc," Hunter barks on entering the Silver Room. He joins the others sitting around the table still in some shock. "Those two idiots have a listening device next door and have to upload useful conversation. Croc, listen to it and edit; leave nothing except family chat and stuff about Macey being a great artist. Add more shit if you need to, get Stan ranting on about burgers, and Macey about art. Upload it, but trace the upload route."

"The microphones are in water," he replies.

"Dry them out."

"Stan, Macey," Croc encourages, as he collects the glass of water from the windowsill.

"Not Macey," Yonan states. Croc and Stan leave without her.

Hunter turns to Yonan curious.

Bedi lifts her empty glass, pushed between them, "More champagne?"

Yonan walks over to a small fridge hidden by another draping white cloth. He opens it and she sees there are about a dozen bottles. He collects several clean glasses from the service table against the wall as he returns.

Kieron makes a late re-entry and takes a flute glass. Yonan opens the bottle and fills Bedi's glass; he then pours for all. He raises his glass to toast.

"It was only a two-channel recorder, so the room's safe now," Kieron reports.

"To Family," Yonan toasts. "My staff think you are my family and friends. It must stay that way," Yonan begins to explain.

"We are," says Bedi drinking her whole glass and waiting for a refill.

"I had to ensure that you, as mercenaries, which you are…"

"Like El Cid," Bedi interjects.

"Had not been bought by them," Yonan finishes.

"El Cid, good analogy," Kieron says. Bedi clicks her glass with him.

"Who's 'them'?" Hunter asks.

"I only know two. You have just caught them. But that is how close they are."

"Where does Macey come in?" Hunter growls, knowing Yonan has had a plan all along.

"Hello, I'm here," she says.

Bedriška is watching and listening far more keenly. She is the ruthless protector of the women in CSCI.

"Macey, your talent is as an extremely good, newly discovered artist," Yonan starts. "I can cause a noise about you, have a gallery tipped off about how good you are, and that I am looking to buy your work. An agent or gallery will take every piece you have and invite me to see them. I will buy them whatever the price. Your status goes up, the price of your work goes up."

"Simple," Macey mocks.

"People like me keep the price of art up, it is our duty."

"So you exploit young artists. That how you get your real money?" Mary accuses. She turns to Bedriška having noticed her motherly instincts. "See, I look after my girls too."

"You won't be there when they out in the field."

"I ain't working in no field," Macey says.

"Mary, no amount of risky young artists would pay for this room, let alone the ship," he explains.

"So why is this your favourite room? The one where you always hold your meetings?" Philips asks.

Yonan sweeps his arms to show off the exemplary space. Macey shakes her head, 'no'. Her disagreement attracts the three investigators' attention. She has a nose for something quite different.

"What. You don't like the room, girl?" Mary asks.

Bedi lifts her eyebrows to question her, respecting her fellow female's take and waiting for her instincts. Macey points to the wall behind them where a large abstract painting hangs.

"Something's wrong," Macey says and they are all intrigued.

"I told you I wanted Macey. The rest of you come free," Yonan smiles.

"I ain't free," Mary interrupts.

Macey stands examining the Kandinsky hung on the wall.

"I was jesting, Mary. I expect a price for your services, as I expect to pay for art. My pride and joy are my ships, but it is the art that gives them life."

He turns to Macey.

"I bought it at Christie's auction of 'Impressionist Modern Works of Art', in London a few years ago. I paid thirty-eight million dollars."

Mary chokes on her champagne, spurting it. Yonan's fast reaction with his hand covering her face saves his painting.

"Sorry," Mary says.

He takes a white embroidered napkin from the table.

"Best Russian art," Bedi states strongly.

"Hmmmm?" Kieron Philips dares to throat hum, disagreeing.

"It Wassily Kandinsky. What is problem?" Bedi demands.

"Well, he's actually from Odessa, a city founded by the Ancient Greeks. They left behind their love for art. It's more Mediterranean than Russian, heavily influenced by French and Italian styles. Even some of the buildings are a mixture of visions; Art Nouveau to

Renaissance and Classicist. That's where his artistic freedom came from."

"He still Russian. Odessa is Russia."

"It's in the Ukraine," Kieron continues to play with her. The two were bed partners on their last mission and they have a special bond and playground.

"For him, his home was fourth largest city in Russia," she concludes. "No Ukraine."

Yonan offers the bottle to fill glasses, a way of stopping the exchange. Kieron lets her win; she is right. Yonan fills Hunter's glass last.

"Don't normally drink this stuff, but if these two keep going at it, I might share another bottle with you," Hunter says to Yonan.

Macey holds up her glass to be filled. Yonan fills it, and she toasts the painting.

"Young lady, you're under twenty-one," Hunter reminds her.

"This is a private residence," Yonan protects.

"And I'm her mother," Mary says, giving Hunter the shut-your-face smile with lips firmly closed and her head tilted.

"Quasi mother," Philips says.

"Don't you start any of that British shit with me."

"My ambition," Yonan announces, "is to own his 'Painting with White Lines'."

"No chance," Bedriška says confidently. "It is most expensive. Painted in 1913."

"It's a beautiful piece. I've seen it in books; love to see it for real," Macey says, genuinely.

"I hope one day you will," Yonan says. "Such works of art only appear for sale about once every ten years, and there is a rumour it will appear. Perhaps you will join me at a pre-auction exhibition in Hong Kong?"

Mary throws her shoulder in, determined to show she has a purpose.

"I would but I'm busy, trying to save the train-wreck your team will have made of my restaurant," she says. "Anyhow, I like a painting to be like a picture, you know. He just throws paint at paper," Mary says.

"Kandinsky invented modern art," Kieron says. "It makes him one of the most important painters in history."

"Yeah?" Mary questions, looking at the work on the wall. "What the hell's he thinking?"

Macey is still mesmerised by the work, "He was thinking that painting didn't need to be a particular scene, or shape; that it was philosophy or music."

"Exactly, not at all Russian," Kieron says, turning to Bedi and trying to resurrect their game.

"I have a small print of his," Macey announces.

"Let me guess?" Yonan asks. "His 'Yellow, Red and Blue', 1925? Or is it 'Vibrant', 1928?"

"Vibrant," Macey laughs. "I love it. Sadly damaged because it ain't framed. I wanted to enjoy it, so I pinned it on my wall. Damp wall. Now, it under my mattress at home with my works. I like to think there's a Kandinsky next to mine."

"That's vibrant alright," Mary says, pointing at the Kandinsky on the wall.

"Most of his compositions are too busy, and heavy for me. I like his simple mad spontaneity," Macey says, in a world of her own.

"It's spontaneous alright," Mary says. "Looks like his paints exploded."

Macey gets close to the work and she starts to speak softer. She is talking about something she loves.

"Sometimes it looks like he attacks the canvas," she says.

"You can say that again," Mary adds.

"Fast, positive, expressive brushwork giving a sense of freedom and hope."

Mary is going to chip in again, but Kieron stops her.

"It's free even when his brush glides like a signature," Macey glees. "Like 'Lyrical Rider on a Horse'. I tried to do it; it ain't easy. Throwing oil paint on does one thing…"

"Causes a mess," Mary manages to get in before she is stopped.

"When it's free the paint has a shallow wake. If it's done slowly and accurately, the wake in the oil is thicker. At least when I do it. This is making me rethink his style," Macey says, leaning in at the work.

Kieron looks from Macey to Yonan inquisitively. Macey is going somewhere.

"Where do you keep the original locked up?" she asks.

"This is it," Yonan replies.

Mary turns and grins. She doesn't believe him.

Everyone, not least Hunter, Kieron and Dwight examine the rich man's face wondering if this is why they have been summoned.

"The original was there. I didn't notice it had been swapped," Yonan smiles. "You're a good team."

"We need to be. Stolen art hard to find. I know," Bedriška says, walking back from the small fridge with another bottle of Dom Pérignon in one hand and her glass in the other.

"How is it you know about art crime? Are you an art expert?" Macey questions Bedriška.

"Well, as I already reveal to my employers," she says, looking at Kieron and Hunter.

They both no whatever she is about to say, nothing will stop her. Hunter nods nonchalantly.

"I was 5th Directorate KGB agent. Artistic affairs."

"She never tells that story when she's sober," Kieron says.

"Excuse me!" Bedi says.

"Didn't you do censorship and internal security against political, religious and sexual dissension?" Hunter asks. "Did you ever see a painting?"

"You on dangerous land, I mean water," she says, threatening Hunter.

"Bedriška is right," Yonan says. "When art is stolen, more often than not, it vanishes. That would make most of my collection worthless. It is possible all my ships are being systematically robbed. And I am building one in Italy and filling it with art, or am I? They might all be fakes. But, I can't reveal I know that. I can't go inspecting my pieces or the thieves will know I'm on to them. I can't call the police. I certainly can't even call forgery experts to inspect my collection; it is a small industry; everyone would know withing days. Is this Kandinsky switch a one-off, or have I become a target."

"This ain't real, I know it," Macey grins.

"I knew you'd know. I need your talent to join a cruise; come and paint on any of my ships. The Baltic, where you would love the cities and the art. St Petersburg; they have the largest collection of art in the world. But, as you don't have a passport yet, this one leaving Miami tonight is best."

"What? Because I knew that was phoney?"

"Only one other person knows apart from this team. He can teach you a lot. No one else can know we know. Not even my man can go looking because if they are in my ships they will see him inspecting them. While 'whoever' is successfully stealing from my ships, if they are, my art is safe somewhere. Macey will know, and she has a talent that will intrigue them."

"We need to find them, and art before they suspect we after them, or they vanish," Bedriška says. "Art will be gone forever."

"And I'm bait?" Macey asks.

"Yeah," Hunter drawls slowly.

"You are a star artist, I believe in your talent," Yonan says.

"High end crime, highest risk," Macey asks thinking.

"It's dangerous," Kieron says. "We can do this without you."

"No. You couldn't. You won't," Macey states.

There is a cold moment as she looks at Yonan.

"I'll make you a star," Yonan says.

"Long as I live, right?" She replies.

8 - POSITIVE AND EXPRESSIVE

Miami-1645

Stan is cleaning the grill, though he can't see a mark on it. Mary's look at 'her' team demands answers. Hunter Witowski, Commander Kieron Philips, Prisha and Bedriška are there, thinking hard. Wild Mary has to break the silence.

"You telling me he gone and lost forty million dollars and still smile?" She asks. "Can you figure what that feel like?"

The others exchange knowing glances of loss.

"I think we got a good idea, Mary," Hunter growls.

Mary's look digs into them as the penny drops. She takes another minute to examine them. She might not be able to interpret paintings, but she can read faces. She has hit a nerve, a very expensive nerve.

"So those little bundles of one hundred dollar bills you send me when you on holiday; where you get them?"

"You know our trips are work, not a vacation," Hunter informs her.

"Some pirate been digging in the sand and leaving you buried treasure?"

"Something like that," Kieron says.

"Why am I flipping tomatoes, when I could be digging in the sand?" she asks.

"Mary, you ain't flipped nothin' on this grill for years," Stan says bravely.

Mary looks sternly at Stan, with one eyebrow raised, then turns back to the CSCI team.

"You telling me, it's just one of them days when I hear about two lots of forty million dollars?"

The bell rings and the door slams. A customer walks in and heads for the counter. That puts an end to chat about money. Macey catches the door before it closes and bursts in behind him with gusto and many large books under her arm. She weaves around the guy who is about to order.

"Macey, stand back girl. We got a paying customer here. Haven't I taught you manners?" Mary says. She turns to the man who is pleased he was not gazumped. "Sir, what can I do for you?"

"Can I get one of those special burgers in a brioche bun with yellow peppers, shredded Iceberg lettuce and sliced fresh ripe tomatoes?"

"Stan, man wants you." Mary turns back to Macey. "Mace, what is it, girl?"

She opens the Kandinsky Modern Master book.

"Look. 'Painting with White Lines'," she offers.

Mary looks at it. She turns her head one way then the other. She tries twisting the book.

"That one of them colour-blind tests?" she asks.

"No, Mary, it's brilliant."

"Can't see no white lines. If that's forty-million-dollars I'm gonna start painting."

The customer is also looking at the picture and he is confused.

"What day was it yesterday?" Mary asks him.

"Tuesday."

"That burger's the Tuesday-special. We see you next Tuesday?" Mary says, encouraging the guy to leave. Stan looks at her confused.

"What you want, Stan?" she asks, as the doorbell rings. The confused customer has left.

"That the first time I ever seen you turn a customer away."

"We don't do them fancy broach buns."

"You should've checked with the chef first, Mary," he tells her, insistent she starts to respect his new position.

"Oh yeah, and what would the chef have said?"

"I need a moment there, Mary," Stan says, and he shuffles off into the back.

Mary looks at the CSCI team who have not stirred.

"Did you hear Yonan ask if we understood how difficult his life is coz he's got so much money?" Mary asks.

"Tough," Dwight adds, speeding in from the technical room. Croc is behind him but goes straight behind the counter, takes a bun and makes himself a burger.

"Wash your hands, boy!" Mary exclaims, but it's too late.

"Who should he trust?" Kieron asks.

"No one," Dwight agrees.

"That's the point. He's lost faith in everyone," Hunter adds.

"Except us," Macey glees.

"Best damn investigating team in the whole cruise-world," Dwight boasts.

"Only investigating team in the cruise-world," Mary interrupts. "With a star artist, put through art school by yours truly."

"Star artist, I wish," Macey dreams. "He wants me as a forgery adviser."

"Whatever, you talented, girl," Mary adds, flipping pages in the Kandinsky book. She gets nearer to the beginning where she finds a painting of a woman singing in front of a piano, wearing a black and white striped dress and holding a posy.

"See, he can paint. Not well, but he can," Mary says, turning her head to examine it. "He can't do faces, not like you Mace."

"Think that's what Yonan was implying about your work. Become a star, and even your early works become precious," Kieron says.

"Yonan's building a new ship. The most luxurious ship on the sea," Dwight reveals. "And guess the USP?"

"You 'S' what?" she questions.

"Unique selling proposition. He fills it with original art. About ten-million-dollars' worth with six paintings in each suite."

"Well that coronavirus didn't knock a hole in his business," Mary adds.

"I can't look at that many pieces; I can't judge one. I only did a semester on forgery."

"They even gonna have large pieces in the restrooms," Dwight adds

"Why would anyone put art in the restroom?"

"I wager much will be systematically stolen before it gets hung in the ship," Kieron suggests.

"We systematically gonna rob him one big fee," Mary says.

"I normally dream up a number, but I don't have a clue here," Hunter says.

"We're his special agents; he said agents get five-percent upwards," Mary ventures. "Five-percent of forty-million is…"

"A car for Macey, happy birthday," Macey says.

"My birthday too," Croc says. "She can buy her own car now."

"Two-million-dollars," Bedi says. "Four ships at sea. Now, new ship full of art. He big target."

"Yeah, more important art's gonna go missing, and he knows it," Hunter says.

"I meant he's a target for an important fee."

"Wonder who the one other person is who knows it."

"We've only got until they find out we're looking for them," Kieron says. "Dwight, let's get legal passports for everyone. Including Big Dog."

"One thing about that fee. People kill for a lot less, a lot less," Hunter coldly says, putting it all into perspective. "We know from the drug heist we solved."

"What drug bust?" Mary asks.

"That's how we met, Mary. It was a heist, and it was all about drugs."

"Posh art thieves is posh ruthless killers," Kieron says.

"I ain't playing," Macey says.

"There's a limousine waiting outside for you, girl," Mary says.

"I'm not ready."

"He said to take nothing except your oils and brushes," Hunter says. "Man's gonna dress you like his 'Pretty Woman'."

Stan returns.

"We out of them brioche buns, Mary."

9 – THE SHIP

Miami-1830

Paparazzi take pictures of Macey as soon as she leaves the limousine. She is in her painting dungarees with her hair up as usual with paintbrushes in it. The flashes continue as she collects her cruise card and climbs the gangway.

"Mai, any comment?"

"Mai, are they your painting clothes?"

'May?' she thinks. 'They've got a cheek!' But she shows restraint as directed.

"Macey, do you always have brushes in your hair?" a young photojournalist asks.

She nods to him, at least he called her Macey.

"May I?" he laughs.

She stands and looks straight at him. Only him. He frames up super-fast and is laughing.

'What is so funny? Is a brush hanging out?' she wonders.

"My mama always told me to brush my hair," she leans over to share with him. He has the headline, the others could hear nothing over the shouting.

"It's Ricky," he shouts, as she straightens to look at the others.

"Macey, New York Press, how do you feel about the commission?"

So many questions are shouted at her. It is like Croc with a gun. She smiles nicely, and ensures 'thank you', are the only two words she says to the mass crowd. Her three cases, her easel and painting bag are carried for her by the ship's staff.

"Are you in the middle of a new work?" a reporter shouts.

Macey nods.

"What is it called?"

"Shoes," she answers breaking her directive again.

She has already walked through the atrium on the way to the earlier "family" lunch, but the ship cannot fail to continually impress even the hardest cruiser. Now that it is full of people it is alive. She has never cruised before and relies on a host to take her to her cabin and show her how to use the key card.

"Are you new to this ship?" he asks.

Macey can only nod her head; she cannot believe how nice and helpful he is.

"I will send your cabin steward along. Have a great cruise."

On entering her room two things hit her hard. The sheer luxury in every detail of her 'mini-suite' and the huge balcony. Her bags, not that she had ever seen them before, are already on case mats on the bed ready to unpack.

There is a welcome arrangement of flowers, a bottle of champagne, and on the TV screen it says 'Welcome May.I.see'. That catches her out. The computer has got her name wrong. She looks around for a phone. There is one by the bed and one on the desk. She lifts to ring reception but stops and reads the name again. Her staring at the name is broken by a knock on the door. She opens it to see a small cabin steward, probably Filipino. One thing she is good at is faces. She is an artist living in multi-cultural downtown Miami.

"Miss Ricca, welcome. I am Zeete, your cabin steward. My pager number is on my name card and if you need anything, at any time, please ring or page me," the man says beaming with a genuine offer of help.

'Wow', Macey thinks. 'What on earth might I want?'

"Your presence is required for cocktails in the sunset bar at the aft of the ship, deck eleven. They will perform lifeboat drill there before drinks."

"Lifeboat drill?" she asks in shock.

"It is standard, mam. Maritime law insists it is always done by every new member to the ship before we can sail."

"What shall I wear? No, sorry, I shouldn't ask you."

"Yes, Miss Ricca I am here for everything. Tonight will be 'evening smart casual', this afternoon will be a relaxed smart casual. Would you like me to help you choose?"

"Yes, and call me Macey," she says opening the door wide to let him in.

"The first day is always relaxed. However, some guests' idea of casual is very smart. Tomorrow night is a black-tie night."

"What does that mean?"

"It means after 6pm all the gentlemen will be wearing a Tuxedo; ladies will mostly be in a long dress."

"Tuxedo? On a ship? Where does that come from?" Macey asks.

"The word Tuxedo comes from Tuxedo Park in Orange County, New York. Male diners there would dine in a dinner suit. Tuxedo became the acquired colloquialism for dining in the park, then became the name all over America."

"Is that a story they tell you?"

"Yes, Miss."

"You've never been to that park?"

"No, miss. But I believe it is true."

"So, I meant where does the idea of dressing on a ship come from?"

"It is a cruise tradition, and before that on the liners. Most ladies love to dress. It is often their only opportunity."

"Well, I ain't ever worn a long dress."

Zeete lifts a beautiful sequinned style dress that would fall well below her knees.

"This is adorable, Miss Ricca. You must look perfect in this."

"I wouldn't know, Zeete. Never worn it. Some fancy Associate bought everything in these cases. What I own could go in my knapsack."

Zeete starts to hang clothes for her, examining them as Macey does the shoes.

"I ain't gonna wear all these."

"Oh, you will, Miss Macey. If you don't, I will," he says jovially.

"Macey will do fine, Zeete."

Zeete looks at the array of dresses.

"Today, maybe you should express yourself."

Macey dives into her knapsack and pulls out a dozen fine paintbrushes. She pushes five or six more into her bun at different angles.

"Too much?"

"A few too many, it looks cluttered."

She removes a few. Zeete takes a minute studying her wild look.

"Now, how is it?"

"Like a communication satellite."

"And?"

"Just what this ship needs."

Macey sees the world in pictures. She has never been good with words or socialising, but she can express herself in art. She is a people watcher, observing the crew member performing how a life jacket goes over his head. The piece of equipment that would be essential if the ship was sinking is being ignored. Macey would not need seven short blasts and one long blast of the horn to tell her it was tipping sideways, but she wonders why media and the public always reference the Titanic. Since working at CSCI she has read all sorts of trivia about ships and cruising. When the SS Eastland banked sideways and went down, more than eight hundred perished. Far more than the Titanic which must be remembered because they were all rich.

Her cruise card is scanned to prove she attended the legal necessity and she is handed a white frothy cocktail. The house photographer lines her up for photo after photo. She excuses herself and turns to join a group to escape.

One woman can't help but look her up and down. Until then Macey was confident in her self-styled look.

"You had a good stare. Now you must have a comment?" Macey asks, pointing out her rudeness.

"Is that a new fashion?" the lady asks, now trying to be as clever.

"Well, you certainly wouldn't know," Macey smiles, leaving the group she never joined. 'I shouldn't have said that. Even my mother would have told me off for that. But that woman had no idea about art or fashion. She'd be shocked if I was wearing a 'Lolita dress'! I wonder if the assistant found me one of those?' She thinks feeling very excluded for the first time in her life, and it seems to be a money thing, a class thing.

Feeling uncomfortable, Macey forces herself to try and join another group. Failing, she heads back to her mini suite, sobbing, but she'll not let anyone see.

Clément, a stylish Frenchman with a handlebar moustache, walks into the party by the door at the other side of the terrace bar. He sports a cravat and a tilted beret. All very much a cliché, but what you see is what you get. Looking for Macey, he walks into a group with no self-consciousness.

"'ave you seen May.I.see?" he asks, almost joining up the letters. "Famous painter, petite, black girl?"

A man nods asking, "Brushes in her hair?"

"Mais Oui."

The man leans over to look at the group Macey left.

"Camilla, where is Macey, the famous painter you were chatting to?"

10 - KERCHING, DING, DING

Miami-1800hrs

It has been a sunny day, not that anyone noticed in the CSCI hub. Now it is a beautiful evening and the low sun cuts through the park's palm trees. Like all the recreational areas between the city's tower blocks and the sea, it is popular. Many people are out walking dogs on leashes with a poop-bag in the other hand. Kieron sports his growing beard and a Kookaburra sun hat. Walking next to him in a Dolphins' baseball cap and sunglasses is Yonan, who has slipped his guard.

"Art is an investment, your fee not so much," Yonan negotiates, as he and Kieron Philips walk the path nearest the sea.

"Every dollar spent is an investment."

"Do you know how much money we are referring to?"

"It's five-percent, the lowest agent's fee. It shows your confidence in us and that we're invested in recovering art."

"Five-percent is quite a hit to take. On forty million dollars that's two million dollars."

"We did the maths and realised this is money people kill for. Probably have killed for it. And, five percent of nothing is nothing to a dead man," Kieron adds. "Or woman."

CRUISE SHIP ART THEFT

Conversation has stopped dead and they walk on. Hunter walks slowly on the other side of the park, often stopping to check his phone and type a reply. Mobile phones make ideal covers for a spy. Sitting on a park bench is Prisha with the uncomfortable Mary who is swinging her short legs.

Back at the restaurant, as proud as a lion, Stan is in a chef's hat. Croc and Izzy are laughing as much as he is enjoying wearing the present they bought him. A customer is taking a picture, first on Izzy's phone, then Croc's. Stan pulls his phone out.

"Hey, please. I want a picture for me. Me and the kids I love more than anything in the world."

"And your new hat," Izzy says.

He hands his phone to the customer.

"This is an old Nokia, Stan. It ain't doing nothing but taking calls."

The chef takes his phone back.

"I'll get it printed for you, Stan."

"And framed?"

"Sure."

Croc holds his phone out. Stan is seen in his new chef hat with his arms around the students. They couldn't be closer or happier.

"Wow! I'm glad I got me that before you all get old and go away," Stan exhales.

Izzy kisses him on the cheek.

"I sent it to Mary," Croc announces.

"Don't you be doing that. She t'ink I bought me this proper chef hat meself."

"No. I told her, we bought it. It's sent, Stan."

Stan gasps with horror.

"What you done?" he worries.

They burst into laughter.

Feeling bored Mary is itching to get away from the park bench.

"This what you investigators do all day? Sit around? What we looking for? And why is a black woman sitting next to an Indian woman in Maurice's park."

"Well tell me something about it," Prisha delves to keep Mary interested.

"Nothing to tell, it's a park. I never been here."

"It's the Maurice Ferré Park, opened in 1976. Sometimes called the Bicentennial Park because it was opened in the same year."

"How you know that?"

"There was a plaque on the way in."

"Bet you're the first person to read it."

"It's an investigator's job to know everything, report everything.'

"Well, you can report that I'm bored and my butt is aching."

Prisha picks up her phone and finger-types a text.

"I didn't mean tell them that!"

"I didn't. I sent a message to Kieron about my brother's company."

Mary's phone beeps. They both look.

"What? They go crazy when I'm not there. What they got on their heads?"

"One is a lobster, one is a fish…"

"I can see that, Prisha. What they doing? Fancy dress?"

"No. It's a phone app. They don't have anything on their heads. The phone does it."

"I'll put something on their heads when I get back. And that Stan ain't never gonna wear one of them stupid hats in my diner!"

Kieron checks his phone and adds to the deal.

"We also want a refrigeration contract"

"A repair stop for ships in Mumbai," Yonan smiles. "I wondered when you'd ask for that."

"You know we have an investment there?"

"I know you have millions of dollars stranded on a ship and one of the only ways to get it off would be inside a freezer unit. It's a good plan. If I give you the contract and persuade others to do the same, your plan becomes real?"

"You assume a lot," Kieron says running through flashes of his first foray into cruising. He solved a drug baroness trying to use the cruise ship for passage with money whilst holding his now partner's wife at gun point as collateral. Together, in an untidy resolution that involved his adopted daughter being held on the ship for a while, they reached an ending that saw her handed over to authorities and them keeping the money. Kieron owns two properties in the Caribbean Island of Bequia with Bedriška's partner and he and Hunter have about sixteen million in a trunk on another ship. They also used most of their splash cash to invest in Prisha's bother's business in Mumbai and if ships start to use him for maintenance in that part of the world, they just need to get the money into a freezer and the freezer off the ship for repair.

"There had to be money with a drug lord's wife escaping south America, and that money had to go somewhere," Yonan says. "I make it my job to know everything about the cruise industry. Now that is worth five percent."

"You don't know where your paintings are," Kieron says as a rebuttal whilst coming to the conclusion that 'he has read all the press, been thorough checking the company's staff and family, and he's assumed the rest. He doesn't know how much they have if anything at all'.

"I know that any cash in India is useless. You don't live in India. The best way to wash any amount of money is in art."

"You imagination doesn't negate the need for our fee. Let's get back to that and get started."

"Half a percent, a weekly fee and all expenses covered seems fair. That is still a lot of money."

"This argument is stupid, there is a job to do, and as soon as we find the thieves they'll be trying to kill us. Two-and-a-half-percent, expenses and a weekly retainer of ten-thousand-dollars. Plus the contract in India and your help on that."

Yonan stops and looks at Kieron.

"I get the first option on all Macey's work, and half a percent when she sells."

"For how long?"

"Forever. I will make her a star."

"You're making Macey vulnerable."

"That ship's sailed. She's onboard."

11 - SQUARE

DAY2-Italy-1145hrs

Sitting in a small, barely decorated waiting room, amongst a dozen or so hoping for a job at the ship building dock this office block serves, is Hunter Witowski, sporting a new square military-like haircut. Ignoring him is Kieron Philips, sitting about four men along. They bask in the early morning sun that cuts through an opposite window. Neither stand out like they normally do; all the candidates look ex-military or similar.

The door opens and a stern-looking lady raises her clipboard. It is to be a simple job interview.

"Bedriška Kossoff," she says, adding an almost silent 'i' before the last 'o' with such a heavy, rhythmic, Italian chant she makes the name sound Latin Block.

Bedriška goes through to the equally basic office. There are no decorations to describe, it is just a meeting space with a long, inexpensive wooden table where three places are set. Each has a pile of cv's and a pad on which to make notes. She recognises her newly created life story that only hours ago she was handed to learn whilst mid-flight on a private jet from Miami.

Yonan is one of three people on the panel. He too must have taken a private jet, but on a scale of jets, his would have been nearer the top of the range. Neither acknowledges each other but she knows she is assured of the job.

"Bedriška, my name is Mia Murina and I'm with Human Resources for Bianchi Ship Builders."

'I don't care who you are, get on with it', Bedi thinks.

The new security guards drink coffee as they watch a short induction film. The interview room is now back to a training and conference room. The film shows how half of a new steel cruise ship was towed from the other shipyard and welded to the half made here. When the hull was ready and the propellers attached, the dry dock was flooded, and the ship sailed out.

"Why not all work done in dry dock," Bedriška asks.

"Good question. It would be too heavy for the shallow waters, so it's floated out to a deep-water berth before heavy materials are fitted," the chief engineer explains.

"What heavy materials?" she asks. Bedi is playing and Yonan knows her well enough to enjoy that. He takes the stand.

"I am Yonan. This company is style and luxury. The mini suites are mostly marble. We have developed a strong but light corrugated board, which the thinnest sheet of marble is attached to. But, like everything on the ship, it is still heavy, Bedriška. Thank you all for joining. As the interiors begin to complete, we start hanging art. In the meantime, it is delivered and stored. The pieces are all expensive; some are worth millions. You follow any piece when it leaves the warehouse until the Gallery Assistants have hung it. Never let it out of your sight."

That is the last they see of Yonan.

They are each issued an Access-All-Areas pass in the security office which is to be a home away from home. The new five instantly bond with the three security team members in there.

"We got one on the gate, one on the warehouse. Five are Italians, I'm American. Another shift is at home sleeping," Mike explains.

He has short military hair like Hunter's. His short-sleeved, open-neck white shirt reveals that he is covered in ink. The tattoos also extend up to his neck.

"You'll pick this up quickly, ain't complicated. Dock's patrolled day and night," Mike says. "Inside the ship, stay out of the workers' way. So, on every other tour of inspection, just do the decks, it's a big place to cover. Twelve-hour shifts, you'll see we don't have a man spare."

As the meeting breaks up, Hunter Witowski holds his fist up to Mike, as another American who has also served.

"You got some ink there, soldier. How d'you get away with that?"

"You're old school," Mike says.

"But there are still regulations, Tattoo not to be two inches above the elbow and one inch below. Not on the head or neck," Hunter reels off.

"That's army. I was navy and they relaxed the regulations."

Hunter smiles a salute to acknowledge the explanation. However, he's not convinced and less impressed that the security team are lounging in the office. They are shown the sixteen security screens, but not all are in use. Scanning the room, he sees a box of unfitted cameras. The ones that are installed and working are high wide coverage of the dock and the ship berthed alongside. Not one screen shows the inside of the ship.

"Do you have any coverage in the ship?" Kieron asks, not feeling a bond with anyone. "Or, of the inside of the art vault?"

These are perfectly understandable questions because they are a security team.

"No," Mike says. "The ship security system is still being installed. They said it would take another two weeks. Until then we patrol inside. Hard work, long hours and people don't last long."

"Two weeks to fit a security system?" Kieron questions, thinking it was not him who expanded the team but Yonan.

"Listen." Mike starts as if sharing a secret. "This is a big payday. The contractors may stretch things out."

"Can't we put a man in their team?"

"No, we don't have the staff and can't do what we ain't invited to do."

Mike is younger than Witowski or Philips and far more relaxed. Most site security is relaxed. Few have ever worked in the highly disciplined end of the secret service or special divisions; that is obvious. Mike might have the hair and far too many tattoos, but for Hunter's liking, he is less navy each time he speaks.

Leaving the building, Hunter holds back and uses his phone.

"Dwight, first up, search Mike Peeke, US serviceman, maybe navy. Also, get me the full revised service regs on tattoos. Especially neckline."

"Hunter, before you hang," Dwight says, catching him. "Macey's not happy on the ship. Like a fish-out-of-water. Hates the monied, posh people. She's locked in her cabin enjoying room service."

"And our man on the ship, Clément?"

"Yeah, I spoke to him. He's weak. Look, here's an idea. I fly Prisha down to Key West and she joins Macey in the morning when they stop?"

"It leaves you thin in the office."

"I got it covered."

"OK, I love it, roger to moving Prisha."

His phone call is short because he wants to catch the others, especially Mike. Mike is still a puzzle to him and no doubt a mercenary, so a dangerous puzzle.

"Mike. We carry a sidearm?"

"It's Italy. Police carry guns, we are dock police. With terrorist threats, the green movement and so much trouble, we might need them anytime."

"You ever shot someone?"

"Oh yeah. No problems there," Mike says confidently.

12 – BERTHED

Italy-1215hrs   Miami-0415hrs

As the security team walk through the dock towards the sea, the sight of the ship is no less imposing and impressive than of any ship already in service. The hull has already been painted well above the plimsoll line while in dry dock. It's a special paint that stops micro-organisms adhering to the hull. Growth on the hull slows the ship and causes higher fuel usage which can lead to fines. Eco-friendly paint slowly releases particles, taking any sea life with it. Painters are now completing and adding more coats above the waterline. Next to them is their work cage which is instant deja-vu for Kieron. It is like the one Ronnie Cohen used to hide Georgie's bag in when she boarded with the planted money harvested in the heist. 'That was the bait to get us all involved; so we had to be compliant as the real heist went on. Well, she was the compliance officer. I wonder what she is doing now.' Kieron thinks to himself.

Their AAA passes are checked, and each of the five new security guards on tour is issued with a hard hat and safety glasses at the top of the gangway. There is no opulent atrium to walk into. The shape is recognisable, but it is mostly bare steel. No carpets, few wall panels. The reception counter stands in sections, still wrapped in card and polythene. Seeing the inside of the ship looking like a steel building site is such a contrast to a cruise, it is a shock. Cables hang from the ceiling and the security guys can be forgiven for wanting two weeks more.

"I bet they could sell tours to cruise fanatics. They would love to see this," Kieron suggests.

"We not want to see them," Bedi says.

"She's right. This work is twenty-four hours a day, and it's an unsafe site for visitors," Mike says.

As they walk past an area where wall panel installation has begun, security issues begin to reveal themselves. Gold leaf is being applied to the ornate decorative ironwork that has now been fitted above the pillars and on the new panels. As each job is completed, the next scheduled worker steps in and the next task begins. Two gold workers, in full face mask and safety glasses, hold full sheets of gold leaf which they tap into every groove and crevasse with a small brush. All around them drills blast, welders flash, sparks fly, and more panels are swung into place.

"Seen enough?" Mike asks.

"No, I'd like to walk all the decks, like our team do six times a day," Hunter says, starting to question how much of the work they do.

The deck above has the first of the six-hundred mini suites. Neither saw them at the lunch event yesterday. They are two rooms with en-suite and double balcony space. Carrara marble panels are in place around the washroom. Bath and shower are being fitted.

Kieron raises his phone to take pictures, "OK, Mike?"

"Sure. You could do it when you are by yourself; why not now? Mr Schmeichel is proud of his ship at any stage."

Kieron videos the whole space and is streaming it live to Dwight, who will have got into the Miami office early.

The Captain's Bridge is in a finished state because the ship has run early sea trials. The other new guys are impressed with all the equipment and Mike is only too pleased to pretend he knows what it all is. The three investigators are looking at the view forward.

"Did it pass its roadworthy tests?" Hunter jokes, pretending he knows nothing, although he understands way more than his tour guide Mike. If any of the tests are failures it can set the maiden voyage back months, or indefinitely.

"Passed with flying colours and got certificates. But, it's not exactly the first ship of its kind."

"They would worry about the vibration test," Hunter shares only with Kieron and Bedriška.

"Vibration only happen when I am angry," she says.

"That's a thing?" Kieron asks Hunter, looking through the window in the floor of the bridge used when docking.

"Vibration will have all the guests asking for refunds," Hunter states. "I'm told it's propeller science."

"Science?" Kieron asks.

"Systematic study of structure and behaviour by observation or experiment," Bedi informs like a robot. She edges forward to a microphone that hangs from a complex transmitter and receiver.

"Russian scientist Alexander Stepanovich Popov invent radio."

Hunter shakes his head slightly.

"No, he's not Russian," Hunter says convincingly, but it is a tease.

"Popov definitely Russian genius," she stamps.

He is joking, but not expecting her to be so instantly angry.

"When SS Lusitania sailed in 1907 she had a terrible ass wobble. They tried adding loads of weight in the rear, but no good. The propeller was wrong and now they know it's to do with the bubbles created," Hunter explains.

"I'm glad I asked," Kieron says.

"Good information," Bedi says positively, after Kieron's dismissal.

"Mike. Does the Captain have a private residence?" is the question Hunter has been waiting to ask.

"Above, follow me. The owner's suite is almost complete, and Mr Schmeichel uses it on occasion."

Mike leads them out and up a flight of white-steel staff-stairs to the deck above.

"I don't like him," Bedi tells Hunter.

13 - BEHIND CLOSED DOORS

Italy-1530hrs   Miami-0730hrs

Back out on the dock in Italy, and without their safety hats, the CSCI pair look back at the ship.

"You two can double up for the night shift. 'Till you get used to it," Mike says pointing between Hunter and Philips. They wonder if he is asserting his authority as head of security, if that is what he is. He might also be the only one who speaks English as well as Italian; a useful combination.

"We go see art warehouse?" Bedriška says.

Mike is having to learn that even when he thinks it is a question from Bedi, it never is.

"Do you want lunch first?"

"No," she says for everyone.

"You're a bit sharp," Mike says to her, leading them away.

"I cut hard."

"Can't wait to see you with a gun."

"You like women with guns. You are pervert?"

'Only she could get away with that remark', Kieron thinks, walking behind them.

"You'll get your uniforms tomorrow, with side-arm. Then you can go anywhere. They'll know you're security," Mike announces to the group.

"Surely they're supposed to know from the pass?" Kieron asks, testing how effective the pass is for the security team.

"The uniform works better."

Kieron starts to drop behind with Hunter. Bedi has Mike engaged enough for a war to break out behind him and he not turn.

As they near the warehouse, both Hunter and Philips note the closeness to the main building where they have their office. An internal road runs between them, but the cables that are slung between them are on an overhead gantry which interests Philips. The old walkway looks very unsafe. He videos it all, sending it live to Dwight.

"Don't suppose you have any building plans or know what the cables are, eh big man?"

"Good morning to you too," Dwight replies.

Hunter takes Kieron's phone and points it at the TV aerial and satellite dish on the roof above their office as he speaks.

"Dwight, tell Macey she's an investigator now as well as a painter. But as a painter, those annoying rich people are her customers. She should look at them with dollar signs. Oh, and good morning. The Englishman's got no manners," he says, pushing the phone back into Kieron's hand.

"Good morning D…," Dwight has gone.

Kieron catches Mike and Bedi up as they enter the so-called 'extra-secure bonded warehouse' without any pass key or test. Bedriška immediately starts to take notes, drawing a plan of the external wall and fire doors. Kieron is still filming and sending. He is concentrating on the roof structure and walkways until he walks towards Hunter at the start of a hundred metres of art standing in line.

They reach the end, and a protruding toilet block and ugly boarded-up offices that are all nailed closed. They walk back stopping at an over-confident-looking young man who had positioned himself to interview them in conversation.

"All this oil paint and canvas, cost dollars at the art shop?" Hunter says, taking his trap and deliberately disrespecting the value of the art.

"Yes, give it a go," the young Englishman is quick to snap back. It must be a well-rehearsed standard answer.

"Hi Ben, says Kieron, inspecting his name badge. I'm Kieron, from Pinner. North-West London," he says in response to a similar accent.

"Bentley, not Ben. And I'm not sure I would refer to Pinner as London."

"Even though it is?"

Bentley is quiet.

"Explain your filing system," Hunter says.

"Please."

"If I'd wanted to say please, I would've done."

Bentley shakes his head at the American's ill manners, and his answers are more directed towards Kieron.

"Those are all grouped as completed. Six paintings for each suite. We need six hundred groups."

"How are they grouped?" Hunter demands.

Bentley looks up as if to say that is rude, he is rude.

"Normally by artist; that is the easiest. Sometimes by styles or a mix of styles. It can be colours, or the colour it implies."

"So, there's no fucking sense to it at all. You all get paid for complete bull."

"I was an art assistant at the National Portrait Gallery in London."

"So?"

"The first Portrait Gallery in the world, founded in 1856."

"That mean I'm s'posed to be impressed that you're an art assistant."

"Only as much as I am impressed by security here."

"What do you mean by that, Bentley?" Kieron asks.

Bedi arrives and saves him having to answer.

"Why fire doors locked?" she powers as a real question.

"They always remain locked to protect the huge asset in here."

"Not always locked. Oil on lock is new. Scratches new," she says.

"I have no idea, I'm only an 'assistant' in this strange place," Bentley delivers, looking at Hunter.

"You like it here?" Hunter says, as a question as well as a threat.

"It's a fabulous job, if it wasn't, I'd be at any top gallery."

"You are special?" Bedi asks.

"Very special. I am Bentley." He offers Bedi his hand.

The two men are dreading what comes next.

"Or is it three kisses and a hug?" Bentley says, politely. "I worked in the New Hermitage. The Spanish and Italian art collection. The second-largest art collection in the world."

Bedi shakes his hand in a greeting and showing respect.

"Bedriška Kossoff."

"Bentley Crouch-Fielding."

The three investigators nod at the young man's confidence.

"We done here?" Mike shouts from the open doors. The three follow Mike out of the double doors with the other two new security guards. They acknowledge the security guard posted at the door. The van backed up to the warehouse and new pieces being carried in steals their real interest. Bedi takes a photograph as she walks past, then sends it to Dwight.

"Dwight. Run licence plate BB81869 Roma," Kieron says, also seeing it. "And, a 'Bentley Crouch-Fielding'."

"How about good morning Dwight? Please? Thank-you Dwight? Seems like only us Americans have manners. I'm up super-early coz you're six hours ahead."

"I want floor plan of warehouse. If I want to say please, I will," Bedi replies for all. She hangs up and turns to the others. "It his job, right?"

14 – BREAKFAST WITH A FRIEND

Italy-1700hrs   Miami-0900hrs   **Key West-0900hrs**

Macey has had a horrid night on board ship. She hates the movement, feels seasick, and is repulsed by the people. The day should be starting, but she is drifting into a deep sleep when there is a knock on her stateroom door. She jumps out of bed to see her only friend on the ship, Zeete. This time he can help to put all the dresses back in the case so she can jump ship as soon as it docks. Excited, she opens the door but instantly deflates. Her mood changes to one of shock.

"Clément?"

"Klee-mont," he immediately corrects her.

Macey is deflated, allowing him to push in. With his finger to his lips for quiet, he raises another hand and waves a wand-like tool. She watches him scan each wall, the ceiling, the TV, lamps and the kettle. The bathroom does not escape; however, he comes up with nothing. He turns to face her, pleased with his search; but she thinks he looked like a complete amateur missing so many places. She shakes her head in disgust, snatches the wand and covers the room far more carefully. When she can confirm nothing, she turns to him, annoyed.

"Clément, I'm Macey, not May.I.see."

"We need to talk about a few things," he says, speedily dropping the accent.

"Hey!" She says, in a greater shock. "Where's the sweet accent gone?"

"Does it matter? To everyone else I'm French."

"French! French!"

"A respected French art critic and collector with class. To you, I'm also from downtown."

"Downtown?" she questions. "Toy town!"

"East London, near the old docks and shunting yards in Leyton."

"You're phoney. Should I be talking to you?"

"I introduced you to Yonan Schmeichel."

"Bet you sold him that painting?"

"Sure. I'm an art dealer."

"How much?"

"For what it was worth. For what he thought it was worth."

"That was my rehearsal piece."

"It was a very good painting," Clément insists.

"He offered me thirty thousand for the eventual master," she says, now confused.

"He bought your first attempt, the original work signed 'one of three' with your 'original name', before you became Mai.I.See. All of special value."

"How much?"

"Twenty-five thousand dollars."

"What!"

There is another knock at the door leaving her statuesque and confused.

"I ordered breakfast, but don't let him in the room," says Clément.

"What if it's not?"

"Don't let anyone in."

"What if they push?"

"I'm here."

"You wuss. What good is that?" she says, opening the door slightly.

"Room service ma'am," the waiter says, prepared to wheel the trolley in.

"No, no. I got it, thanks," she says, rudely taking the trolley and letting the door swing closed.

After ensuring it is closed, Clément follows. Finger to lips again, Clément begins to use the wand around the trolley.

"You're not a magician, give me that wand," she whispers in his ear.

Macey snatches it from him and goes around the trolley. She holds the wand much closer. Eventually, it gives a silent alarm; diodes flash up and down. Macey tentatively opens the white cover draped over the trolley. She isolates the offending pot of long-life milk sachets. The jug of fresh milk makes the sachets unnecessary.

Clément takes the bugged pot outside the cabin and walks it a few doors along. He places it on a used breakfast tray by another stateroom. When he returns he lifts the covering cloth, then the silver lids.

"Tad-ah!"

"You're still not a magician."

"Trust me, that's exactly what I am."

Macey ignores him and looks in every excessive dish.

"What a waste of food."

"Not if we eat it, Macey. Enjoy."

"If we eat all that I'll need a doctor. It's not normal?"

"You can have room service whenever you want," he tells her.

"The cost, man!"

"Everything's free once on board. Well, not free, coz you paid for it all in your holiday cost. Not you though."

"I could stay in this room for the whole cruise, watch TV and order room service?"

"No, eat, we're getting off."

"I'm good here thanks."

"Prisha is waiting for you on land."

Macey's eyes widen with joy. She wants to leave.

"Sit down. Eat first, then pack that easel and get the brushes in your hair."

"Hit me with a little more of that English accent. What d'you really do?" she asks.

"I work for Yonan as an art and talent scout. The perfect find would be a young artist with a lengthy career potential."

"You ever found one?"

"One. You. With you I hit gold."

"Shut the front door!" she says, to avoid swearing.

"You're more than a dash of surprise. You're a star. Please eat," he beams with enthusiasm.

"Talent scout?"

Clément digs in, serving himself more than enough breakfast.

"How many people you eating for? Looks like you've got five loaves and three fishes there," she says in disgust.

"What a great image," he says, looking up. "Your vision is amazing. Painting a table full of cruisers, each with five loaves and three fishes."

Macey takes some food but is far more conservative with what she chooses. She may not be stick-thin, but she enjoys being small.

"Back in Miami. All this wealth is in the dock. Four blocks back, people can't afford to eat."

"This industry employs hundreds of thousands and runs apprenticeships and special programs."

"What's wid' the May-I-see?" she asks.

"Genius. It is..."

"I know what it is, but it don't say, Macey."

"It does, it works, trust Clément," he says, diving back into French. "We are a team while on the ship; you paint, I promote and sell. I want one painting on the wall with a ridiculous price tag."

"From me?"

"Yes, and do not trust anyone else. I mean anyone."

"Zeete, my cabin guy?"

"Especially not him. And we scan the room each time we come in."

"No. No, we."

"Eat. Pack your paints and we go ashore."

"Why am I getting bugged? Who's listening to me?"

Clément shrugs like he doesn't know.

"I'm in danger, right?"

Clément grins, 'maybe'.

"Well, I'm going ashore, and I ain't coming back."

15 - KEY WEST

Italy-1830hrs   Miami-1030hrs-Miami   **Key West-1030hrs**

Macey runs down the pier. On the other side of the secure customs area, she can see Prisha waiting. They hug as if they have not seen each other for weeks. Macey only left yesterday afternoon, but she has never left Overtown, Miami in her life before.

"Prisha, I hate it."

"You've not even been onboard a day."

"Hate it, not going back."

"Well, you're going to love this island, it's paradise."

"Island? It's still part of America, right?" Macey panics. "I don't have a passport."

"It is nothing like Miami," Prisha says, consoling her with a nod.

Just as Clément arrives with her folder and easel, the girls are off. He stands ignored as if he was never there.

"Hello," he says pathetically to no one, then hurries after them.

Prisha leads Macey by the hand into a circus of roads, colour and smiling faces.

"The light is fantastic, the air so clean, and the sky so blue," Macey says.

"What do you want to see first? Houses, beach, or boardwalk? You have beaches in Miami; let me show you the boardwalk," Prisha decides, without waiting for a reply. She is dragged off again as Clément arrives.

"Hello," he says again, with his French accent, but missing them. Feeling hot in his cravat and beret, he looks like a mad artist, but he feels like a roadie. He rushes to catch them.

"The fish are amazing, and there are Manatee, basking right under the boards."

"How long have you been here?" Macey asks.

"Last night. But I was so excited, I was up at first light."

They walk past the brightly coloured electric Conch Train as the driver shouts and pulls the chord slung above his head. The whistle sounds, sunshine is everywhere, and they instantly feel welcome and relaxed.

The boardwalk is so close, they are there in minutes. Stopping to look over the edge at the fish swimming in the crystal-clear water allows Clément to catch them. He offers Macey her easel.

"Not yet," she says.

"Is this your assistant?" Prisha asks looking at Clément. "Would you mind having him move my bags from the hotel to the ship?"

"No," Clément says as the two girls talk to each other.

"Why?" Macey asks, ignoring him.

"I'm staying on for the cruise. Isn't it exciting!"

They hug again.

The boardwalk with classic wooden rail does not excite Macey, nor do the many tourist bars, so the group moves back into the streets. She does love the picture box houses and takes some shots with her camera.

"Are you going to paint these?" Clément asks.

"Only if the rest of the world disappears," she says, decisively.

"I thought they were nice," he says, feeling chastised.

"The word nice means it's not good enough," Macey says.

They walk off with Clément still carrying the kit.

"I'm not a roadie."

Having arrived back at the circus via a very interesting road full of bars and eating houses, they turn up towards Ernest Hemingway's house.

Here Macey is fascinated. She listens to the stories from the guide. She studies the pictures of his family who all died insane. But it is Ernest's portrait that grips her. His dark eyes look back at her wherever she moves in the room. She gives up moving and lets him look at her.

The vast number of cats in the house disturbs her. She has never been a cat person, possibly because she can have a reaction to their hair. Unimpressed by the story of the sea captain giving Hemingway a polydactyl kitten called Snow-white, she steps out and stands on the balcony. The wooden steps go down to the garden, but from the top, you can see into his writing room. She is transfixed. Clément is watching her; he has seen that look before. Not often, but he has seen it. He has worked with enough artists to know when they are entranced, but none like Macey. He approaches her slowly and offers her pad and easel. His instincts were right. Now he is the perfect assistant because he can smell a masterpiece, even though the paper is blank. Macey frames the portrait within the window of the house as if she were standing close and looking in. The room behind is swiftly outlined in detail, but only to be forgotten. Then the magic happens. Somehow Ernest Hemingway begins to come to life under her brush. The sketch is instant and perfect. Hemingway leans across his desk on his left arm, which envelops his pad. His bespectacled, bearded face concentrates down, waiting for inspiration. The pen in his hand hovers as he awaits orders from his head. Macey does not need to wait. All of this and more leaps onto the paper. Clément watches in awe and must break his trance to photograph Macey sketching Hemingway's room. He hits send to share it with Yonan.

The woman who looked her up and down at yesterday's cocktail party stops behind her, looking at her work. She does not have the self-restraint of the others, who are giving the artist space to work.

"How can you paint him when he's not there?"

"I can see him, can't you?"

The woman looks again, into the window.

"He's dead."

"I see dead people."

"Oh, you're going to love New Orleans," the woman says.

Clément decides to put an end to this.

"She's very at home there. The home of Voodoo," Clément adds, with a slurred French accent.

The woman scurries away.

16 - WRECKED

In Italy, all the guards are still celebrating their first day. As they begin to leave, Bedi gets a very pissed attitude.

"Go home. Me, I find hotel."

"What happened?" Hunter asks, knowing very well nothing happened. It is all an act.

"Owner says he rent to someone else."

"Here," Kieron says, throwing his keys. "Bunk in our place till you find somewhere."

"So, there is one good Englishman."

Kieron gets up, grabs a pen to write the address down, but what he writes is, 'keep the bed warm'. Bedi looks at him with an empty expression.

"Good job we on opposite shifts, we never see each other."

The three investigators will live together now. Everyone knows it, no one will question it. The day shift leaves late and Hunter and Keiron grab a coffee before starting rounds.

"I feel wrecked," Hunter admits.

"Jet-lag and lack of sleep. I could do it when I was younger," Kieron says.

What their contemporaries don't know is that they got an overnight, Miami to Italy, flight last night and lost six hours.

"Is this lunchtime, breakfast time or what?" Kieron asks.

"It's work time," Hunter says as his call is answered.

"Prisha, how's Macey?"

"She's spent the last two hours painting Ernest Hemingway."

CRUISE SHIP ART THEFT

"I hope he sat still for her, I heard he was a dreadful sitter."

"It's all good here. I'll report to Dwight later."

1530hrs-Key West

Prisha pockets her phone and waits at the bottom of the stairs at Hemingway's house in Key West. The sun is still high, but Macey is protected in the foliage at the side by his writing room. About ninety minutes from first starting, Macey comes down, shaking Ernest Hemingway from her head. She had been possessed, trance-like while the others waited. Prisha reference photographed all the pictures throughout the house, and what could be seen of his writing room. Clément stayed in touch with Yonan.

A crowd forms beside the crystal blue swimming pool. A guide is telling the story of how Ernest went away to cover the Spanish Civil War as a correspondent.

"He left his second wife, Pauline, here at home. She heard of his affair with fellow journalist Martha Gellhorn. In spite, Pauline had his boxing ring torn down. It sat in the garden where now sits the swimming pool she had built with all his money. As the island had no running water, at enormous cost she had it filled. She threw huge parties with the rest of his money. On his return, he threw his last penny at her, which is now set in the concrete patio."

Tourists await their turn to see the coin. Macey does not; she can see Hemingway smiling at her. He is back haunting her. His smiling cheek seeps through his anger and the coin spins in front of his face. She sketches again. As before, the amazed Clément and Prisha both protect her from tourists as she works.

"I won't be very long," Macey says, to stop them from worrying she might be in a huge session as she was for the Hemingway upstairs. "I want to go somewhere else before we go to the ship."

Using less detail, she paints quickly until few tourists are left. Time is running out. Ships must leave within the working day of the port authority. Today the all-on-board time is five-thirty, but Macey has been hearing about wrecking ships all day; she wants to know more.

The island is small, and they find a house/museum dating back to that time. They enter, and both the interior of the house and the couple that greet them are in period dress.

"Welcome. Before your tour, please note that photography is not allowed," the old seafarer says.

"Very clever, I see what you're doing; cameras have not been invented yet," Macey says, with humour and edge. It is as if she has been taking lessons from Bedriška.

Clément follows, with no further complaints about assisting the master. He has seen her at work. She is a woman of passion, a woman capable of expressing herself, the likes of which he has never seen.

The man in costume shows them a grand three-mast sailing ship in a case.

"This is a true model of one of the ships sunk on Key West reef. The heroic wreckers, as the trade became known, went out in boats to save the sailors," the man explains.

"Was it the sailors they went to save? Or the cargo?" Macey asks, changing the tone in the room.

"They saved hundreds of sailors."

"But it was a trade, they made money from the cargo. Huge sums of money."

"Both the cargo and life had value," the man smiles. It feels like an answer he has rehearsed and used a few times in the past.

"So, what of the odd description of it being piracy? What of tales that navigation beacons were purposely moved to entice ships off course and onto the reef?"

"Untrue," the man interrupts.

"So how it is that after the beacons were replaced by a lighthouse the trade ended? Was is not like mass murder, driven by greed? Like slavery?" she asks.

"We are closing now," the man says, looking at his watch.

A cruise ship can be seen from many places on the island as the height of buildings is restricted. They walk towards it at a healthy pace.

"I wasn't expecting that," Prisha says.

"That room was full of dead people, they all wanted me to say it."

"Now they want you to paint it," Clément says.

"For other rich people driven by greed," she replies.

17 - NIGHT SHIFT

Italy-0145hrs   Miami-1745hrs   Key West-1745hrs

In Key West, the ship is going through a procedure of letting ropes go. Macey has never seen this, nor heard it. The side thrusters push the ship away from the dock until it can turn and power out to sea. It is leaving Key West.

"Are you seeing pictures?" Prisha asks her.

"My life is one big cartoon," Macey replies. "The story ain't worked out too well yet."

Prisha can detect she is down and lost. Sadly, although Macey is a friend who needs consoling, she has been sent to keep her inspired and working.

"With you as the Warrior Goddess, it will end well."

"Now who is it with the imagination?" Macey smiles at last.

Prisha leads her from the rail at the side of the ship to the inner deck rail overlooking a Calypso-themed party around the pool, still bathed in sunshine.

"What's this?" Macey asks.

"The sail away party. It happens when we leave each port. Now, show me our suite," Prisha demands, pulling Macey away. "And tonight, we're going to see the Supremes!"

"No, we're not. Berry Gordy broke that group up."

Day3-Italy-0200hrs   Day2-**Miami-1800hrs**   Key West-1800hrs

The blacked-out windows create an ever-dark bat-cave. They would not know the sun was going down. Croc and Dwight lean into the same screen. It shows a dark picture of cables and a prehistoric terminal box.

"Can you get any light on it?" Dwight asks.

"Ain't gonna help us, bro, I studied Information Technology and Electronics, not history!" Croc says.

Day3-0201hrs-Italy   Day2- Miami-1801hrs   Key West-1801hrs

In a very different kind of darkness, Kieron and Hunter are up on the skywalk of the old warehouse. This building in the Bianchi shipyard is used to store the huge wealth of art. They have a camera phone looking at the terminal boxes where cables enter, slung across from the main building.

"Croc, these are definitely telephone cables,"

Kieron says.

"Telephones have cables?" Croc asks from Miami.

"OK, they might be alarm cables. This coax cable looks like an old TV cable, and these guys look like power, but three-phase power must come in at floor level," Kieron reasons. He might be talking to himself but they are listening in Florida. "Maybe it's generator power.'

"Don't touch to find out," Dwight warns, though it would seem obvious.

"I'm gonna use the coax for picture, and two of the unused phone threads for power. Red stripe for positive, blue with pale blue stripe as negative."

"We'll try and find the other ends in the main building," Hunter adds.

A commotion breaks out below. Amongst the obvious art assistants with their artistic easy style of dress are two harder, heavy-set guys pushing one of the assistants around violently. The others back away watching; the assistant is helpless as he takes a very light beating. The thugs obviously don't want to hurt him. This visit is simply designed to frighten. Hunter films it on his phone. Intervening would gain nothing but pull in a couple of low-level soldiers working for someone else.

"Apart from 'who are they?' and 'who do they work for?' How did they get around the security gate?" Kieron asks.

"And why is there no camera in this warehouse?"

In the technical centre, Dwight is already focussing on their faces. Multiple facial images spread across two of his screens. He gets rows of different angles. Croc sits down at his screen and invokes a facial recognition search on each of the pictures. No sooner has he kicked the search off, Dwight has sent over the second guy's frame grabs from Hunter's phone. They are loaded into facial recognition.

Dwight zooms in, scanning their belts for weapons and their chests or sleeves for an ID badge.

For Kieron and Hunter at the Italian warehouse, the risk of being found out gets higher every minute. On an old outside platform, they watch the two heavies walk straight out of the main gate past security. It looks like they could have stopped and engaged in a conversation. Security was useless or paid off, they can't report this because they don't know how far it goes.

Back on the ground, a small kitten is crying for attention at the door, meowing, with his tail up.

"You reckon that's the office cat?" Kieron asks.

"If that's your new love affair, I approve."

"Look. I'm normally a one-woman man," Kieron pleads.

"The problem is having one woman each contract."

Kieron pours some milk in a saucer for the cat, which it instantly starts to drink. A chunk of smoked-tofu from inside his sandwich is dropped beside the saucer. The cat sniffs it and goes back to the milk."

"Cat's not a vegan," Hunter mocks.

Hunter's phone rings.

"Dwight, what you got?"

"Watch yourself out there."

"Why?" Hunter asks switching to speaker so Kieron can hear.

"Those two might be SISMI."

"Military Intelligence?"

"Looks like they were involved in a few major issues, including the abduction of Abu Omar in Milan, 2003."

"You sure they're not with one of the domestic crime agencies?" Hunter asks.

"Doesn't look like it. We still hacking for anything to confirm it, but most of this stuff's under wrap?"

"I wouldn't have nailed them as Secret Service," Kieron ponders.

"From a first look, they could also have been involved in planting the yellowcake uranium documents on Saddam Hussein," Dwight reports.

"Wow, that's a bit strong," Kieron says.

"Just reporting what we found. But this stuff was easy to find and you know what it means when it's easy."

"Probably ain't true," Hunter offers.

"Look, he's eating it. He is a vegan," Kieron says, as the cat bites into the chunk of tofu. He looks up. "Sorry, remember, that branch of the service was disbanded back in 2007."

"If these guys are building a false CV to find work, using stuff that can't be corroborated, they're rogues, because no one would go to that much trouble to get this job. Other than you... So, assume they are nasty bastards," Dwight says via the phone.

"Like us?" Hunter toys.

"I didn't say that. You find out why they're beating a student. I'll find out who they are," Dwight says and signs off.

18 - NO WORK

For some, finishing a night shift is a feeling of release. For others they are tired and they want to sleep. However, finishing at eight in the morning and having to walk past shops emitting smells of fresh bread and coffee is hard to resist. Both Kieron Philips and Hunter Witowski are tempted into a delicatessen.

It is a long narrow shop, with a pale green tiled counter running down one side, with shelves full of tinned and boxed foods behind. The glass counter displays are full of freshly filled enticing salads and all kinds of pastas. Hams are hanging from the ceiling. Underneath they have little tin trays to collect the excess fat, which is reduced by the natural humidity. There are a few tables at the end near matching double swing doors that lead to the kitchen and back rooms.

Breakfast starts with coffee, fresh bread, cheeses, and a glass of wine with the owner. It is way gone nine o'clock before they leave. Kieron has three bottles of wine between his fingers as well as nearly a bottle in his stomach to help him sleep. Hunter carries a pack of eight beers. In their defence, to a night shift worker, it is their version of an evening walk home with a few drinks.

They would turn the key in the lock but the door is open. Both of them change immediately from merry men, into sharp watchful investigators. Their shopping is placed on the floor quietly, the door closed and the chain put across so no one can leave fast. They climb the stairs, taking each room one by one. They don't shout clear; that is for the movies. Shouting anything would give away their position. Kieron's bedroom, empty. Hunter's room is last. The door is flung open and they see Bedriška splayed across the bed with a bottle of vodka still in her hand.

"I can see what you saw in her now," Hunter says.

"Bedi, wake up. Wake up," Kieron tries.

"Was sex always like this?"

"Bedi!"

Kieron lifts her.

She coughs awake but the dim bulb is too bright for her eyes and her head hurts.

"She's a mess."

"She's an alcoholic. She needs help, self-confidence," Kieron says to Hunter, knowing her past. He turns back to cradle Bedi. "Bedi. You've missed your shift."

"What time is it?" she slurs.

Hunter waves the air, "Wow. Stay away from naked flames."

"Macey is fireball," she slurs.

"Macey?" Hunter asks.

"She told me she doesn't like The Supremes."

"Never my favourites either."

"She said they weren't from Detroit."

"I think they were," Hunter says.

"Why so little security for so much money?" she slurs again.

"Get her out of here, I want to sleep," Hunter says. "You know how to deal with this."

"I have never seen her like this. I dread how much she must have drunk to get in this state?" Kieron says, lifting her dead weight.

"Bedi. Come on, we've got to get up."

"I'll go to work," she says.

"No, I'm going to get you to bed," he says.

"And figure out how you're going to convince her she has a drink problem," Hunter says, helping to lift her.

"Sorry," she says.

"You have a drink problem," Kieron says, taking all her weight as he walks her out.

"I know, I heard Hunter say."

19 - THE JOB

Italy-1900hrs   Miami-1100hrs   **Gulf of Mexico-1100hrs**

There is a small space in front of the sales desk in the art gallery which is often used for art lectures. They are well attended. However, if those lectures were set in any of the large entertainment venues it would feel empty and lose atmosphere. This space works well.

Macey is setting up her easel and placing her paints. As always, her small brushes are in her hair. She lays out her part-started works, 'Hemingway', 'Last Penny', 'Yonan's Shoes', 'Stan's Hat', and 'Balloons and Junk', on a small table next to her. There is little room but there is a certain thrill to be sat in a gallery. The manager, Jill Quant, is not much older than Macey and did a similar art degree, but in Boston. She is looking over Macey's shoulder at the unfinished works. Jill moves between 'Hemingway' and the Manhattan alligator skin shoes Macey has sketched in some detail.

"I wish I had your vision," Jill says.

"Looks like you doing fine. I work in a burger bar."

"Not for much longer."

"Love your imagination about my career. But I got no temptation to let my imagination run away with me," Macey smiles.

She has an instant connection with Jill.

Prisha arrives with two coffees.

"Sorry, I should have got three."

Jill shakes her head, no worries. She hands them the one-sheet ship's 'News Back Home'. On the front is a headline about 'May.I.see, America's hottest art talent boarding the MS Overlord'.

"It says more about the ship than me."

"One minute you want to hide, the next you want the limelight."

"I'd like them to get it right. Wrong name, no detail."

"The luxury cruise ship that only takes 1,250 guests, all in suites. They got that right," Prisha reads.

"Seems poor reporting."

"It's because no one knows anything about you."

"We should have ordered room service," Macey says.

"As much as I am desperate to do that, there'll be time," Prisha says.

Macey is never self-conscious when she paints. But here, each passer-by offers a forced smile and she is surrounded by art she hates.

"Wouldn't you love to have your paintings hanging on the wall in here?" Prisha asks, enthusiastically.

"No."

"No?"

Macey turns Prisha to a cartoon-like pink pony with a bow tied in its mane. The two girls look at it.

"It haunts me. I keep turning to it. It makes me want to throw-up," Macey says.

"That's a consistent best-seller," Jill shouts over.

Macey is exasperated.

"I'm so void of artistic inspiration, I dare not touch any of these," she says, turning to her unfinished works.

Macey drops down hard and rough-paints portholes across her sheet with the speed of a modern art great.

Prisha collects the unfinished works, "I'll take these back to the suite, I feel they are otherwise in danger."

A group of four people slow as they walk past and offer what is now a predictable polite and very forced grin. Their faces might have been trying to smile but they didn't quite make it through the imperious stature and heavy Botox.

At last, Macey feels something. She outlines the four, then slants their mouths. As two others pass she does the same, adds another four behind. Then another two in front, four more behind until the procession fills the paper. The light bursts through the portholes behind them. Now she has inspiration.

Clément arrives with yesterday's newspaper: Southern Independent News. It is open at the inner page of Macey, 'Downtown art star boards ship'.

"What is that?" he asks in character, with the heavy French accent.

"I haven't decided whether to call it 'false smiles' or 'Botox'. See it at the end of the day."

"You are still a little edgy; please remove it from your system. We try and see the good in this ship. And there is good."

Macey stifles her laughter by a tightly restrained face. All she can hear is the east-London son of a dock worker.

"What's this? More about the ship?" Macey asks. Pointing out the newspaper headline and sub-headline.

"My mother always told me to brush my hair."

She might be angry, but the huge picture is of her face, including bun and brushes; her radiance bursting out.

"This photographer found a rare connection. You look amazing," Clément says.

Macey releases a proper smile, the first in ages.

"Yes, he has."

"So, focussing on your morning on stage. Your competition is line dancing, step-fit, and a Knit and Natter. This afternoon; Deck Quoits and short cricket."

"Why am I here?"

"To make a noise."

"You want me to scream?"

"No. No! I want, what that young photographer saw. I want what you felt yesterday. But, in the meantime, I need to get all your past paintings. Everything. Everything you have ever done; from doodles to oils, sketches to watercolours."

"Hundreds; most are at my mom's."

"Someone will go 'round there."

"Ain't gonna be that easy."

Clément looks at her, eyebrows raised, head tilted, questioning her remark.

"She ain't gonna let one of 'em go if she thinks she can get a solid dime for her next fix."

"How about a friend going to get them," he asks.

"Izzy, she knows my space, knows my mum. We have been friends since kids, but good luck to her."

"We need to do it before you hit the news in Miami. Your success is happening faster than we expected."

"Wow. That's sick."

"You need to trust us," he says. "Today, you are the star attraction. Or maybe it is me."

"You? We still don't know what you do."

Clément holds the newspaper up.

"Now, you will see. I will entertain while you paint. Our morning session starts at eleven, and we restart at two in the afternoon. But, not 'ere. This is not big enough. We are off to the atrium."

"It's a staircase," she says, shocked.

"It is an amphitheatre."

20 - FALLEN STARS

Italy-**2300hrs**   Miami-1500hrs   Gulf of Mexico-1500hrs

The investigators slept well for most of the day after their twelve-hour night shift. Back at work, they check the record book; the guard on the gate logged nothing, neither did the guard at the warehouse door. It confirms their suspicion that they are all on the art thieves' payroll. As always, their default position is to trust no one.

The ship is all lit up. The noise of work fills the air, but it is still very peaceful. After they do their tour of the ship and yard as required, they have lunch.

"We should stick our nose into the warehouse, say we heard someone got roughed up last night," Kieron suggests.

"You can ask. They don't like me," Hunter says.

Italy-2300hrs   **Miami-1500hrs**   Gulf of Mexico-1500hrs

In Miami, Izzy enters Wild Mary's Diner looking deflated and upset. She walks around behind the counter.

"Set me up with a drink, Stan."

"Will that be coffee or cola?"

"Strong coffee."

Stan pours her a coffee as Mary strides over from table service.

"What wrong wid you, girl? You missing Macey?"

"I've been at Macey's house. Her mom won't let me in. Won't give me her paintings."

"Oh, is that right?" Mary says, her anger building.

"She just no good, Mary, like my mom. They're the wrong side of '95."

Mary leans over the counter to Izzy.

"I feel obliged to put a little balance to this, Izzy. Feel I owe it to them."

"Amen," Stan says. "Amen."

"Let me tell you, and you hear me good before the storm."

"Tsunami," Stan says, from the grill.

"They were fine church-going women back in the day when the Lyric was our church. That was the most beautiful theatre in the whole of the south."

"Ain't gonna help me get no paintings back."

"That was the place for good black folk. All your mamas were good trustworthy women when you were young. That why they adopt you. Church went and closed. The worms get into people. Your mamas all crashed bad, and they ain't coming back. But," she says, building up a head of steam. "That don't mean the bitch gonna keep Macey's paintings."

Mary flings her apron off as she goes around into the back.

"Drink that coffee fast." They hear her shout.

"Real fast," says Stan. "And I hope you got your running shoes on."

When Mary comes out she has her coat and her best church hat on.

"Oh my," Stan says. "Freight train heading down them tracks."

Izzy follows her out. Stan hits the intercom.

"Hello, hello. Chef Stan here from next door. Croc can you come through and help me, please,"

The door to CSCI opens and a surprised Croc looks out.

"Woz-up Chef?"

"Left on my own."

Croc looks around the diner.

"Where's they gone?"

"Steamed off to see Macey's mom."

Croc runs out the door. The bell pings behind him. Stan is left alone.

"I run this place before, I can run it again."

Mary is marching at a pace as they pass the Lyric Theatre on 2nd, two blocks down.

"I used to love Ethel Waters."

"Who?" Izzy asks.

"I should have got you earlier; she sang 'Stormy Weather', sang at that beautiful theatre right there."

"Thought you said it was a church."

"That before it was a church."

They leave North West 2nd and head up 8th to the bridge under i95. There is no turning back now.

"Can't believe what this place has become."

Izzy has to jog to keep up. Croc is running behind to join them. All three students technically live there, but Mary knows they spend almost no time there and she keeps them at college or in her diner as much as she can. What Mary doesn't know is they spend the rest of the time somewhere else.

Overtown is infested with junkies, dealers, drunks, hookers and pimps. Gangs not only run the corners, but they also run the streets. There is no racial tension here, just tension from out-of-control bullies. Mary is walking straight into the crime ravaged ghetto, where police fear to tread.

"It be a great day when they bulldoze all this, to build David Beckham's stadium," she rants.

"Where the people gonna live?" Croc asks.

"Find another bridge to live under. Even our president Trump says this America's scourge. You three should've listened to me long ago. Said I'd pay for a place of your own."

"You spend more than enough money on us, Mary," Izzy says.

"Why we going to Overtown, Mary?" Croc asks.

"Because we need the pictures. We crime investigators now. Did my training in that park with agent Prisha."

"Hunter nor Commander Phillips would come here without a gun," Croc explains. "Let's go back."

"I got my throwing knives with me. Why you think I wear this coat in summer?"

Croc shakes his head.

"Your knife-throwing act ain't gonna work up here," Izzy says, scared.

"Yeah, well, you can't live here no more," she says, turning to the bridge people, under a huge graffiti, 'Black Lives Matter'. "Let them build Miami Beckham United!"

"Mary, it would be wise if you kept it quiet in here," Croc suggests.

"Get them golden-balls here!" she shouts.

"Mary, please be quiet," Izzy pleads. They rush past more graffiti, 'Welcome to historic Overtown, established in 1896, fucked up in 1996'.

"Ain't no Banksy, is it?"

"Who's Banksy?" Croc asks.

"You ask Macey. She got a book on him. She gotta book on everyone. Like you all got books."

As Mary powers on ahead, Izzy stops by an ugly concrete two-story derelict block that used to be yellow. It used to be a motel.

"Mary!" Izzy shouts.

Mary turns. Croc a moment later.

"What?"

Izzy points.

"What?" Mary asks again.

"She live here," Izzy reveals.

"Here?" Mary screams. "This place ain't even standing up. What happened to that nice house she had?"

Mary walks back slowly, suspiciously eyeing the block. Below it is a demolition site that seems to have taken the garages and structure away from underneath.

"This ain't affordable housing, this is housing they pay you to live in," Mary says.

"This is it. First floor, two doors back."

"I ain't gonna walk up there. It ain't safe."

"Nothing safe round here, Mary," Croc says.

The railings are failing in many places making Mary feel nervy. The holes in the walls bodged up with newspaper and cement, look like a film set that couldn't possibly be in the USA. Mary knocks on the door and steps back. As her rear finds the railing it gives way. She steps forward fast. The door opens. A bent, ill woman, high on drugs.

"What you got for me?" she says.

Mary is silenced by what she sees. The woman looks up.

"Oh, it you. The young queen who had nothing who got herself some money," Mrs Ricca says with spite. "You never came by, you never sent money."

At ground level, Izzy and Croc both walk forward to listen to the intriguing, strange conversation unfolding above them.

"You want this?" Mary asks, holding out a small clear bag of white powder.

Mrs Ricca snatches at it. Mary pulls it back.

"Not so fast."

"Mary's got drugs," Izzy says in surprise.

Croc is wide-eyed.

"Oh shit, it ain't her corner."

The bent woman lunges again.

"Do that again and I leave. And this comes with me," Mary says.

"You always want something, wanted your daughter back, but too late. Too late, she's mine."

"Fuck," Croc says below. "Mary is Macey's birth mom? No way!"

Izzy puts her arms around Croc's arm and holds tight.

"I feel sick," she says. "Do we tell Macey?"

"How?" Croc chokes.

"I want all her paintings," Mary says.

"Why now? You never show no interest. Everyone wanna take everything. Be taking me clothes next. You just like the others."

"Like who?" Mary demands.

"Ones who took the pictures yesterday. I told 'em; no value 'cept to me, her mom. Even though they's shit. But I owed, so they took 'em. There ain't no point in beating a good customer like me."

"Any paintings left?"

"I don't know, you look," the junkie says, trying to grab the bag of white powder.

Izzy runs towards the derelict apartment. Croc runs after her, one step behind.

Mary walks inside, the lock on the door was kicked in long ago. There is nothing, no cupboards, no bed, nothing. The inside is bare. They stand back looking at Mary's shock.

"Macey ain't here much. Her mom sold all she had for drugs. Sold most of Macey's clothes. My mom's the same," Izzy says, but she goes straight to the old air conditioning hatch and yanks it open. Izzy pulls out a bundle of paintings and hands them back. Croc squares them together carefully like they are gold dust. Izzy lifts the mattress in the corner. A rat runs away leaving a family of babies. There are no paintings.

"He took them. Said I can have them back if I pay."

"When was he here?"

"I got nuttin' else to give, nuttin'. They've got everything. I had a nice house."

"How much do you owe them?" Croc asks.

"Seventy dollars."

Crock gives her a hundred dollars.

"If they come back, you get the paintings back. Say they're your daughter's; you wanna to keep them, coz she moved out. All you got left of her," Croc says.

He has grown so much in confidence since CSCI moved in and started employing him.

"She moving out?" Mrs Ricca asks.

"Can't think why," Mary mutters.

"You gonna try be a mom to her now? Like you should've. Too late. She won't know who you are."

"I'll take that risk," Mary forces out, her emotions mix as guilt and sadness add to her anger.

"You didn't just cut the cord, you left her at the church."

Mary can't speak as she see's Croc's shock at the discovery, he takes over. His emotions are mixed too, but they are all anger.

"What's your dealer's name? One who got the paintings?" Croc demands of the woman, throwing glances at Mary.

"I can't tell you that," she says. Unable to stand, she falls over. Rolling over, she looks up at them from the floor.

"Leave her," Izzy says.

Mary holds out the bag of white powder.

"Name?" Mary demands.

"Troy. This his street," is the sad reply from Macey's adoptive mother. She is a very broken woman.

Mary flicks her head for the students to go, backing off herself. She leaves the bag on the windowsill by the door. The junkie can't get up.

"Run, before one of her dealers shows their ugly face," Mary says, trying to hurry them to the stairs.

"There's no need to run now, Mary," Izzy says.

"There is. That's flour in the bag."

"Damn," Croc says.

They follow Mary down the stairs not ever looking back. Croc and Izzy start to jog away until Croc stops.

"Izzy, this ain't a place to be seen running."

"Trust me, everyone run here. You been gone a long time," Izzy says.

"We gotta do it," Croc says to her.

"We gotta do what?"

"Find our real moms."

"No one round here knows their real mom. Next, you be trying to find ya dad. Good luck with that one." Izzy is off again, running.

21 - RIGHT ROYAL SETTING

Italy-0100hrs   Miami-1700hrs   **Mexican Gulf-1700hrs**

Macey is in the middle of the dance floor at the bottom of the atrium. Not only is she relaxed in front of a crowd, but she is answering questions as she paints. Around her head, under her paint brush-bun, is a head-microphone; the type dancers wear. Her portrait of Hemingway leaning on the table looking at his pad has come to life. His eyes look down in frustration. The strain in his hand shows that his pen is about to move. His clothes, the room, all say something. His silver beard is an incredible work of hairs. It's a finished masterpiece she is now painting two people dancing.

"Do you have another question?"

A lady holds her hand up; Clément goes to her with the microphone.

"Is this painting personal? Is the girl you? Is a white man dancing with a black girl, so intertwined, a political statement?"

Macey jumps in before Clément can soften the blow.

"The point is, it shouldn't be. So, my statement is not them dancing together, when you look closer, what is deliberately provocative is that the people around the edge watching have no eyes: that is woke. Black lives, same as white lives."

Clément joins in, with such a heavy French accent not all would understand. "What a fantastic day…"

A guest quickly stands and walks onto the floor, "Please, the last question?"

Clément points the microphone towards him.

"It's about the order. Why paint her wonderful hair, then attach so much detail above it? The swirling stairs, the chandelier, what if the paint were to run and spoil all that fantastic work below?"

Clément takes the microphone back.

"Fantastic last question."

He is the consummate entertainer and salesman who understands the commerce in art. Hemingway is in danger of being usurped as her best work yet. If she sells a masterpiece, the ship will take twenty percent. It collects from all vendors right down to the cabaret acts selling their DVDs. It does not end there; each session has the bar takings monitored. She has held an audience captive; Clément has ensured they have been drinking.

"Ladies and gentlemen. I 'ope you all to toast our wonderful May.I.see. She is a star artist, the likes of which you will never see again. She cares about what she paints," he says.

"May.I.see; ze last answer today."

"Clément, you've talked so much I can't remember the question," she says, and the crowd laughs. She has got the measure of him and them and been funny all day.

"Ze hair, ze order of ze work?" he reminds her.

"Mistakes are allowable. It's part of the art. Some artists will deliberately distort their work to give it energy. Paint runs are real," she says, striking fast and furious. "My style is different, often angry so order doesn't matter, it is what I see. He might smile at me, he may talk to me. She might have let her hair down for the first time in years. They're in love, nothing can change that, not any run, not any mistake, nothing except destructive people watching who have no ability to see. It's about heart, not paint runs on the page."

"Ladies and gentlemen," Clem jumps in before she gets too political. "May.I.see will be back later in the week. You may have questions and she will sign her catalogue. Please allow her to enjoy the ship today. Once again, let us toast, May.I.see."

There is roaring applause as Clément walks over to her and folds the easel as she takes loving care of the paintings. Jill comes in from the side to help.

"You were incredible, incredible. But dangerous."

"I love it. They inspire me," she says.

"You are a natural. You will be a huge star. We need a catalogue to sell and sign," Clément says.

"Really?"

"Yes," Jill agrees. "It's a part of you they take home. A catalogue of your paintings," Jill says, looking at her Hemingway. "Both amazing! The shoes next?"

"Maybe."

"I'll carry these back to my desk; I'm going to be swamped with enquiries. I wish I had some of your pieces to sell."

Jill leaves. Macey is on cloud nine.

"Do not forget. Also, we 'ave to look for forgeries ere on the ship," he whispers. "Just like you found upstairs."

"Why can't you see them?"

"I found the first four months ago, at dinner with Yonan. But, me inspecting all ze art, zey will know I am on to them. You 'ere can 'ave an excuse for an art tour; you are double agent."

"What do I know about forgeries?"

"You 'ave zee eye. I teach you what they never teach in college."

Clément collects her easel and the Hemmingway.

"Works of genius," Clément says looking at them.

Macey continues to pack her brushes and paints away.

"Those here for ballroom dancing, gather on the floor for a waltz," is a new voice heard on the sound system.

Macey turns her head in disbelief. Clément aids her from the dance floor.

"Every minute of the day, entertainment," he explains, as an officer in whites walks past giving them a very large thumbs-up.

"He enjoyed our show," Macey says.

"No," Clément says, shocking her. "Mais oui, but, 'e is the food and beverage manager. We did good bar sales."

"I perform a show, sell drinks and look for forgeries? Anything else?"

"It is my life."

"But, I don't get it. How do they steal hung paintings from a ship?"

"I explain."

"Try," she teases. "And maybe keep it short."

"Seventeen paintings from the Prince Charles collection, on display at the heavily guarded royal properties, are said to be forgeries."

"How? They must have security."

"Exactly, but no security can work. A £50 million Monet loaned to him is a fake."

"Loaned to him?"

"A bankrupt gold bullion dealer loaned it to him along with a Picasso. It is alleged they could be the work of Tony Tetro. Do you know who he is?"

"Sure. I'm at art college. We did a semester on forgery and he came up. He's so brilliant, he's done everyone. Rembrandt to Dali."

"Yonan paid $41 million at Christie's for Monet's Le Bassin Aux Nymphaea's."

"I love his water lilies; where is it?"

"It is going to hang in his suite on the new ship. You will see it. But we have a problem, with forgeries. You spot them; let your investigators chase the thief."

"I can't understand why Tetro doesn't paint his own work," she says, naively.

"Money. He gets well paid without the hassle of trying to become a star."

Money, money, money," Macey groans.

"An avaricious monster has figured that Yonan is a soft target. Tetro probably did that Kandinsky. We need to know what else they 'ave got."

"What's avaricious?"

"An insatiable greed for wealth."

"That makes this a super dangerous job!" Macey concludes.

22 - SNAP

Italy-0130hrs   **Miami-1730hrs**   MixicanGulf-1730hrs

The CSCI office sits between; the Port of Miami, or Dodge Island as it is known, and Overtown on the other side of i95. Feeling safe in the dark technical room, on the right side of the freeway by two blocks, Croc dials out.

Dwight is sorting through the paintings that his team have so far recovered. He snaps each one on his phone, building a digital file.

"She sure can paint."

Croc doesn't need to look at them, he has seen her talent, watched her paint.

"What good is it to a black girl from the ghetto?" Croc asks, waiting for his phone to be answered.

"Big Dog! It's Croc, man. Got a job for you... No, there's no tricks. It's on your own turf."

He waits but the answer accuses him of being a stranger.

"I'm calling you now! You never pass by, same flick, bro'."

He waits, having crossed swords about the lack of contact.

"Lean on Troy. King of the westside projects."

But Croc has no answer. He wouldn't normally be offering Dog anything; Dog is a street-king himself. "You know him, it's easy," Croc adds.

Dwight is a great reader of a situation. He wheels close to Croc and indirectly addresses Dog with a directed shout.

"Where's my hero. That boy been too busy to visit his home?"

Croc smiles and the help, he is part of a great team. It makes Dog soften at the other end and ask what the favour is.

"Yowl," Dog offers for more information.

"Junkie owes Troy seventy dollars, we want you to pay him," Croc relays.

"You want me to do dat?" Dog asks, knowing that can't be the job.

"Junkie's Macey's mom. He took some paintings 'til he got the money. They's her college work. We need them back. You know Macey, she's your sister here."

"Pictures gonna be worth a lot more that that now, you know that."

Croc mutes the microphone.

"He thinks it's an art sale."

"They worth what we have to pay for them," Dwight says, resigned to the deal they may have to make. "That's what the man in the fancy shoes says. Tell Dog to keep it tight."

Croc goes back to the phone.

"Big Dog. Troy's got his seventy. Premium can't be more than your holding."

"You must want them pictures," Dog says and the call ends.

"I've got no idea how much he's got in his roll," Croc worries. His attempt to be street like Dog has gone too far.

"Lucky for you, he won't play that big," Dwight tells Croc.

"It's Big Dog and I told him he can play," Croc worries.

"That boy's seen the good life just a few blocks from the wild side and he wants out of the streets. Now, stop worrying, you've been strange all day."

"Well, I got a question," Croc postures.

"Don't mind you learning," Dwight says.

"How do me and Izzy go about finding our birth moms when records are old school and ain't online. I tried before and found it used to be done by the church. Church went a long time ago."

"You sure you wanna know?"

"We might get lucky."

"Let's assume you don't. Think; What if you end up having to feed a junkie's habit and watching 'em die?" Dwight asks.

"Guess that's the risk. Same boat as my other mom."

"It's a ship, we don't do boats. Ship's bigger, problem's bigger."

Mary storms in and breaks the conversation.

"Izzy went and left me. Seems she don't like answering questions about where she live. Guess you gotta do some talking, Mr Crocodile."

"Mary, you gonna have to wait; we busy, the boys are in some trouble," Dwight slides a print-out to Croc. "Tell me what you think of that guy. You too, Mary"

Mary walks over and looks.

"I tell you. He looks like a thug," she says.

"A very professional thug, Mary, Croc's helping our boys stay alive at the moment."

She doesn't like that kind of busy, so turns away.

"Hope they live coz I can't wait too long," she shouts back.

"Thanks, Dwight. Who's dat?" Croc asks, picking the agency sheet Dwight has printed.

"Oh, that's Mike. The head of security at Bianchi Ship Builders in Italy. That's the agency that got him the job."

"There's an 'and' coming, I can feel it but I can't see it."

"You ain't looking and you ain't thinking. Got your head full of 'finding your mom'. Wipe it clean, Croc."

Croc changes gear and studies the sheet.

"It looks the same lay-out and run-down as the other two sleaze bags," Croc says.

"Which means?"

"They all on the same team?" Croc asks tentatively, half knowing, half questioning.

"One inside, one out," Dwight says, wanting Croc to deliver more.

"That's a team. That's a team with something in mind. Organised. Organised theft."

"Inside and out; a deliberately placed professional team of killers," Dwight stresses.

"Killers?"

"Killers."

Dwight spins himself around. "Now, I gotta meet Yonan."

"Shouldn't we warn Kieron or Hunter?"

"They knew from the moment they met Mike. Now, you think Izzy will pretend to push me around that park? You keep an eye from the other side?"

"For a killer-looking thug?"

"You need to find her fast. Time's an issue."

"I know exactly where she'll be."

Mary had not left the room; she was listening at the door. Having heard killers, and that Croc knows where Izzy is, she looks disturbed as she slides back into her diner.

CRUISE SHIP ART THEFT

23 - NOT HIDING

The padlock is open. Croc checks back and forth before he opens the rear door of a commercial unit. It is three units up from the CSCI office. He enters fast and pulls the door to. Switching the light on reveals paintings all around the walls. The beds and cupboards are made of pallets and it looks like a very classy well-kept squat. A camp stove is on a makeshift worktop next to a sink left hanging off the wall that still works. Izzy sits on a bed in the corner, sobbing. He goes straight to her.

"Hey!"

"Macey rang and asked me to get more pictures of Yonan's shoes. I wanted to tell her we found her real mom. I tried but the words stuck in my throat," she starts, very upset. "Then Mary questioned me about what I said to her. Over and over. What did I tell her? I wanted to question Mary! So many questions I'm bleeding inside."

"Slow down, sis."

"Macey's lucky. So, so, lucky. She's found her birth mom."

"She ain't found nuttin', not till she told it," Croc points out. "Mary gotta be the one to tell."

"Tell what?" is the bellowing voice they both know. Mary has followed him up from the diner and now stands in the doorway. She steps in slowly, mesmerised at the dwelling and all the paintings on the walls. Then down to Izzy and Croc.

"I'm so glad you guys don't live in the squalor I just see. But this ain't a whole lot better. Wish you'd taken my offers to get you a place!"

"What's gone, is gone," Croc says philosophically.

Dwight wheels in behind her and manoeuvres around the space. He photographs yet another set of Macey's paintings before Mary starts to pull them from the walls looking at each one.

"What was this place?" he asks.

"Laundry. They left that one coz it didn't work. Took me ten minutes to fix," Croc says.

"Quite a place you made for yourselves. Might move in with ya. First, we got a job to do," Dwight says, to get everyone to focus. "Izzy, you're off the bench."

Mary is mesmerised by a painting of a mother and her baby, sitting on the steps of a ghetto. A few of the paintings are 'mother and child'. One after another she collects them all, feeling guilty. Izzy watches Mary. She sees a mom proudly looking at her daughter's work.

"I ain't ever had a mom hear me sing or read what I wrote," says Izzy.

Dwight observes Izzy, Mary, and Croc. The chemistry is powerful. He can feel a lot of passion in the room.

"Does she ever stop painting?" Dwight asks.

'The girl's got drive. Take after her mother," Mary says proudly.

Dwight spins and leaves. He knows something has happened about mothers. That means his whole team have their heads in the cloud, even Mary. She's out last, clicks the padlock closed, but can't walk away. Her face is full of guilt and hurt.

Italy-0310hrs

In the Italian shipyard's security room, as undercover security guards, Hunter Witowski and

Commander Kieron Philips, are on their break. Hunter is feasting on crusty bread and Prosciutto, the thin-sliced cured ham. It is washed down with a beer. Philips, who avoids meat, has Fontina cheese and a bottle of Corte del Lupo Bianco; a local Ligurian wine. Kieron fills his paper cup again.

"This is very good. Not a wine I'd normally drink. I'm not a fan of oaked wines."

"They make wines from oak?"

"No, they mature them in small oak barrels."

"Seems a waste of water. They could be making beer," Hunter says, lifting his bottle.

"A very bohemian feast."

"I got an Italian deli in Gables; whole of Italy in there."

"Like Epcot, eh?" Kieron asks. "Thoughts? Other than on the production of wine and whether Italy is in Florida."

They are both harmonising towards the same conclusion.

"One: canvases get switched before delivery; home-run. Two: switched on ship," Hunter throws out. "Here, in the shipyard, it sounds like a slam-dunk."

"But if switched on an established ship at sea, they need a thief, but would they trust them to switch a canvass?" Kieron asks.

"They need someone like Bentley with a double-barrelled name; who ain't a thief, couldn't dodge security, or deal with cameras."

"Here they nurture teams: badass assistants, and badass security. And if an art assistant gets out of hand," Kieron postures.

"They get slapped back in line," Hunter hits home.

"Dwight needs a list of art assistants, past and present, and who have cruised," Kieron says.

"And their cabin steward while onboard. Just a hunch," Hunter says.

"It's a good one."

"And our 'nasty bastard' who assists the assistant. Hiding below decks, or a guest?"

"I don't think they'd feel a need to hide," Kieron says.

"We still need to lay low; this is far from solved, and they'll be on to us soon if they're not already," Hunter says.

"Then the art vanishes."

24 - BICENTENNIAL PARK

Italy-0315hrs   **Miami-1915hrs**   Gulf of Mexico-1915hrs

As the sun forces itself to stay in the sky, runners and dog walkers are the last in the park. Croc runs with them, jogging circuits. Mary sits on a bench some distance away, swinging her legs. Full of guilty thoughts, she feels alone. She brought bread for the birds, but they're not eating it and she is just littering.

A young woman squats in front of her.

"If you need the food wagon, it's here. It moves on at eight o'clock."

"What? Food? I ain't hungry!"

"Our next stop is Bay City. If you get hungry, it'll be there until ten."

"You think I'm homeless?" Mary says, in shock.

"We help everyone," the girl says, careful not to upset in any way. She is used to resistance and having to be politically correct, so hangs for a moment longer.

"I'm good, thank you," Mary says angrily.

The woman leaves, but, like a madwoman with no home to go to, Mary mutters to herself.

"Homeless. I ain't homeless. Huh. Maybe I'm good at this undercover work. Nailed it. Yeah, I'm damn good at this investigator thing. They think I'm Pigeon Woman in Home Alone. Well done Mary, damn clever idea feeding the birds," she mutters. "My second mission and already running solo. Don't know why them investigators get so much money. Even Stan could do this."

A bird flies down, pecks at the bread but flies away.

"What you want, one of them brioche buns? You want the yellow peppers? The shredded lettuce and fresh tomatoes? You ain't getting it, you come back Tuesday," she shouts, tossing the last of the bread onto the grass for tomorrow's birds.

Yonan sits crossed-legged on a park bench, facing the sea on the other side of the park. It's like he's waiting for an old friend who no longer arrives. He wears a hat, tinted glasses and a scarf wrapped around his neck. The temperature drops after the sun has gone in. He hasn't been offered food.

Izzy stops Dwight next to the bench, then she sits the other side of Yonan.

"You're late, Dwight."

"Ain't no one running a clock on me, not even you," he replies.

Izzy gets busy snapping shots of his raised shoe, then the shoe on the floor. Both unblemished, highly polished, expensive-looking brown shoes with two buckles.

"I got your report. I'm not surprised there's a team working the shipbuilders. What does surprise me, is that it's inside the security. I had hoped security people were trustworthy."

"Paid mercenaries and killers."

"Killers?" Yonan worries.

Dwight turns to him slowly. A face with no expression. It reminds Yonan who he is working with.

"We need a list of all art assistants past and present and cross-check if any of them ever cruised."

Yonan looks at him, then relaxes after his shock.

"I'm surprised you suspect my art assistants, but I guess I shouldn't be."

"If they cruised, we wanna know their cabin stewards."

Yonan is nodding.

"Be careful. They might have a plant in Human Resources."

"No, it's been the same woman since I built my first ship there, sixteen years ago."

"As I said, be careful. They might have a plant in Human resources at the shipyard."

"There's a new art delivery due. I did some buying. New paintings all from the same source. Two at the very reasonable price of under half a million."

"Very cheap," Dwight says sarcastically.

"A Wolfman. Value around $4.5 million and another, at an undisclosed price. That will cause huge interest. Dealers always flock to those rumours."

"Should I be impressed?"

"It's your painting from above the jukebox. I'm only borrowing it."

Dwight looks at him more like a killer than before. It disturbs Yonan.

"Let's label it as on loan, from the collector Dwight Ritter," Yonan says, trying to calm the situation.

"No!"

"Too late, the purchases are travelling. Paintings will be in Italy within hours."

"How?"

"My private jet."

"Yeah. You better mark it as a loan."

Dwight's anger is not going to diminish. If he wasn't on a mission, there is no guessing what state Yonan would already be in. Probably a dead old man on a park bench. Yonan must ignore that reaction.

"How did you buy my painting from the same source?"

"I asked a gallery to acquire it. They paid a quarter-of-a-million.

How much?" Izzy asks.

"Good art should be expensive. It must be expensive to make it special; to protect it and make it exclusive. Expensive art makes my ships expensive, deliberately expensive. Macey's painting was a costly acquisition. Undisclosed means the rumours will spread. It also means I can leak the price later for even more press coverage. There will now be interest in it and her. It is a good test."

"How can it be a loan if you bought it?"

"Good point. But, it's still yours."

"Good. Coz, I ain't got no money from a sale, and I don't trust you, Yonan. Not one bit," Dwight says strongly. He leans into him. "As far as I'm concerned, that painting's still mine."

Izzy jumps up to retrieve Dwight.

"I haven't finished. I need to come clean," Yonan says.

Izzy sits. Dwight leans back and listens. It never surprises him when he hears that line. He sits and waits, watching the sun play peekaboo with the horizon; a game lost within seconds. The pools of light from the park lamps now look far more important.

"The Kandinsky they stole was a fake."

Dwight raises his eyebrows.

"The real Kandinsky sits in a vault. They stole a very good copy, a much better copy than they replaced it with, the one Macey detected. She may also have noticed my original fake, but I doubt it," Yonan says.

"She would've," Izzy says.

"Clément will be a good teacher. She'll be a far more experienced artist by the end of the cruise. I hear she's already working on her best piece to date."

"You saying, all your expensive pieces are fakes?"

"Not all."

"How we supposed to do this job?"

"If the thieves realise the effort they've put into stealing forgeries; they won't be happy."

"Fuck, yeah!"

"Do you need me to translate that for you, Mr Yonan?" Izzy asks.

"No thank you, Izzy," Yonan smiles, very controlled. He and Dwight are playing thought chess. "They are such good copies, the best science would not know," he explains.

"Science?"

"Forgeries are detected by X-rays. They show black and white images of the paint layers, and what is under them. Most artists re-use canvases, there is a picture under the picture. New particle accelerated X-rays see those previous attempts in colour. My forger paints the under painting first, then the expensive work on top."

Dwight has a lot of information to digest and report.

"I need to see Macey's other work," Yonan says.

"You're annoying."

"It has to be now, I'm afraid," Yonan says.

Dwight spins his chair but waits.

"Izzy, the man's riding shotgun."

The three make their way along the path, in and out of the light to where Dwight parked his car.

"Could your forger be in on this?" he asks.

"Why would he steal them? He knows they're not real."

"If they're stolen, don't they have more value?"

"No. He is the best forger in the world; paid millions," Yonan explains.

"He could afford to be working with the best, most nasty, heavy killing crew money can buy. Like the one we've discovered."

"No. The best industry forger could afford to buy the crew that you still haven't uncovered."

Dwight swings himself into the driver's seat and looks up at Yonan, "Whoever, they've already contracted one nasty bunch of killers and infiltrated them to work for you as security in Italy."

25 - GRADUATION

Hunter cannot work out what the art assistants do all day and all night. They move paintings back and forth but haven't hung one in the ship. Kieron is comfortable amongst them. He smiles and nods whilst taking an interest in the art. Hunter watches as Kieron stops by an attractive young female assistant.

"Hi, I'm Kieron."

"Why am I not surprised?" Hunter mutters to himself, from a distance.

"Rosemary," she says, looking worried because he is security. To a young English girl, anyone carrying a gun is frightening.

"That's a beautiful British name. Is your surname a classic?"

"Addington."

"Well hi, Rosemary Addington. Do you know Bentley?"

"Everyone knows Bentley."

"Where is he? I can't see him."

Rosemary looks around, but she fails to see him.

"I don't know," she says.

"He works for your team?"

"Not my team. He's mega experienced. I only graduated last year."

"Congratulations."

"I'm amazed at everyone's dedication here."

"It's hard, but working in a gallery sounds worse."

Hunter comes over and joins them.

"I'm not doing anything wrong, am I?" she asks.

"I came over to warn you about him. He's old enough to be your grandfather, but he doesn't see it that way. Nothing secure about that old security guy," Hunter says to her with a smile.

"Hunter, this is Rosemary. It's her first job, she graduated last year."

They nod at each other politely. Hunter now knows why Kieron has chosen her: she is naive and vulnerable. They will get more from her than the others. Hunter looks down at the painting on her table.

"Nice," he growls.

"Beautiful, isn't it?" she agrees.

"Shame about the frame."

Rosemary inspects the frame.

"What's wrong with it?"

"It's…" Hunter stalls.

"It is a pretty poor choice of frame for that painting," Kieron agrees.

"We do reframe some paintings. But not if the frame and canvas are wedded together by history," she says.

"Canvas changing? That must be great fun for you," Kieron asks.

"Not me. I did it in college, but never on a real canvas. I hope to one day."

"Bit like a teaching hospital. Not operated on a real patient yet," Hunter says.

"I never thought of it that way," she says.

"How long would it take you to change a frame?" Kieron asks.

"Me? Forever. I'd be so nervous."

"How long would Bentley take?" Hunter asks.

"He's quick. Very precise and fast. He would have it in and out, in no time."

"You sound more English than Kieron," Hunter laughs, but he is reading a text from Dwight. He pulls

Kieron out; they are finished in there. "Four new paintings arrive early hours."

"We need that camera up," Kieron says.

Yonan has paintings spread over every surface available in the CSCI hub.

"We should've done that in my diner, you would have all the tables you want," Mary says.

"Good idea, Mary. Let's go next door," Yonan says.

"No. I was jokin'. Stan's rushed off his feet in there."

Croc opens the interchanging door. He shows in the young journalist who took the pictures of Macey on the gangway.

"Come in, Ricky," Yonan says.

"Not you, Croc. You get back to work," Mary fires out. She turns to Yonan. "And you. When we gonna talk about licencing my recipe?"

"He'd steal it from you, Mary. You'd have a hole where your heart was," Dwight says.

"Not at all, Mary. My ships take on a lot of vegetables we ripen during the cruise. Tomatoes being an obvious one. Often, many won't ripen."

"Green; that's my kind of tomato."

"Exactly, and I hate food waste. We need to talk, but not tonight. Tonight, I need to make a start on these paintings," he says, showing the ones he has already collected to his right.

"You gonna steal them next?" Dwight says.

"Dwight, please, we have a deal," Yonan pleads.

"You bought my painting? Who from?"

Embarrassed, Mary fidgets and points to the young man standing at the door. "Who's he?"

"Ricky, come and meet the team. This is Ricky Hedgemont. He took that wonderful picture of Macey. He's going to write a short piece on each of the chosen paintings for her catalogue."

Mary uses Ricky's movement to slip out.

"Who chose them? She needs to choose them," Dwight demands.

"OK. Send my selection over to Macey for approval."

"That's not what I said."

"But while she looks through them, let's get the history behind them."

"Yeah. It would be good if I could talk to her," Ricky says, with a sparkle in his eye.

"No way you upset Macey with this. I'll get one of my team to ask if she is ready," Dwight says firmly.

"I need it all by tomorrow morning, latest. It would be better if I could talk with her, one to one," Ricky suggests very firmly.

Dwight wonders what authority Ricky has to make demands. He is like Yonan.

"No fucking way," Dwight says.

"In the absence of Izzy," says Yonan, "please be assured I don't need that translated."

"You're getting too smart," Dwight says.

"I'm still the paying client."

"You're building Macey's hopes up, what're you up to?"

"I know what I'm doing, Dwight."

"It's obvious you planned every step of this, long before you even engaged us."

"Every step so far. It's soon going to get very unpredictable."

26 - SEEING CLEARLY

The new ship looks different each day. The counter for the reception is in place. The wall-panels are in and the downlights are currently being fitted. Telephone and computer cables are all being weaved in.

Kieron and Hunter are on the main habitation deck, where most of the mini suites have taken shape. The carpet will be laid soon, and the furnishings are waiting in the storage decks.

"Those assistants are gonna have to do some work at last," Hunter says.

"When paintings start to move, we won't have as much freedom. We need that camera up tonight."

Hunter hangs out of a small loading hole at the top of the main building. He is pulling in old cables when distracted by headlights at the main gate.

"Van's at the gate signing in," he shouts to Kieron inside.

"That'll be the new paintings," Kieron says, leaning to pull him back in.

Hunter re-sets the handcuffs in his belt and holsters his gun. Dusting themselves off they both head for the wooden steps.

Although the yard is huge, within a minute or so, they have moved from the top of the main building to the warehouse to see the van opened. Two assistants jump in and relieve the ropes that hold the crates. Three boxes are taken, one to each table. The senior assistants have the table furthest away and must have the Wolfman.

"Four. Text said four," Kieron mentions to Hunter. The van is empty. He watches the driver tie the ropes to the walls.

"Did you stop anywhere?" Hunter asks the driver.

"No. I came from Genoa airport."

"Only three cases?"

"Yes. Three came off the plane, I was parked adjacent to it."

The driver is Eastern European, not Italian, and speaks English well as he probably does many languages. They investigate to see if any crate contains two paintings, but each has only one. Kieron rings back.

"Croc. Dwight told us four paintings," Kieron reports to CSCI HQ in Miami as they start to question the young technicians left to run the night shift.

Hunter is at the table, cell-phone out in photo mode, "Is that what you were expecting?"

"Oh yes, wonderful," a bearded male assistant says, seeing the Wolfman for the first time.

"I meant were you expecting only three?"

"Four, but often one turns up later. Sourced differently."

Hunter takes a photograph then dictates into his cell-phone.

"Wolfman; crate opened at 0345hrs."

They do the same for the other two and realise the one that is missing is the one that all the fuss is about. Macey's.

Hunter photographs a shift rota on the senior assistant's table.

"Interesting. Bentley is rostered to work tonight," he says.

"It was never in the van. With the camera, we'd evidence that," Kieron says.

"Bentley's gone, Macey's painting is gone," Hunter says.

Gulf of Mexico-2245hrs

Prisha is on her cell-phone in the atrium. It is late. Many people take the trouble of getting dressed up, only to eat and then go to bed. The late show is out but the bar empty. She is scrolling through pictures on her tablet.

"Hunter, how are you?"

"Good. You with, Macey?" he says, fishing.

"God no. After the 'less-than-super Supremes', as she called them, there was no way she was going to a show tonight."

"Harsh."

"I thought so."

"Her painting was due to hit us in Italy. The other three did, hers didn't. Any ideas?" Hunter asks.

"No. I could ask her, but she doesn't know it was re-sold." Prisha says.

"Best not to worry her. What you doing?"

"Going through Macey's paintings with Yonan. Again, Macey doesn't know."

"What's that for?" Hunter asks, not having been looped in on that.

"A catalogue. I must explain it to Macey tomorrow and show her the ones Yonan likes. They want her talking about them. I feel a fraud, she's my friend."

"No friends in this game, you know the job."

"But, we're not at war, Hunter."

"You be careful; a lot of bullets flying around. Can't help feeling that they're gonna get real soon."

27 - STAR-CROSS'D LOVERS

Italy-0800hrs   Miami-0000hrs   Gulf of Mexico-2300hrs

At sea, Macey's ship is nearing New Orleans and its midnight. At 2am time stand will still for a whole hour; the ship will cross into Central Daylight Time. Those on the ship have an extra hour in bed, the two investigators never do. The shift finishes at Bianchi in Italy, it is 8am.

Kieron and Hunter enjoy the walk back to their apartment. The day is fresh, punctuated by the smell of coffee and bread.

"Dwight's not liking Yonan," Hunter says.

"Yonan stole his painting."

"Hmm. Not so much that he stole it. But he felt he had a right to."

"This is all about stealing paintings, and that's exactly what he's doing," Kieron ponders. "At least the camera's up and working in the warehouse."

They walk past a tourist shop where a man is hanging tee-shirts out for display. They exchange greetings. Everyone has time to acknowledge each other. Not many tourists explore this end of the docks. They arrive at the delicatessen, but Kieron stops concerned.

"Why is Yonan rushing out a catalogue?"

"Eating in, or eating out?" Hunter growls, thinking.

"Home. I didn't see Bedi at the shipyard." He turns to the man waiting to serve. "Two ciabattas and selection of soft cheeses. Surprise me."

"And focaccia, and some of that ham, if you wouldn't mind, sir," Hunter says. He enjoys pointing out his politeness when Kieron forgets.

Kieron turns to him. "You don't like focaccia."

"I love saying the word."

"Can you get these? I wanna get something in the other shop."

Kieron catches Hunter at the apartment door. He takes the sticks of bread as Hunter fights with the old lock.

"Get what you wanted?"

"I did, but it could be the wrong move," he says, as they climb the stairs.

At the top, in the small living room, Bedi is lying across the armchair asleep. She is in contortions only a drunk could form. If missing her shift again was not enough of a statement, the vodka bottles are. The bigger crime is that she has drunk Kieron's wine.

"The 2007 and the 2013."

"Didn't know you numbered them," Hunter says, as a deliberate joke. He gives Bedi a little kick. She does not move. "Breakfast first, or wake her? Though I'm not sure there's any point."

Kieron holds the bag, thinking.

"What you got?" Hunter asks.

Kieron shows him a printed tee-shirt. 'Potrebbe contenere alcol'.

Hunter has no idea.

"May contain alcohol," Kieron says.

"Good luck with that."

Bedriška wakes up, sees Kieron and strains to read the tee-shirt.

"Very funny, but I like," Bedriška manages to say. "I will wear."

Kieron relaxes and turns away letting his guard down. She launches at him. He turns and catches her, taking her down. It is both swift and hard. He kneels over her and leans forward, pinning both arms down.

"Bedi, you have a drink problem."

Her leg comes up, over his head and spins him over. She beats him, mercilessly.

"I'm thinking the tee-shirt didn't work," Hunter offers.

Kieron stands to face her but she is fast. Hard accurate blows, kicks and elbows knock him back, sideways, and over.

"I have drink problem. You have bigger problem," she says, looking down at him.

Hunter stands over him nodding.

"I think we need to deal with this another way," he suggests.

Bedi swings hard at Hunter's face but he catches her arm. It is held firmly and she knows that the game has ended.

"We'll deal with this. Between us. You either accept help or walk away," Hunter says, staring hard into her eyes. "I'm going to bed now. I suggest you two lovers do the same."

28 - BREAKFAST IN BED

Italy-1800hrs   Miami-1000hrs   **Gulf of Mexico-0900hrs**

Prisha bursts into Macey's room wearing the soft comforting bathrobe supplied.

"Mace, try yours," she says, showing it off.

"I saw it. My old teddy wasn't that soft."

"Paintings have downloaded."

"I'm surprised they got them," Macey admits.

"Not all, but you can tell me if these are the best."

There is a knock at the door which breaks Prisha's head-of-steam. Breakfast arrives and the previously lethargic Macey checks for listening bugs whilst restraining the excited Prisha.

"You can't imagine how different this is to crew quarters."

"You mean you don't get room service and robes?" Macey mocks.

"Nothing. My cabin was only as wide as the bunk beds. It was about half the size of your bathroom. And no safe, nowhere to keep your money or tips."

"You got tips? I didn't."

Macey takes Prisha's phone, which she doesn't know is recording sound. She swipes through the pictures.

"Where were you when you painted that first one?" Prisha asks, performing the uncomfortable task.

The girls eat, and Macey goes down memory lane with each of her works. Prisha feels a huge sense of guilt with the phone back in her hand. She hovers over a live recording of their conversation. She needs permission to share and she feels the guilt for coercing her friend.

"The stories you told, are as important as the paintings. Dwight was your first customer; he'd love to hear. Can I send them to him?"

"Sure," Macey replies before she has thought about it.

She ends the recording and presses send, her permission to do so.

"Yonan loves those too. Oh, by the way. Izzy sent new shots of shoes."

Macey smiles and takes the phone. But she looks up in shock.

Prisha freezes. Has she seen a voice recording has been sent? Will she lose her friend?

"What?" Prisha asks, frightened and full of guilt.

"These are double buckle brown shoes."

"Guess the man can afford more than one pair of shoes," Prisha says relaxing.

"But these are not crocodile shoes."

"Der!" Prisha is lost, she has no idea why Macey is so perplexed.

"It's a Miami thing. They still have the Louis Vuitton button in the heel, but they are nowhere near as classy."

"He was playing homeless. Disguising himself," Prisha offers.

"The man doesn't have a clue how to get down," Macey says ignoring the shoes and joining Prisha at breakfast.

"I would like to go to Jill's lecture on the works of Olivia Lomenech Gill."

"And she's important?"

"I see her painting as political. Maybe I'll be disappointed but I see sympathy for slavery in her works: 'War Horse' and my favourite, 'Lampedusa', inspired by Caroline Moorehead's book Human Cargo."

"That sounds deep. Hey, I sent your notes. He says Yonan might put them into the catalogue of your works."

Clément knocks on the door and makes a timely entrance. He takes Prisha's signal to be quiet. For him, he appears unnaturally subdued.

"Tell Yonan not to use any old work until I approve it. There's some rubbish in those piles."

Once again, Prisha has recorded it.

"I sent him what you said, it couldn't be clearer."

"Your paintings say what you were thinking when you painted them, and you are outspoken in your work," she says.

"Mais oui," Clément says.

"Give that French nonsense a break in here, Clément," Macey says. "You don't have all my paintings. Not the best. They're at my mom's; some very dark pieces. It was the period when I had to either leave her or go down with her."

Prisha looks at her phone, she is recording very personal memories.

"I'm sure they'll get them," Clément says, as the Englishman. Prisha hits send then nearly chokes. Dwight will also choke, but on Clem's English.

"A book is crazy, eh, Clemmie?" Macey laughs.

"It is a catalogue of your work, and some stories. Yonan has the young journalist to write it."

"Who?"

Clément takes two fingers. He mimes, his eyes to hers, back and forth, to mean contact.

"The paparazzi kid I saw getting on the boat?"

"Ship. And yes, Ricky. You and he had a connection."

"No. He knows Jack-Shit about me," Macey says.

"He's a young man who needs a break, like you. Or he has no future. He's talented and he cares about you. Yonan wants to use his picture of you on the cover. You have the final say on what he offers, and he gets a commission, no?"

"Sure, but."

Prisha presses send again.

29 - INVESTIGATOR

Dwight is amazed at Prisha's investigative work; she even obtained recorded approval.

"She's good," Croc says. "I gotta get out there and prove myself."

"Why? You're an analyst. You leave the ghetto to Big Dog," Dwight drums home.

"I'm goin', I'm from the ghetto," Croc says walking to the door, determined.

"Send in that young kid as you leave."

"He's keen," Croc says.

"You gotta mirror? Look at yourself."

Ricky is sitting on a barstool next to Izzy. He is an attractive young man with piercing blue eyes. Macey was captivated by him, Izzy is now. Stan is at the other side of the counter, cooking and chatting.

"So, if Mary is her real mother, that makes you her father, Stan?" Ricky asks, taking notes.

"Yep, guess it does," he says, turning in thought. He passes the young photojournalist a plate of food. "You mind taking that into Dwight. I ain't sure I can find any more answers for you, boy."

"Stan. You have the most attractive and talented daughter. Her face says so much, as do her paintings."

Croc has been watching and listening. He sees Izzy's punishing look lock Stan in a freeze of guilt.

"Ain't many kids in Overtown know their father," she accuses.

"You knows, Izzy. I couldn't have done more for that kid if she knew," Stan says slowly and softly. "If either of us knew." Whatever decisions were made appear to have been Mary's.

Izzy doesn't agree, she wishes she had a father.

The journalist passes Croc with the plate of food after listening.

"Hey. You can't put none of that in the book," Croc says as they pass. He hadn't heard much but he can see Izzy has heard a lot more and Stan is acting strange.

"Croc. Didn't mean to ignore you. But, I've no power. Not any more than you."

"Don't tell Yonan any of this. Don't go into her mum living in the Ghetto, nor Mary, nor Stan nor any adoption. Things like that don't happen legally here; the church do it all. They do it for good reasons and you'll cause trouble. We don't know if any of this is true."

"If Yonan finds out I was withholding information, and he will, I'm finished. This is my big break. I'll be woke, trust me. But I need my name on it somewhere."

Ricky enters the hub.

"What can't you put in a book? You ain't writing a biography, are you?" Dwight asks as he enters. He has still missed all the conversations about Mary and Macey and none of that has been reported to the CSCI HQ.

"Hell no. In a day? The paintings are causing all the fuss."

"Why don't you tell me what Croc don't want you to write?" Dwight asks knowing he is missing out on something.

"About Stan and Mary." Ricky half engages.

"What about them? They're good people."

"Why did they have Macey adopted?"

"You got that the wrong way 'round boy. They adopted her, done everything for her. Put her through college."

"Why let their daughter live in a squat three doors up?"

Dwight is not sure he heard right. He's confused and that overrides him not knowing the real drama. Ricky must be confused.

"Can I get a face-to-face with her? You can get her on-line for me now. She knows me. I need to know her."

"No."

30 - A PINK PONY

Italy-2045hrs   Miami-1245hrs   **Gulf of Mexico-1145hrs**

Jill's art lecture ends with her being swamped by guests. Macey stands in awe, but also realises how clever Clément was by ensuring she was not mobbed after her double session in the atrium. Jill did her show all by herself. She knew so much about the body of work and the history of each of the paintings. Macey looks at her watch. Eleven-forty-five on the dot. Clément did that; they finished on the minute.

Macey studies this week's special piece of art, locked in the ornate display case that oozes, 'hey look at me, I'm special'.

"I hope pink donkey is never in here," she mutters to herself.

Jill joins her.

"It's a LeRoy Neiman, that Yonan bought for an undisclosed considerable sum of money. No doubt a very large sum."

Macey loves it. She loves minimalist abstract art.

"How do you finish on time, to the minute?" Macey asks.

"If I don't many will walk out because the buffet opens at twelve."

"Are you serious?" Macey asks, aghast. "But they only had breakfast three hours ago."

"Little and often," Jill says, as a perfect defence.

Macey looks back at the star painting, continually being amazed by cruising.

"What are you working on now? 'Shoes'? I think it will work. It's so out-there," Jill asks.

"Izzy sent me photos of the wrong pair."

"A diptych; that always has dealers fighting. I had one-of-a-pair of Swatch watches once. I was always looking out to see if someone had the other."

Macey is fidgeting at the painting, something disturbs her. Jill shows her knowledge.

"LeRoy's wonderful imagination comes from a mixture of Swedish and Turkish parents and being brought up in Minnesota."

Macey turns back.

"I swat up before a special piece comes on board."

Macey thinks of what she told Prisha this morning. That is what people will find out about her. She panics and wonders what she said.

"You expose their life, just like that?"

"Artists, like actors and rock stars, are public property. They paint, they promote, they sell."

Without comment, Macey is drawn back to the painting.

"I'd love to see the real Avenue Victor Hugo."

"That would be a river-cruise. Paris by cruise ship, it would dock at Le Havre."

"No idea what Havre is. This is my first time out of Miami, and I ain't seen much of that."

Le Havre is a port, which is a two-hour coach journey to Paris. Small ships may get up the Seine to Rouen, but that is only a little further," Jill explains.

"I saw Paris on the TV show, Vikings."

Jill takes her attention back to the prize painting.

"Do you like this?"

"I love it. It's such a fantastic copy."

"That's because it's the original," Jill says, smiling with an air of supremacy.

"No. It's a copy," Macey insists.

"Macey. It seriously is the original. Yonan paid a lot for it."

Macey looks harder at it.

"You gotta magnifying glass?" she asks.

"I'll get one from the diamond store next door."

Jill rushes off, leaving Macey to continue studying. She is ready for the glass when Jill returns with it. She studies harder.

"Look here, and here. What do you see?"

"Nothing," Jill says. "It's a great work."

"That paint stroke, right or left-handed?"

Jill studies it again.

"Right-handed."

"And LeRoy Neiman?"

Jill shakes her head.

"That's the bit you didn't read. He's a lefty."

Miami-1350hrs

Yonan is pacing a meeting room, which is ornate in a minimalist modern way. It is not there to impress cruise passengers, but investors and board members. The pictures around the walls are not from his cherished art collection, but of his ships. They show both inside and out and they are an impressive collection of 'art'. Ricky sits at his laptop, which is on a rubber mat to save the highly polished wood. He is typing from notes. Yonan's cell-phone is on speaker, which Ricky finds very distracting.

"I need the books printed and delivered by tomorrow. Half here and half to the MS Overlord, Erato Street Cruise Terminal, Louisiana."

"But that's in New Orleans," the printer states.

"I know where it is."

"Drop every other job you've got. Cost is not a problem. I'll pay for priority."

"It's not cost, it's drying them."

"We dry them on the engine deck. It's hot down there."

"But transport, we gotta get them there."

"I'll have a jet standing by. Keep the Miami half to dry there."

"I need the rest of it, now. As in hours ago."

"Additions will be emailed within minutes," Yonan says, ending the call, expecting the service.

He looks at Ricky, a look that says finish.

"I have to sleep," Ricky dares to say.

"Not when you work for me."

31 - AFTERNOON ART

Italy-2230hrs   Miami-1630hrs   **Gulf of Mexico-1530hrs**

A crowd that is far too big to manage follows Macey and Jill around the art on the ship. Macey has it easy; she is the star. Jill explains the painting; she is very proud that she knows everything about each piece. It leaves Macey free to discuss the artist's style and what she likes about it. Jill is somewhat peeved at the superior position Macey's has taken on 'her' ship.

"This was his last piece…" Macey starts.

"Macey, he also painted two others before he committed suicide, like so many artists have done. One was entitled 'Round Heads', a rather hurried piece. The other, unfinished so he felt, but amazing to the art world who consider it a complete piece, is called, 'Forgotten'. Many think the latter, his last, is a reflection of his demise because his suicide was planned."

Jill looks at Macey with a smug smile. It is a side of Jill she has not seen before. Macey hides her shock in her study of the piece as art critics can do.

Clément takes Jill to one side. She expects a dressing down which she is prepared to take. It was worth it.

"Jill, Macey seems to have caused a little upset over the LeRoy."

"Yes 'an upset'. She thought it was a forgery."

"I have corrected her. She is right, 'e is left-handed, but it is little known that he loved to be 'Inigo Montoya'."

"What?"

"Inigo resided in the fictional country of Florin."

"An artist?"

"Mais oui. But with a sword."

"Fictional?"

"Yes, fiction is the art of a writer, and should never be underestimated by an artist of the canvas."

"But…" Jill tries to interrupt.

"The sword is like a brush. LeRoy loved that saying. Inigo starts to fight, the most brilliant swordsman of his day." Clément speeds up excited.

"But, he's not real?" Jill says, amazed.

Clément is now slow.

"Real enough to feel hurt. At the age of eleven, his father was killed by a swordsman who wanted to cheat him."

"Where's this going?"

"Exactly, you are like the man in black."

"Inigo is left-handed," Jill says, confused.

"Until he changes hands."

Clément waves his left-hand magician-like and changes to his right hand.

Clément wafts past her and joins the group, still moving like a swordsman.

"Do you think that is a forgery?" a guest asks, as they look at the last painting.

Macey hesitates. She does not wish to answer. She knows it's a forgery. Jill notices there is a problem Clément is shaking his head no, inferring that she cannot cause a disturbance, cannot break cover.

"Jill?"

"Absolutely not."

Macey slides away and the guests follow.

32 – A SIMPLE ADJUSTMENT

Italy-**2030hrs**   Miami-1630hrs   Gulf of Mexico-1530hrs

Commander Philips and Hunter Witowski have split. The camera they installed in the art warehouse has a bad connection and needs to be lined up again.

Standing outside the roof of the art warehouse and looking along the exterior footbridge which the cables run on, Witowski can see the problem. The footbridge has dropped with years of decay, and the wires that span it are strained, if not holding the bridge up and fractured with the stretch. He needs to walk along the footbridge, cutting each the cable-tie free, and look for a break. The bridge, however, does not look like it will hold his weight. He steps forward and cuts the first cable tie. The strain is off in an instant, the bridge jolts down. He tentatively steps again and cuts a second cable tie. It jolts down again.

"Yay! Better picture!" Kieron says.

In the security office at the shipyard he has his feet up on the desk, watching the screen on the far right; the one fed from this new camera. He pours himself another glass of wine and picks at fresh bread and cheese. The picture starts to break up again.

"Nope."

Hunter is holding on as the footbridge cracks and drops.

"Kieron buddy, I might need some help here."

However, Hunter is talking to himself as he cannot go for his phone. Creaking sounds and another small drop. The waist-high cables he released on the way out are now neck high and he is expecting the bridge to collapse. He looks forward and back for an answer to his survival. With it stable for a moment, he runs the last bit, with it folding down a lot more beneath him. He turns and looks back at the fractured and useless footbridge.

But there are two more ties to be cut. Behind him is the old lifting crane. He tugs at the cable to release it, but it is a fight. He hooks it to his belt and steps on the bridge, and stretches to the near cable tie, not adding any further weight or strain to it. He slits the tie and the cable lifts. Now only one tie is left. His belt feels feeble, so he gently twists weaving himself in it. The bridge drops a few inches again and it pulls the cranes from the wall, debris dropping. The wire is doing nothing.

"OK, if it goes, hold long enough to jump and run clear, right?"

He is still talking to himself as he tries to reach for the last tie.

Kieron's screen shows more sidewall than warehouse.

Security staff saw the camera yesterday when it was first fitted and the imperfection has caused much banter. Kieron's phone rings.

"Camera's moved to the wall partner. It needs to go eyes right," he says, thinking it is Hunter.

"Macey blew her cover," Dwight says. "Clément did a patching-up job. I asked how, but trust me, you don't want to hear it. I hope it worked. They are artists; all weird."

"Who did she break to?"

"Jill, the gallery manager. And, to put your mind at rest, the three paintings you got; three's all you should have had."

"Where's Macey's?"

"Well, 'my' painting is not hanging above the jukebox. Nor do I have the quarter of a million the press say it sold for. My painting is going to New Orleans to meet her ship."

"Not bitter? We should have sent someone with it."

"Do we have more staff? Who? Where?"

"Croc, or Big Dog, and all his crew. They were right on the nail when we closed the Laundry job."

"They were supervised by senior investigators. And, they're busy working on getting the other paintings back. The travel arrangements for my painting were Yonan's call."

"No one with it?"

"Mr Bentley Crouch-Fielding. The guy your report says went AWOL last night. He got the private jet back here after it delivered the three paintings. The plane has now landed in New Orleans. Not sure where he or my painting have gone."

"Ah, the plot thickens."

"Indeed. I've a friend who works at Miami airport. He can make himself very busy when I ask. Four paintings were loaded onto that plane to Italy."

"OK. We'll send you Bedi back to help with staff. She's drinking too much here."

"That's very kind of you."

"Arrange a private jet. We're not doing much so one of us will skip off and get her to the airport. Oh, and make sure there is no alcohol on the plane."

The picture on the screen bounces away from the wall.

"Hang on Dwight," Kieron changes to the other caller on his cell-phone. "Hunter. Perfect picture, still wrong camera angle."

The wire stretches freely between the two buildings, the bridge below hangs helplessly down, and Hunter grips onto what is left with his fingers.

"One, two, three!" Hunter heaves and scrambles up only just faster than it drops down, and with a leap, he grabs the platform the walkway was attached to. He hangs at full stretch and looks down to the buckled metal crashing on the floor below.

"There's no using that again," he says to himself.

33 - GETTING DOWN

DAY5-Italy-0700hrs   **Miami-2300hrs**   Gulf of Mexico-2200hrs

Nothing is nice about the ghetto. Young children run around, playing, and chasing each other but their innocence is challenged from the start. Croc watches, wondering how they survive with such neglect in a world of drugs and crime. Many are just old enough to walk but are left to learn in dark, poorly lit streets. That it is almost midnight has no bearing on their lives.

Big Dog approaches Croc with a small crew.

"You come to babysit me?" Dog asks.

"No man. I didn't want you to feel alone."

"Welcome back. Ain't you glad you got out of here?"

"I ain't never left, bro."

"You left alright. You ain't got the right smell now."

Croc shadows him down the street and around the corner. It is obvious where they are going because an opposing crew lurks protecting a building. They notice the Dog's approaching team and one slips inside.

"He knows we here now, Croc. No turning back," Dog says.

Croc's confidence starts to waver with each step. The two crews infuse, back slap, hugs, and fist bumps.

"Don't be fooled, this turn ugly as quick as you lost that erection," Dog tells Croc.

Croc is rocking back and forth very slightly with his shoulders and head. He is trying to stay local.

"Sure, you wanna do this?"

Croc makes his nod of agreement a little more obvious.

"Let's go inside. Keep your mouth shut."

Five exterior steps up and they are through the street door. There is no artificial light, but Dog knows the way. He opens a thick door and goes down. The inside street-soldiers he passes give a nod or fist bump him. He has respect, and their allegiance is to whoever keeps them fed. It isn't a case of them, and their families fed, because they don't have families; they have 'bitches' who live off the scraps for sex. One is hanging off the guard at the bottom. Like Croc's mom, she ate less than she fed her habit. Dog was right; Croc has left the streets. He should not have come. They cross a room and step through a hole knocked in the wall to the next house, where there is a low-level sex and drug den, and on the far side another hole in the wall. They go four houses along, the holes functioning as hide and shoot defence barriers. Troy, the king of these streets, is well hidden.

"Big Dog, my man!" Troy says, with a grin of obvious gold teeth. He lays naked with a woman on a floor strewn with mattresses. Old curtains cover the scatter cushions that don't match. Everything is the result of plundering those who cannot pay him. The shock is that Macey's paintings are hung all around the walls. Troy focusses on Croc.

"Got yourself Big Dog. Good move, kid."

"Paying my respects, Troy," Dog says.

"Where you from, kid?"

"Mom lived four blocks west."

"Didn't ask where yer mom lived."

Croc knows they were ready for him.

"May…I…see," Troy says, the stretching the parts of Macey's name out revealing he knows more than they hoped for.

"Let's roll with the seventy-five and load a C-note, easing the pain on Macey's mama," Dog says.

A crew member takes the money.

"Respect bro, we even now," Troy says, pushing himself up to fist-bump Dog.

"I here for more."

"Me know," Troy says, nodding.

Croc is getting high on the increasing smoke cloud, but he must stay sane and keep quiet unless pushed. He's already said too much.

"I gotcha all the way. What's the hustle?" Dog asks.

Troy pulls himself up and sits back against the wall.

"Special purchase items," Troy says, throwing him the newspaper that told him Macey had boarded the ship.

"I wanna get me on one of them ships."

"Do I look like I own a ship?"

"No, but do I look like an art dealer?" Troy springs life into himself and plays surprise. "Actually, yes I do."

Dog has been inside a ship, but only working for CSCI and only once. He knows there is no way any of those guests are his people. Troy has that hard grin, the one he uses when negotiating.

"You need a tux, bro," Dog uses. He is sure paying him off would be better.

"I get me one of those."

"Your bitch needs one of them long dresses every night."

"Troy looks at each of the girls in his harem.

"I get me a classy bitch."

"She needs to be classy, and no monkey to climb. They got security everywhere."

Troy opens his hands, 'so what'.

"Bitch don't come without the sauce. I get me a new rupansh *(drug addict)*. Not an enthusiast."

"You ain't no art dealer."

"Oh. Seems I could be the ship's amilly *(dealer to the rich)*."

"My man here needs to go upstairs and make a phone call."

"He can take the short way out."

One of the crew leads Croc out.

"How 'bout I cash you out?" Dog tries.

"I was coming to that."

Troy opens the newspaper at the article.

"Nice. Snap by Richard Hedgemont; these paintings worth money."

"How much you think a cruise cost?" Dog asks.

Troy stands up, "Me an expert on art, not cruising."

"That right?"

"This one's ripe," Troy says ripping a painting from the wall to look at it.

"Who know the price?" Dog asks.

"Oh. I know the price. I'm selling."

Above ground, Croc is breathing deeply to clear his lungs. He is on his cell in the middle of a conversation with Dwight.

"A cruise ain't right, Dwight. But I am obligated to ask."

Croc looks around for the nearest crew member, but they are showing respect by giving him space.

"He's an animal, man. He can't mix with cruisers."

Big Dog arrives from below. He has one painting, the one Troy ripped off the wall. He is smiling. Croc wonders why.

"Is what it is, Croc?" Dog says, holding his hand out for the cell.

"Dwight, my man. It's an art auction," he says, looking at Croc while waiting for a reply.

"Who's he gonna find to auction with?" Dwight asks from HQ.

"He may sell drugs to lowlifes in the ghetto, but he move up when he has to," Big Dog informs him. "He'll find another buyer to join the game."

34 - VINTAGE

DAY5-Italy-0830hrs   Miami-0230hrs   Mississippi-0130hrs

Kieron and Hunter sit in their favoured classic Italian deli. The dated green walls and cupboards make them feel at home. Their end-of-shift treat is also a celebration of the camera being up, focussed and working properly. It has become a long breakfast.

"You know, this place reminds me of the pale green '56 Chevy Bel Air convertible I had at college. Beautiful chrome stripe, dark green rear end," Hunter says, looking at the imposing colour.

"Whitewall tyres?"

"One of them was."

"Sounds like a neat vintage motorcar," Kieron replies.

"Would be now. Back then it was just old."

"Like that gantry, you broke."

"I nearly died on that."

"No," Kieron grins.

"OK, not as close to death as when Bedi jumped you," Hunter reminds him.

"We need to get her into a clinic."

"Yep. And get you some self-defence classes," Hunter drawls, enjoying the game.

"Pilot confirmed she was in the air but with two bottles of vodka from duty-free. She's getting worse. I'm worried."

"Do you want to talk about it?" Hunter says in the kindly tone of a therapist.

Kieron is getting annoyed.

"I feel she's gonna kick up a storm back home."

"And when did you start getting these feelings?" Hunter continues.

"Can we focus on the job?" Kieron asks.

"Would you like to talk about things that frustrate you?"

"You're not funny, Hunter."

"I hope this session has helped you. Same time tomorrow?" Hunter says standing up.

Miami-0145hrs   New Orleans Day 1 – 0045hrs

Yonan is awake, waiting for a call. The team failed to get the last of Macey's paintings back and Dwight is wondering how to break the bad news. It will be a thin catalogue.

He needs all the facts and a plan to solve the problem. The problem is that it won't be tonight. Yonan will no longer be able to annoy the printer by adding more pages of more paintings.

Big Dog arrives back at the CSCI office. Izzy is relieved that Croc is safe. Dog has missed being the great assistant he was in the mission now known as Laundry Wars. He would love to be an investigator, but what he brings to the table is his street army. He can't leave his crew in Overtown unless he can show he is invaluable in other ways. Tonight he failed. However, there is respect between gangs and although he could not take Macey's paintings from Troy, he expects a call when there is another player to bid against.

Croc is stumped. He left the ghetto so long ago they see him as an outsider. He looks and speaks differently now as much as he might try to get-down.

"If Troy wants to sell, Yonan's the best buyer. Where would Troy try and deal?" Dwight asks Dog whilst typing.

"We don't get much art in the ghetto. He be using a burner from his crib. He make his fence, Joey, visit and see the merchandising," Dog offers.

Dwight prints a map of Overtown. "Put a pen around each gang's area, write the king's name in the middle."

Dog looks up. He would never give that information, but he badly wants to be an investigator. He carefully draws a line on the streets between each hood. He hesitates, then crosses the location of Troy's crib. Then his dealer, Joey.

"Joey's here, on 69th down near Baywood, right near the beach. Nice area. He has a bungalow opposite a high rise. Easy to find, it'll be the only one with a red drop head Bentley in the drive." Dog writes 'Joey' on the map.

"He's gonna deal art?"

"Dealers are dealers. Bentleys is Bentleys and they open doors."

Dwight dials Yonan as Izzy and Croc both capture the map on their cells.

"Yonan," Dwight starts. "He's stepped up from drug dealer to art dealer. Name's Troy, he wants to sell, We got his address and the fence he'll probably move it to."

Dwight covers his phone and looks at Croc.

"Let's second guess this Joey. Find me art dealers anywhere near North East 69th."

Dog watches Croc work the computer and wonders if he could ever learn that, but he is more muscle.

"I'll be in my car within minutes," Dwight says curtly to his open line. There is no picture on the video call, just Yonan's name. "But, let's make it the first bench in Centenary, there'll be no one in the park this time of night." Dwight rudely ends the call.

"Izzy, we're a team again," Dwight says, already on the way out. "Croc, share the map with Yonan. I'm off to see him."

"Do you need me?" Croc asks.

"No, you man the office, you too Dog. It's about time you learnt how boring this job is. Until it gets nasty, and I feel us getting real close to that."

"Do we need Wild Mary?" Izzy asks.

"No, we going to be in and out of that park. Nothing we can tell him, but there might be more he can tell us."

With Dwight and Izzy gone, Dog looks around enjoying the hub and that he might learn something. Croc enjoys his superiority.

"This is my desk. I search phones, pinpoint them, take down information including their messages. Ain't much I can't get off a phone."

"What if it's a burner?"

"No different."

"What if it vintage?"

"Same."

"What if it's locked?"

"I can open it, lock it with a new password and shut it down?"

"Yonan won't get near Troy's crib. He gotta use the dealer," Dog insists.

"He won't go himself. Big money gets big muscle, gets anywhere."

Miami-0215hrs

Dwight sits next to Yonan, who is well disguised as always; hat, dark glasses and a scarf wrapped around his face. It is pitch dark as all the park lamps switch off on timers. Instantly Dwight knows Yonan is not pleased that the mission failed. The atmosphere between them is cold

"Map," Yonan says, flatly.

"Croc sent it over."

"Send it again, I've got a new number."

"I'll text it now," Izzy offers taking the information from Yonan's cell.

"Sent."

Yonan studies it while Izzy surreptitiously takes photographs of his shoes.

"Dealer's on Baywood. The other cross is Troy's den," Dwight explains.

"Where are the paintings?"

"At Troy's tonight, but we expect them to be moved to a dealer within a day, two at best."

Yonan nods, gets up, but Dwight stops him leaving.

"One thing more. Macey found another bad forgery on the ship."

Yonan walks away.

CRUISE SHIP ART THEFT

"Did he seem interested? He told us nothing. What was the point of meeting? I like that man less and less each time I see him," Dwight says, quietly to Izzy.

35 - NEW ORLEANS BY AIR

Because of the early arrival, both girls were in bed as the ship made its way up the Mississippi River. They may have missed that, but the excitement about arriving in New Orleans is evident at the breakfast buffet. It is a breathtaking, dramatic city that lives and dies by the water. Ravaged by extreme floods in August 2005, after the storm Katrina, its levees were breached in over fifty places. No answer has been found and it stills suffers floods to this day, but the waters feed the city.

Today the sun is shining, and music played in the streets, greets the tourists. Long gone is the memory that Mardi Gras tourism was to blame for the huge spread of Coronavirus there. Tourism is still a major source of income for the many musicians, bar owners, voodoo museums, and shop owners. New Orleans is one stop where cruisers, who never usually spend, dip into their pockets.

For the rich who live in Louisiana, those with land and money, the area is gold. Spouting vast pockets of petroleum and natural gas, partly due to thousands of years of decaying wetlands, it offers many support jobs to the energy industry.

The wetlands offer guests airboat rides through waters with some of the best plant growth in America. Clément has arranged three tickets for Macey, Prisha and himself to experience an airboat. He warns the girls that it will be very noisy, windy, cold, and wet, and tells them to wear waterproof clothing and that Macey should not try to paint. Macey is the kind of girl you can't control. If she had not discovered art as a major, she would never have survived school. That is thanks to Mary; she did not want her to drop out of school and fall into the cracks of Overtown. Macey does have a coat, bought for her by Yonan's assistant, and the pockets are full of sketching crayons. She has her hair in the brush filled bun and carries her pad of canvases.

On seeing her work, Clément is rapturous inside. He is beginning to know how to work her, and that is his job.

Following the Stephen E Ambrose Memorial Highway on an endless bridge crossing Lake Pontchartrain, they turn off the i10 and head into the huge park area. The coach drops them at the boat dock, and they are soon loaded into a much larger craft than either of the two girls expected. Fitted with ear defenders, Clément organises Macey in the middle. If she is hit with an attack of genius, they can give her support or room.

"I guess we don't have to wear life jackets as the Alligators will get us anyhow," Prisha jokes, but with a touch of concern. They have all failed to notice the two tall heavy-set men who sit behind them. They alone consume their bench.

As they speed away from the dock, the wind excites them and Prisha and Macey link arms. Macey notices the more sedate riverboat filling with the less able guests on the ship, and others gliding away from the dock in canoes. Macey points at the canoes, but speaking is pointless.

CRUISE SHIP ART THEFT

When they stop, the native Cajun tour-guide, McFee, moves to stand at the front. He is full of information on the wetlands and the Honey Island Swamp which is part of America's largest and most mysterious swamp ecosystem. He looks like a most seasoned seafarer, one who has had the wind in his face since he was a young lad. No need for a plastic surgeon to pull his skin back. Macey sketches the very healthy man, who enjoys the outdoor life and this swamp. She has the wonderful ability to put an air fan in the bottom left corner, the seats all compressed, and him still the power of the painting. The smaller details will challenge her later.

McFee moves to the side of the craft and kneels to look into the waters. He is perfectly distanced from her and she turns to a new sheet of cotton canvas and again, quickly starts to sketch. It becomes evident why he stopped there, an alligator drives up from the water and snaps at his face. Prisha screams. Not reaching him, it sits in the water with its jaws open. McFee was in the middle of the page, but Macey repositions him and starts to over-crayon the rest. The woman in front of her is as amazed by Macey's work as she creates the alligator.

Off again, McFee turns the boat at speed. Macey begins to sway until the man behind her has one hand on each of her shoulders. He holds her steady. When the boat straightens, she thanks him with a glance back.

Macey is spoiled for choice, seeing mink, turtles, wild boars, egrets, herons, and bald eagles as well as moss hanging on the gnarled cypress trees, flora, and fauna, which is all explained by McFee.

Somewhere in the many sketched sheets, Clément hopes she has another masterpiece. In her own mind's eye is a series of paintings. Excited by the day, Macey, Prisha and Clem think nothing of the two tall bulky men who help them off the boat. They do not notice being followed to the coach nor those two guys getting into their Jeep. Clément smiles as he texts Yonan. The coach heads away from the Pearl River Wildlife Management area, back to the ship. Macey is still accurately sketching from memory; no detail, the journey is too rough.

"I don't like alligators," Prisha says.

36 - WELCOME HOME

Italy-0115hrs-Italy   **Miami-1915hrs**   New Orleans(1)-1815hrs

Bedriška enters the dark headquarters of CSCI. Dog has been sleeping there all night, as have Croc and Dwight after his meeting with Yonan at two in the morning. She is well inebriated.

Dwight wheels in behind her.

"Bedi, great to have you home!"

"Why? You babysit me because I drink like Russian?" she says, angrily, and with a stance that shows it.

"No. We got a major problem, and I'm in a chair."

"What?" she says, softening up.

"Drug lord has a bunch of Macey's paintings," Croc explains.

"Why? You owe money?" she demands to know.

"No, Macey's mom's a user, he her dealer," Dog explains. "Hey. I never got to meet you on the last job."

Dog moves forward, being friendly. He offers his hand. Croc and Dwight have seen her Russian greeting and wonder what will happen next.

Bedi grabs his hand and pulls it, Dog blocks it down instinctively, but his block is spun away, and he is pulled in. He goes to nut her, but she avoids it and holds him tight while she kisses his cheek and his other, then back again to the first cheek; three kisses. She hugs him hard. He pulls a gun out of the back of his belt.

"Put gun away, or I kill you. That was Russian greeting to friend."

"Don't try that on Troy," Dog offers, stepping back and trying to keep his street dignity. "Although, you never gonna meet him."

"Why? I love drug lords," she says, and no one knows how to take that.

"Yonan wants the paintings. Let him buy them via Troy's dealer," Dwight says.

Bedi looks at him in amazement.

"Dealer has dealer?" she asks.

"A fence to move stolen stuff. Yonan knows he has to move fast," Dwight explains.

"Why?"

"Any more press about Macey and the price goes up."

"So, what is major problem I am here to solve?" she demands confused.

"Nothing. You won't get them back. We just be calm, stay in the middle of this trade," Dog explains. "But none of that kissing and hugging."

Dwight cringes as Big Dog has spoken out of turn. Bedi moves to Dog and grips him hard around the shoulders.

"I like, he honest. Now, how much mom owe dealer?"

"She doesn't. We paid him," Croc says.

"Yeah, he's cool, he's all paid up," Dog agrees.

Dwight is watching her keenly. She notices the map behind him on the desk. She lunges forward and collects it.

"We no pay twice. We get paintings."

"Ain't that easy," Big Dog says, worried now she has Troy's address in the ghetto.

"Very easy, I go and get paintings from nice man, Troy. That why Kieron send Bedi back."

"He ain't a nice man, and you can't go in the ghetto," Dog says.

"True," Croc agrees.

"Who said?"

"Jim Crow said," Dog tells her.

Bedi lunges to the safe and spins the dials and opens the door. She pulls a gun out and slides it in the rear of her belt.

"Don't carry a gun in there," Dog says.

"Agree. I carry two," she says, pulling a second hand-gun and spare clips.

She closes the safe then opens the fridge.

"Milk, milk, milk. No Vodka?"

Bedi storms out.

"Oh no," mutters Dog.

"Hey, I'm coming," Croc shouts.

"I can't be seen with them," Dog admits, looking at Dwight. He is uneasy, pacing in lumbering circles.

"You're in the shit," Dwight says to him.

"No, that's why I can't go. The Russian's flying solo, off the grid. I ain't a part of it. I'll go and fix the mess." Dog says forcefully. "No way Troy can know I give up his address."

CRUISE SHIP ART THEFT

37 - ALL JAZZED UP

The excursion takes all the guests back to the ship, which allows the two girls to eat and change for an evening in the city. Macey might think that the amount of food eaten on the ship is gross, but she knows she missed lunch. Her hair is fashioned into a new brush-bun, and she has the same oil crayons and pad ready to go. Waiting for Prisha to finish, she pulls out her 'Shoes' painting and lays it on the easel set by the window to the balcony. She sketches above it and through it a crocodile. Prisha comes out and stops in her tracks, watching her work. She has watched her create many times before, but not destruct.

"You've changed it?" she says.

"It wasn't saying anything. I knew it could but didn't know what. S'why I kept asking Izzy for more. This what it needed."

"Crocodile shoes," Prisha resolves, nodding her head.

"Correct. And the other ones that are calf leather, I'll do the same. Then the paintings are the pair Jill wanted," Macey says standing up, keen.

"Go for it."

Twenty-two wild-life sketches have been left in her room. It is unlikely that they will all make it to becoming finished paintings. Just as it is unlikely they will get any of the old paintings back from Troy, however hard the team tries. Handing the problem over to Yonan and his desire to get them might work for a ridiculous financial compensation; the like of which Troy will never have seen. Enough for him to pay for his own cruise.

Flashing their cruise cards at the top of the gangway sees the three of them free to discover New Orleans by night. The two girls are so excited, they do not notice the two guys tailing them again.

They skip away from the ship. Clément is hoping Macey will be inspired to create more works. At the same time, way over in Miami, Bedi will try and recover her old works.

Although it won't be dark until about seven-thirty, they are keen to get to the Bourbon Street area early. Having heard from other crew members that the bars which have live music become crammed by about six-thirty, they want to choose one and settle an hour before that. The vast selection of bars makes the choice hard. Bourbon Street stretches thirteen blocks from Canal Street to Esplanade Avenue.

"Jill would have liked this. We should have asked her. I never thought," Macey says. "I asked her about a street in Paris and she knew all kinds of stuff. Now we're in the French quarter."

"This is not France. Want to know about Paris? Mais oui. I can tell you about Paris," Clément offers, inferring he knows as much as Jill.

"If you say 'mais oui' again, I'll punch you right on the nose," Macey laughs. She pulls them into a bar.

"But I know this street dates back to when Frenchman Jean-Baptiste Le Moyne de Bienvielle founded New Orleans, back in 1718."

"You must feel very at home here," Prisha says.

"Because he's French?" Macey laughs.

"No, because he's old."

Clément orders another round of drinks. In less than half an hour, their chosen bar, has become very crowded. It would be impossible to get a table and three seats like theirs. By the time the drinks arrive, it is dark outside, and the band has started. After a few songs Macey is uneasy; it is not what she expected. The band are playing rock music, but quite poorly. She wanted to hear jazz or funk. It is obvious they have sat in the wrong bar. All agreed, they give up their table and head outside to the street, which is already loud and raucous. All the bars with great music are crammed. They listen and watch from the street until Macey pulls them both away so she can be heard.

"You know what I'd like to do?" Macey announces.

The others turn, puzzled.

"A cemetery tour."

38 - NOT PAYING TWICE

Italy-0440hrs   **Miami-2040hrs**   New Orleans(1)-1940hrs

Bedi is in the room of an empty derelict house. Rubbish and used needles are everywhere. She is watching a car on the next block, and one block beyond is Troy's pad. It is now unguarded.

"Forty-five-minutes. The guys in the car have not moved," she says, to Croc who leans against the wall nervously.

"Well, if Troy's being watched by Five-0, we should crack back."

"No, not the police. Police would have more back up, they are not stupid. These guys are stupid."

"Oh," Croc says, confused.

"Three men in car. One is driver, he stay there. Only two to go into drug den. Very stupid."

"But there's only one of you."

"But, I have secret weapon."

"What?" Croc asks.

"You."

"Oh," Croc says, lightly as a choking response.

"They wait for men to come out, go to car. It break them up. Then attack."

"Good idea," Croc says.

"Shit idea. We hit Troy before they do."

Croc nods, but thinking she is completely mad. She can see his confusion.

"Men both sides of street; hard to enter."

"Yeah. Always."

"All gone inside. They seen men in car, they go inside, set house like fort, impregnable."

"Oh, right. No way in?"

"Correct, except for?"

"No idea."

"Through front door as guest."

"You won't get past the car, let alone inside the house. You see a white person anywhere?"

"Can black man have white woman?"

"Yeah," he says.

"You got very lucky; show me some love," she says, dragging him outside, arm in arm. She is also dialling on her cell.

"Police. Big gunfight. Overtown. No, I mean war. Ovitz Block. Guns everywhere. Dead everywhere."

She hangs there, glancing left and right. She cleans the phone, removes the battery and drops it into the drain. She takes Croc in a grip and is holding him up as well as dragging him along.

"Is that how black man walk when he has wonderful white woman like me?"

"No. I mean I don't know. I'm shitting myself," Croc bumbles in fear.

"Act."

They turn into the house and she walks up the steps, turns and runs down the internal stairs into the cellar unnerved.

"Don't touch anything," she says.

Croc lingers at the bottom of the internal stairs. The first soldier from Troy's crew crosses Bedriška.

"Move, I not here for have sex with you. I look for Troy."

He does not expect her to brush him aside, then the next member of his shocked crew.

Croc has his head in the door watching but can't believe her nerve and ducks out.

"Stop bitch," the first soldier says behind her.

She hears him cock a gun. She has two men in front of her by the hole in the next wall and a closed door beyond. The reach into their belts. She turns, pulling a gun and with two shots, she hits each guard in the centre of their forehead. Her trailing arm is up, aiming behind her. Her head snaps around. She shoots, taking out the next two before they can aim. But she is nowhere near as accurate.

Croc dares to look in and watches her step forward, between the two guards lying near the next wall. Her arms hang down; she shoots both guards simultaneously. Croc tentatively follows but gasps as three worried crew look out the next gaping hole. Their guns are up, but they see no obvious target, no assault from a gang. Croc ducks into the first room, out of sightlines. The walls are perfect cover. The crew do not see her guns held low behind her ass-cheeks.

"You have problem. Two men from car. Both with guns."

The three push past her and she sees two street gunman appear by the next wall. Her obstacles appear never ending. She raises both her guns and shoots the front two, turns in an instant and takes out the three she let pass, knowing will have turned back at the exchange of bullets.

Dumping the magazine from her right gun, she reloads, and moves to the door.

"What's happening?" is the shout from behind the door.

"I am Russian woman. Your crew chase two men with guns up to street. I am frightened. They need help."

The door cracks open and she barges in, catches a punch aimed at her. Her forearm blocks it before it lands and she twists it painfully against the elbow joint. Her arm comes back to the top still holding a gun, and she shoots while using the twisted body as a shield. She does not need to look. Her left arm is up and shoots the two crew members.

She kicks the final door in and as if she is at a shooting range, she takes everyone in the room out. Except for Troy; the king-pin in the middle. She leaves Troy.

"You art dealer now?"

Troy is frozen with fear.

"Art is big money. We don't fuck about like street punks. We clean up. Where are all paintings?"

He points at the walls. She shoots him in the knee, he does not respond, so she shoots the second knee.

"Where?"

Troy points to a gap between a cupboard and the wall.

"That is no way to keep art," she says.

She shoots him dead.

"Croc," she calls. "Croc, get in here."

Croc runs in stepping over the dead. She signals him to the paintings squeezed into the side of the cupboard. He collects them, then the ones off the wall.

"Problem now, gotta get out with the pictures," she says.

"You don't have a plan?" Croc asks.

"No."

He squares them up and rolls them gently.

"You came in here without a plan?" he asks.

He removes his coat and pushes the roll down his sleeve.

"Good. Very clever. You make good agent. We go."

Croc knows the short way out.

"This way."

"No, we go back this way. We check. Everyone must be dead."

"Oh, they're dead," Croc confirms.

Bedi leads him to the end watching for any movement. She stops and wipes both guns clean, very clean and drops them one by each dead guard. She squeezes their hand round the handle of each gun and finger into the trigger.

"Act very injured. Like shot. We struggle out. Don't touch anything."

As they struggle out, the two men from the car have taken up positions each side of the gate.

"Who's in there?" One asks her.

"Many men, big argument over paintings. They are going to burn them."

"What? Don, we've gotta go in."

The men pick up each of the guns from the floor so they have two guns each and they move down between houses.

Continuing to act injured, and exaggerating their friendship with the two men, Bedi waves at the get-away car. She points down to where his friends went. The car speeds in and skids. He opens the door and steps out.

"What?"

Bedi floors the man with two blows. She gets in the car. Croc gets in the back and they screech away.

Police cars power in from both sides, blocking the sidewalk. An ascension of policeman get out with guns raised.

Bedi drives. Croc is still in shock.

"We were lucky to get out of there."

"I still drunk. My aim not good. I think time to get sober. Time to get help."

"Your aim was great. We're alive," Croc says in awe.

39 - EMPTY MAUSOLEUM

Italy-0440hrs   Miami-2040hrs   **New Orleans(1)-1940hrs**

Clem and Prisha follow Macey's lead, turning down St Peters Street. She remembers guides looking like they were off to a student rag-week fancy-dress party, hustling those waiting in the huge queue for the jazz show in the Preservation Hall. The three of them complete a quota and their tour leaves immediately.

"I feel dead people already," Prisha shares.

"No," Macey abruptly replies. "The guides are actors in costumes playing a part. Like Clemmie."

What Prisha may have been feeling was the presence of the two guys still shadowing them as they walk up towards the Louis Armstrong Park.

"Now I can feel dead people," Macey glows, as they approach the St Louis Cemetery number 1. Suddenly her legs buckle as if she has been shot. Prisha grabs for her but misses. Clément drops the pad and catches her. The guys behind accelerate, but slow when they see her trying to stand. Macey grabs Prisha and walks with her aid.

"I'm feeling very uncomfortable. Very weird."

However disturbed Macey is feeling, she insists they turn in with the others. Most of the cemetery consists of raised mausoleums. The guide stops his audience to look at a new build.

"This belongs to the eccentric actor Nicolas Cage"

"He's not dead, is he?" a tourist asks.

"No, but he plans to be."

The crowd laughs.

"He bought two plots in the cemetery for when he does die. On them, he has had built this remarkable pyramid you can all see before you. No ghost here, but it's eerie. Built and waiting for him."

Whilst the cemetery sports historic sugar pioneers, chess champions and musicians, the one crypt they have all come to see is that of the famous voodoo queen and renowned hairdresser, Marie Laveau. They crowd around the lifeless, plain, ugly concrete shed sized box.

"Now, there's a lot of confusion over Marie," our guide continues. "Because, she had a daughter, actually two daughters. All three have the same name. Marie Laveau the 2nd, is entombed in the Catholic church. She too was a voodoo priestess. But, Miss Laveau the first, is here in the Glapion family crypt - Christopher Glapion being the man she lived with after her first husband mysteriously disappeared. And after her lavish funeral, it is said that she rose from the dead and still walks the streets of New Orleans. Spookily, she is always spotted at the Mardi Gras."

He says it with such a haunting poetic restrained thunder, that it sends a chill down everyone's spine. That is, everyone except Macey.

"Despite being a devout Catholic all her life, Marie Laveau was the Witch Queen of New Orleans. Herbalist, midwife, and snake keeper. Her snake was called Zombie."

Macey is sketching, but jerks, taking a hit bigger than outside. She buckles but remains standing.

"My paintings are causing problems."

She jerks again, feeling the hit of every bullet Bedi fires. Prisha holds her with concern. Clem gets behind her and his arms wrap around her, in genuine affection and concern, he holds her up. Outside the gate, the guys tailing them enter the cemetery.

"The Voodoo Queen had many wealthy patrons. Marie is said to have had power over them, the information she gained from their servants, striking even greater fear into them."

Macey starts sketching again. It is the box, with Marie rising. Marie's features fill in both quickly and easily, and Macey, in an uncomfortable trance works fast. The guide cuts through the crowd.

"That's her, that's exactly Marie Laveau," the guide says, in an astonished, partly fearful voice.

"How do you know?" Clément asks, in his French accent.

"I saw her, only once, but I saw her. Risen from the dead. She rolled away the stone and rose. No one believed me."

Macey looks at him as they all watch her work. She sketches him in the lower corner, looking up in awe. His features fall into place fast.

"Wow!" says a member of the crowd. "This girl's possessed."

"No," Clément says, authoritatively. "This is the very famous, May.I.see, she is brilliant. Her work sells for hundreds of thousands.

There is an "Oh" from the crowd.

Macey looks up again. Her expression shows she can see something.

"Oh," the crowd gasp again.

"Now you have seen her twice," Macey says.

She looks around the cemetery slowly.

"I can see them all," Macey whispers.

She is genuinely seeing the dead. She hears them in her head. Bewildered and unable to read the signals she drops; dizzy and confused.

"This is part of the act," one of the crowd suggests.

Clément is holding the oil crayoned work.

"Not an act, brilliance is exhausting. You 'ave witnessed more than a ghost, you 'ave witnessed the inventiveness of artist at work."

Prisha holds her up on the stone steps of a tomb.

"I have felt death, I've painted it, but never felt this close. Never felt it so personally."

Clément offers her his hip flask. She drinks it and cringes. It is very strong.

"We go back?" Clément asks.

"No, they want me to finish."

Macey sketches out a wider shot of the cemetery. She shapes the ghosts she sees hovering above each tomb.

"They don't rise freely from the dead as Marie can," Macey says, with no idea where that came from.

Clément is on the phone to Yonan.

"These sketches will be worth a fortune. Maybe a gallery here should show them for sale, what do you think?"

Prisha looks at Clem.

"What did Yonan say?"

"For the first time I know 'im, 'e was speechless," Clem struggles. "I 'ave never heard him like that."

"But if he was speechless, what did you hear?" Prisha asks.

"Nothing, 'e could say nothing."

One man is outside the cemetery, the other is at the back of the crowd, both watch Macey, waiting.

40 - FEISTY

Italy-0540hrs   **Miami-2140hrs**   New Orleans(1)-2140hrs

Izzy walks back to the computer hub, holding the coffee she has made for Bedriška.

"She's fallen asleep."

"I'll take that," Dwight says, and Izzy hands him the mug. "Energy just goes after a big mission."

"Yeah, I'm surprised I'm still standing," Croc announces.

They ignore his remark.

"Big mission!" he insists.

"She'll also have jet lag after the flight out of Europe."

"I could have been killed!" Croc says.

He is ignored again.

"Who gonna move in on Troy's patch. There'll be a war for that," Dog offers.

"You want it?" Dwight asks.

"Not me bro, street drugs ain't my thing. I serve the rich."

"Still drugs," Dwight hammers.

"No bro, the rich women like my crew and they ain't twenty-dollar hits."

"Bedi's gonna need to go to ground. I mean now," Dwight says.

"There ain't no one left to come after her," Croc explains.

"Police come next."

"She covered her tracks."

"And she can come live in our unit," Izzy suggests.

"Bless you Izzy, but she needs to be dug deep. I got her a place reserved at the Hazelden Betty Ford Clinic."

"Where?" Croc asks.

"Two hours away on the Gulf coast. By the time you get there, Dog, it'll be morning. It's your first solo run."

"Me?"

"You wanna join the unit? We do some boring shit. Getting her into a unit sure won't be boring. When you sign the papers, you back the date up two days. Croc will change the technical."

Dwight pulls out a set of license plates from under his desk.

"Get these on Croc's old car. After you deliver her, scrap the piece of shit. Get back here without being seen."

Dog is nodding.

"Scrap my car?"

"You get a new one, eventually."

Croc watches Dog collect the plates.

"She said she needed to sober up coz her aim was out – it didn't look out to me. They shot right here," Croc offers, putting his figure to his forehead.

"Did she use her left hand?" Dwight asks.

"Yeah," Croc says, twisting his body to show one gun forward and one gun back "Like two at once."

"Did the left get headshots?"

"No, she had to shoot them again," Croc says, acting out the move again, both hands down.

"She meant her left hand wasn't so good."

"Oh," Croc says, confused that killing is so acceptable.

"She's some feisty bitch," Dog says, crossing the room.

"Bitch! Who call me a bitch?"

Dog leaves quickly.

41 - JUNIOR

Italy–0555hrs   Miami-2155hrs   New Orleans(1)–2055hrs

In Italy, it is nearly six o'clock and Hunter Witowski arrives back from a foraging mission, pre end of shift. He has fresh bread and an array of cheeses that he opens on the coffee table. They have found a baker who has loaves out of the oven by five-thirty in the morning. Kieron Philips is spooling through footage from the warehouse camera and speaking on a conference link with Dwight and Croc on the speaker.

"Let's eat up here," Kieron says, which infers he has found something. Hunter moves the two coffees, a bread to be broken and thick slices of cheese.

"I don't know how they managed without a camera on the warehouse," Kieron offers.

"They didn't want one," Hunter says settling in.

"That's confirmed. Look, this is yesterday's footage. 0930hrs, after we'd gone off shift."

"Good morning, Hunter," Dwight says from Miami.

"Yeah, good morning. What time is it there?" Croc asks.

"Hi, Guys, it's nearly six in the morning."

"Croc are you still seeing this?" Kieron asks.

"Yes boss, I've got the live feed plus a lot to download from the hard drive."

On-screen, an art assistant takes a painting, loosely covered, from the central set of divisions made to keep the paintings apart; a bit like a plate rack in a dishwasher.

"That's the atrium section, see that?" Hunter asks.

"Yes," Dwight says, highlighting the rack on his screen.

"And what's the betting it's the four-million-dollar Wolfman?" Hunter says.

The assistant walks to the back wall, behind the protruding toilet block and he does not reappear.

Kieron leans back on his chair, enjoying both the bread and cheese as well as his discovery. Hunter eats as he studies the floor plan.

"Thought you said they were boarded up?" Croc asks.

"They were when we checked them," Hunter says.

"Well, Witowski, you were duped there," Dwight pokes. "Not often you boys get sold a curved ball."

"Yeah, those doors open," Croc says. "We nail the boards on our unit so it looks closed, but it ain't."

"He's used an end door, one obscured by that toilet block. Makes sense," Kieron suggests. "They'll have a release inside."

"Hate to break up your posh breakfast," Dwight says.

"We're going," Kieron says.

"We're watching," Dwight says as the Miami team gather around the screen. "But, there's a back door out to a service road."

"I'll drop down into that rear reception area from the gantry, here. I'm good on roof gantries," Hunter says sliding the mouse to show his route. Whoever's inside, painting…"

"Forging…" Dwight says from Miami.

"Inside, allegedly forging. Is trapped," Hunter says.

"Before you rush off, Bedi did a little painting."

"What?" Hunter asks.

"Every damn room in the house."

"Didn't she leave anything for anyone else?" Kieron asks.

A photo of a tunnel of dead bodies pops up on the screen. Hunter looks at Kieron. Neither is surprised.

"Not a single room left unfinished, even the skirting boards," Dwight explains.

"Will Yonan will be pleased?" Hunter asks.

"He seems a little unmoved. She's going across town for a check-up," Dwight replies.

"Give her our love," Kieron says flatly.

42 - PHONE A FRIEND

Hunter rounds the gantry as Kieron walks amongst the assistants, as he often enjoys doing. He likes to ask about the pieces. Tonight, he has a fixation on some of the table-top sculptures.

Hunter slips down the metal staircase at the other side and out of sight. He has gone dark.

As expected, it leads down to the back corridor. There is one door, a side entrance for offices or a fire exit. All the fire exits had been locked as the front doors were always open, but Bedi found one of the padlocks had been oiled and used recently. The chain is looped over the emergency push bar. The padlock is hanging sprung open. Hunter takes a photograph and presses send, as he flattens against the wall and pulls his gun. From his taut face, he is prepared for more than a painter.

Kieron walks to the rear office door in the warehouse. He tries it but it is locked and appears to be nailed closed. On closer inspection, the boards are only nailed to the door, not the wall next to it. He pulls a gemmy from the back of his belt and begins to force the door. That should not be difficult because the internal door would only be wood. Staying to the side, he rams his bar into the gap harder, using it as a pick and digging out a gap between door and frame. It is not easy and makes so much noise the assistants in the warehouse are all watching. He forces a separation but drops hearing a gun cocked inside. The door starts to break open. Two gunshots sail through the wood over his head, missing him. He rolls away knowing that was not his partner.

Hunter holds the phone up filming next to his gun as he turns into the room. Seeing the back of a gunman still aiming at the other door where Kieron must be, he shoots him in the gun-arm elbow and thigh. The man drops and Hunter is straight in to hit him across the head with his gun. He collects the cell-phone he dropped and films the face of the man on the floor then the artist at the desk who is frozen with fear.

"That's the low-level soldier we saw on our first day. He was pushing one of the assistants around pretty violently; then the two who walked out without being stopped by the in-house guard on the gate," he says.

Hunter props the cell on a shelf by the door. He drags the guard to an old-style radiator. Using his utility belt handcuffs, he secures him to the pipe. The artist gets up to run. Hunter pulls him back with a firm hand on the shoulder and shows him to the camera, before turning him around and slamming him down to the desk.

"You're going nowhere." He puts his knee into the young man's back. "Dwight. Forging room. Armed guard. Artist is armed."

Hunter pulls a sidearm from the assistant's pocket and keeps it.

"The Wolfman and an unfinished copy," he reports, showing them both to the camera. The artist reaches for them, but Hunter is quicker. His painting-hand pounded onto the desk and Hunter moves both pieces to the wall so they can't be damaged.

Hunter puts his boot on the artist's hand while cable tying the other to his fixed table easel, the trapped hand is cable tied to his own leg folding him over. He cable ties his other ankle to the guard's ankle.

Kieron comes under gunfire from behind in the warehouse and rolls away to the toilet unit wall.

"Stop, it's Officer Kieron Philips. We found a forging room," he shouts, exposed to the oncoming guard. The guard continues to shoot at Kieron.

"Under hostile fire," Kieron reports to the open line.

He dodges the bullets by moving back behind the edge of the protruding washroom building. It is the one that blocks the new camera's view of this far office door. The block serves as his cover.

The assistants in the warehouse are running away.

"Mind the paintings!" The older bearded one shouts.

Another security guard appears making army gestures to the first. Kieron sees him cut through the tables as the other creeps forward.

Kieron listens carefully. The second guard runs through the tables. Kieron drops to the floor and finds him through a forest of table legs. He shoots and the gunman's knee bursts open in a splatter of blood. Kieron rolls back up to the cover of the washroom, considering his next move. He waits, listening for footsteps.

Hunter kicks the door out behind him, gun up. In the surge of confusion, Kieron rolls out, shooting the guard in both thighs. Hunter shoots taking out his gun arm.

"Do you think our cover's blown?" Hunter asks.

Kieron goes to secure the injured man kicking his gun away first. Hunter does the same to the one in the tables.

"Dwight, I think it's time to call our friends at INTERPOL. Reveal the international art forgery ring based in Italy. I think the police will take us in, you need to get us out," Hunter says.

Kieron has his phone photographing the shot guard.

"All precision defence shots."

"OK, there's no need to show off," Dwight replies.

"Any guards not turning up for work, or any assistants who vanish must be considered unfriendly. And warn Yonan, our cover's broken. We need to find his art, and fast."

Hunter drags his man towards the forging room leaving a trail of blood.

Kieron cable ties the other shot gunmen as he shouts instructions towards his cell.

"Dwight, we don't want too much thinking time in an Italian lock-up. It's kicked off now. We'll need INTERPOL to get us out," Kieron adds. "We gotta find the art fast."

There are screams from the forging room.

"I think Hunter's on that," He hears Dwight say.

43 - FRENCH MARKET

DAY6-Italy–1900hrs   Miami-1100hrs   **New Orleans(2)–1000hrs**

Clem has no trip or excursion planned. They are free to discover the City, unlike Hunter and Philips, who have now spent ten hours locked up in an Italian police station. Luckily for them, it is after a night shift so they have used the time to sleep.

In New Orleans, Macey didn't sleep much. She has produced the beginnings of new masterpieces. Whilst the jazz clubs inspired nothing, her fascination with the dead has. The 'Witch Queen of New Orleans' is the guide seeing Marie Laveau rise from her tomb. 'Graveyard' is a very dark piece. The long night has produced four other very spooky works. The most outstanding one is of Marie Laveau, risen over her mausoleum. She dominates the centre, and the risen dead from all over the cemetery surrounding her. They are all reaching up for her, either adoring or growling and scratching at her. The painting is distinctly haunting. The wildlife trip produced twenty-two sketches, although missing Macey's cutting edge, they may stay unfinished. Clem's job will be to get her focussed on finishing some of the most meaningful works during the following two days at sea. 'Keep her happy, keep her working' is Yonan's brief.

As they walk along the seafront, the first eye-feast is a large red and white paddle steamer. Prisha and Macey enjoy having their pictures taken with it behind them. Clément directs the session, or tries to, but he has no power to stop them from pulling shapes and kicking their legs up. Macey has recovered from last night's exhausting work in the graveyard.

"You should paint this, c'est incroyable," he says, of the red and white paddle steamer called the City Of New Orleans. Macey is not interested. He turns her to see the magnificent historic boat with the iconic cantilever 'Sunshine Bridge', that spans the Mississippi, sitting in the background.

"Or, zis."

Macey looks at it.

"Nope," she says, "pink ponies," and she turns away arm linked with Prisha like two young girls.

"Maybe tonight, 'red sky at night, artists delight'," she shouts.

"Zis way," Clément encourages them, giving up easily because he knows they need press photographs of her. He has something else up his sleeve for the morning. Plus, tonight the bridge will be an impressive profile against the most beautiful sunset.

"We start in the French market."

"Why?" Macey asks, with a straight face.

They both break into laughter and walk along the seafront path, performing numerous silly walks. The sea wall is separated from the city by train lines and the Toulouse Station. Clément points them across the line into the market.

His cell-phone camera is up, and he catches them looking back, in a silly walk, halfway across the tracks. The classic crossed 'Rail-Road Crossing' sign and the red triangular 'Yield' sign underneath with New Orleans behind, offer a May.I.see press shot. He continues shooting, catching them dancing across the tracks.

"The beginning of the French Quarter," he shouts.

Macey waits for him, pulls him into her and Prisha.

"But, you're not even French."

The two girls scurry away laughing. They turn right and walk through the market without stopping. At the other side, Macey turns to him.

"Is this what France is like?" she asks, pulling a very animated, weird and disappointed face. "Oh. Sorry, you wouldn't know."

She turns away laughing, pulling Prisha with her.

"How about that? Look, the 'National Jazz Museum'," Prisha offers.

"No. I would like to go to a voodoo museum," Macey says.

"We walk through the Jazz Museum reception and out the other side," Clément offers.

He is right, as he is most of the time. Both girls are intrigued by the old instruments and bands. Macey, however, is captivated by the singers and those who played the instruments. The dead.

She turns to Clément.

"What a shame they didn't theme it here. They've rammed history into a modern office and killed any atmosphere."

On the other side of the hall, hidden behind the sales counter, they find the New Orleans coin museum. It is overcrowded but affording the exhibits less space allows them to produce an atmosphere. Here the history survives, refusing to allow itself to be swallowed up by the modern architecture.

"Do you want to see more?" he asks.

Clément's question is real but for the first time, his attention to them is not 100%. Out of the corner of his eye, he has seen someone. A man he is sure he saw in the airboat yesterday and he is searching his brain. This man has been around too much.

"No, I still want to see the voodoo."

They exit the other side and walk straight past the unknown man who Clément cannot resist glancing at. The three cut back towards the sound of a jazz band playing in the street, with him following. Clément is no secret agent and would be useless in a fight, especially against someone with that build, but he does know to stay in a crowd is safer.

44 - SEEN YOU

Approaching the gangway to the ship, Bentley carries a wrapped square parcel. Its size suggests Macey's painting is now framed and boxed for travel.

The other of the two guys glued to them is also in the secure area, watching Bentley walk across the dock towards the gangway. He flicks open his knife. He edges around the other side of the pallet. It has a mixture of boxes and parcels cellophane-wrapped together to form a load, and it affords him cover. Bentley is not watching for him. The man is not even being watched by those behind him loading the ship with forklift trucks. A truck beeps and the driver waves at him to move. Not because he should not be there, but because he needs to drop another pallet.

Bentley gets to the officer at the bottom of the gangway and he is now safe. Taking his 'visitors cruise card' he walks up to the ship.

When the truck has gone, the man slits the layered wrapping. He pulls out a thin catalogue. It has Macey's picture on the front, and a quick flick through shows a collection of her work. He pulls his cell out and speed dials.

"Painting's arrived, it's onboard. Books have arrived. All we gotta do is sort the girl out. Where are you?"

There is an eerie pause.

"Ok. I'll get on board. I'll find him."

The man advances to the ship, closing his knife. Producing a cruise card, he nonchalantly passes the officer. He slides the knife up above his wrist into the long sleeve top, under his jacket. Turning to the side, looking back and forth, he reaches behind him and moves his gun from the small of his back to his hip. It is far more obvious there if anyone were looking. It is also harder to draw. He is taking his light denim jacket off as he shows his cruise card and is bleeped in. The gun is unseen below the level of the plinth; there is too much going on with the card and the jacket. The man puts the book and his denim jacket in the tray and bides his time, checking his pockets as he watches the tray go through. He puts his wallet, some coins, and his watch in a second tray and releases it. Like the few cruisers returning early, he coolly walks straight through the x-ray detector, big smile not a care in the world. His gun is in his belt, the side adjacent to the x-ray belt and away from officers.

The alarm is triggered, so he has to act fast. Ignoring the bleeping his left hand takes the gun from his belt and slips the weapon under his jacket as he collects it from the tray on the X-ray belt. His right hand releasing the knife from his sleeve and hiding that too.

"Please step back, sir."

"Oh, sorry," he says, turning back, recognising the alarm and the call he has left both weapons safely behind him.

He takes off his belt, and as he passes back through the protection arch. He puts his belt in a third tray. Pulling both sleeves up to his elbow to show no tricks he quickly waltzes through the arch. There is no alarm and an approving nod and smile from the guards. A female guard is about to lift his jacket, and he had planned for that too.

"Did my money come through in the small tray? I can't see it," he says directly to her, advancing fast.

He scoops up the coat and ensures both weapons are held in as he rolls the coat under his left arm. She passes him the smaller tray.

"Thanks," he says, pocketing the money. She passes him his belt with a teasing, huge smile. He smiles back, but he wants her to hurry. He has noticed that the head of security is taking a special interest in him.

"Excuse me, sir."

The guard leaves his desk and walks straight towards him. There is no need to react until there is anything to react to; the first rule of undercover engagement.

"May I?" The security guard says, pointing to his right forearm.

"Sure," he says, knowing the weapons are under his left and if required he could drop all the guards in the vicinity and get off the ship. However, that is not his assignment.

The security chief adjusts his sleeve up to the elbow revealing the full tattoo. It is a skull with a green berry on.

"That's no voodoo souvenir, right?" he asks with a knowing smile.

"Right."

"Says just enough," the guard says.

"Obviously says too much, but it was done after I left," the man shares.

"I thought you guys never retired," he says, and the moment has lightened as long as he doesn't ask to see the other arm. He might notice the careful transfer of the loaded jacket.

"We do, then we cruise. Looking for a single, rich, sassy woman."

"Do you mind if I take a picture? I like to collect special forces ink?"

"Knock yourself out."

"What's on the other arm?" he asks.

The man looks at the guard and smiles, without giving anything away. 'Is he being super clever and wanting the parcel to change hands?' There is only one way to find out; the hard way. The man crunches the coat with his left arm to feel both weapons are in his grip, he goes to transfer. The security guard's hand comes up.

"Let us help you. Mina, take the man's coat for him."

The guard's eyes stare at the man. Is this a game of chess? The man has no option other than to speed-up the transfer.

"I got this thanks, Mina. You're not rich, are you?"

"Only in India, when I go home," she laughs.

The man reveals the other arm is ink-free.

"I'm so disappointed."

"No, you're not. You weren't expecting the first one," the man says.

"What regiment were you from?"

"Can't tell you that, I'd have to kill you," the man says, laughing with them.

It is not easy for a tall well-built ex-military guy to walk onto a cruise ship unseen. If the man had any hope of not being noticed, that is over.

45 - VOODOO CHILD

Walking up the narrower streets of the old quarter, all the houses are two-storey with iron-railed balconies. Macey feels very at home in this part of town. It is full of stories that she can feel, crammed with visions that she takes in. The voodoo museum comes as a shock because it's one of the small houses in commercial use. Her cell phone beeps; it is Izzy. Yonan has another pair of shoes on. It is a top view of a pair of loafers.

"What's that?" Prisha pries.

"New shoes. Another new pair."

Clem raises his eyebrows at the thought of three paintings in a set, but he says nothing. He follows the girls into the voodoo shop.

Each room and connecting passage is decked out with voodoo related items. Every inch is used to excite the tourist and encourage them to buy. There is even a wishing stump that requires a dollar to be poked into it. It is adorned with the same strings of silver balls used at Christmas. There are crosses all around and the connection to Christianity is implied everywhere. A primitive drum continually beats out an eerie rhythm.

Whilst it is the French Quarter and its roots are French, Clément sees nothing familiar. He has also seen it before, and for him, it has zero attraction the second time around. His only interest is what it does for Macey.

"We have magicians and fortune-tellers in India going back way further than this. Thousands and thousands of years," Prisha says softly to Clément.

Macey chooses a voodoo doll and passes it to Clément with a beaming smile.

"You want it?" he asks.

Macey nods her head.

"I think I'm going to need it," she says.

Prisha and Clément have both seen enough and people would like them to move to allow others in. Many are waiting to walk around the centrepiece of the room, which is a skeleton sitting on various cases and a small coffin. Each of the cases has shelves conveniently built, showing potions, lotions, and dolls for every mood. More worrying are the takeaway ritual kits in coffin-shaped small boxes. Death and skulls are common themes.

Macey has her pad out. She may be small, but she is causing a jam. Not because she is standing there but because others are standing watching her sketch the skeleton that sits proudly in the centre. She is now putting a skin onto it; dotting the earrings, a bow below her neck, her hair is parted the middle and edged with the most delicate hairband. It is a haunting woman. Her dark-skinned face is young and innocent with perfect features. Macey finds herself reaching out and grabbing a small bag of herbs, marked Tanna Leaves.

"That's the young Marie Laveau," the shop proprietor gasps, pointing at the sketched work. He has come to move people on but is mesmerised by Macey's work.

"No," one says. "Nothing like her." Indicating a picture on the wall.

"That picture is her daughter, Marie Laveau 2," the owner says. As they all look, it does say clearly that it is Marie Laveau 2.

"This is the real Marie Laveau."

Macey starts to shake. Her work has been so fast and furious, the acceleration ends in a trance and she collapses, holding up the leaves. Prisha goes to Macey, Clément goes to the picture.

"Give it to me," the proprietor says, trying to snatch the painting away. In the feud that breaks out, the big man walks between them and the shop owner, firmly pushing him back. The man, giant-like in the small shop, helps Macey up slowly. He takes the painting from the curious Clément who has seen him before.

"That is my picture; it was painted on the premises," the shop owner shouts very angrily.

The man looks back at him. His huge muscle-built stature says the matter is over, without a word needing to be spoken.

The owner follows them to the door, his face red. He is enraged.

"Lord knows: she's a voodoo child," the owner shouts after her.

Clément pays the woman at the counter for the doll Macey chose.

"Clément, pay for the Tanna Leaves," the Big Man says to him.

"Of course, she needs Tanna, she is possessed," the owner shouts.

Clément pays for both and runs to catch them.

CRUISE SHIP ART THEFT

46 - BOOKED

Bentley finishes hanging May.I.see's painting in the art gallery. The special feature case is closed and locked. Jill watches his every move.

"She's a very lucky girl."

"And some, but she's good," Bentley says, moving the unfinished Hemingway next to it, and the ghost of Marie Laveau in the cemetery to the other side as bookends to her star piece.

"We need frames for those two. The three would look so powerful," Bentley says.

"You know I don't have the luxury of stock," she says.

Bentley opens her small stock cupboard at the side of the gallery. He pulls out two pieces and holds one in each hand.

"Perfect."

"They're sold."

"With frames?"

"Yes," she says.

"I'll put them back before you dock in Miami," he says.

Bentley is senior to her. His pocket-tools are out and the paintings removed and rolled in no time. He lays the frames in front of May.I.see's two most recent masterpieces. Begrudgingly Jill gets a long card roll from the cupboard and puts the two sold pieces in to protect them.

"We don't get to keep the LeRoy," Jill jokes. "I would have liked it until Miami."

Bentley turns to her.

"You're surrounded by fine art."

"I know, I'm lucky."

"Do you want to get luckier? Lunch with me?"

"You ask so nicely," Jill answers, sarcastically.

A crew member wheels a sealed parcel into the gallery.

"For you Jill," he says, tipping it off his trolley.

"I've been waiting to see this, Bentley says, rushing to it.

"Jill rounds the desk and takes a pair of scissors from the drawer and starts to cut the polythene grip that wraps it.

"Now we'll get to see how talented she is," Bentley says. He opens the booklet and studies it page by page.

"She certainly has an eye and an edge. Even a little political," he says.

Jill lifts a pile of catalogues onto her desk from the open wrapping, a second pile is spread on the table below the painting. She pushes the rest under the desk and takes one for herself. Bentley has his attention deep in the booklet. She has to nudge him.

"Sorry. Yeah. Sure. I'll look at that over lunch."

He frames her two paintings easily, and finishes, looking at his watch.

"Perfect timing for a jazz brunch," he suggests.

Italy–2130hrs   Miami-1330hrs   New Orleans(2)–1230hrs

Hunter is pushed back into a new police cell. He has been separated from Kieron. He goes to the door and calls out through the grill.

"Kieron!"

"At least they're not soundproof," is the reply from down the aisle.

"They said there was nothing on the hard drive from the art warehouse camera, and the guards said they were shot unprovoked; they hadn't even pulled their guns. They were trying to stop us from stealing a painting."

"Dwight is taking his time getting us out," Kieron says.

"It feels like the police are in on this too," Hunter thinks out loud.

"We've got to find where the paintings go before the trail gets cold."

"They want us out of the way for as long as possible."

Italy–2200hrs   **Miami-1400hrs**   New Orleans(2)–1300hrs

Dwight spins his chair around. He often does when he is thinking, especially when he wants to see the faces of everyone in the room. Izzy, Croc and Mary, essentially the staff of the diner, perch in the dark.

"What worrying you, boy?" Mary yelps at him.

"My main investigators are in an Italian jail, and INTERPOL is not playing ball. My other investigator's in rehab. That leaves me with…" Dwight ponders, leaving his question open.

"Me," says Croc.

"And me, fully trained by Prisha," Marys says.

Dwight looks at Izzy.

"What?" she powers at him.

"You the only one in the room who's not an investigator? I'm giving out badges," Dwight encourages, but he is being sarcastic.

Mary nods in approval.

"Now, investigators. Yonan's gone missing. His wife never saw him last night, his office has not seen him this morning."

"They said that's not unusual," Croc offers.

"No, but he always takes my call," Dwight insists.

"Don't know why. You hate him," Mary says.

"And the kid, Ricky can't get hold of him. I want you to get out there and find him," Dwight says.

"Ask Macey to call him? He gonna pick up the phone to his star," Izzy concludes. To her it seemed simple, the job is over.

"It lunch-time, the diner's gonna get busy. My induction ceremony and badge gonna have to wait," Mary says, leaving.

Izzy gets up.

"Never said I was an investigator, but I solved that." She follows Mary out.

Dwight looks at Croc.

"What?" Croc asks.

"Where's Yonan?" Dwight asks him.

"How about you find him?"

"I'm trying to convince Interpol to get involved."

47 - NO SURPRISE

Italy–2240hrs   Miami–1440hrs   **New Orleans(2)–1340hrs**

'The City of New Orleans' is a wonderful example of a paddle steamer and it is available for jazz brunches while berthed. If you thought there was a lot of food on a cruise, this ship might beat that. For not much money, there is chicken and sausage soup to start. Then a choice of salads before Creole Grillades, all finished off with a Mardi Gras Bread Pudding and rich cinnamon custard. Alternatives are available.

It is a long thin dining room, as the shape of the boat dictates. The squared plaster ceiling is classy, as are the white tablecloths and silverware. It is easy to see how, in times gone by, the rich sat here and gambled. Jill and Bentley dine at a table for two; a band plays on the stage.

"How does a young girl's brain have so many ideas?" Jill asks, looking through Macey's catalogue.

"She's angry, and it all stems from her life story. Read that. You weren't born in slums; you can't see slavery or oppression. You know who your parents are, and your foster mother didn't lose the family home to pay for a drug habit," he says paraphrasing. "It's hard to imagine what she's been through, but it'll make her a star now."

Ricky may not have written a biography, but under Yonan's tutelage, with a very light touch, he has written enough to make the reader weep, even if not openly. It is a piece that might bring him a lot of attention because his name is on it.

"Macey thinks she found a forgery," Jill admits, looking up. "She's gone from street-wise to paint-wise."

"Is she looking for forgeries?"

"No, a customer saw it first. They asked her."

"How did she reply?" Bentley asks.

"It's what she didn't say. It looked obvious, she agreed."

Bentley flicks through the book.

"She's staying on?" Jill asks.

"Yonan was going to take her off here, but he went quiet. Maybe Cuba. Yonan's not replying, so no plans have been made beyond today."

Their dessert plates are cleared and their cups are pulled to the centre ready to be filled. It's a fast, efficient, well-organised event driven by good service.

Waiters, on any ship, are only allowed to work so many hours. They clock-off after lunch, and clock-on to serve dinner when the boat leaves its berth for the river cruise.

Both Jill and Bentley have coffee and leave long before the end. Unlike other guests leaving early, it is not because they want to see the rest of New Orleans. For Jill, it is their ship's second day in Louisiana, and she has work to do before it leaves. For Bentley, he has to collect the LeRoy, then he's leaving on a jet plane. He has no idea when he'll be back again.

"If I don't make it back, you'll have to do your first canvas frame-change."

48 – SURPRISE

Italy–2250hrs   **Miami-1450hrs**   New Orleans(2)–1350hrs

Bedi walks into Headquarters. Dwight doesn't turn his head.

"Why am I not surprised?" he says, without looking.

"Clinic very good. Good treatment. I am cured."

"That doesn't surprise me either."

"You pleased to see me?"

Now Dwight turns, and Izzy has crept in behind Bedriška, confused. She listens.

"Very pleased you're better, even more pleased you're back. What did you do with Big Dog?"

"He left, then I left."

"Croc, call Big Dog. See if he needs you to rescue him."

CRUISE SHIP ART THEFT

Croc is very pleased with the implied status. Dwight addresses Bedi as Izzy walks forward and perches on the edge of Croc's desk. Years of working together, growing up at Mary's together, has made them, together with Macey, very close. That is why both are so distressed at the discovery that Wild Mary and Stan are Macey's real parents.

"We have some problems. The first; Yonan is missing," Dwight shares with Bedi. "I hate him, but he's the paying client."

"How long he gone? Bedi demands.

"Just over a day."

"He has apartment with mistress."

"His mistress is art."

Bedi turns to Croc.

"You track his phone?"

"Only to Little Haiti, then the phone went dead," Croc says.

"OK. Try this phone. He slip me number at first lunch meeting. Say it his private cell."

"Why am I not surprised?" Dwight grins.

"You don't get surprised much," Bedi says to Dwight. "Name art galleries in direction of phone," she demands.

"Three," Croc says, sliding her the print-outs. "Going further there are more."

"They steal art off ship, why go far?" she states. She has the answer to most things.

"Hang on," Dwight says, thinking hard. "This is one of the few ports where a ship might dock for two days. It allows them to get a painting off, copy it, then get it back on."

The room goes quiet.

"But nothing on wall for two days?" Bedi says, abruptly.

"OK, someone would notice that," Dwight says.

Izzy beams excited she has the answer everyone is looking for. "There's two copies. Like Macey had two rehearsals of Dwight's painting."

Croc is still confused, but Bedi gives a rare smile.

"You are an Investigator, and a damn good one," Dwight tells Izzy.

"If they've already got a copy, why do they need to make another one?" Croc says, still confused.

"The temporary one is an inked over photocopy. Macey hates them, always going on about them and calling them painting by numbers," says Izzy. "She's always harping on about something with Dr Zeus."

"But how do they complete a proper world-class painting in less than two days?" Dwight propositions.

"Macey could," Izzy says.

"She could, but she'd never do a copy," Croc adds to the game.

"But good painter with no imagination would," Bedi explains.

"They're forging pieces somewhere. They need privacy, room, and good light. Possibly a skylight," Dwight reasons. "Second problem; the boys are locked up in Italy."

"Not problem. I am here. Boys can look after themselves. Well, Hunter can."

"Get me art framing houses, painters' workshops. I look at all. I start. Call me if other cell gets results," she says, walking out.

"Is she going to kill someone again?" Croc asks.

"Maybe. Do you want to go with her?"

"No," Croc is quick to answer.

Izzy turns to him, inquisitively. She does not know the story behind Bedi and Croc's mission to get the paintings back.

49 - ENOUGH

Hunter starts a commotion in his police cell. He has seen the layout and the route to the interview room.

"What?" the guard asks.

"I've decided to talk. I'll tell everything, in return for a plate of spaghetti."

"What?"

"I said I will tell them all, before I forgetti," Hunter says.

In the other cell, Kieron is almost bursting out of his retained laughter. He knows Hunter is up to something, and together they are about to attempt a breakout.

There is a bell and the outer gate opens. The two interviewers march in again. They enter the interview room on the other side of the aisle to the cells. An officer drops the chain of keys to hang down after opening his door. Hunter has to stand with his hands on the wall. The guard reaches and cuffs both Hunter's hands. Hunter is led towards the interview room. Before they reach the door, in the moment of a turn, Hunter takes the guard's loose hand. He bends it up back against the wrist, the way it does not go. He twists the thumb inwards and over. It is a disabling move. The pain is excruciating, making the guard, trapped, useless and speechless. He cannot even draw a breath. He is Hunter's puppet and his body follows his buckled wrist everywhere Hunter takes it.

First Hunter takes the wrist towards the guard's chain of keys. The guard takes the keys with his other hand, the pain is too much. He opens the door and Kieron steps out.

"Say thank you to him. You English forget your manners," Hunter tells him.

"Thank you," Kieron says.

"Now gag him."

Kieron rips his shirt and makes a super tight gag. He un-cuffs Hunter and they cuff the guard. Witowski knocks the guard out with one blow and they lock him in the cell.

Hunter moves to the interview room and quietly turns the same cell key in the door, locking the interviewers in. Philips goes to the access door for the cell area and flattens himself against the inner wall.

"Let me in," Hunter shouts to the interviewers. He bangs on the door.

The nearest interviewer comes up to the door, puzzled that Hunter is locked outside. He tries to open the door and fails. Hunter feigns helplessness. He doesn't understand. Every question they ask, he shrugs and mimes the same.

"I can't get in."

The interviewers try to open the door. They can't. Hands behind his back, as if cuffed, Hunter acts as if he is beside himself with grief that he can't get in.

Within seconds the area door opens. Two police guards bust in. They pull up, seeing an innocent-looking Hunter, with hands seemingly manacled behind his back. Hunter snatches one, Kieron claims the other. Both guards are whipped around, spun off balance, and knocked out.

Philips holds the door open, Hunter checks for other policemen. The Italian police carry guns outside the cell area, so it will be a very different situation upstairs. They will be targets.

"Let's go."

The door locks behind them, but they have only seconds to get out of the building before alarms start. They run up the stairs; to be trapped downstairs would end all chances of escape. They duck down out of the sightline of the door window into the main street level floor. As it bursts open and the first officer runs forward to the stairs, Philips drops his shoulder underneath him. He rises, flipping the officer up and over, then rolling down the stairs. Hunter has the second shocked officer from behind, steals his gun and as Philips stands aside, he sends the second officer down the long stairs. They both move through the door quickly into the main open plan work area and they flatten themselves against the wall in gaps between the filing cabinets. They know that within seconds the two officers downstairs will raise the alarm. They do not know where the doors are or which way to make a move.

Hunter hits the fire alarm and they wait watching the confusion and panic in as police officer are instructed in an emergency drill. The door becomes obvious, but they wait until the last police officer is in line to evacuate. Commander Kieron Philips picks him off before he leaves, as military-efficient as the day he was forced to retire. He renders him useless and takes his gun.

"Sorry about this."

Kieron hits him with one anaesthetising blow.

"Now you find your manners. But first, you should have asked where they keep our wallets, phones, and passports."

Kieron leans over the policeman.

"Wake up, wake up."

Kieron can't wake him, so takes the man's phone, warrant card, wallet, and car keys. He watches Hunter blast out of the emergency exit and go past a group of policemen who are being fire-marshalled on the other side of the car park. They are not expecting to have to draw their guns as this is a town where not much happens; the quiet end, away from the container docks and cruise terminal. The shipbuilding yard is the only industry this far north, and the shops, for the most part, live off it. The police are too slow to pull their guns. Hunter shoots at the tyres rendering parked cars and vans useless as he sprints along the side of the building, taking cover. It causes a commotion as the police take cover. Luckily he has run the correct way, towards the street. He occasionally reveals himself. He wishes to draw them away, so he runs, fast.

Philips waits until all the police have been tentatively drawn after Hunter then slips out left. He is pushing the stolen car key-fob for a result. One car must open up. Eventually, a red Fiat 500 shows itself. Philips could not be more peeved but he has no choice. He pops the tailgate open and rams it up. A second ram sees the hinges twist into the bodywork. It will never come down again. He slips in the driver's seat to find that it is at least a sport version with all the kit a small car cannot normally expect. He wheel-spins out. Recovering from a slide on his turn he guns the car forward with no concern for the officers who leap aside. One is too slow and is jettisoned over the top cracking the front windscreen on the way up and getting stuck on the open tailgate. Philips turns hard right and the officer takes his second theme-park ride smashing into a parked car. Kieron accelerates up the street, assessing the local layout. He slides the car into a 180-degree about-turn and guns it back into trouble. Unexpectedly, he weaves into the police forecourt straight into gunfire. Hunter runs out shooting back and leaps into the open tailgate. He awkwardly rolls and raises his gun.

"What the fuck is this?"

"I got the cheap hire," Kieron shouts, "Backing up?"

"Go for it."

As the officers step into the road to shoot, the car cracks into reverse and goes full speed out of the forecourt into the road, hitting the brakes and locking hard left to send the car straight down the road, front first.

"Did you pass your driving test?" Hunter shouts.

"Sorry, forgot to check mirrors."

Hunter is shooting out of the back. The local police are not brave enough to run after them, but they can hear car sirens. Witowski watches the ones with airless tyres skid out of control into parked cars. The wreckage causes a temporary road blockage.

"Ideas?" Philips asks.

"Ship?" Hunter Witowski says, checking his body for any blood or wounds. With adrenalin high; they might not feel shots with the small calibre guns the police use.

"Agreed, we won't get away from them in this," Philips says.

He weaves through roads they know because they have walked them before and after their shifts. They turn along the dock road, and straight into the shipyard, that they know better than the chasing police. Their car smashes the barrier down; past the sleeping guard who is as ineffective as they expected. They power on towards the ship, skidding so close they nearly hit it. Both leap out and rush in, uniforms showing their security status even though their passes were taken.

The police might be close behind, but the two investigators are in a warren that they know well, one they patrol nightly.

50 - LEAVING ON A JET PLANE

Italy–0205hrs   Miami-1805hrs   **New Orleans(2)–1705hrs**

Bentley sits in the private jet Yonan has afforded him, still captivated by May.I.see's book, and the unfinished works he saw in the Gallery. He picks up the phone, one of the luxuries of this stunning plane.

"Who is that?" he asks when his call is answered.

"Ricky" is the reply.

"Can I speak with Yonan?"

"He's not here."

"Why are you answering his private line?"

"He is going to ring me on this number. He's deciding on the other paintings. I hope."

"There are more?"

"Lots more."

"A second book, or a reprint?"

"I think we toss those books and reprint. I have set pages up ready."

"I'm sending you two pictures you must include. Two-part works. Hemingway and Ghost, framed. They must be included. They are magnificent," Bentley reveals.

"This has to stop at some point. Send them to me. I'll set them up for when I hear from him."

"Oh. I loved your mini-biog of her." He ends the call.

The plane powers up to take off.

Italy–0210hrs   Miami-1810hrs   New Orleans(2)–1710hrs

"Thanks for your help buddy," Hunter says into the stolen phone, sarcastically relaxing for a moment in one of the ship's part-finished mini-suites on deck ten.

"INTERPOL's not playing ball yet," Dwight replies.

"We're out, on the run, in the ship."

"Chopper to the pad would be nice," Kieron shouts.

They are both in poached workman's clothes, wearing hard hats, and they carry basic tools. It is a kit that should not register as missing until there is a shift change, and they hope not to be onboard that long.

"Be prepared to get us out of Italy when we're done, here," Hunter suggests.

"We need to move. We're slouching in a suite but dressed as deck painters."

"10-4." Comes back from Miami.

Knowing their way around a ship is handy. Few people do. Even cruisers who think they know a ship and have read the fuller maps on the internet showing some other routes, can have no idea how complex a rabbit warren it is. Wearing the overalls, even if they are seen, should befuddle police. They run up two decks worth of crew stairs to the pool area and get to the pump room. Inside they close the door and take grease from a tin to apply as 'make-up'. Less is more, as Macey says, and she would be proud of them.

Back outside, they pass the empty pool; netted for safety as it would be for passengers. Workers are afforded the same safety where possible. They move along past a team painting handrails.

"Good cover, we could go anywhere as painters," Hunter says.

"But we need paint."

They search all the crew openings, but cannot find paint or brushes.

"Stores?"

They descend crew stairs, turning each half staircase to drop one deck straight, then into a policeman. They separate, splitting his attention.

"Name?"

"Constantine," Kieron says.

"Full name."

Hunter puts him down without effort. The policeman is out cold.

"Emperor Constantine."

They rip his shirt, gag him and tie him and use his cuffs. They now have a second small firearm, another cell-phone and a radio. They open the fire hose door and squeeze him into the small gap over the hose. The door is closed.

Kieron's plundered phone goes.

"Ten Minutes out," is all Kieron hears, and he knows they need to stand-by at the top.

"We just got promoted."

"Oh Yeah?" Hunter asks.

"Paint inspectors."

On the helipad, they pretend to check the paint on different areas of the handrail. The chopper drops in like an Afghan troop carrier and the two men run under the blades on the far side. Police rush to the rail back from the landing area, guns out, but too scared to shoot at the jet chopper. It lifts and drops down towards the sea and away. It is a manoeuvre all pilots love to do.

51 - FORGOT

Italy–0300hrs   Miami-1900hrs   (leaving)New Orleans(2)–1800hrs

Prisha picks up the wand and starts to check the whole room for bugs. Finishing, she moves to watch Macey paint a calf behind Yonan's second pair of shoes. The 'Alligator eaten by Shoes', as Macey currently calls it, is on the table next to it, so she can ensure they are a pair."

"Do you think they work? I've never done a pair."

"I think you could make it three with his new shoes."

"I forgot them," Macey says, going into a tizzy as she searches for the message from Izzy.

"No surprise; how many sketches do you have?"

"Too many to finish," Macey says, as she opens the pictures on the phone.

The first is shot down on the top, she saw that briefly before. She puzzles over the shoes.

"Don't tell me," Macey says, trying to think of the name.

"I won't," says Prisha.

"The buckle: LV."

"Not getting it."

"Louis Vuitton again, Yonan must love Louis Vuitton shoes."

"You would," Prisha adds as a throwaway.

"They bought me three pairs, look in the closet."

"No! Are we the same size?"

"Take them."

Prisha runs into Macey's room.

"Major loafers," Macey shouts, guessing the shoe type. "They sell for about three-thousand-dollars."

"How much?" she shouts, as she returns with three pairs.

"There are cheaper versions," Macey shares.

"Oh, good. How much?"

"About seven-hundred-dollars, but I don't think Yonan would go for those."

"No."

"But, this pair is amazing."

"Why?" asks Prisha.

"That is alligator, that is calf, these are a mixture of the two. Now I have a set of three, I'm more excited."

Macey turns to see Prisha zipping up a pair of Janet Ankle Boots. They have a side zip and three dress bands, two of which are buckles for sizing.

"Janet Ankle Boots. LV does very few heels and they picked them."

"How do you know so much about those shoes?"

"I am doing an art degree. I thought of going into fashion, I love fashion, but I prefer to create my own statements."

"It's not just fashion, it's ridiculously expensive fashion. Right?"

"I studied them all in a project I called 'Money'. None of them excited me; not to paint. Not until I saw them being used. And those look great on you."

"They'll look great on you, too." Prisha says, parading in them both, and slipping back into the room to find a full-length mirror.

Macey looks at Izzy's next picture of the loafers. It is side-on.

"They are beautiful shoes, but if I had the option, I wouldn't wear calf, goat or alligator," Macey says, holding her arm out so the shoe is next to her easel.

"You are not joking!" Prisha says from the mirror.

"Clément says they want me to turn heads. And these people know fashion."

"So do you," Prisha says, running back and sitting in the chair. She cannot wait to change, to slip on the white ankle boots, with a criss-cross black lace. They are as low but with an added higher thin ankle strap. She handles the third pair.

"Not so keen on these."

Macey looks. They have a heavy square heel, patchwork, and a sandal front.

"I don't know those," Macey says.

"Well, you can't have liked them either."

"I do actually. You can keep the white ones. I hate them."

Macey studies the third picture from Izzy. Her face is one of concern as she tilts her head.

"What?" says Prisha, not for the first time.

"Throw me those Janet Ankle boots."

Prisha passes her the darker pair; she hasn't taken the white ones off now they are hers.

"What are you looking for?"

Macey goes back to her phone for confirmation, then shows Prisha the picture.

"These are fake."

"How can you tell?"

"The small stud on the heel, look," Macey says, giving her the cell phone to study the picture.

"It says LV," Prisha offers.

"It shouldn't be there on loafers."

"Is it not on all their shoes?"

"No."

Macey is already ringing Dwight in the Miami office.

"What else is fake?" Macey says while she waits for the call to be answered.

52 - WHAT ELSE?

Italy–0335hrs   **Miami-1935hr**   (leaving)New Orleans(2)–1835hr

"Macey, how was New Orleans?" Dwight asks from the CSCI hub.

"I loved it. I was so busy I never looked at Izzy's pictures," she says, on speakerphone to the office.

In the darkness of the Miami office, Izzy opens her hands as if to challenge the trouble she went to in to obtain them surreptitiously, safe that her best friend can't see.

"Of Yonan's shoes?" Dwight asks.

Izzy is nodding yes.

"Except they're not. Those shoes are fakes. He wouldn't wear fakes."

"Are you sure?"

"Are you sure he's real?" Macey challenges him, sure that Yonan wouldn't be seen dead in them, and she has been seeing the dead.

"No," Dwight stumbles, thinking hard. "Macey, you impress me more and more. Leave it with us, this job has jumped up a notch. You look after yourself," Dwight finishes.

"No one can get us on the ship, and we'll be at sea within hours," she says.

"Watch yourself," Dwight warns again before ending the call.

He turns to Izzy.

"That wasn't Yonan we met, was it?" She asks him.

Italy–0340hrs   Miami-1940hr   (leaving)New Orleans(2)–1840hrs

Macey is used to all the investigators ending calls abruptly. They rarely have time for small talk.

"It's still a good picture though," Macey says, looking at the other two.

"Don't put the stud in," Prisha says.

"Or do I, to attract attention?"

"No, that would be the wrong attention. Enough is going on with the message," Prisha advises.

"Maybe I put the stud in the side of the calf and the alligator?"

Prisha is still parading in her new white ankle boots.

"Are you ever going to take them off?" Macey asks.

"Never."

Italy–0345hrs   **Miami-1945hr**   (leaving)New Orleans(2)–1845hrs

Dwight turns to Izzy and moves towards her.

"He never said much to me, did he, Izzy?"

"Very few words, I remember it well. Does that make me an even better investigator?" she asks.

"You said you never wanted to be an investigator."

"I want the badge now."

"Croc, assume he was phoney. That means Yonan was taken at least the evening before our current 'vanished' timeline."

"I'll go back another fifteen hours on the trace," Croc says, and turns to get back to work. "Hope that impresses you too."

"Guys, you all impress. But Macey was a painter. Never did anything except paint, now, she's a natural."

"She learned off me," Izzy says.

"OK Izzy, tell me what I revealed to him?"

Izzy leaves quickly because she can't remember.

Sitting on a stool eating at the counter in the diner is Ricky.

"What you doing back?" she asks, hoping the little twinkle he had in his eyes might have been for her.

"I realised I hadn't eaten in ages."

"What, we the only food joint?"

"No, I wanted to speak with Macey."

"Why, what you put in the book?"

"I was worried because I put in the stuff Croc told me not to."

"What's that?"

"Yonan edited it."

"Or did he?" She says wondering for a moment if that was the real Yonan. "What did he say?"

"That she didn't have to have come from the ghetto, that Mary and Stan were her real parents but had her adopted."

Izzy fills with shock, "What?"

Ricky understands her panic, and it converts to his fear.

"Macey doesn't know that?" Ricky asks, dropping his burger. All colour has drained from his face. He leaves her for the hub next door.

"Dwight, I gotta speak to Macey."

Macey is on the back of the ship, with her easel out. Prisha has a new place to parade her new boots. It was a grey day when they left the berth, but the sun has dropped, and a red glow breaks through the cracks in the sky and backlights the Sunshine Bridge.

"That's not fake," Macey glees.

"No," says Clément. "You 'ave produced so much magic."

He looks down at her work to see a watercolour painting of the sunset sky in all its beauty being haunted by a portrait of Marie Laveau.

"Did you want a pretty sunset with the bridge?"

"I pictured that," he hesitates, "but then I am not a star. I couldn't what you have there."

"And what worries you? If this will sell as well as if I just did the sunset?" She asks.

"No. The volume of work. How will you complete it?"

"Two days at sea is not enough, I need another cruise," she says.

Prisha arrives with two cocktails. Clément coughs. He turns and waves a waiter over.

"I would like one of those, please," he says, handing over his cruise card, point made.

"We go to the theatre tonight," Clem heavily suggests.

"It's a tribute act. I have had enough fakes for one day," Macey says.

She turns her sheet over. She has painted in rather an abstract night sky full of stars.

"Can you read the stars in this?"

"I'm not an astrologer," Clément says surprised at the work.

"Look closer, what's in the stars?"

Clément looks closer.

"They all say LV," Clément observes.

"Is it about forgery?" Prisha asks.

"No, it is about wealth, and trying to reach for the stars. They are all phoney."

53 - MOVING ART

Italy–0415hrs   Miami-2015hrs   at sea–1915hrs

The police have gone. Kieron and Hunter wait for a group of Mike's men to walk away from the ship. The two investigators sneak out, hiding behind the pallets waiting to go onto the ship. They move from stack to stack. There is a huge truck that gives them cover and they are away.

The two had dropped down from the flight deck onto the safety walkway that runs all around it, rather than get into the helicopter. The bird took off too quickly for anyone to notice that Philips and Witowski were not in it.

"We're up against time; they must have traced the flight path and have the pilot by now," Kieron says, as they approach the art warehouse.

"Mike has an excuse to put a bullet in us now, front or back."

"The Wolfman's our only lead," Kieron says.

"It's not quite unfinished, we'd may have to wait."

"Let's see."

"I guess it could also prove our innocence," Hunter suggests.

"You think? I get the feeling no one's listening."

"The original will get collected soon. That's who we're after, the guy at the top. One of us needs to be in a vehicle, outside the gates ready to follow. The one inside here might not be able to. This could be where we get split up," Hunter says.

"The one outside could get arrested in a stolen car. They are looking for us," Kieron says.

"You're outside. Try and do better than a Fiat 500!"

At the rear of the warehouse is where the side door and reception is, the escape for the forger. A white van sits waiting by the door with its rear doors open.

"Trojan horse. You've gotta be on that van," Kieron says.

"You've gotta get a vehicle fast and follow me."

The two men crab down the side of the warehouse to the van which is decked out with a full wooden interior with sash chords hanging in abundance. A huge pile of blankets sits at the back with a pallet thrown over them.

"Go, I'll sort this out."

There is movement in the reception and both men leap inside. They rush to get under the blankets and drop the pallet on top. Both pull their guns out.

Hunter is peeping through a crack in the materials. The driver appears at the back with the same artist he smashed into the table and tied down. They push a crate on. The driver throws a blanket over it and ties it to the side, just inside the door. He pulls the sash cord tight and the doors are slammed shut with total disrespect for a four-million-dollar painting.

Kieron slides out and films them pulling away from the forger's room through the rear door window and leaving the shipyard. He films the painting in the back and presses send. Hunter types a report.

"What was the van license plate?" he asks Kieron.

Kieron shakes his head, he didn't take it.

"Rookie mistake, eh. We're getting old." Kieron whispers.

"No, I got it. Just wondered if you did. But, like your fight with Bedi, you're losing that edge," Hunter mocks.

Kieron takes the military banter, but also knows, they are genuine observations. Although Hunter didn't say it, they both know he has been a little slow since his big head injury acquired on the Serial Killer job. Although he is better than he was even on the human trafficking job, he is still not 100 percent.

54 - INNUENDO

DAY7-Italy–0535hrs   DAY6-Miami-2135hrs   at sea–2035hrs

Being off the main road, weaving and the noise of huge engines means they are in Genoa Cristoforo Colombo Airport.

"Not what I was expecting," Kieron says, flipping his phone up and texting.

"Me neither, I'd have packed a case. Dwight better order us a plane," Hunter tells Kieron.

"And passports."

"He probably has a forger here at the airport, working on them now."

"He texted me back a 'roger that', so it's all under control. Sit back and take a load off," Kieron says.

"You know, the driver was by himself," Hunter announces.

"I know what you're thinking. If he was good, he will have noticed the pile of blankets was bigger."

"I'd notice," Hunter says.

"Me too."

"You sure, you're not just saying that?"

"No, I'd have noticed it. Ignored it because I was alone and had no idea what was under it, but I would have called it in," Kieron explains.

"Yeah, but you know what happens when you're at a dead-end like this with no way out?"

"You find a way out."

"Correct, I find a way out."

"I'm watching with interest,"

"Watch and learn, buddy."

"Unless there's a spare jet here and now, we're going to get left hanging, that's if we don't get arrested. Or shot," Kieron says, starting to mock his possible plan.

"I'll find a jet."

"What do we say to the pilot, follow that jet?"

"Yeah, just like jumping a cab. And I'll get the registration number of their ride, coz I know you'll never remember," Hunter says.

"No. I was thinking, we get on their plane," Kieron suggests.

Hunter shoots him with a look that says he thinks Kieron's suggestion was both stupid and mad. But, he is thinking about it.

"Just in case, Dwight will get us a jet," Kieron adds.

"Cancel that jet," Hunter says with determination.

It may be banter, but it's two military practitioners thrashing the problem out. They both know surviving this situation is going to be hard.

"The driver won't be getting on the plane," Kieron continues.

"Deliver, go home. He's gonna wanna slam the doors and…"

"I got that," Kieron says, stopping him from swearing.

"That lock looks smashed. No lever to open it from the inside."

"One of us needs to climb in the crate with the painting," Kieron says being silly.

They are about to have to make the split-second decisions that could see them killed. Their adrenalin rises ready to burst out with an incredible frightening force, but that would destroy the objective. The objective is to find where the paintings go, living is a bonus.

The door opens, and both men gently peep from between the blankets. No one stands with a gun on them and the driver is instructing two ground staff who slide the crate out. Predictably the driver swings the door to slam shut as he walks away. Kieron is faster, he throws a blanket to the floor and it slides to drape over the edge. The door bounces off it.

"Gotta go," Hunter says. "He'll be back."

The driver follows the painting to the plane. Kieron is watching through the gap in the door.

"Go," he says, taking the empty clipboard from the wooden side of the van and jumping out immediately after him. The van shields them from anything to do with the plane.

"Ground crew. I don't see anyone else," Hunter says.

They are both still in security uniforms, but without any utility belt or boot laces: all taken, as were their passports when arrested. They have no hard hat, like the airport staff, but it is dark, only certain areas are lit and that may help. Kieron watches the two men waiting for the door on the hold to flip up so they can load the crate. The driver walks up behind them and starts to argue. There is a problem.

Hunter walks off at speed, takes the steps up to the door of the plane, says hello very nicely to the male and female air stewards then enters. Kieron is much slower but tries the same. Being slower, he meets the Captain who appears at the top of the stairs. His presence blocks Kieron.

"Hello, Captain. It's a very expensive painting, and the Art Assistant has orders to ensure it travels inside, not in the hold."

The Captain looks at Kieron.

"Make sure it is strapped in, and double-check it," he says.

"OK, sir. I've got this. Commander Kieron Philips, security," Kieron says, by way of introduction.

The captain turns back into the plane. Kieron eyes the male steward as a flirt reading his name badge, 'Enrique', then he concentrates on the men below.

"Bring the crate in. I've got it cleared," Kieron shouts down and waves.

The driver thanks him, Kieron is now in the game. He watches the two ground crew carry it up the stairs. He enters the jet in front of them. He folds the armrests up.

"Enrique. Do you have a blanket to protect the seat?"

The male steward quickly finds one and spreads it. "On the blanket, please. Then both seat belts over it, and lock it down," Kieron tells the ground crew. "Double check please, Enrique?"

Enrique smiles, nodding. The ground crew are released and Kieron follows them to the door. The driver throws them the van keys and climbs the stairs to the plane.

"Welcome, sir," Kieron says.

"Thank you for your help," he says.

He sits in the plane near the painting. Kieron must remain bold and walk past him quickly before he reads any of the actual badges on his uniform, or he will have to explain why shipyard security is in the plane. Though that might be possible.

Kieron slides the curtain and joins Hunter in the service area.

"Well done," Hunter says, congratulating him. "But now there's no one in Italy, thanks to your drunken girlfriend leaving us shorthanded."

55 - NOW WHERE

DAY7–Italy–0645hrs　　　　DAY6-Miami-2245hr　　　　at sea–2145hrs

The remarkable thing about private planes is the crew often don't know all the passengers, and the passengers rarely know all the crew. No one has set seats, and there is no set routine. Hunter still hides in the service area.

"Are we off now?" he asks Kieron as if he were aircrew.

"In a moment, sir. Just doing the final checks," Kieron says lifting his empty clipboard.

"And where are we going?"

"Who knows, it's one of those mystery two-centre holidays," Kieron replies.

"Without passports."

Kieron tilts his head.

"That's something else we should find time to worry about."

The two stewards step in, a little taken back to find them in their area. Enrique, the male air steward is rather pleased to find Kieron.

"Gentlemen, would you like to take your seats?" the female steward asks.

Kieron puts the clipboard down and pulls out the Italian police warrant.

"We're today's air marshals. Your company is aware that we're on a case."

The male steward's face lights up; he is impressed.

"Big fella aren't you?" Kieron says to him.

Enrique smiles back and Kieron turns to Hunter.

"No," Hunter says, guessing what Kieron thinks should happen next.

"When we land. At least one of us needs to be able to walk anywhere in that airport," Kieron confirms.

"The office never told me about this," says the female steward.

Kieron now makes it obvious he is looking at her badge.

"Inese, is that…" he pauses to let her answer.

"Latvian."

"Inese, the general office don't know. This comes from much higher, and they told us to rely on your help. INTERPOL has liaised with your company owners. For your own safety, don't say anything to anyone about me."

She nods minimally, still concerned. Enrique has a huge smile.

"Enrique; such a romantic name," Kieron starts, and Hunter is almost shaking his head, with an inkling of where this is going.

"Do you have a good book?" he asks.

Enrique dives into a cubby hole and pulls out 'Cruise Ship Heist'.

Hunter closes his eyes, further disbelieving where the day will take them.

"It's brilliant, have you read it?"

"I sped through the plot, ducking the bullets," Kieron jokes.

"I worked on a cruise ship years ago. Nothing like this ever happened."

"Me too, I worked on a cruise ship," Kieron plays.

"No, you didn't," Hunter sneers.

"I did."

"No, you were never staff."

"I was."

"I love the way you old married couples bicker, I told Barry, he's my partner, we should get married, settle down and start to argue," he flirts.

"Take your clothes off, let's get this over and done with," Hunter orders, to stop any further gloating from Kieron because of the position he has wangled himself into.

"Read your book, I'm doing your job for this flight."

"Can I wear your clothes?"

"No," Hunter insists.

"He has to," Kieron smiles. "I'll be outside. Inese, come sit with me; Let the boys change clothes."

Kieron and Inese step out through the curtain.

"So, we must follow the package and watch it go through customs, but we have no idea where it is going. We were told of no logged flight plan," Kieron fishes.

"I know, the Captain was so annoyed. From what he has been told so far, he is sure it's Prague. I love Prague."

"Almost taking you home."

"I don't wish that," she smiles.

The plane starts to accelerate up the runway.

Kieron leans back and gaps the curtain.

"Can I get a glass of champagne when you are ready, steward?"

"Please," Hunter reminds him.

"Please."

"No, I meant please shut the fuck up," Hunter whispers, leaning through the curtain and flashing a Spanish passport.

In Flight–0705hrs   Miami-2305hrs   at sea–2205hrs

Inese is managing to sleep in the service area. She is used to the uncomfortable crew seat that Hunter can hardly sit on. Hunter should sleep; two rules of engagement at any level, eat when you can, sleep when you can. Kieron has been sleeping for hours.

Hunter strides back from serving yet another brandy on ice to the driver who is escorting the crate on its journey. As he walks towards his curtain Enrique is fast asleep, he stops and lifts Enrique's arm and lowers in across Kieron's lap. Kieron opens his eyes. Gently lifts it back, but Enrique wakes.

"Anything I can get you, sir?"

"A flight plan, we must be way past Prague."

"Inese took the pilot's food earlier and he said we're over Latvia."

"It'll be Russia," Enrique says, rolling back to the window, sleepy. "This flight is always St. Petersburg, seen it, done it."

"Russia. Can I get you a vodka?" Hunter says looking at Kieron who is wide awake.

"No, but you could get me a passport," he whispers.

"I could, but you look nothing like Inese."

"If you need a passport, look in the top drawer. Passengers always get drunk on these planes. Always leave passports and wallets on board. We keep the famous ones, like collecting signatures, but I want them back," Enrique says.

56 - FAKE

Bedi is on 69th Street. It is wide and busy running all the way down to the beach after some big high-rise apartment blocks. Three of Miami's respected art galleries are in the area, where some experimental art is shown. Bedi can see no obvious clues there, but she saw a framing shop which intrigued her more. It had a visible workspace and materials, with no doubt more space at the back. Miami is vast, and she is not a local, so it is confusing. Realising she is hungry, she eats in a Greek restaurant on 71st and drinks ouzo. She calls Dwight, who has no further information, so checks into a small hotel and sleeps. Unless they wake her with better clues on where Yonan might be, and if he has been taken, she will probably sleep straight through.

Dwight quite expects her to sleep when she has the chance. He would if only he could.

At sea, the ship is back in the same time zone and later will pass the line of Miami as it heads to the Caribbean Sea. The show in the theatre tonight is at 8.30, repeated at 10.30. The second show would be far too late for Macey, Prisha or Clément; they have all had a very hard day. New Orleans is exciting but physically draining, especially with the trance-like painting. Macey, now far more relaxed in the enormous dining room, has promised to dress up and dine with Prisha tonight. The first night she was shocked by its sheer size and the hundreds of people, the glass lampshades, and chandeliers. The wealth of silverware on the table and the service was all too much for her. Now she knows which knife and fork to use first and that her bread plate is on the left.

"You can't be surprised if some guests did not see your show," Clément whispers to her. "Look how many there are. Impossible in the atrium. Maybe only three or four hundred saw you. There are over a thousand people on the ship."

He is sitting between her and Prisha, and always orders the wine. His cruise card is swiped like all the guests, but his bill comes up as zero. Yonan meets all his expenses.

The woman sitting next to her did not hear Clément explaining, but during the meal, she did discover who Macey is as if the brushes in her hair were not a clue.

"I'm sorry I missed your show, but I didn't miss your shoes as you walked in," she says, delighting in the fashion.

"You like shoes?"

"I do, but I'm not an expert. The dangling jewels spelling out his name kind of gave it away."

Macey smiles. The woman is funny even if she didn't see her paint. It is also amazing, that a few days ago she dreaded painting in front of people, and now she is put out that someone did not see her show.

The woman across the table is dying to see.

"Oh, please share," she says.

Macey is shocked and confused: she can't want me to take a shoe off and show it at the dinner table. Even she knows that can't be right.

"Come on, the dinner's over."

Macey feels encouragement from others and seems forced to slip a shoe off. Before she can retract it, the shoe is passed around the table, the gold letters dangling.

"They are lovely shoes," Prisha says to her, trying to draw attention to hers.

"Melody Platforms," the lady says as if she wants a prize.

"Yes," Macey answers.

Prisha waits, but still, no one asks to see her boots. However, they soon realise the woman only wanted the chance to play top trumps.

"I looked at those but preferred these. Jimmy Choo embryoid-crystal."

"Oh, you win. I nearly didn't wear these. They were a gift. I would never have bought them. They are baby goatskin." Macey knows the woman has eaten lamb, "They are slaughtered at 16 weeks old, just like lambs."

Clément wanders around the table and collects the shoe. Macey slips it back on while he waits. It is time to leave as she is getting edgy and political again.

CRUISE SHIP ART THEFT

In the theatre, while other guests seem to hog the edge of the rows, Clément and the girls sit in the centre. Macey has a few sheets of cotton canvas left in her pad which she turns over and sketches the carvings on the theatre boxes and the lights. Like the stage, her sketch has no performer yet.

The curtain lifts to a huge build-up and a Michael Bublé tribute starts. He is excellent, the moves and his voice are faultless. Clément looks down at Macey and does a double-take. On her stage, she has sketched James Brown in a spin, his cape blowing in the wind.

Macey grins, "Look, bubbles can go on the other side." She starts to sketch Michael in.

When the show ends, there appears to be a rush to leave, but Macey stays, taking in all the detail.

"Why is there no James Brown tribute?" she asks Clément.

"You had the Supremes; it is not a racist thing."

"I know, that's all cool, but they are safe acts. These people need shaking up. Look, they are not excited, they are not leaving talking about the show. They'd talk about James Brown."

"He's not on the list."

"What list?" Macey asks, standing up.

"His act is too wild," Clément reveals.

"These people lived through his musical career. They will have danced to him. Let me talk to Yonan," Macey enthuses.

Walking through the gallery on the way to their suite, her eye is caught by the catalogues on Jill's desk. She grasps one, keen to see what is inside. She flicks through the pictures, but her painting of Dwight featured in the 'come look at me case' steals her attention. Her head drops from one shoulder to another and she studies it. In a whirl of rage, she discards the booklet and snatches at the case, ripping the door off and pulling it from the wall. As it drops, she wrenches the frame out. She tears out the budget canvas and smashes the frame repeatedly in sheer vengeance. Neither Clément nor Prisha can stop her until it is too late.

"That is a fake. That is not mine, it's a forgery."

57 - UNROLL THE CANVAS

In the air Europe–0900hrs   DAY7-Miami-0100hrs   **Ship at sea–0000hrs**

Prisha cuddles Macey who has her head on Prisha's shoulder. They are on one of the love seats at the back of the 'After Midnight Bar'. It is romantically lit in a red glow, also reflected by furnishings. Most guests never stay awake late enough to justify its name. A few serious drinkers are sitting at the bar systematically going through the gin cocktail menu, and four guests are sitting across from each other discussing American politics; they might be there all night.

Clément sits across the table from Macey and Prisha, looking like the gooseberry in a romantic interlude. The waiter brings a new round of drinks.

"The bar will be closing soon, sir."

Clément nods to acknowledge.

"Please, bring another round, but put the ice in a separate large glass. Merci."

Clément has often stayed up late selling art in these bars, and the waiter knows why the ice is separate. He walks off to the circular bar. The bright bottles and glasses are lit as if the centrepiece were a spaceship from a seventy's movie.

"You can't wear those boots in bed, Prish," Macey says, looking at Prisha's ankles.

They all enjoy a restrained laugh. If she can laugh now, Prisha and Clément know she has, at last, calmed down.

"I can. I'm never taking them off," Prisha says. She shows the white ankle boots to herself, for her own enjoyment.

"Macey, you may have made a mistake," Clément says. "You've improved as an artist so much, your work is maturing so fast. Maybe the portrait struck you as inferior to 'Hemingway', or 'The Dance'."

"I know my work, that was a fake."

"Jill will spend the night repairing it. Take another look in the morning," Prisha encourages, as she sits up and video calls the office in Miami.

Between them, they appear to have quietened Macey down.

"She'll never repair that," Macey says, no longer shouting. "It was my best work and the first one I sold, you can tell Dwight."

"Most of the damage was to the frame. That smashed completely," Prisha says.

"Good."

"I'm sure Jill will have it back by the morning. Her first job was as a restorer. She's worked for some of the top galleries so she must be good," Clem explains.

"I'll smash it again."

"No, no, you mustn't," Prisha says.

"I'm on this ship to find forgeries, and my painting gets copied!"

"Exactly. This is our chance. Now, we have a forgery's journey and a timeline," Prisha says.

"If it was copied," Clément attempts a rebuttal.

"If it was copied?" Macey repeats. "It was."

Prisha untwines herself from Macey and stands up.

"So, Jill was a restorer?" Prisha asks, holding her phone up at Macey so Dwight can see. He has been listening for a little while and now joins the conversation. The waiter places the extra drinks and leaves.

"Conservator," Clément says, "she said her title was Conservator."

"Hi guys, it's Dwight. Macey, how are you? Hate to hear you're upset."

"Thanks, Dwight. But they stole your painting."

The bar is empty, they are tucked at the back, so no one notices they are all speaking to a cell-phone.

"Hey, as long as you're OK, Macey."

"You're so sweet," she says, sitting up straight and waving at him on the screen. She takes the cell-phone affectionally. He is a friend and they have a bond.

"I caught the end of your chat. So, if Jill mends paintings, she could reproduce anything? Is that what you're saying?" he asks.

"Restorer, conservator, assistant, forger, all the same thing, Dwight. Someone copied yours, then stole it," Macey says.

"So, we should not trust Jill?" Prisha asks.

"No," Dwight replies.

"Jill is too young," Clément says, kicking the idea back.

"That's not how we work, Clément. Trust no one, everything is possible. So, you two art experts, explain to me how the industry works? How do they start?" Dwight fires at them.

"They start when they leave college. If they are lucky enough to work for a hugely successful artist, they do all their master's leg work and more. Sometimes they even create a whole piece that goes out in the master's name," Macey says.

"That's a bit harsh," Clément accuses, relaxed in his natural accent.

"It's like your phoney accent, Clem," Prisha mocks him to silence. "In India, when a big star sings a song, they demand most of the writing credit."

"In art, the masters take all the credit," Macey says. "I was offered numerous jobs in my final year. I was not prepared to do that. I have my own voice."

"To be so bold was very risky, Macey," Prisha says.

"No. I'd never been on a cruise, never lived like this, never had more than one fork. I had nothing to lose."

"By masters, who do you mean?" Dwight asks. "Explain it. Do they have workshops full of workers?"

"Yes. Take Leonardo DaVinci – He painted in his own master, Verrocchio's style; layers of clear acrylic, so light reflects through them to give an eerie effect. It is accepted he painted the curly-haired boy in Verrocchio's 'Christ with John The Baptist'. But all the students painted in that style, many will have gone to work with Leonardo. In turn, Leonardo's students painted in his style."

"Eventually, great students find a style of their own," Clément says.

"Most can only copy," Macey explains, hitting the button.

"Da Vinci…?" Prisha asks, knowing the least about art in the west.

"DaVinci was a brilliant engineer. His other art he left behind. So many paintings were unfinished. Now, who is to say the unfinished works are not those of his best students? Students who hoped Leonardo would choose theirs to finish. That's my theory. If I could write, I'd write a book about it."

"But experts have looked at them," Clément says.

"So, art is judged and named by experts?" Dwight asks.

"The experts weren't there when they were painted. Experts are like teachers marking schoolwork. Teachers teach because they can't break into the real world, no matter how good they look."

"No, that is a huge leap," Clem insists.

"OK, take DaVinci's most famous painting."

"Please no," Clem says worrying.

"No, I want to hear," Dwight says.

"What is it?" Prisha asks.

"The Last Supper?" Dwight suggests.

"Correct. The best version of it hung on the wall of Mauldin College, Oxford. It was there for 25 years before being returned to the Royal Academy of Arts."

"But that is a copy, made by his students," Clem says.

"How do you both know all these things?" Prisha asks.

"I studied art, I study everything about art. Even so, that painting of the last supper is always big public news," she says.

"But, the original is a fresco on the main wall of the monk's dining room of Santa Maria Delle Grazie in Milan," Clem explains.

"I like Leonardo, he's political. He challenged the very religion that commissioned him. I find that refreshingly intelligent. He saw how women were put down by religion."

"Macey please. This is getting very deep!"

"No, you like my work because of my voice. I'm a woman and Christianity puts women down."

"Are you saying that the fresco on the wall is not the original? Or that it has been repaired and restored so much it is no longer his, no longer the original?" Dwight asks.

"Good question. It took a huge team to try and clean and repair it, but people think one man painted it? What a joke, eh? A little naïve! They should grow up."

"It's still his art," Clément says.

"Doesn't sound that way," Prisha says.

"You've seen me work. I sketch, and sketch over the sketch, then paint. There are no such sketches under a fresco. Why? The work is known, it is a copy. You can't risk sketching over sketches on wet plaster."

"Macey, what has this to do with our fakes?" Clem demands, feeling slightly irritated that she has gone off on one of her political tangents.

"It might have a lot to do with it," Dwight says. "Let her run with this, I'm intrigued."

"Da Vinci gets commissioned," she continues. "He sketches a rough on something small. It gets approved. He sketches on a huge canvas and his students paint it from that rough guide. Leonardo vanishes, that is a fact. He disappears. Meanwhile, the plaster on the wall is drying."

"So, the one at the Royal Academy of Art is the master, the original?" Prisha asks.

"No," Clément says.

"I am suggesting it is," says Macey. "Leonardo comes back. He copies from the canvas as quick as he can but he's missed his chance."

"Wow," Dwight says. "It's one fucked up business. But why become a forger?"

"Because art assistants earn less than a nurse's starting pay."

"I gotta tell you something else, Mace. That Kandinsky they stole from Yonan's apartment and replaced with the not so good fake? They stole a great copy, left him with a bad copy. The original is in his vault."

"The copy of my painting was shoddy work. Is the original in his vault?" Macey asks.

"Good question?" Dwight says.

"Yonan would not do that," Clément defends.

"Can I wind back. Why had Leonardo 'missed his chance?'" Prisha asks.

"Because the plaster was dry when he arrived back to manage his team to paint on the wall, to copy the approved canvas the students had painted. Plaster needs to be wet to paint the perfect fresco. They'll never repair that one on that wall because it was done on dry plaster. About twenty percent of it is left."

"So, he had a team of forgers?" Dwight asks.

"If you believe that theory, and that is not the accepted one," Clem says.

"They were his young students," Dwight says.

"Was anyone there? How do we know?" Macey asks.

"You love controversy, Macey," Prisha says.

"You don't have a team on the ship," Dwight says.

"Don't need a team for small paintings, they would get in each other's way. But, is Jill someone's student?"

"So, one person could do this onboard the ship? A person with access to the paintings. One who can take them down for cleaning, whatever? One person who can replace them," Dwight suggests.

"The ship's curator," Prisha concludes.

"Don't get me wrong, I'd love to go and see all this art, I'd love to go to Milan and Florence," Macey says.

"Macey, stay focused on the job. Put your opinions into your paintings," Clem says.

"-What tools would Jill need for restoring and forging?" Dwight jumps in asking.

"Most would roll into a canvas pouch. Maybe two, maybe a roll of scalpels, cutters and shapers."

"Pouch?"

"Like my one you see all the time in Mary's diner. Except hers would be bigger, more expensive. She would have two, the second for brushes. Plus, oils and liquids."

"The ship would get those for her, they know she has to repair stock," Prisha says.

Clément looks at her as if to ask how she would know.

"I worked in the main hotel office behind reception, for nearly nine years," Prisha tells him.

"Does she have more brushes than you?" Dwight asks.

"Maybe, maybe top of the range. But she can't use them; all the gear and no idea."

"What do you mean?"

"She has no ideas. I'm full of anger, but she's a rich kid. She never suffered any hardship, never actually made a friend with a rat. You think Michael Jackson could have written Ben if he'd never seen a rat? His whole family lived in a two-room house in Indiana."

"Sorry to keep asking, Macey, but I'm learning and I love the way you describe the business."

"This business is perverted and twisted and may never get back to art."

"OK, what do you mean?"

"Kandinsky had talent. Now people throw paint and hide behind clever bullshit."

"What's that?" Prisha asks, her eyes now wide open at what Macey is revealing.

"There are those who see, those who see when they are shown, those who never see, and those who only see with their ears," Clément says, now joining in.

"I'm getting how a second-hand car dealer like you clicks in here," Dwight says.

"Harsh," Clem says. "But true"

"People now buy with their ears. What they are told is expensive," Macey says forcefully.

"You need to understand the power of art. Last year art was a sixty-billion-dollar-industry. Institutions now lend against these investments," Clem insists.

"Not Jill's. I've seen one of Jill's paintings, and she paints 'lobby art'," Macey says spitefully.

"Lobby art?" Prisha asks.

"I hope you are taking notes, Dwight," Macey says, now chuckling, as she gets so much off her chest. "Lobby-art equals elevator music. And once in the lobby, you never get out."

"I can't write quick enough, so I'm recording it. Does Jill work on an easel?" Dwight asks.

"Restoring: on a flat table. Painting: on an easel. She might have a table-easel, one that folds up; or a tilt table with drawers if she is super lucky," Macey answers.

"Find that room, report back."

Dwight ends the call, but Macey is engaged as a fellow investigator.

"She copied my painting. Where?" Macey looks at both of them for answers.

"She has numerous art cupboards, I would need to ask the hotel manager," Prisha says.

"Some behind false walls near the gallery," Clem reveals standing. As he stretches out, he notices two men across the other side of the round bar. He is sure they have been following them.

"We need to catch her at work and find my painting. It's here somewhere," Macey says.

"OK. I pretend there have been huge offers for the 'Hemingway'. See where it disappears to at night," Clem agrees, looking across, but the men have gone.

"I could eat breakfast," Macey says.

"Way too early for that," Prisha says.

"Don't the clocks go forward?"

"Not that much."

58 - MAYBE NOT

In the air/Russia – 0905hrs   **Miami-0105hrs**   Ship – 0105hrs

Croc and Dwight are pulling an all-nighter, not because they chose to, but because days elongate when you have other agents in a different time zone whose day starts eight hours earlier. Croc is also trying to get any useful information from a new cell-phone that is rarely used. The office phone rings.

"Hunter can't make his mind up whether to be a rock star or a footballer. We're buckling up now, approaching Pulkovo Airport," says Kieron.

"Croc needs passport details to change the PAX."

"Might be going dark until we land," they hear Kieron say, although Hunter's new picture and details appear on their screen.

"Good luck with that," Dwight says, but they have gone so it is only to himself.

There is a flashing alarm outside and the cameras show the four different angles of their front door. It is Big Dog, waving and shivering in the cold of the night.

Croc opens the door personally and there is a simple 'slap and fist bump'.

Big Dog walks around into the digital display areas. He sees Dwight moaning to himself. Dog thinks he is best left alone.

"Wassup, boss?" Croc asks.

"I get them a chopper they don't use. I fly a jet and passports up from Rome; they don't need it. They jump the wrong jet and pretend to be rock stars."

"I'll fly in and help, me and a few boys take the pressure off."

"Dog. They're landing in Russia."

"Oh."

"You ain't got a proper passport, and you can't even take a parcel to the West Coast."

"I delivered her, man. Even did the sign in and checked the place out; her room and everything. Good place, except they thought I was the patient. We fucked up their expectations."

"Yeah. She got cured fast and came straight back here. Where you been?" says Dwight, slightly angry.

"You said, dump the rubbish and skip normal transport."

"So you walked?" Croc asks sarcastically. "And my car wasn't rubbish."

"Croc, get back to tracking your phones," Dwight says, then looks at Dog to finish his excuse.

"I had to wait for a sister to pass, no white drivers stop."

"If she brought you home, where did the time go?" Dwight asks.

"We had to get to know each other."

"You wanna be an investigator; know your time is special."

"Yeah. She thought so. Your man Kieron seems to stop to bite the cherry."

"He's a lot quicker than you."

"For sure, then I fed some zeds' after I was milked, then I found some chicken."

"Bedi beat you home by half a day."

"How about sending me out to the ship? I could go as Macey's special half."

"That's my job," Croc says firmly. If there is a ship-holiday, he is determined it is going to be him.

"You're a confused-zebra; she needs a real man."

"Croc, concentrate on that passenger list. They'll be walking off that plane. None of you are going to the middle of the ocean. She's safe there."

"Really? We had a heist, a serial killer, and human traffickers; which one is she on?"

Dwight shrugs, arms out.

"You can't go on with your team, Dog"

"I got my tools."

"No one ever gets a weapon on board."

Dog is left nodding, thinking hard.

"I need to learn me some of that crazy kick-arse ballet," he says, defeated.

"We can sort that. You too Croc?"

"Yeah, seven days a week, I'll be there," he says, as his screen bleeps and a dot flashes.

"Someone's trying to call Yonan but he's not picking up."

"Where's it from?" Dwight asks.

"That's the interesting bit. It's from out at sea," Croc says, as the call stops ringing. He spins his chair to Dwight. "You sure Macey's safe in the middle of the ocean?"

59 - SAINT PETER

St Petersburg, Russia–1030hrs   Miami-0230hrs   Ship–0130hrs

When a ship docks for the first time in a high-security country like India or the USA, guests must be processed. It is long and boring. Customs officers visit the ship, seeing each guest face to face. This is for at least two reasons. One: everyone is kept on the ship until cleared of being a rogue. Two: customs don't have the staff to deal with large numbers of cruisers on a dock where there could never be enough capacity.

Russia is different. Russia is high security but very easy by cruise ship. St Petersburg is more westernised than traditional Russia. However, many of their Russian ways seem strange. Drivers of coaches and taxis cannot be expected to help with a walking aid or chair. Neither can the palaces.

There will always be more than one ship berthed. Normally three in high season. Most ships stop for two days and most guests will get off for day tours. Those who have been there before are unlikely to get off again in the evening. Few shows meet up to the expectations. The ballet tour is not to see the Bolshoi. It is performed by a young company and is specially for tourists. The music is similar. The free glass of wine is barely OK, and if you wish another, the bar will only take cash in the local currency. Tours are essential to get into Russia easily. Getting a visa is costly but becomes irrelevant if you are on an organised tour. It is ironic that once in St Petersburg your tour guide lets you go, with a card in case you get lost. It says, in Russian; 'I am lost, please call this number.' The office will have you picked up quickly. Hunter might be able to use this.

For cruisers getting in and out of Russia means passing a basic set of custom booths and although there is a stringent check, it is nowhere near as strict as the airport. He knows, in the morning when cruisers are heading out to meet tours, where fellow Russian workers are earning money, passing through customs is fast. Returning at night, for example, from the ballet, will be slow and with long queues. Cruise ship entry is what Hunter knows very well.

A private jet still needs to get a parking spot and for that, the airport needs to have had a PAX. A passenger list. No sooner has their plane stopped, than it starts to refuel. Croc rings through to Kieron.

"I can't change the slot time, bro'. Slot time is done by the coordinator. Your plane ain't stopping."

"How long are we here for?"

"An hour at the most. No passengers are staying."

"Think we are," he tells Croc.

Kieron and Hunter, the two ex-special forces veterans now complement each other perfectly, but Hunter's experience of working on ships after he left is of no use to them now. They could be on a mission in the Middle East, but this is Russia, and neither has worked behind the lines here. They slip off the plane as the crate is being unfastened and fussed over knowing one of them must stay close to it. If the crate is staying in St Petersburg, they will have to as well. How they get out of the country is an even bigger problem.

They enter a private VIP lounge which is in the number-one terminal. The clubroom is exclusive to them. It may be part of the main passenger terminal, but the entrance and exit are separate and there appears no connection to the public passenger area. There is a circular area of well-spaced lounge chairs that they are unlikely ever to use. The row of four chairs, against a half-height hard-walled segment of the circle, have lamps to the side of each chair, but it looks like a hairdresser's salon from the eighties rather than the luxury it is meant to. They stand at the side, backs to the wall, under the floor above which intrudes about six feet into their open ceiling. It produces a smaller circle and opens in the middle to give them a glass-domed roof. That would be ideal to crash in but is no way out. They make their way to the bar and buffet, which is unmanned, everything is free at this level of comfort. They have noticed the few cameras and are working out their angles and the safe areas. The niches around the edge of the circle, that run under the floor above seem to be safest. They hang in one as two ground crew enter in yellow hi-visibility tops over heavy clothes with heavy boots and yellow hard hats.

The ground crew acknowledge them with no concern and Kieron and Hunter return the greeting. They notice that they both carry a jemmy. That can only mean they are here to open the crate. There must be a hand over here, and they have to become involved. The door on the Russian side opens again and a customs officer enters followed by an armed policeman.

"Do you speak Russian?" Hunter asks Kieron.

"My second language," Kieron says.

"I'll leave this one to you and get myself a beer."

Kieron follows Hunter to the buffet. Hunter looks at him.

"There will be a magical moment," Kieron says.

Hunter's eyes open wide, he is waiting to be enlightened.

"It ain't yet," he says.

"I think it is. The customs officer is looking at us and he wants something," Kieron says.

The airside door opens and the driver walks in, quenching the need for someone to exchange officialities with. It is a familiar routine for the driver and he watches a jemmy pushed into the wooden crate, and it creeks open. The customs officer checks three canvases stretched on wood but not framed. He checks them off his list, initials it and gives the driver the top sheet. The driver leaves, the customs officer and the policeman leave.

"Our ride's about to push out," Kieron says.

"Time to become a local," Hunter suggests.

"Go on then."

"I can't."

"Why?"

"I am an international rock star disguised as a cabin steward," Hunter says.

"Good point."

Kieron walks over and objects to them nailing the crate down. He takes the hammer to show them what he wants them to do. Except he doesn't. He hits down hard on the first radio then the second, both smashing to the floor. The second man swings his hammer at Kieron who must swerve to miss a punch. The first guard captures him and holds him. The hammer is swung at his head but both legs come up and kick out to take the blow. He struggles against the man restraining him, reaching back he squeezes his cock and balls. The other man lunges at him. Kieron gets under the blow, and flips him over. The arm he still holds is ripped out of the shoulder. He hits the other attacking man under the chin and sends him back, unconscious.

Hunter walks over casually and collects the two jemmies and drags the first man towards the washroom. Kieron follows.

"Thanks for your help!"

"I figured you'd never manage to drag them both."

Inside the washroom, they strip them, take their wallets, cell-phones and ID. Within minutes, Hunter and Kieron walk out dressed as ground crew with passes. They close the crate and carry it to the door into Russia. They send the shortest of texts to Dwight.

'Leaving airport as ground crew + 3 x paintings'.
They swipe the security passes and leave the VIP lounge.

60 - VERY SPECIAL

St Petersburg, Russia—1130hrs   Miami-0330hrs   Ship—0230hrs

Almost all airports are the same. Check-ins, departures, coffee shops, taxi ranks and duty-free. Private jet lounges do not have a duty free; the passengers there can afford to have whatever they want, delivered at whatever price. However, the door system between the customs side and the exit is always a mini-maze folding out. It is often through another section of duty-free, but always with walls to stop anyone outside from looking in. Families, friends and taxi drivers all must stay behind a barrier and watch for the passengers to appear from behind a screen.

Hunter and Kieron have seconds after leaving the lounge, before hitting the curious public.

"One and one?" Hunter asks as they pause, putting the crate down. They cannot be seen from either the lounge inside or whatever is outside, and that could be anything.

"Yes."

"Who goes?"

They agree, and Kieron already has his hard hat off and the yellow vest is being discarded to the floor.

"I'm the only who speaks fluent Russian," Kieron says.

"I didn't get that impression on the last exchange."

"The Russians don't get it either."

He rips off his Russian shirt which ensured he got out of the lounge doors if approached. Underneath he has kept the shipping company security shirt on. It is a choice, whether to overdress or not. On this occasion, both have kept the first clothes on under the Russian ground crew uniform which Hunter still sports.

"Ready?" Hunter asks.

Kieron nods. Opening the wallet taken from the ground crew, he gives Hunter all the Russian money. They lift the crate and march. Outside is as private as the lounge. Two large men are waiting and hold their arms out for the crate.

"Thank you," Kieron says to Hunter, making large gestures to match as they separate. Hunter walks off, never looking back, and he stands by the window looking out. Kieron refuses to let go of the crate.

"No. I go with the crate. I never let it out of my sight."

The two Russians are perplexed.

"No, never."

"There is an expensive painting in there."

"Who cares. Many expensive paintings come."

"This is special, there's a May.I.see inside."

"Who May I see?"

"The most expensive one you've ever had. I go with it, or I take it out, and it goes back with me."

The two Russian guards think. They look at his shipping yard security shirt and begin to nod.

"Good. You carry," they agree.

Hunter slips out in front of them and edges towards the taxi rank. Everywhere there are policemen carrying guns.

One of the Russians walks a safe distance behind Kieron in case there is a move they are not expecting. They stop at a people carrier where the back seats are already down. He watches Kieron and his partner lay the crate in very carefully.

"You wear this," the rear guard says, holding out a cable tie and expecting his wrists.

"This was not part of the deal."

"Part of my deal."

Hunter slips into a taxi.

"Follow that car."

"This not New York," the driver says, reluctant to do it.

Hunter pulls out some notes from the small wad Kieron gave him a few moments earlier. He hands them to the driver.

"This is not England."

"Where the fuck do you think it is? You tell me the price," Hunter says, getting angry with him and about to change cabs. He snatches the money back and opens his door.

"OK. More money."

Hunter gives him all the notes from Keiron's roll.

"More, this not 'follow-money'."

Hunter opens the wallet that he took. It is a bit light on notes. The taxi driver leans back and snatches all the notes.

"You have card?"

"Yeah."

"Good you pay for ride at end," he says, pulling away.

Hunter has one eye on the road and one eye on texting until his battery is out. The phone he stole is locked.

"I don't suppose you could charge my phone?"

"Ten thousand roubles."

Hunter gives up, knowing he has no money left and he is no way going to use a card that can be traced. He sees the black people carrier turning into residential back streets and looping back, which suggests they are nearly there. He throws the driver a twenty-dollar bill so he can get out fast.

The black people carrier drops them outside a block in the middle of the canal district. Kieron is still manacled but insists on walking around the car to watch them unload the painting.

"Hey, easy with that," Kieron says, to establish his position.

He follows the two men into the block lagging behind to tie a shoelace while keeping his rear in the door until Hunter arrives. They walk in together as if one, so the porter ignores Hunter. Kieron rushes to catch the two Russian men up, Hunter takes the stairs. In the elevator, Kieron bends to tie the lace he just untied.

Hunter runs each flight as fast as he can without making a noise, each time looking at the elevator floor indicator. It must be going to the penthouse. The stairs end one floor below it. He checks back and front of the hall, but there is no way up.

Kieron is inside the amazing apartment. He watches the owner nod to have the crate opened. He wears a light lounge suit, expensive slippers and he has three women lounging in the room but his interest is now Kieron.

"Why did they send you?"

"Something new, a new artist. Everyone is trying to get her works."

"Who?"

"May.I.see."

"I've never heard of her."

"Because you're not right up to date?"

"Let me tell you. If I have not heard of her, she is no one."

"Why did they send me to ensure it arrives?" he asks, holding up his wrists. The oligarch nods for the cable tie to be cut.

"You delivered the painting, I have the message, now go and be a tourist in this beautiful city. Your work is done."

If that was a cue for Kieron to leave, he does the opposite. He walks to the spectacular bay window and looks out. They are surrounded by canals and bridges!

"What should a tourist see?"

The man follows him to the window.

"If you came on a cruise ship you would have a tour. Over there is Isaac's Cathedral, the Mariinsky Theatre and there," he points, "the wonderful bell tower of St. Nicholas Cathedral with spire. This is the modern cultural centre of New Holland. This canal deserves more recognition. It joins many other canals, has beautiful granite embankments and stunning old bridges. A canal boat tour is the best way to find all the attractions and they will no doubt tell you much of the history. I think it is the best way to see and understand the city."

Kieron notices a hand grab up at the rails. It must be Hunter, having climbed up from below. He will have to pop his head up next, to see if anyone is looking, and they are. Kieron turns into the room and changes the subject.

"Thank you for your hospitality. An incredible apartment. I love the sparse romantic style you have brought to this building. What is it? Neoclassical?"

"Yes," the man says efficiently, not wishing for any further conversation.

"I can't help observing you have no art on your walls. For someone who loves art, I find that strange."

The man smiles, the conversation is over. He is now suspicious of Kieron and indicates his men should show Kieron out. As they grab Kieron, Hunter throws a huge pot plant through the penthouse window and bursts in.

The two Russians are well experienced and trained fighters. A maul of legs and punches are thrown and engaged. Powerful bodies heave about, smashing expensive furniture and wrecking the opulent apartment so fast, the likes of such destruction of wealth has not been seen since the Russian Revolution. Hunter leaps clear of his would-be capture and having had more than enough for one day, his aggression is merciless. He hits directly forward, no circular swings; into the throat, up under the nose, up under the ribs, and the final one straight in the middle of the ribs with such a force the guard's heart will without question stop, even if the previous deadly blows had not killed him. Hunter turns to Kieron who is interlocked with his guard. He hits the guard with a sharp, wicked, knuckles-out jab to the side of the neck. The guard drops dead.

"What were you messing about at?" he asks Kieron.

With two dead men on the floor, and women screaming, they claim the oligarch and pound him into the floor, head up, throat exposed. Kieron sits in front of him.

"Is this a big ring, or just you?"

"Me," he chokes.

"You certainly appear to have no personal love for art. Where do the paintings go?"

The door bursts open and Russian special police pile in one after the other, guns up.

61 - RISE AND SHINE

Prisha is up early and with no hangover. From someone who was brought up to drink no alcohol, she can now hold her drink with the rest of the team. Having checked in with Dwight, she knows both Hunter and Kieron have been out of contact for too long. She realises that there are no half measures in this occupation; she must be strong. She walks with confidence around the wonderful atrium, which is beginning to buzz with guests. She walks down the Cinderella stairs and past reception. Behind there is the hub of the ship, the accountants, housekeeping, logistics, guest transport, lost luggage, and planning for what comes on and goes off the ship and in what order at each port they visit. She knocks on the hotel manager's office door, which is a few doors back from the main reception doors.

"Come in."

He pays far more attention when he realises it is someone he doesn't know. Prisha walks forward with her hand out.

"Prisha Nah, I work for Mr Schmeichel."

Her hand is shaken firmly and she is offered a seat.

"Jordan Blake. How can I help you?"

"Simple request, complex background. Which do you want?"

"The request."

"I would like a ship's map, with all of the art cupboards and art areas marked, by yourself if you don't mind, as we are on a need to know basis. And I need the keys for each of them."

"Oh," Jordan replies, a little shocked.

"In short. Art is going missing; I can say no more. Jill is a suspect, as any of your staff could be."

"Oh."

"Mr Schmeichel wants this solved and cut dead at the source."

"Sure. I need some time; I should ring him."

"By all means."

"Can you come back at 1430?"

Prisha agrees and is up. With a business smile, she thanks him and leaves, knowing her request will be dealt with efficiently.

Clément is with Jill at her desk in the gallery. Macey had not been taken to either meeting for safety reasons. She is a wild card now, even more so than she was before. It may be early, and she may be angry, but she has taken the time to set brushes in her hair. They are all small, not the selection in the canvas roll she uses to paint. The paint on these is dry and the colours can be chosen to suit her mood. Her hairstyling comes from her second art pouch which should be called her hair and make-up roll.

She is set up on the balcony and has taped the three 'Shoe' paintings across her French windows. She is working on her LV, high heeled sandal from last night. The heel has formed the hind legs of a goat, the front is still being sketched. Each attempt to touch one of the others in the set presents her with 'painter's-block'. She returns to the heel because she knows she hasn't done it justice yet. They are all being subjected to her new anger, but there is no magical common thread other than the obvious one. That is not enough. She turns to the high-heel work and seemingly wrecks it. She is turning it around. It is now a young goat sitting on its back legs, the upstretched head is the heel and it is suckling from its mother. She starts to jewel the teats.

On the coffee table sits the unread catalogue book; the Pandora's box that needs to stay closed or she will become far more enraged.

Clem is studying May.I.see's work in the repaired featured case of the gallery.

"Great job, Jill. Your talent is incredible," Clément starts, making her feel good. Compliments always work, and as a salesman, he knows that! "Have you any canvas, larger than the ones Macey works with? She is restricted by her pad, but she is ready to explode to a much bigger canvass, I feel it," he asks Jill, his last three words hitting the French accent hard.

"Maybe," Jill says, "but doesn't she have enough to get on with?"

"I wish she would finish one, but no."

"You see, I am organised, methodical but how I wish I had what she has!"

"Maybe, one day?" Clément asks her.

"No. Some call it education, some call it upbringing, but it is really grooming."

"There, brilliant idea, say that. Be freer. That is something Macey would do. You have a theme. Grooming. Paint a series; the many ways a child is groomed."

"Where do I begin?"

"Organisation is a talent," Clément says.

Jill stands up and walks off thinking, he follows.

"That is my pink pony cupboard. The best sellers, Macey would hate those," she says, passing no more than a wall panel between two hung paintings. The only clue to the door is that there are no paintings hung on the panel.

"I have some odd stock in this one. Things that are useful for bits," Jill says, finding a key from a ring of about fifteen all on a large circle with a wrist strap. She turns the key in the wall. The door opens and a few things fall. Clément lets her collect them as he takes in the contents.

"This is not organised or methodical," he says with a twinkle.

"Not my mess. I don't think I've opened this door more than twice. If there is nothing here, I have some other options."

Clément feels the room has many very useful things in it, but it is the dust he is looking at. It is far too uneven, and some areas have moved and not others. It has been opened recently. If Jill isn't opening it, someone else is.

Macey is standing on the balcony. The goat is fully formed and she is taking broader stokes and attacking each of the four paintings with the same uniform anger. She stops, feeling someone behind her. She picks her moment and turns. The two men, once mysterious are now very familiar and in the next suite. With the compartment-wall between suite balconies relaxed they are watching her work. She smiles.

"You have a wonderful talent. The side was not locked closed, so we took the liberty of watching you paint."

"We'll go if we're disturbing you?" the second man says.

"No, you're welcome to watch."

"What you did with the shoe, I love it."

The door opens and Clem walks in with a large canvas and plundered items.

"Clem," she says smiling, "Come and meet our neighbours."

Macey turns but they have gone.

"That's very spooky. I'm going to work upstairs."

62 - LAUGHING

Bedi arrives back at the office, sparky and refreshed, which wakes Croc. He was sleeping at his desk. It is such a normal position he has a pillow permanently to the side of his keyboard.

Dwight doesn't wake so easily. He is in a reclining armchair with hard sides. It is one that also tips forward slightly to give him an edge when using the power of his arms to swing into his battery-powered wheelchair. He rouses himself from a heavy, long overdue sleep.

"Croc, push me into the desk. I'm gonna use my armchair for a moment."

"I'm sorry to wake you," Bedi says.

"No, I should be awake. I've been up once to Prisha, but couldn't keep my eyes open, had to grab the peace-train with the desk on alarm."

"Why on alarm?"

"I haven't heard from the boys for…" he checks his watch, "six and a half hours and they're behind enemy lines."

"Where?"

"St Petersburg."

"Russia! Why you not call me," she says, in shock.

"They followed three paintings out of the airport, leaving the two ground crew tied up in the toilet of the VIP lounge. Nothing new. I gotta visit the washroom, push me back to my chair please."

Bedi obliges as she digs deeper.

"Where?"

"They could have been picked up, with the buyer, or the buyer's guys have them," he says, using his strong arms to lift and swing himself into the motorised chair. He powers off to the toilet.

"I go to Russia."

Big Dog walks around, he had been sleeping in the beds at the back. It has almost become a dormitory.

"Dog," Dwight shouts from the back. "Put your sheets in the laundry basket."

"But I slept in my clothes."

"Gross," Bedi declares.

"You can shower and put ya name on a drawer. Leave some clean underwear here." Dwight orders going into the wash area.

"I ain't moving in," Dog says quietly.

"You did last night," Croc says. "It's me that does the laundry!"

Dwight has switched the shower on.

"Is he gonna shower?" Dog asks.

Croc nods his head.

"How?"

"Don't know, never showered with him," Croc says.

"Respect man," Dog offers.

"I should get woman to shower with him," Bedi says.

"I know a few."

"Can you show us a line-up?" Croc says.

She ignores him.

"Do K&H have passports?" Bedi asks.

"I like K&H, cool. Hunter has a rock star's, and Kieron has an air steward's."

"Male, I hope," Bedi says.

"Never asked, but name is Enrique."

"In Russia. Airport very hard. Very strict security."

"How you gonna get in?" Dog asks, being very sharp with demarcation lines and crossing them down in the ghetto.

"Not fly. Cruise ship best way in, best way out. Get list of ships in St Petersburg over next few days. Hunter will know cruise system, they get out on ship."

"What can I do?" Dog asks.

"Get showered," she berates him.

"Take some of my clean clothes," Croc offers.

"Me not catching none of your tuition-raggedy strides."

"They the only fresheners we got."

Bedi is fed up with Dog's positioning.

"Don't come near me till washed." She ignores him and consumes Croc's attention.

"There been three calls to Yonan?"

"He never picked up," Croc says to her.

"How many rings?"

Croc looks at the record.

"Five, five, five rings on each."

"What time each call?"

"1402hrs, 1502hrs, 1702hrs."

"You stupid. You forget time difference?"

"Shit," he says, seeing his obvious oversight. "I was tired."

"Do better, or I kill you for stupid."

"I'll trace them, trace every phone connected."

"How you do all that, man?" Dog says approaching him.

"You shower or I kill you, serious," she points to Dog. "You find connections or I kill you," she says to Croc.

"Leave someone for me," Dwight says, as he returns looking and smelling fresh, still rubbing his head down with a towel.

"No loss, they all stupid. I ring people in Russia, I find K&H. If not, I go."

"Give it a few hours. Sending you to Russia worries me," Dwight suggests.

"Worries me too. I am killed on sight."

"You need help out there, sister?" Dog asks.

"I not your sister. My sister maybe dead, at age eleven she have first drug overdose, working in brothel. I hate drugs. I hate sex traffic."

"You made that clear and sent that message on the last job, Bedi, and glad you did, sorry you had to. You were vigilant in honouring her."

Bedi nods, far from happy at the new memory.

"I also hate Russian police."

Dog wants to say something but a tug on his shirt from Croc stops him.

Bedi's face is frighteningly strong, as scary as it has ever looked.

"I'll go get showered," Dog says.

CRUISE SHIP ART THEFT

63 – SONOROUS

The sky lounge is huge, very formal, and with the most amazing windows all around looking out to sea. A perfect place to watch the sunset, it has a distinctive look and feel, changing from day to night. In the morning it is very quiet, very bright, with only one waiter servicing the few people who are quietly reading. The bar is not open, but the waiter will get drinks from another bar, or as is normal, coffee from the coffee shop on deck 5. The dress code is smart casual, no shorts, or flip flops. In the afternoon it becomes a work area; in the left-wing of the half-circular lounge, there is a small haven past an internal wall. There they have wine-tasting or eclectic lectures. The right-wing mirrors the left but hosts the water-painting classes. In the middle section, there will be a craft workshop with a 'knit and natter' next to it. The ship is extremely inclusive, and the LGBT meetings will be in the raised section in the afternoon if not the masons or other guilds.

Macey patrols the space between the tables all around the half circle, not seeing a perfect place to work. The light is wonderful, the view inspirational, but she cannot use her easel. She is not working on a single painting and cannot tape her work to the windows because they slant out at the bottom and in at the top. They mirror the front face of the ship. It is a harsh angle, not only designed for the aesthetic style of the ship, but also to restrict the vision of the front deck. That is a small area on the front of a ship that guests can never see. It is the crew relaxation deck with a small plunge pool. If the glass of the windows sloped the other way, Macey would manage but the ship would have a huge wind problem. Still searching, by the time she has completed the moon shape, she looks past the unused stage to the redundant bar area. Macey glides up the two steps and cuts to the right on the small dance or performance floor. Standing alone, by a necessary structural pillar, is the room's grand piano. When played it is the feature of the room. She tries to lift the lid, but its release catch is not obvious and it is heavy.

Propping open the lid of a grand piano allows the sound to be louder and richer. Setting it away from the cranny, that the other three musicians use, allows it to be a more focal performance as well as more sonorous. There are often concert recitals in the evening before dinner.

The waiter rushes over.

"Does madam wish to rehearse? There is a guest piano in the wedding chapel on the floor below. That is for rehearsal."

"Madam can't play the piano," Macey laughs.

"A photograph? Let me take it with you sitting at the keyboard."

Macey stops, thinking.

"Good idea. A self-portrait."

The waiter lifts and fixes the lid, then puts his hand out for her cell-phone. He catches her in a range of poses. Satisfied, she stands. He moves around to lower the lid.

"No," she says.

He stands back and watches her lay her strange 'Shoe' paintings on the upright lid, very unsure of this use. When she goes for the tape, his hand comes up.

"No, madam, please. It is highly polished."

"Don't worry. Mr Yonan Schmeichel sent me to paint all over the ship. Check with him."

The waiter is confused but has no option other than to report it up. Whilst he cannot ring the owner of the shipping line, he can ring his hotel manager.

Macey is getting far looser with these shoe paintings. She wants them to be angry. In a few incidents, her oil paint skids off the edge of the paper onto the polished surface. The waiter feels he must engage with her again. Waiters are used to being politely bold; when a guest comes in the wrong dress, they have to approach them with the line, 'would sir, or madam be more comfortable in a bar without a dress code?' They must raise an arm to show them they have to leave. He feels he must do the same with Macey.

"Your paint is going onto the piano, madam."

Macey stands back.

"There, finished."

"But the piano?" he asks, embarrassed that damage has happened on his watch.

Macey gently lifts each of the paintings to a different flat table, then goes back to look at the black polished lid.

"That's not finished," she says examining it.

"Yes, we have to get the paint off."

"That's not what I meant," Macey says, taking her two-inch wide brush and carving large angles on it. The waiter cannot believe his eyes.

By the time the hotel manager arrives. Macey is standing back looking at her modern art on the piano lid. He turns to stone. He has never seen anything like that happen on a ship.

"Graffiti, on the ship?" he asks.

"What is a lid for?" she asks.

"It produces different sounds," he says, in restrained alarm.

"What sound does it produce?"

"Sonorous," he says coyly.

Macey turns and smiles as Clément bursts in.

"This is wonderful," he says.

"I feel good, so good."

"This is outrageous," says the hotel manager, choking on the words, still in shock. I'll have to get it cleaned by this evening. You will be charged for this damage."

Macey turns to the hotel manager.

"I'm on Mr Schmeichel's account, so no worries. Call him before you clean it off and say, Macey has done her first 'Banksy' on the lounge piano lid."

"But this is a Steinway."

She signs it, May.I.see. The first time she has used that motif.

"No, it's a May.I.see. How many of these big pianos you got?" she asks.

"Fourteen, but you cannot destroy any others."

"Actually, I think I can paint them all," she says, feeling like she has been cleansed. She adds to her signature, 'Sonorous 1 of 14."

"What is this?" the hotel manager asks.

"Not for me to tell. The critics know best, they will decide what I had in my head."

Macey takes her pad and sketches a set of shapes that stand out within the work. Clem is smiling.

"Clem, I have never felt so wonderful. So free."

"You have never had fourteen Steinway lids to paint," Clément says, turning to the manager and his waiter. But she beats him to it.

"None of you say a word about this. None," Clément says, instructing them all and forward planning. "Overnight, Macey will paint them all. Tomorrow, Yonan will have a huge news story he wanted."

"But I can't get through to Mr Schmeichel. I have been trying all morning," the Hotel Manager says.

"Don't worry, it will be fine," Clem says. He is shivering with excitement. He hugs her hard, truly pleased for her.

"Welcome to the world of art, May.I.see. Tonight, you become a huge star."

64 – Q

St Petersburg, Russia–1930hrs   **Miami–1130hrs**   at sea– 1030hrs

Dwight is about to start a proper meeting. It is something he, Bedriška and the two agents abroad are used to, but it is completely alien to Mary, Stan, Izzy or Croc. The lunch on Yonan's ship was the closest they have been, but it was so confused it was not a normal planning meeting. Big Dog might be used to planning at gang-level, but this is likely to be different. To ensure formality, Dwight has taken delivery of a twelve-foot circular table. He is the last to roll up. He lays papers on the desk with a bang. Both tricks are to gain attention.

"We're all tired, but that's no excuse for bad work," he starts, looking at Croc. This is a take-no-prisoners type of meeting. "Report everything. Sit'-report. Sit'-report, sit'-report."

"What's a sit report?" Mary asks.

"Mary, I need to know everything you saw, touched and smelt when you were on your mission. It's my job to decide whether it's important or relevant; not yours."

"But what is sit' report?"

"A situation report."

"Like I was in Maurice Ferré Park, opened in 1976. Sometimes called Bicentennial Park because it was opened in the same year?" She asks.

"Yes. Everything. What more you got?"

"Nothing, I only got that off a plaque," she says, to the amusement of the others.

"OK, quieten down. That leads me to discover you stopped and read a plaque. All of you, can you see where this goes. The reading of the plaque is important."

"Why?" Izzy asks.

"In that case, gotta say Prisha read it. She told me."

"Where were you when she was reading it?"

"I was already resting my sorry ass on a bench."

"Then you two split for a while?"

"I see the build, don't see the demolition," Big Dog says.

"I get to see the demolition." Dwight says.

"And me, I break this stuff down too," Croc says.

"But you don't, you stupid," Bedi says back to Croc. "That why we have meeting. Teach you."

"OK, Bedi. It's good teaching, and also a good reminder to you. Yonan slipped you a phone number, you never told me."

"It was private," she defends.

"So what?"

"Sorry. I thought I might fuck him. Then, I tell everyone all detail."

"OK, second time at the park, I was sitting by myself. A woman thought I was homeless. And there were two gay guys on the bench at the other side of the park," Mary adds.

"Yes, Mary. Much better."

"But they never moved."

"Neither did you, Mary," Izzy says.

"Don't you dis me girl, you don't even wanna be an investigator."

"I know they never moved," Dwight says.

"How you know? I never sit-rep'd it?" Mary squeals.

"They both work for me."

"Cool man," Big Dog says.

"You not trust me to do the job right?"

"With all due respect, no Mary."

"Well, where them two guys now, outside with automatic weapons?" Izzy asks.

"No sister, I would have seen them. It was clean outside," Big Dog says.

"You get the hang of it. It's like you're at a AA meeting."

"OK my name is Mary, and I fucked up."

Mary stands up abruptly to leave. She is angry she was tricked and found wanting.

"Where's your team now bro'? As we all letting go," Dog asks.

"They flew to New Orleans to guard Macey there and they boarded the ship. They watch her every move."

"Macey. Mary's daughter?" Bedi asks.

"I don't like this game," Mary bulldozes, and she storms off, then stops. She walks back to the table slowly but with power.

"Why don't you take her off the ship?"

"Her and Prisha are damn good investigators. Now sit down. It's my turn to share. Last time out, Yonan told me and Iz'..."

"-hang on," Izzy interrupts, "man ain't telling me. I was taking a picture of the man's clogs,"

"Correct."

"You ain't very good at this reporting, boss," Dog says.

"We've all gotta get better at it," Dwight says. "Yonan offered to help with Prisha's refrigeration business in Mumbai."

"What?" Izzy says, and they are all dumbfounded.

"He knew it was the only way we might get money off a ship; inside a fridge that needed repairing."

"And he knew you had millions on a ship?" Mary asked.

"Yes and he asked for five percent, and five percent of Macey's earnings for making her a star."

"Seem like he doing a deal with you, not you doing a deal with him. This man a real player. You better count your fingers," Dog says.

"If he got all the originals hidden away, why we chasing phoneys?" Mary asks.

"That's the kind of thing we ask around this table. That's why we report every word. We've been too lax on this job. It ain't straightforward," Dwight finishes and flicks lights on his whiteboard.

They all go and look at the board. There is a lot more information than they have discussed.

"Why he got us chasing fake pictures?" Mary asks.

Dwight points to a card pinned to the top of the information board; 'Find thieves/recover Yonan's Paintings'. "But I've been thinking."

He scribbles on a new card. 'Why? Crime history = value goes up'.

"So, the buyers are buying fakes?" Izzy asks.

"You got it, good investigative journalists think like you Izzy."

"Sounds like one big art con to me," she says.

"Could be, but who? Why? Where? How? You're in charge of our board."

Izzy steps up to the whiteboard and writes across the top, 'Biggest Art Con Ever'.

"Fuck headline," Bedi dismisses, pointing to the card below. 'Hunter and Kieron no contact since midday West Russian time. My contacts hear of nothing. That mean secret police. I go to Russia."

"You risk being killed," Dwight says firmly. He is genuinely worried for her.

"I be famous like Tsar Alexander second."

"Give them more time," Dwight insists.

"No. Get me flight to Helsinki."

"Why Helsinki?" Croc asks.

"Finland. I no fly into Russia; no chance! I take cruise ship in. Get on at port before St Petersburg, it always Helsinki."

"I'll go with you," Dog says.

"You never get in. If you do; you never survive. If you survive; you draw attention to me."

"Then I wait for you in Helsinki. In case you followed as you come back."

"You wait very long time."

"I'll wait," he says.

"Good luck, ship sails to Tallinn."

"Croc, get everyone on the team legal passports; everyone," Dwight says.

65 – JILL'S KEYS

St Petersburg, Russia–2300hrs   Miami-1500hrs   **at sea–1400hrs**

In the ship's art gallery, Jill is starting an almost full lecture. Like her paintings, her performance holds far less attraction than Macey's. As always it will be forty-five minutes and finish before a change in the food shift. This time she plays into afternoon tea.

The hotel manager has called his Miami cruise office again, this time about the graffiti, and he has been told that Mr Schmeichel's whereabouts are unknown and that CSCI is looking for him. Clément and Macey being on board are also confirmed as being his staff so to go with any requests they have. With his arm twisted, he is forced to understand the possible wonder of having all their grand pianos graffitied. However, the number of people who know of CSCI's involvement is expanding. He has allowed Clément the house copies of Jill's keys and given him a map of the art storage areas.

Clément has to be fast, and fast means not getting emotionally involved; Macey has again been excluded from the raid. Prisha, who can find her way around a ship, is his partner. Most of the cupboards are small stock cupboards, hidden in all kinds of nooks and crannies. They are open, photographed and the two move on.

With thirty-five minutes to go, down on deck three, they open up a room. The map does not suggest how long this cupboard is and they are surprised. It is a long narrow area with an elongated narrow workbench. It is a larger space than expected and is being used for something. Not least of the clues is a long flex looping to a strong light bulb hanging over a box. It improves the normal ceiling lighting at that end. They both enter with interest. This is the first place they have opened which is set up as a working studio. Prisha checks her watch, then photographs and sends to Dwight. She is attracted to a box. It is an old-style box in walnut wood with brass straps, hinges and fastenings. She opens it up and the two sides fall into a writing desk, perfect for working on small detail. Under the leather desktop, the inner box is full of drawers and organised material.

"Look at this."

"It is an old seaman's ditty box," Clem says but he is distracted. His gaze is fixed to the bottom of the wall. "I think they date back to pirate times, and what we have here is piracy."

Prisha follows his eyeline to a half-finished copy of 'Hemingway' leaning against the wall next to a large photograph of the original.

I was hoping to find it, but now I'm disappointed," Clem says.

"Five minutes then we leave. Search paperwork for names and numbers," Prisha says as if she has been a hard-faced secret agent for years.

"Now we've found it, what do we do?" Clément says, looking through the pictures.

"Photograph everything."

Prisha goes through paperwork, then an old fashion Rolodex, photographing card by card. One spins up with a St Petersburg address. She sends Dwight the photo, but the texts go in a queue to be sent as there is no service this low in the steel ship.

"Let's get out of here, now," Prisha says checking her watch again.

"One minute," Clément says.

"No. Move. Now," Prisha demands firmly.

"Look," he says.

Prisha moves back to Clément and turns the pile of canvases and each is a start of the Hemingway.

"It is a production line," he exclaims.

"But how? How is this done?" she asks, turning each canvas to see they are all sketched out exactly the same.

Clément leaves her to leaf and photograph. Flat on the floor he finds what he is looking for, four plastic stencils, each performing a different function of the work. Below them he finds tracings.

"Photograph these, then we go," he says to her, knowing the importance of them.

They rush out and close the door, orientating themselves to the stairs.

"We are still not safe. If she finds us here she will guess," Prisha says.

"How long can we stay? We are not inside; we can hear the door above and the metal stairs," he asks her.

"Five minutes, no more. It is more important to report back."

While they are negotiating time, a key is heard behind them. She has arrived by a different route. Clément is desperate to photograph her going into the room. His head appears around the edge of the stairwell just enough to be camera-ready.

"It's not her," he says turning back to Prisha.

Prisha bursts out with her map; a Malaysian crew member is about to close the door.

"Excuse me, where is the medical centre. We are lost. Clément comes out on the word we, as the man looks at her map. His camera is going silently and at chest level as he pretends to slowly bring it up for a text.

"You won't get service down here," the man says. "Up to promenade deck on the stairs."

He smiles. Like all crew members, he is helpful, and as soon as they turn back to the stairs they hear the door close firmly behind them.

"Do we burst in and photograph him?" Clément asks.

"No," Prisha says, climbing the stairs fast, two at a time. "We send the information, Dwight can make that decision."

In her mini-suite, Macey is taking a break from her easel to choose a dress for the formal night. Tonight, she intends to look stunning. At midnight she will change, like Cinderella, back into her dungarees. Prisha and Clément arrive back, and he picks the wand up again and checks the room.

"I've done that twice this morning," Macey says.

Prisha stands firm, with a smirk, and Macey knows something has happened. She follows Prisha to the balcony where they both watch her cell send.

"Wow, why is that taking so long?" Macey asks.

Prisha looks up and mimes for her to be quiet. Clément joins them.

"Macey," he starts, with eyes wide open about to reveal what has happened.

Macey stops him and indicates the balcony next to theirs where she saw the two men taking an interest.

She watches them both sending files back to Miami and waits in frustration.

66 – FRAMED

DAY8-St Petersburg, Russia–2401hrs   DAY7-**Miami-1601hrs**   at sea–1501hrs

In the Miami Headquarters, Dwight faces his remaining team; Stan, Mary, Izzy and Croc are there. He despairs.

"What?" Mary screams.

"I don't know where to begin, Mary".

"You better not begin with that look!"

"I figure the play is to take one, no, two of her paintings; best if they're signed. Go into each of the galleries and ask how much they'll give you for them. Watch their eyes. Someone's eyes are gonna burst. If you draw a blank, go to the framing outlets."

"No worries," Croc says.

"Whoever it is that goes has gotta look like a dealer."

"I'm an art dealer, and I got me a gallery," Mary says.

That makes Dwight stop and consider her position. He hadn't thought of that attack.

"Where d'you buy them?" he asks her.

"They in my gallery, where she works. You wanna see more, come down."

Izzy is nodding, Stan starts to agree too.

"I see a problem," Dwight says.

"Better be a good one, my gallery about to get five percent on a few deals."

"Problem is they will know where you are. They know where to come and cause trouble. They know where to come and smash the place up."

"I gotta get back to my grill," Stan says, and he leaves.

"I still got my throwing knives. You can take the girl outa the circus, but you can't take the circus out of the girl."

"I don't like that idea, Mary," Izzy says. "It sounds too dangerous if they know where we are."

"I agree," Dwight says.

"You gotta better idea?" Mary asks.

"I think a drug dealer should take them in. Got them from her mother coz she owed money. That story feels kind of real," Dwight suggests.

"I could do that," Croc offers.

"You don't look nothing like a heavy, nor a dealer," Mary says to him.

"Just like they don't see you as a brother in the ghetto. Get used to it, you a boffin now," Izzy says.

"They're right, Croc, you look nothing like a drug dealer," Dwight says. "I'm the one who looks mean enough."

"You could even take her catalogue," Izzy says, agreeing with him. "That's safe. No one gonna mess with you; a drug, a player, and you do look heavy. Not in a bad way, but you do."

"One day I'm gonna surprise you. I get nasty when I have to. And, I still have a gun rigged under this chair," Dwight starts. He looks Izzy straight on.

"What?" she asks worriedly.

"Can you dress as my Bitch?"

"No, she can't," Mary bursts out.

"You ain't my mom; you worry 'bout May-I-See. I can easily dress as one hell of a bitch," she says, grabbed by the role play.

Izzy turns to Dwight and here head drops to one shoulder and her twang gets very street. "You think you're the man here in Miami; we can play."

"Well you ain't got time to go buying no clothes, man needs to go," Mary says.

"I don't need to shop for that," Izzy throws out.

Izzy is out walking the streets of Miami in her ridiculously high shoes that she so rarely finds an occasion to wear. She swaggers as if she wears them every day, and her skirt has ridden as high as it dare go on her thighs.

"How long does that battery last?" Izzy says, feeling Dwight is hanging back a bit. She is looking like one hell of a bizzle. If she stood still for a moment, she would have cars pulling up asking her if she is 'working'. She loves showing she can act the part, especially as she has a legitimate excuse.

"It's all good. Enjoying the view," Dwight says.

"I should have had my nails done. They let the girl down. Maybe I'll get them done on expenses in case we do this again."

Dwight ignores her as they enter the second gallery. The first one they called at thought they were being turned over, not having heard of May.I.see yet. The frame shops only offered a price to frame.

A smart looking male dealer approaches them with a smile.

"Let me know if I can help you. Art is a great way to invest your money, with far better returns than any financial advisor will find you."

"Me think you're right, dude," Dwight says.

The dealer smiles, excited at the prospects of a new client.

"How much are you thinking of spending?"

"I'm selling."

"Oh." The dealer says, the wind taken out of his sails.

"Other galleries near bit my fingers off."

"Oh. What is it you have?"

Dwight tosses the catalogue, making the dealer move fast to catch it. His eyes open wide, he doesn't even open it.

"Good book, you should read it."

"I've already read this book," he says, handing it back.

"Not interested?" Dwight says, nodding for Izzy to take it. She grabs it and turns.

"We going? I gotta get my nails done."

"Wait, bitch."

The language and size of Dwight worries the dealer.

"Can I ask where you got them?"

"Oh, they original."

"You have more than one?"

"Yeah. How many you want? You buy, I supply, and a little line of livener to sweeten the deal."

The gallery owner is still sitting on the unanswered question, though he is ever more worried about Dwight. The atmosphere in the room has changed.

"You read the book or just look at the pictures?"

"I read it but saw no mention of a dealer. I wondered where they were."

"You get to the bit about her mother live in Overtown?"

"That's rather unfortunate. Maybe when the paintings sell, Macey can buy her a nice house."

"Hate to lose a good customer, but her mom ain't gonna move. I look after her real good where she is. Had the nice house, me took that - long time ago. Got everything the woman own, only thing left was these. You wanna guess how surprised I was when the girl hit the news?"

"How do I know you have them?"

Dwight waves. Izzy bends over to retrieve the art, showing her rear to the dealer. Her head turns back.

"You looking at the best piece of ass in Miami, you remember that."

Izzy slides the roll of two paintings out from under the chair.

"How many have you got?" he says calmly, but keenly, as he studies them.

"Now you want the book back," Dwight says.

Izzy scribbles two numbers on the back. She hands the dealer the catalogue.

"I ticked the pages of the ones I got on my wall. I looking at money, right? Not entertaining a fancy voyeur." Dwight adds, locking him straight in the eyes.

"Damn right you are," Izzy says, to the gallery owner now circling the top number on the catalogue. He holds it limply. She is playing her character very well and thoroughly enjoying it.

"That cell only switched on at three."

"Every afternoon? For how long?"

Dwight grunts a short laugh.

"At night dude, on for fifteen minutes only, at night. You wanna buy-in, you come to Overtown, we negotiate there."

The art dealer nods in reaction but feels fear and ambition fighting with each other in his gut.

"How about a quarter of a million now, for all of them?"

"When you wake, from that head injury that making you dizzy and stupid. Call me."

Dwight nods to Izzy. She collects both paintings, flirting with the man.

"I come a lot cheaper, and me excite you more than this shit."

They both leave.

67 – RAMMED

Day 8-St Petersburg, Russia –0200hrs   Day 7-Miami-1800hrs   at sea– 1800hrs

Tonight is a formal night at sea, and six o'clock is the witching hour when the dress code clicks in almost everywhere on the ship. Prisha is in a dilemma. Time is running out fast and she feels horribly alone and under pressure. She was all but an observer on CSCI's serial killer investigation and joined them for the laundry job. This is her third investigation and she does not have the same military or covert background as her contemporaries. With all senior agents 'dark', the pressure to act is immense. They must find Kieron and Hunter before they are killed in Russia. Their only hope might be to find the real Mr Schmeichel. Jill might be a key to unlock that riddle and she is there with Prisha on the ship. But, if Prisha acts she must silence her or Jill may inform those she works for. A soft move could compromised the whole mission. At that point, the art vanishes, Yonan is killed, Kieron and Hunter fail to make it home. Yonan might have as well gone down the other route and brought in the police and the art experts.

Croc cannot be asked to shoulder a decision like this; she has no option other than to act. First, she has to dress. Anything other than an evening dress will draw attention to her. She opens the dresser, pulls out dress after dress and throws them on the bed, but goes to the telephone and dials.

"Hotel Manager, please." She waits, having to deal with the barrier at reception. "Please tell him it's Prisha Nah, from Mr Schmeichel's office."

She will get the urgent attention she requires, but the circle of those who know more than they should expands once again.

Macey arrives back with canvas and easels, Clem in tow.

"Dress fast," she orders them. "We're going to have to make a move on Jill."

"Have you thought this through?" Clem asks.

"Not enough, and you can open the debate, but we have to act fast to save the key members of our team."

Lack of time confuses; the brain's ability to process and question correctly reduces. A member of house services delivers a brown envelope.

"What are they?" Clem asks, worried.

Prisha rips it open to reveal the requested cable ties and drops them on the table in a rush to look presentable.

"We have no kit, and these are used all the time."

"Where did she forge by picture? If we have to smash the bitch up to make her talk, can I please do it?" Macey asks.

CRUISE SHIP ART THEFT

Jill is on an officer's deck down below guest level in a smart single-room cabin. Clément knocks on Jill's door, not expecting her to be there. It is six-thirty. Her duty is to be appropriately dressed and back at her desk soon after six to deal with guest enquiries.

However, she does open the door, and he is incredibly polite. Having convinced Prisha and Macey that none of them is an agent with torture skills, it is not a raid. He uses all the skills of a salesman, and like a great actor, uses few words.

"Jill, may I come in?"

Jill looks at him perplexed, checks her watch, and thinks.

"Hi, Clément, I should be at my desk, what is it?"

The door is hit with force by Macey and she is in with a burst of force. Macey pins Jill to the bed within moments, shocking not only Jill but also Clément and Prisha who closes the door fast. Macey may be an artist, but they forget where she came from and how much she has had to fight. Her surge of anger shows the paragraph in the catalogue is not an invented PR story. Macey has yet to read the piece by Ricky.

"Why are you reproducing my paintings? And where is the original of 'Dwight at Night'?"

Clément cannot pull Macey off, she has not finished her tirade. Prisha's only help is to turn the television up so the sound in the room is confused.

"Scream, and I will hurt you bad, rich girl."

With her forearm across Jill's throat, she reaches back.

"Tie."

Prisha passes Macey a cable-tie. Jill is rolled over, her arms are forced together and harshly snap-tied. Clem cringes. Jill is spun back. Macey punches her across the chin with perfect accuracy. She slides down and cable-ties her legs together, then pulls her legs over the bed. She rips the storage drawer out, and cable ties the leg tie to the bedpost.

"You ain't going nowhere, so speak. I ain't happy, and you won't be the first person I've hurt."

"Sorry," Jill sobs in shock. It is obvious no one has ever treated her like this.

Macey slaps her, "That's my work. Thief!"

Clem manages to ease her back.

"We need to know who you are working for," he asks Jill.

Prisha steps forward.

"We can stay here all night. Unlike you, we won't be missed from work, and before that happens we will have moved you. At the moment, a quick clean up and some makeup and you'll be fine. If you don't play ball, you will be a mess. Macey comes from the ghetto. Neither I nor Clément can stop her. So, who and where is the Russian connection?"

"Russia?"

"The forgeries must go to Russia?"

"No, we show them on the ship. The bidding for those big pieces is done directly to the gallery in New York."

"No. What happens in Russia?"

"I don't know. Maybe the originals go there."

"Who do you work for?" Prisha demands, realising she is too far down the chain.

"I answer directly to Bentley."

"Bentley?" Clément asks

"Bentley Crouch-Fielding. He painted 'Dwight at Night' before it arrived on the ship."

Macey heaves her up, face to face, her eyes nearly popping out as she reddens with rage.

"I painted 'Dwight at Night'."

"Bentley promised to make me a star. It never worked."

"That's because your painting is shit," Macey says, with no let-up to her venom.

The door to Jill's cabin opens behind them and they all turn sharply. Macey drops Jill, Clément puts his hands up like in an old cowboy movie. Prisha boldly stands her ground.

"We'll take it from here, go enjoy yourself," the first man says. His name is Zack and he is the senior of the two.

"Very good work. Dwight's gonna love this," the second man says. He is far younger, much more handsome, but even more frightening, with a glint of madness in his eyes.

"Who are you?" Prisha asks them.

"Dwight was our commanding officer; still is. We do anything the old boy asks, and we're here for him. He put us on to watch your ass, but leave you to run your own show," Zack explains.

Clément smiles. He relaxes slowly, his hands come down, and he points at the men, now understanding why they have been following them.

Zack points back.

"Nice spot Clément. Name's Zack. We were never hiding or you would never have seen us. We were there to be seen, so no one tried anything. Macey was going to be snatched in New Orleans."

"They know we're on to them?" Prisha asks.

"Seems they know something. This is crazy time, do or die, now your finger's in the pie," the second one says as he lifts Jill up. His finger is in the cable tie around her wrists. It pulls tight on her skin and she starts to scream. He puts his other hand to his lips to quieten her.

"They were due to take her in New Orleans, right Jill?" he asks.

Jill nods frightened of him.

"His name's Billy," Zack tells her. "We call him 'Billy the Kid' because he was the youngest one on the team to ever kill someone. Now, he just can't stop; seems to have got a taste for it."

"You can call me Billy. Tell me, who was going to take Macey?"

"I don't get told that," Jill says in fear, trying to bend her neck back away from his reach.

Billy nods, almost hitting heads.

"Here's the one you're going to answer. Where is Yonan Schmeichel?" Zack asks as Billy widens his smile right in her face.

"I have no idea. I've only met him once. Bentley is my team leader."

"To be clear. It was the question you were going to answer properly. You have no other purpose to us whatsoever. And you won't be able to swim with your new wrist and ankle jewellery," Billy says still in close range. He is more than scary.

"Let's help you. Where's Yonan, where's Bentley?" Zack asks.

"Bentley's in Italy, managing the art assistants. He runs the workshop there. I think the first copy is done there. He speaks with Yonan," she reveals.

"You'll start by ringing him."

Billy drops her. His flick knife bursts open with a snap making everyone in the room jump. Jill whimpers. He slits the cable tie on her wrists."

"Grab your phone, call Bentley, ask him where Yonan is. You need to speak with him urgently to hold it all together."

As Jill takes her cell, Bill snaps one of the large cable ties tight around her wrist, the only thing it holds in is another cable tie which he connects into a loose loop. As the cell goes to her ear, he wraps a tie around her neck, pulling the loose loop in so her hand has little scope. He snatches the tie tight around her neck and holds the end..

"Looks good on you," he says.

Jill dials, Billy snatches the cell-phone when it rings.

Zack is talking into his cell-phone.

"It's ringing, sir," Zack starts.

Billy puts his ear to Jill's phone.

"He's picked up, sir," Billy says with an evil smile.

"Go in now," Zack orders through his phone.

"Bentley is about to tell us where Yonan is," Billy smirks.

From the cell-phones, they hear the doors being kicked in. There is the sound of a gunshot and Bentley howls.

"That's his left knee," Zack tells Jill.

"No, he always does the right first," Billy says.

A second gunshot and a shorter howl from Bentley.

"That's his other knee. Whichever. You see, we shoot first, then ask…" Zack pauses.

"Now you tell us; where's Yonan Schmeichel?" Billy asks, looking completely mad.

Zack nods as his sentence has been finished for him. Both men end the calls. They drop Jill and slit the tie on her feet. She breathes out and tries to relax.

"Guess I'm lucky we don't allow guns on board," Jill offers tentatively, with a little relief.

Zack pulls his gun.

"No. You're lucky I liked your legs. Think about telling us all you know about Yonan, and where these fakes go. Let's go for dinner," says Zack. "Would you like to join us, Jill?"

"No."

68 – HELL SINK KNEE

Day8-**Helsinki – 1045hrs**   Day8-Miami-0245hrs   at sea– 0245hrs

Looking stylish and expensive, Bedriška leaves the arrivals lounge in Helsinki. A small knapsack sits in the middle of her back with a strap over each shoulder. A pair of mega-expensive pumps hang from it, the laces double tied. She carries no other bag. She ignores the hawkers and walks to the nearest café, orders a coffee and waits for it. About twenty steps behind her is Big Dog. He looks slick, but she knows he has had that black leather jacket on too long and slept in it. He has a strapped bag over his shoulder and stands next to her in the queue. He takes a breakfast Danish Pastry.

"Hot chocolate please."

He talks to her as if a stranger.

"Cold weather here, sister," he says. Then he corrects himself. "Sorry, I shouldn't have called you sister. But gotta have one of these Danish things."

"Why? You nowhere near Denmark."

They both carry on a separate breakfast routine, waiting for drinks. Bedi's arrives first and she goes and sits at a table for two with a perfect view of the airport's public area. Dog arrives at the next table, pulls a chair out so he faces the other way. As his head is down, he covertly speaks.

"This right?"

"Yes," she says, the cup held up covering her lips and ignoring him. "Watch everything. Moving or not."

One looking one way, and the other, the other way, the whole lounge is covered.

"Follow me, always watch. See if I followed. Get cab after me. Go to Senate Square. He probably take same route. Go to fountain, look at cathedral, many steps. Look for suspicious. Go up steps, and inside, see me praying. You pray in next row, about 3 meters away."

"Social distancing?"

"Whatever."

Her coffee goes down and she leaves. Dog eats fast rising, having to catch up and follow. Outside, he has a cab two back from her, as the cab rank is busy.

Day8-Helsinki/Russia -- 1045hrs   Day8-Miami-0245hrs   at sea– 0245hrs

Still at sea, backstage in the ship's theatre, Clément is quietly admiring Macey freely paint the open lid of the grand piano. He walks out onto the barely lit stage and stands solo, looking out at the eight hundred and seventy empty audience stalls.

"You could do that piano art as an act, while someone plays. A wonderful show."

"No. I'm done here."

Clément walks back and looks at it.

C'est incroyable"

"I told you I'd slap you if you did any more of that French wobble. You're lucky my hands are dirty."

"We go."

Macey collects her things.

"No, no. Wait," Clem says.

He releases the chocks from around the wheels and pushes the piano towards centre stage. She puts her materials down and helps. They leave it there standing in the middle. The lid is up showing the work to the empty auditorium. He chocks the piano wheels and they both climb down and look back at the work.

Macey's new kit is a larger affair to carry. She may have graffitied one piano from her smaller selection of carried paints, but fourteen pianos require stock. She is using her oil tubes mixed with paint Clément has had to forage. He is good at that. He has a small cart which he uses to tow everything on. They leave the stage and Macey cleans her two-inch brush first in thinners, then in a cloth. Clément has been scattering catalogues along the front of the stage.

"This is not the right way to dry a brush," she says, not happy with the results from the cloth.

"How do you clean the brush?"

Macey moves to the upright metal strut of the trolley and slaps the brush back and forth hard. Back and forth across the metal, like she was slapping Jill in a cartoon.

"Stop, stop," he shouts.

The light spray of thinned paint goes flicking everywhere.

Macey stops and looks at her brush. Now she is pleased.

"It's only thinners," she says.

"I'm glad I took my DJ off. It would be ruined."

Macey marches off, "Seven down, seven to go. We are not getting any sleep tonight."

"Macey. You pull the trolley. I need this on film."

Macey takes the trolley. She waits for Clem to get into position, a third of a way up in the stalls.

"OK."

He pans the camera-phone down from the piano centre stage to her pulling the trolley across the front of the ship's main entertainment stage.

"Sonorous seven. Seven to go," she says to the camera. "Follow me."

She exits. The other side would have been quicker but she understands art, even the art of film-making. Clem checks the shot.

"You ain't getting a second take," Macey shouts back.

"It is amazing, all along the front of the huge stage. It is a show."

"Where next, Frenchman?"

"The atrium."

69 – CHURCH OF ST NICOLAUS

Day 8-**Helsinki/Russia – 1145hrs**   Day8-Miami-0345hrs   at sea– 0345hrs

Big Dog walks into the very white, minimalist Helsinki Cathedral, looking around. Its huge under-decorated arches make it look empty and cold. The altar is almost the only feature other than the three chandeliers that hang on very long chains to form an even centre light source; unnecessary in the day when the sun bursts through clear, unstained, unpainted glass windows.

He positions himself in the stalls near Bedi and bends forward as if praying.

"Never seen nothing like this."

"You never been anywhere. Small Dog."

"True," he breathes out, knowing he is seeing a different life to the one he knows. "No one on yer ass. You're clean."

"Last look from top of steps, then we go across square. Café. Sit with me at table."

"That's a fucking honour," he says, then looks up at Christ on the cross. "Sorry dude." He apologises for swearing but then hits him hard. "But seems like you do look after some better than other good church going folk."

They walk out into the bright sunlight, which hits Big Dog more than Bedi who strides away. He stands, perplexed as a huge military band march in and stop in front of a crowd of people sitting on the steps. The soldiers in ceremonial dress are six deep, ten wide; about sixty soldiers."

"What's this, bro'?" he asks a tourist next to him.

"Changing of the Guard. Daily at half-past twelve."

The frontman spins his mace and they start to play as two very medalled senior officers march in. Dog moves across the front of the tourist on the step below.

"You're leaving?"

"They ain't gonna start rapping, are they?

"No," the tourist answers in some shock.

Big Dog shrugs and leaves.

Bedi sits alone in the Café, surrounded by tables of finished food being picked at by seagulls. Dog enters and sits with her.

"This some sort of zoo?"

"I ordered you hot chocolate and sugar bun."

A waiter comes out and places three drinks and three plates of different food. He shoos away the birds and collects the plates. Dog watches him in amazement as he scrapes plates and keeps adding to the pile on his arm. He shakes his head, then looks back at the table.

"So, who we expect?"

Bedi says nothing. His question is answered by a man who sits down and greets her in Russian. He turns to Dog and shakes his hand. Dog complies but understands nothing. His head goes from side to side as they talk. Dog is in awe of this linguistic tennis match. The man takes a large serviette. Not that anyone sees it. Dog knows he palms a gun into the white cloth and puts it down in front of Bedi. In her own time, she collects it and drops it into her open bag that sits on her lap. The man drinks his coffee and leaves.

"Don't I get tooled up?"

"Yes. Not here."

"Cool. Where?"

"In Tallinn."

"Like I know that place."

"You find it."

"Is this lunch?"

"Yes. Eat. Then we leave. Together. We are safe. He also said we not followed."

"Like you don't trust me?"

"You never saw him."

"Don't dis me. I still learning."

"I not angry with you. I angry because my contacts not know where our men are being held in Russia. That worry me. It worry me bad."

"You sure I can't help?"

Stuart St Paul

"No. You one more person who will die."
They finish their refreshments and leave together.

Helsinki/Russia – 1400hrs   Miami-0600hrs   **at sea– 0600hrs**

Macey is beginning to wane. It might be the last lid to accomplish, but that is no help. Losing steam, both artistically and physically, she sits looking beyond the open lid at the small intimate circular dance floor surrounded mostly by love-heart shaped tables for two. It is a special club hidden down on the lowest passenger deck, behind some shops and the library.

"What's this place?" She asks Clément.

"Like a speakeasy. An old soul joint, where the act comes out and does a few numbers after your entrée or antipasto."

"Starter course?"

"Yes. Then you eat. Great tables; one sits at each side of the heart, service is to the top."

"Not like the tables for two upstairs where the two guests never talk to each other throughout dinner."

"You notice?"

"I notice everything, but they stand out because they demand a table for two and not to share. Why? They hate each other."

"They never eat down here. This is a very different dining experience because it's a cabaret venue."

"Good acts?"

"I saw Madeline Bell here when she was seventy-two and she was amazing. She walked around the tables singing, spoke to people, made everyone feel special. It made my trip truly memorable."

"Not heard of her."

"She sang the classic hit 'Melting Pot', way in front of its time, about mixing people, colours, fading them together until the world is one healthy shade of tan. That was back in 1969."

"Way it should be. Sonorous; a world that resonates with all," Macey says, and she carves out different paint colours on the piano lid. Then she cross brushes them with her two-inch brush, clean and dried. The strokes blend the colours together. But she has left a hole in the middle.

"Find a picture of that lady for me."

70 – FERRY OR SHIP?

Helsinki/Russia – 1500hrs   Miami-0700hrs   at sea– 0700hrs

Walking with Bedi, three blocks down towards the sea, Big Dog is very uneasy. This is not his world. He did not see the gun seller creeping upon them; rookie error. The guy was watching them and made his move when he was ready and convinced it was good to go. Dog likes the hood, but he isn't stupid and he knows this is another level. He is going to have to step up, and fast if he has ambitions. Bedi now has a gun, he has nothing. He feels vulnerable and he hasn't felt that way for many years. They cross the road and into a small dockside market.

"I should have killed a man here, but I was too soft."

"What happened?" Dog asks, surprised she was ever soft.

"Not about killing him, about upsetting a friend. I trick him into drinking poison. I bought ingredients here and mixed them carefully, then sent him away. On a train. I watch him be ill in the compartment as it go.

I sent him away to die on train, but he live. Some slime need to be killed twice."

"Guess I don't need to ask."

"No. I got him at another port."

"Where?"

"Does it matter? You won't know. You never been anywhere," she says to him.

"Just asking."

"Don't. But I think maybe Bruges."

"Look, I need to get me some tools."

"Not here. You get ship across water, into Tallinn. It is two hours. Get hotel, enjoy city, but not too much. Dwight will arrange gun for you there."

In the market at the front, they walk amongst stalls selling fresh fish, fruit, and vegetables. Stalls with textiles and some purely of tourist interest like dolls and fridge magnets. It is all new to Dog and easily distracts him. Bedi is continuously looking around as she buys a ferry ticket and hotel room from a booth.

"That is my ship. I get on now as I must get luggage through," she says, arriving back with Dog.

"What luggage?" He asks looking at the small sack slung in the middle of her back. He is too late realising how stupid he is being again. She has a gun to get on board.

"Where's my ship?"

"That your ship," she says pointing to the ferry.

"You serious? I ain't getting on that. It's embarrassing. I ain't never worn bright green and orange."

"You won't be wearing ship."

"For sure, I won't."

"Tallink Star hold 2,000 passengers. More than my cruise ship."

"I don't care. Why paint a ship like that? Do other ships need to see you? Maybe the brakes don't work?"

"It quicker than other ferries."

"I got time, got days. Maybe I can choose one in a different colour."

"No. It is lovely day, go up to Sunset Bar on deck 9. Forget worries to get weapon in Tallinn, you walk in country free and easy."

Big Dog nods, he knows she is right. He turns and looks at the ship in disgust.

"Except, you have joke passport," she adds.

"That do me fine," he says apprehensively.

"Tallinn; walk into old walled city. Your hotel is on left through arch. Here," she says handing him a leaflet from the ticket booth. "Tomorrow, midday, you go to tunnels. Tourist visit. Wear blanket."

"Wear what?"

"They give blanket."

"What, like local threads?"

"No, blanket because cold."

"I ain't wearing no blanket."

"You will, it very cold. Man will hand you gun somewhere in tunnel."

"How's he gonna recognise me?"

"Don't be stupid. Stupid is job for Croc."

"Tonight. First job of agent; check every route in and out of hotel."

"Standard. Same as when we flush any joint. First, know the way out."

"If not happy, change hotel. Tomorrow go up tower, watch me arrive. I must know if Russians following me."

"What do Russians look like?"

"Good question, because you won't see Russian coming."

"Why don't they hit you in Peter's 'burg'?"

"They not good enough. So, they will follow. Russians love to battle in Tallinn. They still think they own it. Go, your ship long queue. Wave from top, I want picture from my ship."

Bedi leaves him holding a ticket and heads towards her ship but before getting close she is greeted by an officer.

"Hey, how are you?" He asks.

"I am good. Why we stop?" she asks as frank as ever.

"There is a problem. No papers came through for you. And I don't think I can get a gun on," he says.

"I will deal with it," she says, walking off towards the ship.

He follows her. She walks straight past dock security showing an out-of-date cruise-card for the wrong ship, and past the passenger steps where he stops. She walks up towards the loading area where loads are being taken onto the ship up a wide ramp by forklift trucks. She approaches a forklift driver to the edge of the busy area, waiting his turn. He lounges back, checking his cell-phone. She hits him from behind and he falls unconscious. She drags him to his truck's load, a large bin that is only partially filled with items too small to load on a pallet. She steels his hard hat, puts on his high visibility jacket, and takes his consignment papers. He is flipped up and over into the bin. It is all done with the confidence of a very experienced agent who has worked in seriously nasty situations and had to proceed and deal with the consequences should anyone see what they are doing.

Bedi raises the bin so no one can look inside, then drives the procured forklift straight at the ramp onto the ship.

"Get back. Wait," she shouts to the other forklift trucks, then swears in Russian. The drivers and the ship's movement control officer look at her disapprovingly.

"I need washroom. I need deliver. Fast. I have bad period, with blood, must pee."

Bedi is waved on. She swings the forklift round to the officer, hands the papers, and drives on as directed. She turns sharp left and follows directions. Having planted the bin on the floor, she reverses a little. She lifts the fork, tipping the bin. She jumps down to check her unstable load, then pulls the body from the bin. Standing him limp and unconscious, she re-dresses him then drops him on the floor beside the driver's seat. Bending down, she slaps him until he wakes.

"Wake up. Look," she says angrily, pointing to the tipped bin. "Straighten, your load, take truck off. Never fall asleep again. Dangerous."

She leaves him in shock and not sure what happened. He sits himself back on his truck and reverses out, turns and drives off the ship.

71 – SILVER SERVICE BREAKFAST

Helsinki/Russia – 1600hrs   Miami-0800hrs   Cuba – 0800hrs

The two large men, Billy and Zack, are very comfortable sitting at the breakfast table with Clément, Macey and Prisha. It is a table for six in the large dining room. Macey feels it is an unusual place to have breakfast as she has always used the buffet and this is so different. She looks around at how busy it is with people wishing to be served. The attitude feels different to that she finds in Wild Mary's diner back in Miami. Here there seems to be an expectation, and they leave without tipping. She has deliberately brought some dollars to tip. 'Don't they know these waiters were up 'til late last night after dinner service?' she thinks to herself. Her view settles on the empty chair at their table. Will the Maître'd fill one empty seat?

"Is Jill coming?" Macey hits a little too hard.

"No, she's tied up this morning," Billy says.

"Yeah, Jill won't be at her desk for a while," Zack adds. "She's done something to her wrist."

There is a pause of realisation, Clem is the one most wide-eyed.

"Literally?" he asks, shocked. "But, you asked her to dinner last night."

"Yeah. It was banter. She could see the fun in it," Zack replies. "I think?" he questions, turning to Billy for corroboration.

"She wasn't laughing," Billy says, recapping slowly, but very straight-faced.

"No, but you don't have to belly laugh at banter," Zack argues.

"True."

The two men are large units, and the calm with which they exchange these military would-be-funny lines is quite disturbing.

"But she gave you what she knew," Prisha fishes.

She is asking because she is keen to learn. Every day is a school day in her new job as an investigator and Prisha lets nothing slip by. Macey is listening too as she begins to eat. She is also keen to learn. It's only Clem who feels awkward.

"But," Clem begins.

"It's what she thinks she doesn't know that we want," Billy says, pausing from eating to look at Clem. "Eat up, you never know when you'll get food again."

"Dwight decides if it's worthwhile information," Zack adds.

"A very full report," Prisha deduces.

"Sadly that means she stays a little tied up in her studio," Billy smiles.

"We left a note on her saying please leave, live art exhibit," Zack finishes, for the double act.

"Art is crazy, live art is worse," Clem says.

"It's a large piece. We also tied up all her teammates."

"It was a metal bench," Prisha says slowly as the penny drops. She offers a knowing grin.

Zack points at her.

"I can see why Dwight likes you," Zack says.

"The long flex from the light that hung over the table," she continues.

"Correct. Four guys and her. Live electric flex wrapped around their wrist then tied to the metal table."

"They struggle they die," Prisha adds.

"At least they have the chance of killing themselves and all the others," Billy says. "Free will, human rights and all that."

"How did you know that?" Macey asks Prisha.

"Dwight's circulated his report of Hunter's raid on the art warehouse in Italy. Before they were arrested, they were tied to a metal bench by a live cable. It was so genius."

"It's a pretty standard technique," Zack says.

"When we get back tonight, they should be in the mood to talk," Billy smiles, red ketchup running from his chin. There is a worrying madness about him.

"When you get back! You are so lucky. I would love to go into Havana. Hemingway's other home," Macey says. "But no passport."

"You could risk it. They only check cruise-cards in and out," Prisha suggests.

"They clearly announced passports must be taken ashore," Clem states.

"Are you Swiss or English?" Billy asks him.

"I am a French art dealer."

"Why do you use a Swiss accent?"

Clément is worried and confused as he stares at Billy trying to make a French face.

"I'm from Paris, born there. Mum is from Berne in Switzerland. There is a distinct difference and you have the Swiss off to a tee," Billy explains before Clem can speak again.

Clem is in shock. He starts to speak, delivering each word slowly and with thought.

"I was born in Switzerland but moved to Paris. I work there."

"Oh," says Billy.

Macey is entranced by the room. The people's attitude to the waiters is disturbing her.

"Ridiculous that they need such a fancy service for breakfast. These people just want slaves."

"You made 'your' slaves work last night, clearing up the smashed frame, the glass, mending it and getting it back on the wall," Clem reminds her.

"It is a little luxury. They are on holiday," Prisha defends.

"What? So, if the guests liked shooting, for a little excursion they let the waiters run in the woods and set 'tour group fifteen' off after them, shooting?"

"I love your brain. Its freedom is so perfect for true political art. You will reach the hearts and minds of so many, and be reviewed, criticised, and talked about. You could not 'ave a more lively platform. Sonorous Fourteen will be just that, running slaves; but I never tell."

"Running slaves?" Prisha asks shocked.

"I will never reveal. But, maybe, I will imply one day so a critic can see it for themselves. They love that."

"Perverted, crazy shit," Macey interrupts.

"Sounds like a good excursion," Billy says. "Hope it's not sold out."

They all turn to him and he keeps a straight face.

"The shooting one," he reminds them.

Eventually, he lets all their amazed faces relax.

"And I got no idea where that accent comes from. I was born in Peckham," Billy says. "Banter. Don't try it. None of you're any good at it."

"My grandmother was, she used to teach the British soldiers in India," Prisha tries, but she is ignored.

"I have a little present that Dwight sent to his favourite girl," Zack says, pulling a passport out.

"Until they shot her," Prisha says, trying to up the ante, but still being ignored.

Macey takes the passport. She turns the pages in awe.

"Is this real?" She asks.

"What kind of question is that?" Zack asks, with a straight face, challenging her.

"Course it's not real," Billy says, having wiped his face.

"They didn't know she was wearing a flak-jacket and had a gun," Prisha tries, determined not to give up.

"So, I'm off to Cuba," Macey says, excited.

"And, we'll be right behind you. Jill can wait," Zack says.

"They made her a saint," Prisha continues. "Wrong religion though."

"Just a warning. Do not lose us. If they know we are onto them, and they must do, there could be a plan to grab you here. You are the most expensive member," Zack says.

"And the most vulnerable," Billy adds.

72 – HEMINGWAY THE ARTIST

Helsinki/Russia – 1730hrs   Miami–0930hrs   Cuba– 0930hrs

Macey sits in the lounge of her mini-suite, feet up on the footstool, waiting for Prisha. She is looking at 'Hemingway' in her May.I.see catalogue.

"This is going to be a series of Hemingways. But they don't say enough. I need some edge."

"You are too excited to be edgy."

"Do you think it was firewater for him or liquid courage?" Macey asks, fishing.

"He was a prodigious drinker," Prisha shouts. "My mother would say I am now."

"Your grandmother certainly would, she was a saint. She sounded some woman," Macey says with a huge smile.

Prisha puts her head around her bedroom door, annoyed.

"Why didn't you help me. I was trying hard to do banter."

"It was far too funny ignoring you," Macey says, flicking through her catalogue.

Her face changes. The muscles force her jaw straight down and the smile gives way to angered pursed lips. She concentrates so hard, her eyes force forward. She stands upright with a lightning bolt.

"Did you see what they wrote about me?" Macey says.

There is no reply.

"Don't ignore me, Prisha. It's not funny now."

Macey lifts the catalogue and continues to read. Her legs give way. The air deflates from her body.

"Prisha. Wild Mary is my real mother. Have they just made that up for the book?"

Prisha comes out of the room, dressed and ready. White boots and shorts. She ignores Macey.

"Hemingway drank absinthe. They say he was one of the greatest absinthe drinkers of the twentieth century," Prisha says, keeping a straight face and as she moves to the door of the mini-suite ready to step out into the corridor.

"Coming?"

The air is frosty as Macey and Prisha walk up the last of the hill that Finca Vigia sits on. It is 15km southeast of Havana in the San Francisco de Paula area. It could have been a hundred miles away and Macey would have gone, even in her lousy mood. She has her easel strapped to her back, but Clem, who plays usually plays donkey for her, is not there. He has gone ahead to work magic. In front of Hemmingway's house is a pergola full of flowers, but that does not inspire Macey. There are groups of tourists walking around outside, as the house is not generally open to guests.

Guides walk tourists around it telling them stories as they look in the open doors and windows.

"There is also a four-storey white tower which housed his writing room," a Guide says drawing them away.

Clem walks down to meet the approaching group with a huge smile.

"We can go inside."

"How did you do that?" Prisha asks.

"I am a great salesman," he says, very proud of his accomplishment. "Macey is a painter and, his mother, Grace Hall Hemingway was a painter."

"I showed them your paintings of him from Key West. They have asked for a picture, I promised them at least a signed print of what you paint here."

Macey does not react. She remains stoic as she follows Clem up to the entrance. A guide is walking past, and they all hear.

"His grandparents were from England," another Guide says as another group moves on.

"Please don't mention his parents, let's find someone who actually knows," Macey chews, still perplexed and seething.

Having had that curt instruction from Macey, Clem leads and they follow.

"His boat is undercover over there. He had it fitted with guns so he could search for Nazi U-boats; quite a character, no?" Clément shares.

"You made up the painter story?" Macey asks, with a fixed jaw.

"No. They know the history. Ze lady I met says she knows it all. His mother was an opera singer and painter."

"Mine flips burgers," Macey throws away testing them, then picking up the pace to walk away from them. She is intrigued by the house. They enter and follow a charming older African American lady as she shows them around the incredible building she loves. Her ancestors were no doubt brought here as slaves. It remains a very touristy walk until Macey stops.

Realising she is not with them, her small group backtrack and find her glued to a picture of Ernest as a baby held by his mother. Prisha could curl up and die.

"Her name Grace, like mine," the guide says.

Macey takes it very well, to the surprise of Prisha and Clem. They guess that Macey has now discovered about her own mother, and they are unaware of the scale of its damage. Macey lifts her cell phone.

"May I?" she asks, wanting to take a picture.

"Sure. I want you to create some magic, I loved that man," Grace says.

"You say that like you knew him," Macey asks.

"I was sad when he died," she stops. Genuinely sad and fixed on the picture. Macey steals an image of her before she recovers.

"I grew up in this house. My mother was his maid," Grace reveals. "She was like his mother. She was the one he turned to."

Prisha has almost stopped breathing. She may have been introduced to the complication, but the jigsaw is clear. Macey must be hurting.

"Suicide?" Macey asks.

"So they say."

"Depression? I'm beginning to know how he felt," Macey says.

Prisha feels she needs to jump in so Macey can't control the way the conversation goes.

"Is that why he killed himself?"

"No," Grace says slowly, and with a heavy heart. "Me think it because he left Cuba. Left his real family. He loved it here, always returned. Lived here thirty years."

"But he had a form of bipolar madness I read in Key West," Clem says, hitting detail.

"What do they know down there?" Grace fires.

Prisha hopes that is the end and starts to move off, but Macey grabs her arm and fixes her. Macey's eyes search Grace's heart. Grace can sense her genuine interest and feels free to open up to her. These are the moments Macey paints. This is the edge she looks for.

"Nothing?" Macey asks Grace softly. "They know nothing?"

"Me think he was suffering. He always suffered."

Grace points at the picture of Ernest and his mother.

"He put this up, me never know why. Me think it tortured him."

"He wasn't bipolar?" Macey asks.

"Ernest? No!"

Grace turns her head away from the picture of his mother.

"My mother loved him. But, 'is mother....."

They all stand and wait. She is going to reveal more as she steps closer to the painting and fully engages with it.

"His mother was a hard woman. She ran the family, she was the power over Ernest's father."

"How?" Macey gently pursues.

"Money," Grace grunts. "It make some men lords and other men slaves."

Clem and Prisha wait, knowing that not only is this Macey's world, her passion, but there is an intriguing story she will express in oils.

"She had money?" Macey asks.

"Her dad was wealthy, but she was one big famous opera singer. She earn hundreds, maybe a thousand dollars a week. Me, I can't even imagine a thousand dollars a month now."

"His father?"

"Maybe fifty dollars a month. Me sure Ernest blame her for his father's depression, and his father's death."

"Wow," Macey says.

"She always got what she wanted, except with Ernest."

"No?"

"She want a girl. She treat him like a girl. That's why he write from a woman's heart."

"But he was tough?" Clem dares to suggest very quietly.

"His grandmother was tough. Could handle a gun, went fishing, and liked the woods, until she got cancer."

"Ernest could be tough on the outside; maybe had to prove he was tough. I see my mother with him, she knew the real Ernest. The one she had to comfort. Me also think he had that Post Traumatic Stress from way back."

"From his mother?" Macey gently asks, knowing the damage her mother has caused her. Prisha can only stand and watch, amazed at the similarities.

"No. A bomb landed right by his feet in Italy, during the first world war. He was in two plane crashes. The man got that dysentery, had his intestines come right out which he had to bathe. Huh. My mother, she sit with him and listen to the stories he never wrote nowhere. He was quiet. I watched from behind the door. Ma said those were his special times. He exorcised things that haunted him. That's when he needed his mother. But he had my mama, she named Bell. Like For Whom the Bell Tolls."

It hits home again. Macey is stunned.

"Just me thoughts. He left, 1960. Me just ten years old. What does a child know?"

Grace is lost in deep sadness. Macey stands fixed. She realises that Stan must be her father, and he left her. He left her when she was born. Why?

They leave the house and Macey's head is full of a mixture of things. Prisha has a camera full of pictures.

"Y'all have a Mojito before I take you to the tower," Grace says, and they go to a bar erected in the grounds where they crush sugar cane. It has its fair share of ants, but no one seems to care.

"Which was his favourite drink," Prisha asks. "I thought it was absinthe."

"The man had no problem drinking anything, but he liked his Ballantine beer."

"Inspired?" Clem quietly asks Macey.

She sees Zack and Billy the other side of the bar. Zack smiles, Billy raises a toast.

"Empty. I feel nothing. We have a job to do, and that's finding a thief. But it was a nice tour," she whispers to him.

In the tower adjacent to the house, Macey is inspired. She stands at her easel painting Hemingway at the window, a glass in his hand. With artistic license, she has compressed his desk up close to him and the window.

"It is like you knew him, like he is here," Grace says, watching.

Macey starts to paint his mother in the sky, hanging over him as if to say drinking and all his women are wrong. Her eyes are haunting. The paint dries fast in the heat and Macey adds a layer of lacquer blowing to assist drying. She paints, then lacquers again. The dimensions catch the light and your attention. It is as if you cannot escape the eyes. Eventually, she takes a wide dry brush, it must be two inches, and she gently goes back and forth over his mother in the clouds until the woman has blended in, gone translucent, all except her eyes. It is like his mother is not there, but she is, watching.

73 – SHIP TO SHIP

Helsinki/Russia – 1900hrs   Miami-1100hrs   at sea– 1100hrs

As directed, Big Dog goes up to the top deck of the Baltic ferry, deck nine, and gets himself a cold beer to try and enjoy a very pleasant evening. He feels a lot easier about being inside the ship, and not having to look at it. It pulls slowly away from the dock and angles itself to go out towards Tallinn. As is gets closer to Bedi's ship, he finds himself waving, like all the other passengers. Those on Bedi's ship, which is still moored at the side of the dock, wave back. He stops himself and looks around. 'Is this what people do, wave at other people they don't know?'

The shuttle may call itself a high-speed craft, but it sails out of the harbour slowly. A party starts on the ship. For the first time, Big Dog notices most of the women are wearing crowns of flowers. Many of them are in pale pink dresses. He had thought that was a custom when he saw a few in town, but now it looks like a party. Groups are spreading food out on the deck and it appears to be a celebration. They start to sing and gradually others join in. It breaks his hard exterior and he finds a smile.

"What they sing?" He asks one of the prettier young women who seems to have been watching him. He can tell when a woman is looking at him.

"They sing about a little frog."

"Frog? That it?"

"Yes. They have no ears and no tail."

"Right. That all?"

He watches and they are all making weird frog noises.

"Oh, frogs," he says, convinced the world is a strange place.

"Now they sing about little pig," the woman says.

"Guess they're gonna oink, yeah?"

She does not even need to reply; the chorus does that for her.

"Kids' song, right?" he asks, but not seeing too many young children.

"Well no, but they will join in."

"Why? You gonna sing it again?" he asks, because it seems to have finished.

"Yes. Many times. Rejoice, it is midsummer."

She leaves him to engage with others, but always with an eye on him. He watches as they form a circle bouncing around, imitating a frog. Now the children appear and help the adults. She waves him to join in. He refuses but takes pictures with his cell. He would like a picture of her, but she is playing hard-to-get.

CRUISE SHIP ART THEFT

Big Dog looks around, as he has done more than a few times, to ensure he is not being followed. Bored, he goes below to the buffet. He would give anything for some fried chicken, but no luck. He takes the pizza and slides a second cold beer in his pocket so he can explore and eat on the go. He never saw much of the cruise ship he was on before. Not that this is a cruise ship. Before, the theatre was all he saw as his men guarded the stage and followed orders. It was a big payday for them and afterwards, they all partied hard, but none of them made out like frogs. Well, maybe later they'd humped like frogs.

Big Dog is intrigued to see a business lounge where there is a much more formal crowd, working. He tucks his empty plate away and feels the ship accelerate. Moving to the side and looking out, he can see that they are now in the Baltic Sea and the captain has hit the gas.

"Hüüdma!"

Big Dog jumps. He turns and it is the young woman again, high on midsummer. She spins him, but he is not pleased. That is twice he's been crept up on in as many hours.

"What?"

"You say, boo," she says.

"I ain't said boo since I was in diapers."

"You should have some fun."

"I'll pass, thanks."

"Midsummer is very special in Sweden. I have family from Sweden."

"Midsummer?" Dog queries.

"Since old times, churches in Sweden celebrate Johannes day."

Big Dog looks puzzled.

"He was born June 24. So, it goes with mid-summer."

"I get that. Happy birthday Johannes."

Dog raises his beer and toasts him.

"I don't think he drank," she says.

"Oh I bet he did, just never told the wife."

"Now, I live in Estonia."

Smiling she spins him again, high on the celebration. Almost too late Dog sees a knife. A man is thrusting at him as she turns. He instinctively slides to the side and the man stabs the woman. Her dress turns from pink to red and she drops. Big Dog has to move on. His beer bottle is his only weapon. He swings it once then twice, beer going everywhere as he hits the man. He backs away to the wall, hits the alarm to get the woman help.

"Medic."

The knife is jabbed at him. He side-steps it and as the steel hits the metal bulkhead, he nuts the assailant hard with his forehead driven by the full power of his neck. The man doubles over. Dog hits his more static target as hard as he can with the bottom of the bottle. The part that does not collapse, the part that does the most damage. The man drops, and Dog hits him again so he isn't getting up. People are screaming and his instinct is to slip away fast. Now he must hide because as far as he can see, he is the only black man on the ship. He stops, his back flat against the bulkhead and he is haunted by a sense of duty. If he wants to be an agent, he must act like one. Agents would take his phone, and his wallet to report back. Maybe a photograph of his face. But that means a danger of being captured. He looks back around the corner and a few people are screaming. He has to think quickly.

Big Dog rushes in and pretends it is to help.

"Go get a medic. Go. Someone check the woman."

He pulls the man round. "Hello. Wake up!"

He goes through his jacket and palms his phone then opens his wallet. It says some name in Swedish he can't even read, let alone pronounce.

"George," he shouts to him pocketing the wallet and assigning him a new name. "Wake up, George."

He rolls him over as if trying to help, but underneath his fingers are digging into his throat finding the windpipe to end any last chance of life he had.

Knowing he has killed him, he flops him back, takes a photo of his face.

"We need a medic! Where is the medic? I am not a medic," he shouts leaving fast as if looking for one.

His pulse is raging, his blood pressure sky high. Now Big Dog knows the difference between a gang fight and surviving an assignation attempt in the field. His mind is catching up; as an agent he failed to get the flower girl's phone, bag or a photograph of her. He turns back, there is still no officer there, but a growing crowd of red-neckers.

"Medic is on his way." He nods down to the girl.

"I've got her," a man shouts as he pummels hard into her chest to get her heart started again.

Dog takes the photograph.

"Does she have a pulse?" he asks. He slips the small bag from her wrist and feels for a pulse.

"I can feel when you push," Dog says.

"Good. It is working."

"Where is this medic?" Dog says, standing, and he goes off again to look for help, but he never returns.

Big Dog is shaking, he is full of adrenaline, fearful and on a high. All he can hope for is that panic on the ship escalates when they dock. That there is a stampede of two thousand passengers so desperate to get off no one sees a black man. He might even have to instigate panic. All this for a few paintings! His job now is to stay alive, report back.

74 – ELK

Helsinki/Russia – 2030hrs   Miami-1230hrs   at sea– 1230hrs

The ferry docks and as the thick ropes are fixed between ship and shore, Big Dog hits the alarm. There is no sound, it is either a silent alarm or it didn't work.

"Fire," he says, pushing through the crowds of passengers. "Fire. Shout out in Estonian, Fire."

Slowly the murmur starts to swell, but no one has called out.

"Fire!" He shouts louder.

The calls kick off all over the ship and the surge to the doors begins to get rough. As the doors open, the crowd burst through.

"Fuel Oil!" He shouts. "Boat will explode."

Now the cry is translated and repeated and passengers fight to get out. The immigration guards are useless, they are fairly informal at these ferries and have never had to deal with an angry crowd. The gates are opened and people push through. Big Dog can see the police and has spent most of his life ensuring they don't see him. That situation is not going to change now.

Even with the ship behind them, the crowd are still walking fast past some large units. He is approaching the main road, a few hundred yards away. Dog is overtaking most of the passengers on the inside, close to the building and harder to spot. A mass waits at a controlled traffic and pedestrian signal. He waits in the cover of the building as two policemen scan the stationary crowd. The light turns green to walk and he is off, low and to the edge of the moving horde. He is safe on the other side where the group begins to thin out and cross the grass verge.

Crossing the less busy access road to the old town, there is a wait to go through the narrow gate. Inside is a bygone time. The crowd thins out, taking in the wonder of Old Tallinn.

Big Dog stops, flat against the wall and looks around. There are no police in here, and most people walk straight on, although some turn right. He looks up and can see a tall tower. That must be a perfect observation point and no doubt why it was built, also why Bedi suggested he watch her arrival from there to see if she was being flanked or followed.

He looks behind him and can see his hotel further along. He crosses the road and looks at it from the other side. There is only one door. The windows might be the only other means of escape, so he appreciates it only being two stories high. Dog checks in. It is like going back in time. Even the staff wear weird clothes.

Later, in his room, he calls Dwight to reports and take instructions. He is alone in a foreign city for the first time and he appears to be on a list to be killed.

"You've done it as I explained," Dwight is heard to instruct over the phone. Big Dog places a bottle with a shoelace on the table beside the door, then three bottles in front so they would be knocked over should someone try to enter. Hanging from the door handle by his other shoelace is a collection of hanging bottles.

"And make your bed on the floor the blind side of the door. Put pillows in the bed so any intruder hits that first, it gives you a few seconds to react."

"Thanks. These bottles gonna make more noise if they empty?" Dog says.

"Yeah but don't go mad drinking, big day tomorrow. Sleep."

"Sleep?" Dog laughs sarcastically. He climbs into bed on the floor with two beers and an opener. He is sitting up fixated on the door as he cracks the first bottle open.

"Got me staying in a fancy hotel, got me a minibar, and me gonna sleep on the floor," he says to himself.

There is a knock at the door and Dog freezes with fear. It seems an eternity before a young woman's voice politely accompanies the next knock.

"Room service."

'I just got them bottles lined', he thinks to himself.

"One minute, y'all."

Dog gets off the bed and loops the bottles off the handle. His hand is on the handle.

"How I know you room service?" He asks confused. I ain't got me one of those little holes to look through.

"What else would it be, sir?"

"I don't know."

Dog feels like he must trust her, he is hungry for the burger he ordered. Even so, he opens the door prepared for a fight. He calms when he sees a young woman with a tray. She looks concerned when he closes the door behind her and she is in the room with him. She looks around at the bottles scattered everywhere.

"Should I bring sir some more drinks?"

"They all paid for?"

"Yes, your company pays all the bill."

"Yeah, we do some more beers, sister. The burger looks nice. Looks like good fresh beef."

"It is elk, sir," she says as she leaves.

"Elk?"

75 – HAVANA

Day9-Helsinki/Russia – 0030hrs   Day8-Miami-1630hrs   **Cuba– 1630hrs**

Floridita is a large bar on the corner of a block. Macey stands outside, flanked by Clément who is dying for a drink, and Prisha, still on edge over the information Macey must have discovered about her past. Clem walks into the bar and orders three mojitos. Prisha is fast behind him, happy to stand under the swirling fan and feel a rush of cool air.

Macey needs her space, still pondering the contrived birthday parties that Mary organised for her as a kid. The flow of money for her college and support Wild Mary has given her over the years. She ponders on the street corner, uninspired by the bar and not seeing Hemmingway. A huge old classic car skids up and rocks on its suspension to a stop behind her. A highly polished, deep royal blue convertible. Clem and Prisha both turn and look.

"That's a '57 Chevy Bel Air Convertible," the bartender says, taking the money Clem left on the bar.

Classic cars are a feature of Cuba, but it was not the car that caught their attention. A man runs in from each side of Macey. They have all been caught off guard. Clem runs out too late, and too slowly. The men up-end into the rear seat of the car. As Clem reaches the pavement, the driver looks forward ready to screech away. Before it can move, the front of his car is smashed in hard, head-on, by a smaller, modern, red Suzuki Jimny. Glass breaks everywhere. The driver scrambles for reverse, as Zack gets out of the destroyed small jeep-like car and in three strides is on the street kidnappers. One blow ends any sign of life in the first man, and a swipe of the legs and a push sees the second man hit the sidewalk head down with a fierce crunch. As the blue Chevy starts to escape backwards with Macey trapped in the back, another red Jimny powers in and smashes even harder into the rear of the classic car. The Cuban driver knows his car is trapped. Shocked, he looks in fear to Zack on the sidewalk. He has never seen such a killing machine. To avoid Zack, who has finished his fellow walking assassins, the driver scrambles back into his door ready to vault over it. He turns to leap out and almost takes to the air. But, Billy coolly pops him under his chin, powered by the coordinated explosion of power from his twisting hip and his straightening right leg, all working in such poetry. The driver flies backwards over his seat. He falls helplessly, folding, wedged into the passenger footwell so unconscious life may never come back. Billy grabs the head of the man in the back seat who has now let go of Macey. He twists the head around hard with a snap. The man is dead in an instant as Zack pulls Macey free. Billy is smiling over the car to Zack, whose two ambushers are on the floor, also possibly dead. Zack shrugs.

"We needed one alive to talk," Zack accuses.

"Why do I have to let one of mine live? You had two."

The exchange hard looks, then Billy breaks it.

"He's not quite dead," Billy says pointing down at the one crumpled in the footwell.

"He is a psychopath," Clem says to Zack, then looking at him and the two dead on the floor he wonders if Zack is too.

"He's got a kind heart," Zack replies to him, breathing in with a sigh.

Zack kicks both floored assailants to check, but as he expected there is no life. He moves to the driver, trapped in the car and struggling like a crab on his back in a hole. Billy slides around and continues to help Macey out, playing the part of a hero, instructing her.

"Are you alright, Madam?" he shouts, loud enough for all to hear.

Macey nods, confused.

"Anyone else hurt?" He shouts.

Leaning into Macey he shares the next comment with her before pushing her over to Clem.

"Now go, you've nothing to do with us. They're all dead, so, you should be safe."

"Thanks."

"Enjoy Cuba, we'll be right behind you."

Macey takes the spare mojito from Clem and necks it down like a shot.

"I wasn't keen on this bar anyway. I wasn't feeling Hemingway there."

She walks away swiftly, and Prisha and Clem catch up behind her. At the car, Zack has the driver up, held by the head.

"In ten seconds you will be as dead as the other three. I don't care. Tell me who hired you, and you live."

"Cesario. It is his car."

Zack turns around to the crowd.

"Cesario?"

They are so scared, there is almost a chorus.

"Tequila Dance Bar."

Billy has already left. He is on the other side of the road following the at-risk trio. Zack crosses the road, seemingly in another direction, but he turns back with traffic and follows some distance behind.

Prisha is using the smart-map on her cell which tells her Hemingway's other drinking hole is three-minutes' walk away. In the short swift walk, they see old and young men along the roadside sitting at small tables playing dominos.

"Down there," Prisha says, and they hustle down the final street. She jogs to keep up with Macey. "Should we not just go back to the ship? It would be safer."

"We have Billy and Zack. Trust the team, each member has their own job. What was yours? To keep it from me that Wild Mary is my mother?" Macey stops abruptly and turns to her. "Is she?"

"Yes. I found out the same time as you."

Macey thinks, turns, then powers on.

"Croc didn't. He knew." She shouts back, now showing her anger, only softened by the length of time it had been brewing with memories.

La Bodeguita del Medico is a different kind of bar altogether. This is a small bar, a drinker's bar. The counter is on one side with bottles shelved behind it, guests are on the other side with framed quotes on the walls behind them. Few would look up and study the mural above them with guitars and bicycles. Macey does. It smells of Hemingway and attracts Macey to take the step up, and the only other step, past the open wrought iron door guards. She is in. The empty stool she takes is only just inside, but she is both at the bar and adjacent to the road.

"That is where Ernest Hemingway sat," the bartender says, clearing the empty glasses from in front of her.

"I know, I'm talking to him," she beams.

"Then he is telling you to order this."

The bartender places a champagne glass on the bar.

"Three please," Prisha says, joining her.

He adds two glasses and generously pours one measure of absinthe into each glass.

"That's a jigger," he says.

He tops the glass up with champagne. When the glass is full, the liquid develops an opalescent milkiness.

"Good luck," he says and is gone

The bar is heavy with rich, fresh cigar smoke and the noise of friendly conversation.

"Hemingway would have been happy in here," she says, and she necks her drink like a shot and steps onto the sidewalk and erects her easel. She sees Prisha walking over to Zack and Billy on the other side of the road leaning against the wall. She has a beer for each.

Stepping on the ship safely, Macey has the beginnings of two more Hemingway paintings. That could make four. The one at his desk in Key West, and the one of him spinning his last dime towards the viewer. Now Grace in his house and the street bar with old cars. There will be more. In Macey's head, she sees the need for his mother to be looking at him in every painting.

Clem looks back as he goes through the ship's security. Zack and Billy are not there. He worries, but Prisha turns and clocks herself out again. She runs after Billy and Zack, knowing they are both on foot.

"Don't wander off without your back-up," she says, catching them.

"You should go back," Zack stipulates.

"No, I should learn more about the operation."

Zack considers and gives in. Time is too tight for an argument. As usual, the ship will not wait.

At the dance bar, he walks in alone, leaving Billy lagging behind with Prisha. Zack walks straight up to the man seated at the corner of the bar, with guards each side. Billy takes the offer of a Latin girl who begins to show him how to dance. She shows him the moves; he directs her towards the corner of the dance floor near to Zack.

Zack pulls out a US twenty-dollar bill and lays it on the table in front of Cesario.

"That's for the damage to your car."

"My car is not damaged."

"Blue, 57 Chevy. Sounds like a line from a song."

"I have a Chevy."

"It's damaged, front all caved in, back all caved in. Ten dollars towards the front, ten dollars towards the back."

"My men will tell me if it is damaged."

"Four men? Driver, ugly, with a beard?"

Cesario looks at Zack.

"They're all dead. You'll be next."

A gun clicks behind him, but Zack does not even turn. Billy spins away from his dance partner, takes the gunman's arm and folds it up, broken as if he were dancing with him next. Billy has taken his gun.

"He likes guns," Prisha announces to all behind Zack.

"As I said, you will be next. Dead. So, it's worth taking my deal."

"What deal?"

"Who booked you to snatch the black girl? Now, don't waste time, you don't have any."

"Man called Bentley, like the only nice modern car. Money came from Italy."

Zack leans into him.

"Are you insured?"

"Yes."

"Get the car fixed, enjoy the rest of your evening."

The two men walk out. A gun clicks behind them. Prisha beats one gun arm down with both hands but is captured and held around the neck. Billy spins around again gun up, pulling a second gun from the belt of a drinker nearby. Both arms aimed, he shoots twice. The bullets whizz past Prisha within inches of her and make a mess of her capturer and another gunman behind them.

"Game's over," Zack shouts back to Cesario. He has not even turned or stopped walking. Billy nods for Prisha to leave. She passes, he shoots again and again and backs out to join the other two.

"Was that necessary?" Zack asks.

"They flinched."

"Flinched?"

"I think. We better double back to Cathedral Square then loop around," Billy says, already having worked out a route.

"Yeah. I got the feeling this ain't over," Zack says. "And he gave Bentley up far too fast."

76 – FRIDGE MAGNET

Day9-Helsinki/Russia – 0530hrs   Day8-**Miami-2130hr**   at sea from Cuba– 2130hrs

"Well, ain't she the surprise I was expecting?" Dwight mutters.

"If you were expecting it, it ain't no surprise," Izzy says.

Izzy and Croc are both paying attention.

"What you found?" Croc says, sliding across to Dwight's station as he leaves it.

Dwight points at the printer. Izzy is there in seconds and starts to read as it comes out, and finishes as she walks to her huge white metal investigation board which, is in the dark. She has erected a Rube Goldberg set of lights that she switches on, and it lights up. There are some cards in a sparse family tree.

"Izzy, where's that sit?" Dwight starts. "I'll get you some proper lights for that."

"And some more magnets the way this is going," she says.

"Get them all to bring you back fridge magnets," Dwight says, writing at the desk nearest the board. "This board is going to become special."

"How special?" Izzy asks.

"Very special."

Izzy takes her marker and writes 'Izzy's Board' at the top.

"I expect magnets from Helsinki, Tallinn and St Petersburg. I'm gonna start a collection."

"I'm on that," Croc says. Excited, he turns to focus on Dwight's screen. The displayed information sheet is a picture of a pretty young woman.

"Who's this?" Croc asks.

"Write dead on the top of that, Izzy," Dwight says.

"Dead, that's sick," Croc says, sitting back from Dwight's screen. Then he jerks alert. "Is she the flower girl who tried to kill Big Dog?"

"Yeah, Natasha Smenotva" Dwight answers. "Dead at twenty-five. How old are you?"

"Twenty-two, they both say limply."

"How did you find her?" Croc asks, annoyed he was beaten.

"You ain't the only one who can use a computer. What I lack in your modern knowledge, I bleed with contacts and experience. I been there, done it, know how it works and can second guess them. Use that board and apply your skills."

"Sick," Croc admits, as he has to watch Izzy throw him a grin.

"Croc, I'm serious. You need to stay swimming. Lot of bright kids coming up behind you know more. They gonna be more current."

"They won't be as good as me," Croc says.

"Well, I just beat ya," Dwight says. He has cracked a few clues open. They have missed things. "Natasha was in her last year at the SVR/FSB program, still at training college. She thought she was good."

"And she got wasted," Izzy says, still trying to find a place for her on the board.

Dwight is at the empty conference table near the board. He writes new cards as he instructs them.

"She'd be put in one of the two sections after training: internal or external intelligence. She was training like you two."

Izzy stands helpless by her board, less keen to find a home for a dead girl. The small tree has a line by itself on the right:- Yonan Missing, Miami Dealer, Fake Yonan. On the other side, we have Mike and the mercenaries. The more complicated tree also starts with Yonan at the top. A line goes down to Bentley's card. Then it flares out.

"Bentley got a lot of interest," Izzy says. "I reckon he'll be dead next."

"The object of the game ain't to guess whose dying next, but to keep our people alive." Dwight points at the board. "Look, study."

Izzy runs them through it, starting with the spikes out from Bentley.

1. The line down from Yonan.
2. A line to Italy which is obvious.
3. Forgery Team No 1.
4. A line down to Jill, and she has an interactive line to ships.
5. A line to CSCI.
6. A line to Russian Dealer.
7. Hermitage Museum, Russia.

"Bentley is the main spider," Izzy announces.

"Spider?" Croc asks.

"He has the most legs."

"Here," Dwight says, offering a card saying K&H. "Take CSCI off, and put K&H in its place."

"Why's that?"

"They worked in Italy, not for CSCI, they burst into the dealer; CSCI didn't. They got arrested. They may have told the police they were investigators, or maybe not. Put K&H in where it is K&H."

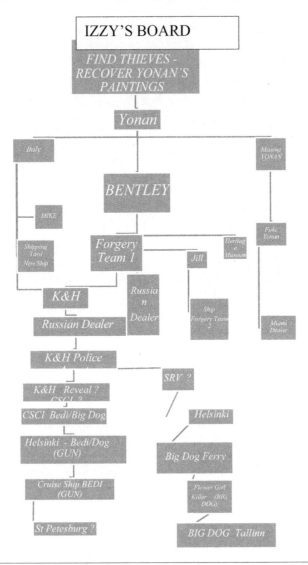

Izzy does that, then tries to figure out why it is so important.

"OK, where does she go?" Izzy asks, holding the Flower Girl. "Under police?"

"Do we know that?" Dwight asks. "That's you thinking like a journalist. Making an assumption to get a headline. We don't know that."

"Where else does intelligence school get things from if not the police?" Croc asks.

Dwight looks at him with the slightest of shrugs making them ask more questions of the board. He hands her another card and continues to write new cards.

"Helsinki?" She now has three cards in her hands again and does not know where they go. "OK, these go where?"

"I have some software that does this a lot easier, and better," Croc says.

"So why am I wasting my presh?" she fires at him, offering the cards back to Dwight.

"Precious what? Time? One: it's not precious. Two: you're learning. And three: you can't beat seeing it like this. And four: you have good friends out in the field gonna be killed unless we get them back."

"True," says Croc.

"OK, Croc, you start putting all this into Sherlock 2 and work together with Izzy. Izzy, from CSCI, put a line to Helsinki, from Helsinki put one way to Bedi slash cruise ship and the other to Big Dog slash ferry."

They first ran their version of Sherlock 2 on the serial killer case. It is a layered computer software programme first used in the United Kingdom to find serial killers. It floats a 'family tree', but picking up on the most obscure of reported or discovered parts of the evidence, floats other trees or puts the top-tree with three-dimensional connections.

"I ran flower girl and the stabber's phones," Croc offers. "Both had sent a report that they had seen Bedriška in Helsinki, that she had a partner. Neither of them posted after that."

"They got a lot wrong! Neither said the partner was black. Sherlock needs that."

"Reporting to who? They really been to college to learn this?" Izzy digs.

"Yes," Dwight says. "Kids don't send reports back for fun. They're trainee Russian spies. But, they called Bedriška 'woman'. That got me thinking they're just doing plat-time missions and this went wrong."

"Play time. Chasing Bedriška is not play time."

"Exactly. They said woman. They'd not been sent to apprehend Bedriška, didn't know it was her."

"Hell no, they'd need an army for that, not a student," Croc inspires. "I've seen her in action. Comic characters get based on that crazy-baby!"

"Exactly, they're students in training. Bedriška was an accident they're office they still don't know about. They were on a training mission, they over-stepped their directive and died on the ferry."

"So, they were like on a school trip?" Izzy asks.

"Bedi would have been taken more seriously, she was a past agent of theirs. I searched Russian colleges, a lot easier to get into than Russian secret service sites. Both of them are SVR students. Their handler would have no doubt been a fellow college student being tested as a project manager. Now busy trying to clean it up; another training mission."

"School trip went wrong for them," Izzy says.

"But a clean up means to get the man who got away. They'll be after Big Dog," Croc surmises.

"He has a school trip trying to kill him?" Izzy asks.

"It opens a door for us," Dwight throws out.

"What door?" Izzy asks.

"How did they get given this job? Where did it come from? Them chasing Dog tells us who they are?"

"So he's bait?" Izzy asks.

"Because their team are dead on the ferry," Croc offers.

"That put's Big Dog at double risk," Izzy says.

"And their controller doesn't even know Dog is a black man yet. You see how important it is to post reports regularly, why Kieron and Hunter do it on the move. Why Prisha stacks her phone to send when it can; she is good," Dwight says.

"Send, in case we are killed, right?" Izzy asks.

"Exactly," he replies very coldly." Dwight approaches the board; it is very serious now.

"But why are we interested in these students?" Izzy asks.

"I reckon its end-of-term exorcises in the field. Picking up on suspicions and low level crime. They must have thought they had found themselves a drug smuggler with Big Dog because he was black. But they didn't know so they couldn't call that in and get it wrong," Dwight explains.

"So what?" Izzy fires.

"So idiot students may have Kieron and Hunter. Use every piece of information. The board," Dwight says turning back to it. "Ferry needs a line to Flower Girl and she needs a line sideways to SVR, the Dog lines go to Tallinn," Dwight explains.

"We need a bigger board," Izzy says, having trouble with the cards. "Then I need a line taking Bedi and her Cruise ship, down to St Petersburg."

"Fantastic, except we don't know whether she'll ever arrive in St Petersburg. The student college will be building a spider-like this," Dwight says, to pull her up again.

"But they have no way of knowing who we are?" Croc says quietly questioning himself.

"No. If they have another team watching the art, at some point, the idiots will join the teams together," Dwight says.

"Three teams. This team on Big Dog. The team that has Hunter, and the art team," Croc concludes.

"Then they join them," Izzy says.

"No." Dwight informs them. "Then it gets taken off them and dealt with by proper agents and handlers. Then we're in real trouble. Find who engaged the intelligence students and why, find the team on our boys and find where the art went before they find us."

That hits home. It is not just about making a board.

"We need to warn Bedi too," Izzy says.

Dwight looks at his watch.

"Ship docks in two hours, let her sleep. It might be the last sleep she gets in a long time. And we're going to be up all night. That's managing, not panicking."

"Trying to keep them all alive?" Izzy asks.

77 – STAYING ALIVE

Bedriška's cruise ship can just see the coast either side as the sky turns blue revealing shapes and waiting for the sun to rise. Sailing slowly up the right-hand fork at the top of the Baltic there is a small but substantial island on the left and mainland Russia on the right. Soon they will be passing the Peterhof area as they head towards Marine Façade the cruise area of St Petersburg docks. This part of the sea is like a small appendix at the top right the Baltic just past Estonia. The brightly lit ship is still the main glow, awake and standing by for guests to wake for breakfast.

Wearing a stolen officer's uniform, Bedi leaves the ship's huge laundry on deck 6. She walks out into the main working highway known as i95. Seeing another officer approaching, she drops down a deck using the crew stairs to avoid them. She looks up the stairs to see if they have followed her. She walks confidently down this lower corridor of the crew quarters. The walls are plainly panelled and the carpet cheaper and less exciting than the guest areas, but they are nice. All the doors say 'Ents Manager', which means they are all doors allocated to the entertainment department. They won't come out of their rooms for a disturbance; they sleep like logs. Bedi has purloined a two-stripe officer's uniform meaning a fairly permanent feature onboard who should be known by most. A higher grade would be known by all so she has rank to give orders, but could be unknown. However, the last person she wants to see is another fellow officer. She carries her small bag in her hand, not slung over her uniform jacket.

She arrives at midships, an open area which could open sea doors on port or starboard. One of the few areas you can walk from one side of the ship to the other. Neither doors are open because she is one deck above sea level; the deck she wants because she knows a door will be open. In front, the opposite side of the bulk head from where she came, is the door to the medical area; she hopes she won't end up in there. She turns down the steel stairs. This low in the thirty seven tonnes of steel she has no cell-phone service and no one from CSCI head office can get through, no matter how hard they try but she does not want a ringtone drawing attention. She lifts her cell and turns it off. Now Miami stands no chance of contacting her. All they have is a text saying 'awake'.

Russia–0530hrs   Miami–2130hrs   **At sea from Cuba–2130hrs**

Macey's ship has left Cuba and the team are all late for diner. With a huge sense of relief at being safe, Prisha and Macey finish getting ready for a late evening out together on their ship. It is on a sea day from Cuba, and there will be another sea day tomorrow up to Charleston. The remnants of room service lay on the table in the middle of the living area. Macey is in her bedroom strapping her shoes on and Prisha in hers is applying lipstick again. Dressed for an evening in the warm Caribbean they look totally different to Bedi operating in the cold Baltic.

"Do you think my lips are too thin?" Prisha asks Macey. "Lips are fuller in America."

Macey is looking at her cell and reading.

"I could get them done," Prisha says, turning to see Macey is not paying her any attention.

"You're not listening."

"Dwight's sent me a text from Ricky; 'pologising 'bout his exposé in the catalogue. Says he never had a clue that I never knew. He admits he feels destroyed at the pain I must be in. Says he's gutted and feels he needs to be here with me."

"That's nice."

"It would have been nicer if he hadn't told the world, but it seems the rest of the world knew anyhow. Did you?"

A knock at the door saves Prisha.

Macey moves to it but waits before opening the door. She flattens herself to the wall remembering something the agents said in the office once about assassins who knock and shoot.

"It's Zack."

"Zack who?"

"Open the door. I got Billy with me and he'll chew it open."

Macey opens the door and the two men come in. The door is closed behind them.

"Bit hot to be that formal," Prisha says, looking at them both in jackets.

Billy parts his jacket and shows his gun.

"Could get hotter," he smiles.

Helsinki–0700hrs	Miami-2300hrs	At sea from Cuba–2300hrs

Big Dog wakes, not at sea. He is in Tallinn in his nest on the floor. He stretches as he sits up. He checks his watch and stands, looking at the perfect bed.

"Hope everyone else in the hotel slept well," he says to himself sarcastically. He walks to the door to start removing the bottles, but stops. He decides to use the bathroom first. He turns the shower on.

"Nice," he says to himself as he looks around the bathroom. "How the rich live."

He dials Dwight. Croc answers.

"I get the assistant?" Dog moans.

"You had students chase you down in Helsinki, but here, you got the head of technology, bro," Croc boasts.

"Don't you bro' me. I just checkin' in. None of my bottles got jingled."

"Jingled?"

"Yeah, jingled. Ain't I up near Father Christmas land?"

"What did you drink last night?" Croc asks.

"I ate me a fine old elk burger."

"You what? You ain't right. You've been poisoned. Them students must 'ave got you with their 'steely knives'."

"No one pricked me, junior. And what's wid da students?"

"The two peep's who tried to kill you on the boat, they were trainee Russian agents."

"No way." Dog measures, then it hits him. "Two?"

"The flower girl. Trainee KGB."

"No way."

"But only trainees. Keep your eyes open. Maybe leave the hotel, have breakfast on the other side of town."

Russia–0700hrs   **Miami-2300hrs**   At sea from Cuba–2300hrs

"Good job," Dwight says to Croc as the call ends in Miami. "No point in panicking him."

"Hard not to tell him everything."

"He ain't ready for that. Tell him what he needs to know. Move on, ask for a report, but my guess is there's nothing new. He needs a gun. He needs to lay low until pick-up time. Now, what's new wid you?"

"Flower Girl was training with SVR, the foreign

Intelligence Agency. They seem to be second to the main intelligence agency, the GRU. GRU is more powerful and respected. Then there is the FBS, the KGB, and the FSKN who are the main directorate for drug control."

"Croc, nice as it is, enough -"

"The police caught Kieron and Hunter red-handed at an art dealer's private apartment. Seems schools out, and they have ended up at a low-level detention place out of town."

"They would have been out of a low-level place straight away," Dwight argues.

"Hang on, Kieron's there to find an art thief. Not get home. You know what they're both like. What if they're staying at the hotel to find information? Reverse interrogation?"

"That's a heap o' croc. Now you know how he got that name, Dwight," Izzy says.

"No. It's good. You might have something," Dwight says inspired.

Russia–0705hrs   Miami–2305hrs   At sea from Cuba–2305hrs

The ship has slowed down. Bedi stands at the open door, just above sea level. Several technical crew stand by the huge exterior hull door, and the senior mechanic stands by the control to close it again.

Bedi gets closer to the edge as the small tug powers alongside the ship. The Pilot stands on the edge of the tug ready to jump on board. Every port insists on a pilot, not just Russia. The pilot will assist the Captain taking 'his' ship, into the 'Pilot's' dock. It is not just that the Pilot knows the waters and the traffic but if things go wrong and a disaster occurs anywhere, in panic language can resort to being local. In those situations the Pilot would be able to understand. Below the grade of Pilot, fewer and fewer staff would speak good English, and even fewer as you get to labouring grades. Small boat handlers and others on the sea may have no English. The tug makes contact, bouncing on the side of the ship. The pilot jumps and is pulled onboard.

"Show him up to the bridge," Bedi demands and she turns and steps on the tug in the split second it takes to pull away; an already effected motion. The door of the ship dutifully closes, even if the mechanics are surprised. But, how could they question a superior double-pip officer? Even if they had the chance to think.

On the tugboat, there is only the driver and one very puzzled assistant who does not speak English and does not know she is Russian. The assistant is knocked down and out. The driver turns and he is floored. Bedi scrambles for some rope and ties both men, legs and arms. There is no need to gag them; they cannot be heard at sea. She turns the tug off-target and aims at the working docks of St Petersburg, then ties the wheel. Next, she takes off her overdressing. She is not going ashore as an officer. Bedi is now in her jeans and tee-shirt. She pulls the gun from her bag and dons a very stylish looking jacket to conceal the weapon in the back of her waist belt. The bag is slung behind her back. She steals money from both men and folds it into her pocket. Taking control, she powers the boat and broadsides it to the fishing dock. There is no chance of it stopping. It is going to crash. Quickly she ties it to go on wide circles out to sea. She pulls the accelerator and leaps out onto the dock before the almost stationary propellers take effect again. The boat powers off out to sea and she switches her phone back on and texts 'in Russia.' She cuts up past sheds with nets and chains and crosses a car park. At the last car, she smashes the window and is in. The alarm is disengaged, and the car started. She is on the road before any form of authority could be alerted.

Approaching the main city, the view changes from the grey tower blocks to the River Neva, alongside which the historic city was built. Unlike any visiting agent, she speaks the language perfectly, she knows the city back to front and knows the geography in-depth, such as Lake Ladoga, where the river starts. She knows the smaller towns along the river: Shlisselburg, Kirovsk and Otradnoye, and also small things like the locals often call the Baltic the White Sea, because the Black Sea is on the other side of the country. However, no one will ever doubt she is from Russia. That is not her problem.

Her cell-phone rings. She flicks it to the speaker. It is Dwight.

"Bedi. Dog avoided a hit on the ferry. Two young SVR student agents. Not sure they had a plan."

"Maybe standard training. They watch at airports for suspicious-looking tourists," she explains.

"Would a student team have got H & K?" Asks Dwight.

"If end of training. All students out on pretend mission to be assessed. They would also look for jobs on police reports."

"The boys might be having an easy ride?"

"No. Students love to pass lead up to main agency. They will look for special commendation."

"If school is out, be careful at immigration," Dwight says.

"I am in city, nice weather, no rain. I will cross

bridge and stop for Russian breakfast."

"How d'you do that? The ship only just arrived in Russia," Croc says out loud.

"I not stupid, Croc. I learn from very best, then kill them." Bedi ends the call.

Russia–0830hrs   Miami-0030hrs   At sea from Cuba–0030hrs

Dwight swings around in his chair.

"I'm thinking Croc is right. Even if the top agency took K&H, they'd be out. They're smart. So, they don't wanna be out. They're with trainees and they are doing reverse interrogation. But the Russians, seeing an ex-agent like Bedriška, might change everything. It's time to get them home before bigger boys do start playing. I've got a plan."

78 – CHURCHES AND REVOLUTIONS

Helsinki/Russia – 1015hrs   Miami-0215hrs   at sea to – 0215hrs

Bedi approaches the huge church which is now effectively a museum for tourists; Our Saviour of the Spilled Blood. It has large round turrets, topped by huge blue and golden onion shapes. It is a typical Russian Orthodox church, but larger and surrounded by tourist vendors.

Bedi checks her watch and enters. Inside she wanders around, endlessly circling the mosaics walls and pillars. She thinks she sees two men keeping watch on her and she stops twice at the fenced-off pavement. It is where Alexander-the-2nd was supposed to have been slain and his blood was spilt. Why people want to see blood on pavement is beyond her. She has seen too much.

She is brushed by a man who stands with his back to her. Slowly she turns a little, staying close to him while looking at the montage of religious mosaic figures. The whole church is mosaic.

"Where are my friends?"

"Your man in Miami found them. I get you there."

"I need three guns and a knife."

"Everyone know you in town after movie-star entrance at docks, you never do anything small. Now you watched."

"I see, they amateurs."

"I think good men. You are legend here. Today, even bigger legend."

"I need weapons."

"Miami paid. We get you guns."

"Where are my friends?"

"At government office in Malaya Street two blocks down from Catherine's Palace. I put you on a tour."

"I am not tourist."

"You are today. You dropped something," he says, as he steps away from her.

"Oh, look," a woman says softly to her husband, bending down to pick up the slip of paper.

Bedi turns, but she has been beaten to it. Knowing it is hers, she looks at the woman who is not thinking of giving it up.

"Mine," Bedi says.

"What is?" The woman asks.

'She is going to make a meal of this; that might be perfect for me but very silly for her', Bedi thinks.

"I dropped it," Bedi says softly.

"What is it?" the woman says, holding it down by her side.

'She is going to keep it', Bedi surmises. 'This can only end badly for her'.

"That is mine," Bedi demands quietly. "Please give it back without a fuss."

"Tell me what it is then?" The woman says, matching her quiet volume.

"Does it matter, it is mine," Bedi says, leaning into her. The woman is making herself look more and more like Bedi's contact in Russia.

"You want it, what is it?"

"Ticket, my ticket."

They now have the attention of the two men watching, who must be thinking this is a handover. That confirms they are agents. The church is so full, anything could be done close up, but it would immediately feature on social media. Police and agents avoid that so Bedi smiles to acknowledge she knows they are there. They start to advance through the tight crowd.

"Give me my ticket now, police are coming," Bedi says as they start to struggle, Bedi is ignoring her and looking at the agents. The woman copies as people take out their cell-phones.

Bedi leans in and whispers, "If you look at the ticket, I will have to kill you."

The woman checks the ticket. Now she is a liability, she can break the mission open by revealing Bedi's destination. The two agents arrive, Bedi takes the ticket in the confusion, shoots the man and the woman and pushes the bodies into each of the agents. Their hands are covered in blood.

"Killers," she shouts.

Bedi is away. The crowd is thick with screams. They back off from the two men and the dead 'tourists'. It forms a tight circumference hard to break through for the men who are now on everyone's cell-phone.

Moving towards the exit, Bedriška feels a pickpocket taking advantage of the distraction and her movement. Instinctively she turns, breaks his wrist as she pulls him in close. She takes her money back, plus every wallet he has in his stash pocket inside his lose denim jacket. She drops him dead and leaves.

Outside, Bedi stays close to a tourist stall as she reads her ticket. It is a full-day tour of Peter and Paul's Fortress and Catherine's Palace. On Palace is written 'half-day, join Peter and Paul's Fortress, coach park, Coach 19. She knows where that is, she knows her way around St Petersburg very well, but the question is, is she being followed? She rings Miami.

"Dwight, I see four follow me. I already made mess in church."

"Lose them. I found K&H. I need you at government buildings near the palace by about 1845. Arranging everything now, uniform, official communications for you to transfer them, you should be able to walk in and out."

"If not I have gun-fight at the Russian Corral?" she asks.

"Lose your shadow," he says, signing off.

The two agents she saw separately inside the church are still behind her, still outside the building featuring in all the tourists' happy photos despite being part bloodied. Another two are to her left along the row of tourist stalls. That leads to Mikhailovsky Square where tourists go to see the statue of Pushkin and the theatre. In front, she sees and hears a female guide in a drab coat, who holds a number 14 on a handheld paddle-like sign. She wears her public address system like a flak jacket. The group of tourists around her are cruisers, they all have blue circular stickers with the number 14 somewhere about their chest.

"Follow me," the guide says.

Bedi accelerates to join tour 14, and follows towards the meadows she knows is the Field of Mars. Perfect cover and the right direction, plus she is now wearing a blue circle with a number 14.

When they reach the Eternal Flame in the middle of 'Field of Mars', she is not listening to the guide. She knows it was lit to commemorate the fighters in the revolution. She concentrates on the agents who surround her, and she knows she cannot take the bridge across to the fortress now, she might never make it to the other side. Four agents are too many. She follows group 14 into the Summer Gardens which were based on the gardens of the Palace of Versailles, in France. The walk through the middle can be a very relaxing day out if one is not on an assassin's list. They stop as the path parts to spread around a square of fountains.

"These fountains came from London." She hears the guide say but she feels a man too close behind her.

"Best you come with us," he says.

Her elbow snaps back hitting him in the diaphragm and buckling him. As he gasps for air, she walks him backwards and sits him on the bench. But, as she turns to sit next to him, she snaps his neck. Her arm falls affectionately around his shoulder but to hold his limp head up. She watches the other three who are planning to pounce. She wags their colleagues head about and smiles.

Group 14 walk off and she is up and accelerates to catch them. Two agents rush to slip in front, leaving one behind. She stops abruptly before the front two get to their point positions. They do not see her tackle into the rear guard and strike him dead. Walking fast in and out of tourists. She winds her way back to the road having lost the remaining two agents. She runs across the bridge to Peter and Paul Fortress and walks swiftly through the fortress to the far car park and coach stop.

Dwight turns around to Croc in the Miami office. It is late and it will be a long night ahead of them.

"I need more time," Croc insists.

"You don't have more time."

"Russian secret service has a tough digital system to crack, plus, I don't speak Russian."

"Great, you got it all in hand."

"No, it's not," Croc panics.

79 – TUNNELS AND PALACES

Day9- **Helsinki/Russia – 1100hrs**   Miami-0300hrs   at sea from Cuba– 0300hrs

Tallinn glows with colour in the very hot summer months. Guests mingle, enjoying the city, the beer and the local food. It could be the most popular of all Baltic cruise stops, with around six cruise ships a day when it is busy. It is also a destination for bachelor parties because it is cheap, so the nearby airport is busy. Everyone is casually dressed except for Big Dog who has his signature black leather jacket on. The square excites him, and he looks at the restaurants offering strange kinds of food. He finds an offering he now knows, Traditional Elk Sandwiches.

"You got one of those to go?" He asks the man out front trying to capture business.

"Of course, sir."

"Ready to go now?"

"Step inside."

Inside, 'traditional' is like going back in time. If he thought the hotel was strange because they were in a version of historic dress, this is back in time without a DeLorean. It goes more than a few steps further. The staff are traditionally dressed, the ales are made with roots like turnips and potatoes, honey ale and birch wood. It is a barn with sawdust and leaves on the floor, but his sandwich is as quick as his local fast food joint in Miami.

Having a liking for elk, he enjoys the chunky sandwich as he follows directions to the tunnel. Why he must go into a tunnel to get a gun is beyond him.

Down under the city wall, next to a road and hidden by another wall is the modern glass entrance that could easily be missed if you weren't looking for it. The flags and signs certainly didn't work for him. Now he has found it he thinks the whole place must be some kind of joke; it is called 'Kiek in the Kock'.

Having paid his entrance and tunnels tour fee, Big Doc waits in an area with interactive television screens, pictures and models that show the history of the tunnels. He shakes his head; surely if there is a tour they'll tell you all that. Some people are already swaddled under blankets. He does not know why, it certainly isn't cold. Though they are unlikely to be dressed like him underneath their blankets. He checks his watch, he is hitting his rendezvous time, noon. He's taking the next tour. No one in the waiting room looks like a killing KGB agent, but neither did the flower girl.

"Please take a blanket," the guide shouts with a pile she is now handing out.

"Do I need one?" Dog asks, trying to avoid it.

"Yes," is not meant to be an abrupt order.

She is gone before he can give it back. He unfolds it carefully in case the gun is in the folds and follows the group through the door. Inside, are a lot of long tunnels only lit by temporary lights. He can't believe how well the floor is cemented level as they were dug in 1686. He remembers that date because they sure are old and they sure don't look it. The soundtrack, low in the background, has gunfire and the occasional bomb going off. The guide explains they were improved in the second world war, then again by the Russians in the 1970's Cold War. 'Maybe that why they're cold', he thinks, glad of the blanket. Some parts of the tunnel are graffitied, but he doesn't recognise any handles. None of the crews from Miami have ever been down there. The guide announces that the tunnels were taken over by the punk movement in the 1980s. Big Dog toys with whether this would make a great pad. The long, straight, flat tunnel was for rolling ammunition down and that could be handy. The concrete stanchions that jut out from the walls are just wide enough for one dude to take cover and shoot. But that always works both ways. It didn't help Troy against Bedriška. He is lagging behind his tour group thinking and planning.

"Your gun, take it! Now catch your group up," a man says, handing him a small handgun.

"Where you come from?" Dog says, annoyed he has missed another approach.

Real gunfire makes both of them jump back behind the concrete stanchions.

"They were watching you."

"Thanks."

The man turns to go, Big Dog looks at the gun.

"Hey, hang! This ain't a gun. I need a hose."

"Hose?"

"Something that sprays. A fire hose. Oil gush."

Bullets reign down the tunnel at them. Big Dog instinctively squeezes hard behind the wall built exactly for that.

"See, that what I mean. A hose."

They both shoot back to slow them down.

"Don't shoot any cruisers."

"What do they look like?"

"They don't carry guns," Dog says, squatting.

Big Dog drops to the floor and peeps around the corner over the sight of his gun while bullets fly. He shoots, aiming a little to the right of the muzzle flashes. A man drops and only one attacker is left.

"Let's go," the man says.

"Where?" Dog asks, seeing the deep dark hole he is suggesting. "Ain't there giant spiders down there like she said, size of plates?"

"I deliver your gun, not give a tour. Now catch up with your group or follow me. I'm not dying here."

Dog crosses over.

"No, no, no. I can't. Not with giant spiders."

"You never see them, too dark."

"Fucking no way."

"You want to die? They have hoses."

"Only one left, I can hear him running."

Big Dog rolls back, flat to the floor and shoots back. The man falls.

"Hey, can you get them to turn the soundtrack down back there." He hears the guide shout back. Dog gets up and steps over the dead man taking his gun, he turns back to his gun provider.

"This is a hose. That's my group. You can keep the spiders."

Dog joins the group, the man vanishes into the dark.

80 – ST CATHERINE'S PALACE

St Petersburg, Russia – 1545hrs   Miami-0745hrs   Caribbean sea– 0745hrs

Bedi enters the Palace and follows her group up the stairs. She is checking the guards they have here, the government building is just minutes away. First, she needs weapons. Somehow this must fit into some grand plan, so she looks up and follows her group. For all the time she spent in St Petersburg she had never seen this palace. She knew it was a fake, like the paintings she is chasing, like everything in life. Fake or hype or both. She knew this palace was bombed to the ground by the Germans in World War Two and was rebuilt for the tourists. However, it is impressive, it is quite special. She turns and takes a picture one in front, one behind, her actions are touristy, but she now sends Dwight both snaps, those following her, and those in front.

A man in a wheelchair is arguing at the bottom of the stairs. He had bought a tour ticket, only to find there is no wheelchair access.

"You only go up if he walks up the stairs or you can carry him," she hears the monitor say. Bedi turns around in shock. She has lived away from St Petersburg and had forgotten how unforgiving they can be. The woman is small and pathetic, there is no way she can carry her husband. They are not getting in. Bedi turns, marches down the stairs and pulls the man out of the chair bends her knees and lifts him over her shoulders. He squeals with pain.

"Shut up."

She too can be a hard Russian. She marches up the stairs and through the crowd, who are busy looking at photographs set in plaster mouldings with vases sat on them.

"Move, move, please move," she demands, as she goes through them.

"Do you want a hand?" A man asks.

"No. I do for tours all day long."

The man walks on, not sure whether to be puzzled or insulted. Bedi folds her load to the floor and holds him as his legs obviously can take no weight. His wife is helped up the stairs with his wheelchair by another tourist who opens the seat.

"Good. We swap on way down. I take chair," she says, as she sits him in the chair and turns to get in front of this new group, but remain behind her old group.

The first room has a 'head' dining room table. It only works for the diners sat on the inner side of the flattened moon shape. The wall candle holders are ornate and painted gold. They all have light bulbs on them but produce little light. The place is an ideal observation trap because everyone is photographing the room back and forth with their cameras. They are all cruisers with their give-away coloured circles with tour-numbers on. Bedi is looking for anyone who might be following her. Or be in front and might be turning to watch her. She also has a new task, to collect as many coloured cruise numbers as she can. She needs at least four. The first one comes off a handbag without effort or commotion. It appears that some cruise guests do not wish to stick the numbers to their clothes, so use them to attract thieves to their handbag.

Next is the grand ballroom to which the table in the previous room should belong. The ceilings are immaculately painted, enough to give any renowned fresco artist a run. These paintings are at least honest; they were obviously painted by a team, to order, and in the last century post-WW2. No sole artist could take credit.

There are ornate windows every few feet down the complete length of each side, between each is a repeat of the candle holders with electric light bulbs. It is a feast of gold plaster carvings and mirrors. Bedi has her phone on constantly and it twists it fully back and front even if she stays looking forward. There is so much to see in the palace such actions are excusable. Bedi however, is filming the crowds of people and Miami is watching even if she is not.

St Petersburg, Russia – 1555hrs   **Miami-0755hrs**   Caribbean sea– 0755hrs

Izzy sits with Croc watching Bedi's live feed of the golden palace. Croc is still trying to break into any system that can send a movement order, to an address he still does not know. It seems an impossible task with little time to go. Izzy is worried by a man she spots in the room.

"I don't mind bling but this crib is bad taste. I mean sad bad, not wicked. Point me right," Izzy asks Bedi via the video call.

Her camera moves slowly to the right, her body does not. She moves enough for it to make sense, though any camera angle can be forgiven.

"Hold it there," Izzy says.

She does, Bedi holds her position.

"Does Croc have my paperwork. Time is running out." Bedi asks and they hear in Miami.

"I know," says Croc.

"That guy. He seems more interested in you than the room, and it is a pretty impressive room," Izzy says.

"I'm impressive even in this room. But, I see him," I am not stupid. Does 'stupid' have my papers?

"Stupid?" Croc demands angrily.

"You will be stupid if I left in Government building not getting out. Get this sorted."

St Petersburg, Russia – 1615hrs   Miami–0815hrs   Caribbean sea– 0815hrs

The rooms of Catherine's Palace become repetitive. There is another almost moon-shaped dining table. The whole side of the house is room after room sitting off a long corridor. Unlike the concrete tunnel in Tallinn, the Palace Tunnel is bright with gold square arches, one at each change of room. Again, walls to be used as protection in conflict, designed for the same reason as in the tunnel. It was also built as an unnecessary show of power and wealth by a German Princess who took Russia and was set on controlling as much of the world as her armies could conquer.

It is obvious from the room's width, compared with the ballroom, that these rooms only use the front half of the house. Behind the back walls must be servant's preparation areas or dressing areas.

With one eye on the man behind, and ignoring the repetitive cherubs, she watches for others now with the aid of Izzy in Miami.

"Bet it's hard to keep warm in winter," she hears Izzy say.

Bedi ignores the chat. Izzy needs to learn it is work. Plus, she is getting annoyed. She hates this side of Russia and she has now been subjected to the whole half an hour of the tour and yet learnt nothing. All she knows is where her two colleagues are being held. She will have to go in alone. The tour is complete and she is now at the end near the red stairs, the stairs no one wants to go down because it seemed far too short. There is a man by a double opened door, and he simply lifts the rope barrier as she approaches and she slips in. The man who had been behind her follows in and the rope is re-connected. This is either friend or foe, kill or be killed.

The man who was following her introduces himself.

"Danut, you never see me, behind you," he smiles feeling very cocky.

'I saw him from here in Miami,' Izzy shouts in her headphones. Bedi pulls the headphones from her phone, making the sound live.

"Say again, Izzy."

"Even I saw you from Miami!"

"Speak later, you work harder." Bedriška ends the call to concentrate.

The Danut's face drops from a smile to one of operational glumness.

"My name Bertoff. We give you knife, three good guns, attaché case for them, and a senior FOS uniform and identification card of FOS agent. Plus papers we make as reserve. That office is of lower security, you should be able to walk anywhere and confuse them for enough time to get the two men out."

"That easy?" Bedi asks.

"For Bedriška, yes. You are legend. Your office should do proper papers on-line and official order. You go in and out. I think, easier without guns," he suggests.

"You think? No guns."

"Problem is security x-ray. Discover you at entrance, job get hard," Danut says from behind as he joins Bertoff.

"You think?"

"Yes."

Danut produces a belt with a pistol from a box on the table behind them.

"Uniform pistol. That you can take in. Often not worn, but you collect prisoners so gun expected. You demand."

"I demand?"

"Wrist bands, leg bands with half stride. They would be expected," Danut says explaining the uniform.

"One gun, walk-in, walk-out?" She pesters, questioning the plan again. "Where am I going?"

"Building, a few blocks away. Not special government building so we are sure they not held by any special force. So, you get in and out as visiting officer to collect detainees. Provided you not recognised," Danut says, and he is very serious. "Because if they know you…"

"Yes. I am target practice for any agent who want medal."

"If online orders arrive, easy…" Beretoff adds.

"If! You have sent papers?" She asks.

"We send Mr Crocodile in your office correct orders in Russian language. He get into Russian computers, we cannot and if we did we would be traced," Danut says.

"OK, the plan is; request to release your men to the superior agency for interrogation. Here your copies of entry paper and transfer paper."

"They not release my partners unless they have had orders online," Bedi says.

"Then you must shoot everybody."

"Thanks for your help Danut."

"I will be outside in car. Unless…"

"Unless what?"

"Unless shooting start."

"One gun," Bedi says. "If they don't demand to keep it at the main door."

"I know," Bertoff admits. "I give extra, I put blade on handle of gun, lay it down on security belt, blade not seen."

"My risk. One; I am recognised. Two; papers not there. Three; blade seen on X-ray. Four; I get bored," she lists.

"Bored?" He asks in shock.

"I joke."

"I trust your office. You turn left, downstairs, left again and they are on left. Walk out. Go home," Bertoff says showing her a sketch of the layout.

"I think only one gun," Danut says.

"I can make a mess without gun."

81 – A PROBLEM?

St Petersburg, Russia – 1815hrs   Miami- 1015hrs   **Caribbean sea– 1015hrs**

Dwight has eventually softened and given Macey, Ricky's phone number. The morning started with angry texts between ship and shore, then the texts calmed down, and for two hours, on and off Macey has been on the phone to Ricky. A very expensive phone call using the 'as-sea' service to call. Other online media has not been considered because this is their first real meeting.

"I'm telling the most dangerous man in the world my life story. I know you are making notes," she tells Ricky with a huge smile he can't see.

"I'm not dangerous."

"You're a journalist. You tell the world. Once it's out I can't get it back," she says.

"No notes, I'm listening," he says.

"Men don't listen."

"I'd listen to you all day and all night. I'll never be sorry enough," Ricky says.

"Are we going to do something today?" Prisha asks, daring to interrupt.

"Please go, enjoy the ship," Ricky says.

"I'll might ring you," she says.

"When?"

"At least thirty minutes. I have to charge my cell."

"Promise?"

"Maybe. I've not forgiven you for publishing my life story yet. A story I never knew."

"One, I didn't know you hadn't been told and two, what if they were never going to tell you. I did."

"If who weren't going to tell me?"

"Everyone who knew; Mary, Croc, Izzy…."

Macey hangs up and turns to Prisha.

"Men always promise at the beginning," Prisha says. "But in fairness, we marry them and try and change them. So they say."

"I'm certainly not thinking of marriage!"

"No one does until they do."

Macey puts her cell-phone on charge, then the two girls walk out. Macey turns and looks back at it.

"Leave it," says Prisha.

"Did you know?" Macey asks her.

Prisha waits fighting for the right phrasing.

"I knew what was in the brochure just before you."

Clem is on the top deck playing short football in the Caribbean sun. The two women watch and cheer on, relaxed. Who knew cruising could be so much fun and encourage you to do things you never would? Clem looks like he has never played the game before in his life.

St Petersburg, Russia – 1825hrs   Miami- 1025hrs   Caribbean sea– 1025hrs

The front entrance of the Russian Government Building sits on a corner. It has six steps up under a permanent awning. The buildings behind are far more boring, though no doubt efficient. They are a disinteresting dirty dark yellow colour, and form an L-shape, with an arch joining the two sides. Bedriška and the driver sit in a hired black SUV parked outside.

"I go in front, exit might not be same, watch for me," Bedriška relays to her driver while she studies the complex.

"Cameras will have seen us. We sit here, we become suspicious, more people involved."

"OK, we go."

Danut, the driver gets out, walks around to her door and opens it. She marches up the steps. He waits dutifully by the car, the bag of guns on the car seat within his reach, the window open.

A security guard stands inside the building door and he salutes Bedriška, the stripes on her uniform command that respect. She hands him the paper, puts her gun on the x-ray belt and walks through. The x-ray officer reaches to take the gun, she snaps to get there first.

"Collect gun on exit," he says.

"No. I collect two prisoners. I keep gun, she says buckling it up. At the moment, she has a gun and a blade and stands inside the building. If they disagree, they will both have their throats quietly cut and she will have limited time. They nod between them and allow the gun.

Bedriška turns and goes straight for the stairs on her left. At the bottom, she ignores the guard at the door and uses her card. The door fails to open. The guard turns to help.

"It is broken," she exclaims.

"No," the guard says.

"Try yours."

The guard pulls his card and tries the door, it clicks open. She holds him under the neck and by his ear. He passes out. She leaves him seated and goes through the door. If he is seen, she will be foraging for weapons to stay alive.

The first office door is open. Two officers sit playing cards.

"What is this!" She fires.

They both stand to attention. She is far senior to them. She sees their guns on the windowsill behind them as she shows them the transfer paper.

"You not get orders?"

They nod.

"Are prisoners ready to travel?"

The two men shake their heads.

"Why not?"

"Orders just arrived; we were..."

"What!" She demands.

"Card game..."

"Get them now! I am expected in Moscow."

She hands them the leg restraints and the two guards rush out and unlock the next door. They bundle the two men up while she stands out of sight in the corridor, watching for other guards, or a commotion outside where she has left the sleeping guard.

The two prisoners are dragged out in the leg restraints. But they are the wrong two prisoners.

"Not these two!" She screams knowing time is running out. She should have killed the guard outside the door as he will be waking soon.

The guards stand in shock. She indicates to send the unwanted prisoners back. The door is closed, and she waits for them to respond. They point downstairs and she knows that as soon as they go through that door they will find the sleeping guard. She holds a firm punishing gaze at them, ensuring her body is in the way and not moving. They back off and go for another internal set of stairs and she has a sense of relief.

Orders are explained to the two guards on the lower floor who check their computer in haste. Hunter and Kieron are brought out.

"We look for new leg restraints," the guard offers as the ones she supplied were used upstairs. Based on cable ties, they are not reusable and have to be cut off. She still has the wrist ties which the guards want to use.

"No, you march them to vehicle. I walk behind, we tie to seat belt," she demands. "Go."

The two men are taken up the prison stairs to the door. They keep a pace knowing she is moving them fast for a reason. They are marched to her car by the guards. Bedriška behind them. The bag of guns is taken by the driver ready for use. The officers cable tie the prisoner's wrists to the seat belt. Even if they discharge the safety belt, they cannot run. The two men are useless until she releases them.

An alarm sounds in the building and the two guards look at Bedriška suspiciously. She puts them both down with shot to their hips. Bedriška backs in, door open, her gun trained at the building. Last, his gun trained on the building as cover, Danut jumps in the vehicle and guns it away.

"Road to airport, fast," she demands as gun shots follow them until they are out of range. "We hope they go to airport. We turn off road and find way to dock."

She spins around with a blade and cuts Hunter's hand ties. She gives him the blade to free Kieron.

"Thank you?" Kieron says.

"We expected you earlier, but thanks."

Kieron grabs her head and gives her forehead a quick thank you kiss.

"Inappropriate. It will be in my report." She hands them guns then sits facing the. "Danut. Faster, get us to cruise ship. Fast."

"No," Kieron interrupts. "The real art is sent here. The dealer who had us arrested, he buys the art from Bentley once it has been accurately copied. They thought we were customs."

"Maybe thieves. They're shit interrogators that 5th Directorate KGB you were in. Bunch of softies," Hunter teases.

"They not KGB. They training. You caught in training programme."

"Whatever. Now we've been sprung they'll know we're serious and we're onto them," Hunter states.

"The art will vanish," Kieron says.

"I should have left you there."

"We go back to the dealer," Hunter states firmly.

Bedriška cuts him off. "No. We go home, I now at big risk in St Petersburg."

"This dealer's the key. So called legal art purchases protected by guards, then the police, then agents. They rang England and were told the paperwork was all signed. The man they rang was Bentley, we denied knowing him," Kieron explains.

"Yeah. He's gone down in my estimation; I wanted to finish the annoying guy before," Hunter says.

"But, there is bounty on my head in Russia," Bedriška says. She pokes the driver. "Tell them."

"Yes. She is famous, she will be killed," Danut explains.

"Bedi, you can sit in the car. We need someone outside."

"No," the driver says. "You do not understand. As soon as they know you escape, they will know it is famous Bedriška. You all will be killed on sight."

"I already been in Russia too long. I will not be allowed to get out," Bedi says.

"One stop. We go back to Anoataly Istov," Kieron demands.

"Istov?" Bedi screams. "Istov? Yes. We go to him first!" Bedriška says now full of vengeance.

82 – THE REAL PROBLEM

St Petersburg, Russia – 2045hrs   Miami- 1245hrs   Caribbean sea– 1245hrs

It is evening when the black SUV pulls up at the art dealer's block. There are two guards outside, lit from behind by the light of the reception area.

"I did not sign up for this," Danut says.

"Suck it up and invoice for it, buddy," Hunter says.

"I know this man," Bedi says.

Hunter opens the door for Bedi. Kieron stands by the driver's door until he gets out.

The four walk straight past the two guards, who salute Bedi's senior Russian uniform that she still wears. When behind them, htye take them down and drag them inside steeling their standard equipment including cable ties and guns. The elevator takes them straight up to the penthouse suite.

They exit the lift, drop both of the guards inside the door, pull their radios off and the driver cable ties them. Kieron notices one of the pinioned guards look up and recognise Bedi. He shits himself with fear.

"Don't kill me, please."

The other guard sees her and turns away wincing. Kieron is very confused but enters where Hunter already has the dealer lifted by his neck.

Danut, with his medical mask high on his face, has corralled five staff as he checks all rooms, rips out communication cables and demands their cell-phones. He removes the simm cards one by one and breaks them. He then rips the top off a water-cooler and drops the phones in one by one.

"You work for Bentley?" Hunter asks the dealer harshly in the main room.

"I report to Bentley. He sends the paintings, I sell them, tell him what is selling and he makes me reproductions."

"If you sold the original, how can you then sell reproductions?" Hunter asks him, banging him into a second wall.

"I have the most trendy gallery in St Petersburg, Anoataly Istov, my name," he says as if that was the answer. His face fills with genuine fear as Bedi walks forward.

"You ask the wrong question. Russia is very different. If art piece is good, if it sell high, everyone want it. Trendy art mean everyone have second original copy, from artist's students. The master original go up in value."

"OK, what's the right question?" Hunter asks.

"Who does Bentley work for?" She asks, edging him to the balcony.

Fearing death, he squeals like a pig.

"His father. His father."

"Mr double-barrel posh Englishman Crouch-Fielding," Hunter blasts.

"No, no. Just Crouch. Mr Crouch. He is father, he is boss. Mr Crouch, famous dealer, he signs all papers," Anoataly squeals to Hunter.

"Where's Crouch based?"

"New York. 'Ouch' Gallery."

Hunter turns leaving Bedi with the dealer, but he sees Kieron looking down at a glass table, smirking.

"What's up with you?" Hunter asks.

Kieron says nothing, Hunter walks around and looks at the table he is looking at. It is a woman, on her hands and knees. Clothes ripped from her, breasts exposed like she has been cruelly abused and is crawling away from her captor. All along her back is a glass coffee table. She is the table and her head comes up through the glass. She is the table. He turns and looks at the dealer who is pulling himself up on the sofa. Behind him Russian Officer Bedriška with her hands on her hips.

"Explain?" Hunter says looking at Bedi holding the dealer.

"Me. Russia's most famous female killer," Bedi says.

"We should go," the driver panics.

Hunter and Kieron are studying Bedriška who is nodding with that impressive pout.

"I make it, I make self-portrait. Now copies everywhere in Russia. I known as whore-killer, that why every collector want table. Very expensive. It women who buy table, they not think I am whore, but I am hero. That table original, that is mine."

She turns to the dealer.

"Take your cell."

The dealer takes his cell-phone out, the only one not collected and smashed.

"Unlock. Put on camera."

Bedi takes the phone and hands it to Kieron. She scoops up the dealer and thrusts him out to the balcony again screaming, and she holds him over the edge. The dealer is in fear. Kieron takes the picture. She throws him inside on his hands and knees, hoists him from the back of his neck and drags him to the table. On all fours he is staring at the likeness of her face.

"You, supposed to pay me, fifty percent of sales. Now I back in Russia killing, table value go up again."

"I never knew how to pay you."

"You give every Rubel, to children. Kieron, tell him charity."

Kieron writes down the address of the children's charity at the church he supports in the Caribbean Island of St. Vincent. They have had hundreds of thousands of dollars he has acquired solving cruise crimes that he felt would be best placed there. He is proud of Bedriška giving all her royalties away like this. Before he hands the paper, he asks her.

"Are you sure?"

"Yes."

Kieron gives the dealer the address and bank details that he knows by heart. Bedriška gets right in his face. She is very intimidating.

"You pay or I kill you. I come to back Russia when I want. No one catch me. They all end dead. You understand?"

The dealer nods. She leaves. Hunter and the driver follow her. Kieron lingers, the charity means a lot to him.

"Look after all the originals you've got. Hear me? That original table, crate it up and send it to Crouch in New York. Tell him to look after it, he's our next visit. Then back here if you don't pay the charity."

Kieron leaves.

In the elevator the Kieron and Hunter hold guns preparing for a shoot-out as the elevator opens.

"I feel we left there very easy," Hunter says.

"Yes. But no," Kieron half agrees. "I don't think he even gets sent the original."

"Agreed. The crime ain't here."

83 – LEAVING HOME

St Petersburg, Russia – 2235hrs   Miami-1435hrs   Caribbean sea– 1435hrs

The witching hour this evening on this ship is eleven fifteen. It is unusual because the ship has already been in St Petersburg two days with one overnight, so this is extended stay on the second day does not happen very often. The tours to traditional evening entertainment venues, Russian theatre, ballet, and music, were last night. This extended day is for tours to time-honoured eating and drinking venues and the ship can leave as soon as all are accounted for, the Pilot is onboard and there is no other marine traffic.

Cruisers enter the ships secure area though a covered entrance. Next door for those in no hurry to join a queue is a souvenir shop. Queues are forming at immigration and the ship's horn puts pressure on the night shift Russian officials who feel above all those who are not Russian or those below their superiors who are few if not absent at night. They feel no pressure.

Bedriška still has her uniform on and immigration officers are not above KGB officers. She walks through the queuing people, directing guests to different queues. She converses abruptly with the officers in the passport inspection booths. They know she is Russian, and she sounds like an officer even if they are confused she is there. If there is a problem, they will have to call someone from another office.

Bedriška walks back past a second booth down another queue and starts ad-hock checking passports in the line, she has made her target, she takes the passport of two tall chunky men.

"I check these, join that line."

She collects two more passports and circles around palming the men's passports she procured to Hunter and Kieron. She then orders them to the front of the queue.

"You two, go there. Senior ship officers."

She bosses them to the front of the queue. When they are in the booth, she walks up to it.

"Hurry, many people to check."

She looks the officer in the eyes with spite and squeezes through. Power and domination work in Russia. Kieron and Hunter walk through.

"Seaman's Log," she demands of them.

She lets them pass but surreptitiously keeps the two passports. She walks back through another booth and hands the passports back to the real owners. Eventually, she goes through to the ship side again. She waits for the two male tourists to be checked. They attend together, being partners. The officer finds a problem.

"What?" She barks to the officer and approaches him.

"They have already left Russia."

"Look!" she says to the immigration officer. "Are you stupid?"

"Cruise cards," she demands from the two men.

They produce their cruise cards which match the passports.

"You make mistake?" She tells the officer.

Fearful of any reprimand he waves them through. Bedi disappears.

The sundecks on the rear of the ship are lit but empty at night. The four decks stack as moon-shaped terraces, with each reducing in size giving a wonderful staggered shape to the back. The bottom of the pattern is a whole rear deck not just a balcony. It has a small splash pool normally either for children or those who need to use steps to walk in gradually as no other pool features that. The bar on the middle of the rear decks is closed and stock-taking is in progress, but Bedi has managed to get two double vodkas in one glass with a little ice. She stands at the back, in just the officer's shirt and skirt. She holds the KGB jacket and is looking out to sea. In the dark, the wake from the propellers always glows white as it is churned over and left behind. She is in a drift of memories, a few good but mostly harsh. Kieron approaches her.

"I wish to be alone."

"No you don't, you want a friend and a man who wants to hold you because he cares. A man who wants to hold you because he understands your hurt and what you went through."

"You can never know."

"I can try."

Kieron stands beside her and gently puts his arm around her and pulls her in.

"It is a wonderful thing you did, giving that money to charity," he says.

"If he ever give it."

"If he doesn't, I promise, I will personally go back and slit his throat. And you know I can and I will."

She looks at him.

"My sister never made it out of Russia."

Kieron is shocked to hear that maybe she is in there somewhere alive.

"I look, and look, and look for her. That why I offered to join KGB 5th Directive and work on sex trafficking. But, I killed so many bad men involved in child pornography, television and press make me into hero sex killer. I become liability for KGB. They worry, some officers paid not to look. But, I look. I kill them too. I end up killing many KGB officers. That is why I am 'whore killer'. I kill more men in Russia than any other woman."

She turns to him.

"Maybe kill more than any man. I would still do it."

Kieron hugs her.

"To us, you're a hero."

She buries herself in his neck.

"You know we are being watched," she whispers.

"Yes. Prisha captured them in some innocent tourist pictures and sent shots back to Dwight. He says they're senior KGB officers. They come to kill me. I always expect bullet in my back."

"Except Hunter is behind them, watching our backs."

"It will get messy," she says. "Just two?"

"We think so."

Day10-At sea to Tallinn – 0035hrs   Day9-Miami-1635hrs   Caribbean sea– 1635hrs

Apart from the disco and the midnight buffet, the only place open on a ship after midnight is the Casino.

Hunter and Kieron sit on different tables; Kieron plays blackjack, Hunter is losing enough at the roulette wheel to have a crowd.

Bedi would look good in anything, and the broken down KGB uniform looks like a blouse and pencil skirt on her. She walks into the casino with a swagger, turning many heads. There are four ways in the fore and aft ends of the area and both port and starboard sides though half the area is a pub and half full of tables and slot machines. Music is always kept just to the same level as the cacophony of gambling noises so the sound becomes addictive. One of her KGB shadows was directly behind her the other slips in to a table near the bar. Both Kieron and Hunter were invisible as players already at the table. She stands close to Kieron, making him look like a film star.

"You look fantastic," Kieron says again.

"I know. I must carve new table. Now happy whore. Or maybe in this uniform. Everyone thinks it is 'fancy dress', bought from tourist shop. I keep it for fun. Now, we go. Before they send your picture, we both go to the toilet."

She walks off at speed, making the two Russian KGB guards attentive. She enters the ladies room. Both guards go towards it, one slips in the ladies behind her, the other stands outside on guard. Kieron walks at him without deviation, he lifts him by the crutch and the neck and walks him backwards the two steps into the toilet. He is so fast the struggle does not begin until inside and he is pushed into a cubicle. He turns him, wrenching his neck and stepping back.

"That's for Bedi's sister."

He takes his agents phone, cruise card and wallet, photographs his face, before crossing into the ladies. Bedi is doing her hair.

"Get out. This is ladies."

He sees two feet twisting out of a cubicle so Kieron leaves. While he waits for Bedi he pulls the 'out of service barrier' across. He connects the Russian's cell to his and presses send. Bedi appears.

"Come, we have more Russian money to spend. We can clear up after the night is over."

84 - EVIDENCE

Macey's short painting show went very well and the atrium was packed from lunch to tea. She understands the seadays daytime entertainment programme as well as the need to create sales. Now back in her suite, made up for the formal night, she is excited and toys with the idea of sending a photograph to Ricky and telling him about her day. Prisha has her phone.

"I know what you are thinking and I ask if you are sure this is right? You are sharing an awful lot with someone you don't know," Prisha says.

"Or, maybe I do know him. Maybe it's him I'm dancing with. Or maybe it's all just press releases about my day and my evening picture. I'm sure someone sent him daytime pictures. Eh?" Macey stops twisting and her eyes accuse Prisha.

"They were press release pictures," Prisha says embarrassed.

"Go on then, send this."

Prisha takes the picture of her in the long silver dress. She is deliberately near her easel. The painting she did of a young black woman dancing with a white man, her hair down and flowing is just behind her. For the first time, she has her hair down and is smiling. She takes the phone back and types, 'off to the Captain's cocktail party', and she sends.

"Miami in four days. I'm getting closer to seeing what he is really like. Then I'll find out."

"Not that you're counting," Prisha says.

"The sea, Charleston, Canaveral then Miami."

"I had that look in my eye once. I ended up a single parent with two children back home with my mother," Prisha admits.

"I don't know how you cope, never seeing them."

"It is the same for almost every one of the crew, on every ship at sea. We can earn enough money to give our whole family a good life."

"Is it all about money?" Macey says, changing her mood. "My real mother dumped me with a woman who is a drug addict, and if she is sent money it goes on crack."

Macey is now thinking about her heritage. She has been deceived for all these years.

"I'm not looking forward to seeing Mary and Stan. Not sure I ever want to see them."

"There's a lot of good to look forward to back home," Prisha says, trying to mediate.

"I'll be sad the cruise has ended," Macey admits.

"So, from the girl who wanted to jump ship in Key West, you have enjoyed the cruise?"

"Apart from the little hiccups, and near-death experiences, I've loved it. Though, we haven't found the forgeries and sent a list back to Yonan," Macey says, refocussing on the job.

"Better than that, you have seen 4 fakes, and we found the forger onboard and the manufacturing team, and the men found a forgery set up in Italy plus the Russian connection," Prisha says. "Our work has been more than successful."

"So why don't the team think the job is finished?"

"We still have time to look at more special pieces around the ship and find fakes."

"Sure, but it's not about a few fakes on the ship is it?" Macey asks.

"No, there's a glue that holds all this together."

"Is this where it gets nasty or it gets easy?"

Prisha freezes stony faced.

"That said, I wonder if Jill and her paint squad are still tied up," Macey asks.

"How could you let them go and give them the chance of causing trouble? You have to think of the guests first. Maybe she will be taken off tomorrow in Charleston."

"But her desk; who'll run the gallery?" Macey asks.

"Seriously, you can't work that out."

The two girls exchange knowing smiles as Macey realises it is Clément.

"He has been there since your show," Prisha reveals.

"Oh no, I wonder what he has been saying and selling."

"Who knows what goes on in his brain? Or yours. I loved you doing the ghost in all the New Orleans' paintings," Prisha says.

"Thanks. After I developed the technique in the first one its easy. I feel Hemingway's mother was a ghost to him. Always there. Just as I am followed by killers, ghosts always on my shoulder."

Day10-At sea to Tallinn – 0230hrs   Day9-Miami-1835hr   Caribbean sea– 1835hrs

"You're still awake?" Dwight asks, from the Headquarters in Miami.

"It appears so," Kieron says. "I'm walking away from the blackjack table. I had a lot of Rubles left over."

"OK. I've sent you detail; the two you put down were both KGB hitmen. We also dropped the ball with Bentley. On every application form, and profile he says his father is dead. That's not wrong, Mr Fielding is. His mother re-married, she has since died leaving Mr Crouch, his stepfather in the game. He owns a gallery in New York. Croc is digging deeper there."

"You want us to go to New York?" Kieron asks via the telephone.

"Not yet. Bentley has booked to join Macey's ship in Charleston. Mike has asked for a room too. That seems weird, and must be to do with Jill being missing." Dwight suggests.

"A security guard is supposed to stay with a painting, but it would never be Mike; he's the head of security. Mike should stay at the shipyard," Hunter says.

"I reckon Jill knows shit that needs to be silenced, that's why Mike's going himself."

"We need to get there," Hunter says.

"I'll arrange a private jet in Tallinn. But, Dog has already been identified there so be careful. Tallinn's dangerous."

"What if we can't get there?" Kieron asks. "Here's an idea, smother Mike's purpose. Have Yonan's office order Bentley to take eight or more paintings to the ship. Say he needs to release some others for a dealer. Then suggest he must prepare others to leave in Miami, so he will need a few assistants. You nominate them so he gets suspicious, and have him include that new assistant Hunter thought I was chatting up, Rosemary Addington. Let's treat her to a day out."

"Good idea. Make it so busy, they won't be ready to travel by then and Mike will have to wait. It gives us an extra day," Hunter agrees.

"Also, do a full rundown on each of the assistants. And pull in all their mobile phone numbers and check them against Jill's phone records. Something bugs me about his whole team," Kieron adds.

"I thought we might sleep," Dwight says.

"It's over-rated, Dwight."

"Clean up the mess you made in the washroom," Dwight orders then ends the call.

85 – TALLINN

Big Dog slept at a different hotel, high on Toompea Hill, with a view out over the City. For all he was the king of his hood in Overton, he has never seen life like this. He is starting to relax and feel lucky. Croc and Izzy have never left the office.

He can see the ships come into berth one by one from the patio where he eats breakfast outside in the early sun. The agents always sit with their backs to the wall so they can see all the doors, but without trapping themselves in. It is the same as he did in his den back home. Applying that here, he sits at a table near the cliff edge. He has a complete view of the hotel's glass bar and dining area and the public entrance from the road. To his back, anyone trying to scale the cliff would be an idiot. However, he has not been good at spotting people creep up on him. It is no fun being a crime investigator; this game is played constantly. He needs to eat. Yesterday he was bold and went for the local dish, elk, and liked it. Maybe he will try it again today, but he needs to move after the waitress has cleared away, unless, it is her that will try and hit on him.

"I can see you like our kohuke."

"What's there not to like? Chocolate yoghurt for breakfast."

"It is curd, which is made with lemon juice. Yoghurt is made with bacteria."

CRUISE SHIP ART THEFT

"Seriously? Bacteria?"

She nods.

"What have you seen here in Tallinn?"

"I saw the tunnels yesterday. They were sick."

"There are tunnels everywhere. It is a limestone hill, so they are relatively easy to dig."

Dog smiles. It is time to go. She is getting way too friendly. He has decided he likes travelling, but this is work and he has to be in the look-out tower by ten. It can't possibly have a better view than he has now but will have a better view of the road in from the docks.

The tower is part of Olav's church. It has a 124-metre spire with no elevator. The entrance is inside the church, opposite the general entrance and ticket office. It is a stupid tiny arch, almost something out of 'The Hobbit'. Maybe it is awkward so attacking soldiers are slow ducking under and are sitting ducks. Yes, he thinks. It is a very clever entrance. He will adopt that back home. The stone steps are narrow and uneven, and a rope as handrail threads through hooks up the centre. It might be early, and it might be stone, but it is hot now and Dog is overdressed in his heavy jacket once again. Well before he completes the 232 steps up, he is sweating, and wondering how people cross each other when it is only wide enough for one. Tourists coming down must have to body touch when squeezing past those going up. No social distancing here. He is breathing hard when he gets to the viewing platform, and glad it is not the added height it was in the 16th century when it may have been the tallest building in the world.

The view of Tallinn and back to the Toompea Hill is impressive, but as he expected, the view of the dock and the ships is one of strategic importance. He rings Bedriška once in place as agreed.

"Bedi?"

"No. It's Kieron. She's in the shower. But, it doesn't look good outside," Kieron continues.

"What you mean? Sure ain't gonna rain today," Dog says.

"It's raining men. We have company: three agents on the gate."

"They students dude, you guys can play ball with them kids."

"No, these are not students, these are proper agents and we have more than a lot of police."

"They stepped their game up because I rinsed the boy scouts they sent yesterday. Was I supposed to run squealing like a pig? I never got that whistle."

"No," Kieron says.

"Oh. Well done Big Dog," he says to himself.

"It's a job."

"'Til the lights go out."

"Yeah."

"Well, one of us is popular because the corner is well populated."

"Corner?" Kieron asks.

"What makes you think you got the teachers come out to play?" Dog asks.

"They missed Bedriška both in and out or Russia. Now it's serious. They'll want to catch her before she gets too far down the Baltic."

"We got double the police on the corner with two big guys working the road. Plus, one outside the archway into the walled castle."

"They're after Bedi, not you."

"I'll relax, take in some rays, get me another elk burger."

"You want the good news or the bad news?"

"You ain't coming ashore."

"You got it."

"I gotta get to the ship, right?"

"Right. Go to the back of the castle, where there are other exits. Get a cab to the docks. Sooner we get you on this ship, sooner you can get some rays and a burger."

"And if I can't get on?"

"There's a private jet waiting at the airport. Get on. It will hop down to our next stop and you'll jump on there."

"How long have I got?"

"Until 1630 to get on this ship or more time for the plane. After this ship leaves, the security here should vanish."

"And get heavy around the airport?" Dog concludes.

"Maybe," Kieron almost sighs as he ends the call.

Big Dog is playing the big game now.

The three; Bedi, Hunter and Kieron, all have clothes newly purchased from the ship's shop which opens shortly after the ship sails. They wait for the Maître'd at the premium Asian restaurant. Hunter turns away to take a phone call from Dwight. He listens.

"I asked Big Dog to stay another night in Tallinn. It splits focus. If the plane is still there they won't know whether to wait in Tallinn and watch the airport, or be in Sweden, or, give up. Bedi can't justify the cost of an army of agents."

"You should be here. It seems she can," Hunter mumbles.

"In that case, watch yourselves in Sweden. The Russians may be less likely to get assistance from the police, but they might be there. We're still researching the Ouch Gallery in New York. It seems clean, but I'll keep you informed. Still, nothing on Yonan but I don't trust him as far as I can throw him. I've put a huge, I mean silly huge expenses bill in for St Petersburg, asking for immediate payment."

"Cool."

"No, it is so not cool. It will need his approval, and it has to be paid today, latest tomorrow."

"But he ain't around."

"Times like this, I get a damn itch in my right foot and that ain't around either. It's a phantom itch. One I can't scratch."

86 – AT SEA DAY 2

At sea from Tallinn – 1830hrs   Miami-1030hrs   **At sea to Charleston – 1030hrs**

Time zones are crippling for the Miami office; Tallinn and Sweden are going to sleep, Yonan's ship off the Florida coast is waking up. Macey is already up, daydreaming.

Another lecture is in the timetable but with Clem at the art gallery's desk, Macey is on her own to figure out her presentation. At breakfast, it does not seem to be her top priority; Ricky is on her mind. After many video calls she is desperate to meet him. Today is her last demonstration, then when they dock it would be possible to leave the ship and fly home from Charleston. It is a hard choice; she would miss seeing the Holy City as Charleston is referred to, and Canaveral, the space city. Prisha keeps telling her that she doesn't even know Ricky and she may never get another chance to see the South Carolina.

Macey must stay. As well as being a romantic she is too politically outspoken in her work not to want to see first-hand the lack of civil rights her people had to survive. But she checks herself; she doesn't know her people, that is going to have to be one long conversation with Wild Mary, if she can force herself to do that. If she can force herself to ever speak to her again.

Charleston, the slavery town, will no doubt present mixed emotions. She loved the 2004 hit movie 'The Notebook' starring Ryan Gosling whom she thinks is a hunk, and she thought Rachel McAdams was lucky. The film was set in the 1940s and shot in Charleston which looks adorable. That is not something she would have known, but for the ship's 'port talk'. That show in the main theatre was busier than any cabaret show she has seen. So much information is fired at you in that forty five minute lecture you need to watch the in-house re-run. They didn't say it has one of the lowest black populations in South Carolina, but that is for the oil crayons tomorrow. Will she be the whimsical romanticist or wild revolutionary? Will she see the dead?

"I'm going to make a tea with those Tanna leaves I bought in New Orleans, and then wish," Macey announces.

"What if they are poisonous? Or worse, they send you into a weird trance and you embarrass yourself in the show," Prisha worries.

"You are more worried that I will look crazy than if I am dead?"

Today, she is looking at the shoes; the animals on your feet and that you eat. She is still worried that it might be too much for cruisers, but it is all about the approach. She can't take in Hemingway, as much as there is a story to be told; his mother haunting him is what she did in her New Orleans presentation. Whatever the response, a crowd will drive her to either anger or pleasure, and whichever way, the paintings are a series and they won't come back from the atrium in the same state as they are now. The crowd's reaction will stimulate changes.

The show goes well. Macey is an enormous success. Like so many of the showmen onboard, Clément has a magic internal clock that hits forty-five minutes. The audience forms a mass, wanting Macey to sign booklet after booklet while Clem packs away.

"I am sorry, we must go to the gallery. This space is to be used for a quiz," Clément says when he has finished and loaded up Prisha as if she were his assistant. He leads them all like the pied piper and they follow, ensnared. Clément will have them alone for about ten minutes before Macey arrives. That brief time allows him a sales talk, in which the chancers move off and the real fans stay. Macey never needs to see that.

Macey enters to tumultuous applause and there is no doubt: if she were selling prints and signing them, she would sell them by the score.

"Mesdames et Messieurs, I present the next sensation in the art world. Macey, darling, join me 'ere. I 'ave only one 'undred prints of this Ernest 'Emingway ere. They will be exclusive. Macey will sign them, and sign them 1 of 100, or 96 of 100, whatever. But what make it special is this work is no doubt not finished. So, these prints will never be reproduced again. She will concentrate on signing them, and all you need is your cruise card. We 'ave arranged with the gallery and the ship to 'ave them at the special incredible low price of one 'undred dollars each. I still can't believe it. Macey, if you do not mind, only sign the selling prints or we never see Charleston."

The crowd laugh, some leave, but it is obvious the prints are going to sell. Macey edges up to Clem.

"That will be ten thousand dollars," she whispers.

"For not the best reproductions," he answers equally as private.

"I thought I saw Yonan on the upper level of the atrium," she says.

"No. Crazy."

"I think I did. With another man."

"Upper level? Three floors up, in massive crowds with lights in your eyes? You are overcome by success," he says.

Macey sits down to sign and she will be a long time, even with the help of two entertainment hosts. They are set across three tables so she continually has to excuse herself to move to the next table. A super clever technique they use when a star chef is onboard. Between her signing the new name; May.I.see. She should text Dwight about her seeing Yonan, even if Clem is sure she is wrong. That won't happen for an hour; she is swamped by an enthusiastic crowd.

Stuart St Paul

87 – STOCKHOLM

Kieron is up early, looking at the sunrise as the ship sails very slowly into Stockholm. It seems a huge river rather than the sea. The river-like experience feels like a team is rowing into the city. Small islands are on each side with a few summer homes. He has been followed around the deck, but ducked into the gym. Back on deck he holds a large circular weight close to his chest. He stands at the front rail captured by the beauty of Stockholm's outer islands.

A man rushes him from behind, but behind him is Hunter who hits him and lifts him, holding him on the rail for a split second while Kieron loops a simple cable tie around his neck and pulls it tight. He and the weight drop overboard and vanish.

"Dolphins!" Kieron shouts for the benefit of any who may have thought there was a man overboard. The few people on deck this early rush to see, but they see nothing. Dolphins are rare in the Baltic but have been seen in these waters. They are always in shoals.

Agents are always in a pair. Bedi approaches the other man who has slipped around to the opposite arc of the deck. She steps in, holding an even bigger weight in one hand. Hunter approaches her to take the weight, but she refuses.

"It my turn."

Hunter rams the man into the rail and holds him while Bedi snaps the weight tight.

"Go," she says.

"Dolphins," she shouts as he sinks.

The three of them walk backwards as if looking for the large fish. They are soon followed. They lead the crowd away.

"Three dolphins," she shouts.

But there is nothing to see.

"I like this game with tourist."

A man approaches them.

"Do you get dolphins in the Baltic?" he asks her.

"Very rare, and special," she says in her convincing eastern European accent.

Hunter and Kieron firmly walk her away.

"Breakfast," Hunter says in his convincing American accent.

As they take their buffet food to a table and sit, Hunter reports. He is the one who has been talking with Dwight.

"Big Dog's not out of Tallinn yet," he relays to his colleagues.

"He found pussy on way across Florida so maybe he is busy," Bedi offers.

"No, Dwight has a plan that he says will come together, but that he's not in control of the speed with which it will be executed," Hunter finishes.

"OK. I trust," Bedi says.

"Means we won't be leaving Stockholm first thing?" Kieron ponders.

"I go to Abba museum," Bedi says.

"Abba?" The two men say almost together.

"Yes. I am big fan of Eurovision."

"I'll go with you," Kieron says.

Hunter looks at him. He thought he knew Kieron, if not Bedi.

"How wrong can you get someone. Abba?"

"No, I wanna go to the Vasa museum. It's in the next block and meant to be fantastic," Kieron says.

"What is fantastic about a boat that could only float for about twenty minutes before sinking?" Hunter adds, equally as surprised.

"The fact that a ship is still preserved and intact after three hundred years."

"We're not on holiday," Hunter reminds them.

"Yes, until they get us plane," Bedi says.

"Do you mind if I don't join either of you?" Hunter asks. "Not sure when I've heard anything so crazy."

Day11-Tallinn – 0750hrs   Day10-Miami-2350hrs   At sea to Charleston – 2350hrs

Back in Tallinn, there is a large square hotel: the Nordic Hotel Forum. The front of it is busy with important cars pulling in, filling or emptying and going. Some look very official, and it is the size of a hotel that could be used to house officials of the European song contest. It also has more than its fair share of military officers, officials and diplomats from all over the world.

Another limousine pulls up outside and the door is swung open, attended by many officials and hotel staff. This one is flying a distinctive flag, on each wing. The green Y on its side, with red above and blue below. Black outlines the yellow wedge of the Y. If South Africa were in the Eurovision song contest, this is exactly how a star might arrive. A Zulu king comes out of the hotel. His long skirt is made of hanging strips of animal skin. His chest is covered with a beautiful embroidered white lace, and he has a leopard skin apron around his neck. He has many beaded necklaces and bracelets, even on his ankles. Around his head is a Davy Crocket loop with skins hanging down, all leopard. This is an important man leaving the hotel, but what would be more interesting is the view Macey would take of him if she was here. Sadly, that will never be oiled onto canvas. He stops for photographs from the press and he offers his phone to a bell boy to take a wider picture than he would with a selfie. The third-world meets first-world.

He gets into the car, it drives away, and the officials disperse. The next car drives in.

At the airport, Big Dog, still in the Zulu King's clothes leaves the limousine and boards the private jet. The doors are closed and it taxis away, ready to take off.

Stockholm – 1230hrs   Miami-0430hrs   at sea to Charleston – 0430hrs

Bedi is in the Abba museum, looking at outrageous outfits when she receives a text of the even more outrageous picture of Big Dog. The caption says, 'Big Dog is travelling. You have a take-off slot at 1400hrs'. In the very dark theatrical building that holds all of a ship and masts standing tall, Kieron gets the same text and checks his watch. It has gone lunchtime and he and Bedi need to get together and travel back. He walks fast, almost breaking into a jog as he goes the two blocks back to the Abba museum. Outside he sees agents and police beginning to assemble.

"Bedi. Stay inside, there's a huge team waiting for you. I'll get back to you," Kieron says, into his cell-phone. He dials Dwight. After a simple report, he suggests a plan. As an experienced special agent, he has often had far less time to react.

"I need every Abba fan site and twitter feed to say Bjorn and Bennie have arrived at the Stockholm Museum on an impromptu visit. They will soon be downstairs."

The two men end the call; they both have a lot of work to do. Kieron sends Bedi a text. 'Bjorn and

Bennie are upstairs, they are going down. Stay there or you will miss them.' He rings her, but he doesn't need to. She is already sharing the text on her phone with the tourists, with excitement to match. She covers more people, from one end of the museum to the other in no time at all.

"Have you seen Bjorn and Bennie? Look, they are coming down," Bedi shouts to start hysteria.

The commotion they want is gaining motion far too slowly. Kieron looks to see if there is any way to escalate it. The ticket office is outside to the right. Inside is a café and escalators down to the museum. He goes out to the considerable queue.

"No. Is this the queue? I can't wait. Bjorn and Bennie are downstairs, I'll never get to see them if I queue."

The queue breaks up and the word starts to spread. The fans, mainly female, rush in and crush past the electronic ticket barriers and fight to get onto the escalator. Why so few countries have women fighting on the front line has always been beyond him. The timed admission to stagger and control overcrowding has gone.

As the room swells, Bedi hits the first emergency door. Alarms go off. She weaves her way to a second. She pushes it open and moves to a third. Fans have found these doors and swell in like expanding foam. Bedi goes into the gift shop, taking a glitter hat and a scarf as she passes through. She steps outside to the chaos where the police are unexpectedly overwhelmed at the side. Hunter pulls up in a car. Kieron runs and jumps in, Bedi is in a second later.

As the three enter the private jet now sitting at Stockholm Bromma Airport, just 9km west of the city, they see Big Dog still dressed as a Zulu King.

"Look at you, the 'Fancy Prince of Con Air,'" Hunter says.

An air steward opens the curtain.

"Please sit and put your seat belts on, we are taking off straight away. Oh, you two," Enrique finishes, dumbstruck as he recognises them.

"Enrique, old friend," Kieron enthuses.

Enrique keeps a straight face. He gulps, controls himself, then continues the legal safety briefing. He is going well until Bedi leans into Big Dog and opens the Russian attaché case of guns.

"Gun," she demands.

Big Dog drops his handgun into the case and she closes it.

"How you gonna get that bag of bullets on the ship?" He asks her.

"Attached to ship supplies going on board with extra layer of pallet wrap." Bedi looks at the dumb-struck Enrique. "What? You forget? Doors there and there, air here, life jacket under seat, seat belt is easy. What else is there? Nothing!"

Enrique raises an eyebrow and continues out loud.

"It is 1400hrs here, only six in the early hours in Charleston. We have an eight-hour flight, so you will arrive just after lunch tomorrow. I hope you all have passports and entry documents," Enrique gives them all a look as if he is finished, but he hasn't. "Because you're not having mine."

Hunter and Kieron throw passports at him.

"What? Is this some tradition?" Dog asks.

"No, they're his. We borrowed them," Kieron explains

"I am reliving a bad dream," Enrique says, failing to believe Dog in traditional dress. "And who is this?"

"We kidnapped a Zulu King," Hunter says.

Bedi leans into Enrique.

"Where is plastic roll?" She asks.

"Plastic wrap," Hunter explains.

88 – SAME TIME – DIFFERENT PLACE

Day11-Plane in the air   **Day11-Miami-0830hrs**   Charleston – 0830hrs

The ship has docked in South Carolina, north of Florida, and although the CSCI private jet is still in the air, when it lands it will be in the same time zone. The investigators in the air are fast asleep; they need it. Although the clock might suggest it has been a long lie-in, it will only be about eight hours sleep. Further down the coast, in Miami, Dwight, Croc and the new enthusiastic recruit Izzy need sleep, but there is even more pressure on them and more work to do than there has been over the past few days.

Bentley Crouch Fielding's travel from Italy has been put back a day. He will join tomorrow at Port Canaveral, a day after port Charleston where he wanted to join. Rather than one extra day to complete his work, he has been given four assistants. He is tasked with seeing eleven expensive paintings all the way from Italy to America. He has Mr Schmeichel's private jet, but eleven is a huge responsibility. The art assistants won't be able to do much more than cleaning and watch him. What the interns don't know is that there are no available cabins on the ship which shows as sailing at full capacity. Some assistants, if not all, will have to fly straight back unless the hotel manager on board can work some magic with unused crew cabins. The ship arrives as they do, early in the morning and it stays berthed for two days in Canaveral. What they will do, during their brief visit, is maybe bunk on the floor of Bentley's room on the berthed night, and get a good look at one of Yonan Schmeichel's ships fully kitted with art as well as find time to play before their flight home.

The underlying excitement amongst the assistants is not the art, but that they might get to see Universal's Islands of Adventure, Disney World or Kennedy Space Centre on the other island-like piece of land joined to the mainland and only fourteen miles away. They are all confident there is time for changing canvasses, cleaning, or packaging alongside having some fun. Apart from Rosemary, they are all adept at the work now if Bentley will trust them to do it.

In the dark Miami hub, Croc is looking at the board, not his computer where he can shift the layers. Izzy moves her eyes from watching Croc puzzle over to Dwight who appears to be inspecting a ceiling he can't see in the dark.

"Your foot's itching, right?" Izzy says to Dwight.

Dwight hasn't had a foot on either leg for some time but the itch tells him to worry. She is one of the few who could say that without worry of a reprimand.

"What if Bentley's not in the middle of all this?" Dwight asks.

"But he is, look," Izzy says pointing to her board.

"No, he's not," Croc says, wearing a huge grin.

"Are you thinking Mr Yonan Schmeichel is in the middle?" Croc asks Dwight.

"But Yonan's been missing for days," Izzy says to disagree.

"Missing? I put a huge invoice in yesterday, super huge. Just checked; the money's in the bank."

"And he should be the only authority for that to be paid, right?" Croc asks.

"You don't like him," Izzy says to Dwight.

"He ain't missing. Time for an even bigger invoice," Dwight replies.

"But what for?" Croc asks.

"Extras! Bullet money; one thousand dollars for every bullet shot at a member of our team."

"How you gonna add that up?" Izzy asks.

"I just did, it comes to two hundred and thirty-five thousand dollars. Type it up Croc. If they keep paying, we'll keep invoicing. We can both play games."

"I'm gonna add that to our standard contract. I like that," Izzy says.

"You like our agents being shot at?" Dwight says firmly to pull her back, then breaks a small smile to let her off. It is a great idea and a serious reality.

89 – CHARLESTON

Day 11 - Plane in the air   Miami-0900hrs   **Charleston – 0900hrs**

The sun is out in Charleston, which is not always the case. They are recovering from a storm and people are shovelling debris and dirt. Shutters and boards are still hammered on many windows. The ship is so close to the town that you can see the damage from breakfast.

Forty percent of slaves shipped into America came into Charleston. Macey knows that but is determined to enjoy the day. It must be deep in their past.

Macey steps ashore, hair down, carrying her two new larger acrylic primed cotton canvas pads of just ten sheets each. The few brushes she uses for blending are in her hair which is up. Clem carries the full set of oil crayons. At the port gate, Macey hands Prisha the pads to produce her cruise card. Before she can get them back, a man in a white shirt and straw hat turns into her.

"Would you like me to carry those for you?" Ricky says.

Macey walks forward and hits him with a stern look, but when he opens his arms she softens and cannot resist greeting him with a hug that is held for a long time. They do have a connection that needs investigating.

"I don't normally do hugs on the first date," he says as they separate. "But I've booked us all on a horse and carriage ride; it looks amazing."

She links arms with him, but to pull him away walking off in front of the others. Now she can grill him.

"I need to know what else you found out about me."

"I'd need to check my notes."

"You're starting this relationship off with a lie, are you now?" Macey torments.

Prisha carries her pads as the group follow, past customs house and up to the main street.

"Who are the two big guys?" Ricky asks.

"My bodyguards."

"You need them?"

"Since your picture made me famous."

"No one's noticed you, look," he says scanning with his arm to tail-end her joke.

"Please Ricky. If you know something more about me, I need to know."

They arrive at the queue for horse and carriage ride where one has just finished. Those stepping away from the pristine period carriage are thanking the carriage driver who has the same hat as Ricky has bought. The driver's hat has a red band around it, matching a red band around his waist which separates his white shirt from his confederate grey trousers.

Having pre-booked tickets, Ricky is ushered to the front of the queue.

"I only booked four places on the carriage," Ricky worryingly says to the ticket attendant wearing the same red bands around her white dress and her styled straw hat. Before he can say anything else, Zack takes over. His huge presence makes a gap between him and the rest. Ricky can only observe.

"We have look after her, wherever she goes, we have to go," Zack says to the ticket attendant with a warm smile. "Let's have the whole ride to ourselves." He hands her enough money for her not to refuse.

Ricky feels their powerful presence for the first time.

"Sit on the bench," Zack says.

Prisha leans in to him, seeing his nerves.

"They'll get on and be sitting right behind you. Try anything, you're dead," she says.

"I'll behave."

Ricky goes to help Macey up.

"Hands off. My job," Billy says in a way that not only frightens Ricky but the whole queue who were irritated over the perceived queue jumping. Billy grins wildly at them after Macey has stepped up. No one attempts to complain.

"You're full," Zack tells the driver, the last to get on. She looks down to the starter who gives permission to leave. Gingerly, she drives the carriage away and starts her commentary.

"Welcome to Charleston. We have ninety-eight historic blocks. We cannot see them all so we're broken into five zones. We will do the main street, then come back to Rainbow Road, the historic houses and then we will see the city jail. You'll see a lot of churches; Charleston is known as the holy city," she grins, pleased with herself. "We have more churches here than in Rome."

Ricky shakes hands with all the group, rather late with his introduction. Macey is looking at everything, the perfect squareness of the buildings, the amazingly clean streets. She listens to every word until they get to the town square where the driver explains the monument to J C Calhoun.

"An important man here..." the driver finishes.

But there is only one thing that hits Macey in all that the driver says about Calhoun, and that is 'he did not want slaves to be free'. It is the way she said it, as if his point of view was as correct as his monument still standing 100 feet high.

Clem reaches over to try and pacify her immediate anger at the towering column topped by his statue still being there in Marion Square. He fails and Macey has jumped out of the still moving carriage as it turns to go back down the main street. Zack leaps out too.

Macey looks at the monument, signalling for her oils. The carriage stops, Clem and Prisha deliver, Ricky watches.

"This is not normally a stop in the tour," the driver says, turning to Billy who is pulling the reins for the team of horses to stop.

"We all have to end our lives somewhere," Billy says, and she sits and waits.

Macey sketches the tall pillar with a man on top, but she puts branches out from the pillar as if it is a tree. Black men, women and children hang dead from the branches. Clem cringes. It's her most strikingly provocative work yet. Macey depicts an angry God in the sky holding loops of more rope.

"I'll do the detail later," she says, storming back towards the carriage.

"Surely that should have been pulled down by now?" Macey barks at the town, but the coachwoman is the only one there to hear it. She remains quiet as she drives on, her horses completing the turn. It is obvious Macey feels that equal civil rights are not considered the norm' in the town.

"Lady asked you a question," Billy says to her. "The guy on top."

"I guess it is outdated," the coachwoman admits.

"Are there plans to pull it down?" Macey asks now the conversation has been revived.

"Best to ask in the tourist office. I don't know the answer. The question has been asked many times."

"You know what I'm gonna do if Yonan makes my work famous?"

"No," Ricky says.

"I'm gonna offer to design a whole group of new statues to sit around that monument and haunt J. C."

"I'm not sure the town would go for that, mam," the coachwoman says.

"It might have to start a movement that puts so much pressure on Charlestown, it will hit their tourism. Art can make that happen. Anyway, why does that sick man have the initials J.C? Is it the same reason you have 52 churches? You all need forgiveness seeing you are a good Christian city with more churches than Rome."

"Mam, we can finish the tour if you feel uncomfortable."

The commentator turns to try and instigate a conclusion, but Macey has Billy looking crazy over one shoulder and Zack over the other.

"We're fine, you finish the ride," Billy says with the look of death in his eyes.

"Got the story you came for?" Macey asks Ricky sitting very close to him.

"I didn't come for a story."

"Don't be cheesy," she says provoking him.

"I haven't taken any pictures."

"I took them for you," Prisha says.

"Me too," adds Billy because they are all watching the couple.

Macey looks disappointed at Ricky missing her anger.

"It's not what I came for," Ricky says, holding his ground.

"OK. Stick your ground. I like that," she says, just for a moment enjoying the fact that he came for her.

"I don't understand," Ricky says.

"You never been out with a woman?" Billy asks from behind.

Macey looks at her sketch, but then turns to him.

"I love that you came to see me. Love it. But, now, this is me. I am this woman. My art is who I am. It has to be inspired. Hatred, equality, ignorance; if I see it I paint it. I wasn't expecting to find this here so I wouldn't be offended if you found a story. Charleston will always mean a lot to me and not just for this painting."

The testy exchange formed no wedge between them, it was part of a process to take in the details after the contract has been signed; they are a couple in probation.

"Maybe in Charleston, the ghost on the shoulder of every black man is J C Calhoun," she says loudly, aimed at the driver. "And I should make him the God of each of your churches. The other God would have kept better watch over blacks if you'd have let him in."

When they get to Rainbow Row, Macey insists on getting out again. She cannot pass the Old Exchange Building and Provost Dungeon, which the guide tells them is where the slaves were auctioned off in the square. She leads an investigation and no one argues. Billy stays with the carriage so it doesn't vanish.

Inside, Macey stands for a long time, looking at the posters of black people for sale.

"Exactly what kind of Christians are they?" She asks, turning to the others. "There is a seventy-five-year-old woman for sale here, top of the list. Her name is Kate!"

No one has an answer. It might not be the most ideal first date, but Ricky is attentive. He admires her politics.

"Macey, would you mind if I wrote some notes about you. Your reaction to all this is so poignant."

"Me? Do you need to?"

"As much as you needed to say it."

Macey smiles.

"You learn more about a person in an hour's tour with them in Charlestown, than a year of conversation," Ricky says.

Macey takes her sketch pad. The others are used to waiting. Ricky isn't, but he takes notes about the building and those who passed through. He feels the same stories as she does.

"I wonder if your ancestors passed through here," Ricky ponders.

"Well, you know more about my ancestors than me."

Walking back from the coach corner, through the shops to the ship, Macey feels that arm-in-arm with a white boy is causing mixed feelings. In the distance, leaving a clothes shop with bags and bags, it appears to be an African King who must have been spending big time. Catching up, they discover it is Big Dog.

"No Way!" Prisha screams.

"Way!" he shouts.

Macey uses the moment to catch Ricky off guard.

"What did you find out about me?"

Billy's mad smiling face pops in between them.

"Well?"

"You have siblings," Ricky reveals.

"I don't want to know," she fires back in shock. "I do, I want to know everything."

"I warned you," he says.

"No more. I need a drink first. But I don't feel like getting back on that ship without you," she says to Ricky.

"Yonan is my boss too, it's his ship," Ricky smiles.

"But he's missing," Prisha says ear-dropping. "I'll try his office."

90 – DINNER AT SEA

Day 11 - Florida - all at 1900hrs

Ricky is unexpectedly overwhelmed by everything he has seen so far. He dumped his bag in the living room between Macey and Prisha's bedroom. He uses Macey's shower after she has finished.

Back in the mini-suite living room, which is bigger than his whole Miami apartment, Clément is kitted with a formal outfit from the ship's shop. But what has impressed him most is Macey's new paintings. He is amazed by them all and the speed she works at. The one he does not see is the one of her dancing, which isn't in the pile.

He is further awe-struck by the atrium at night, which is enough to wow any cruiser from any ship. The money spent on Yonan Schmeichel's MS Overlord, to make the three-story amphitheatre ultra-impressive is, without doubt, the most spent on any ship at sea. However, what he is enjoying is being taken out by Macey. After one cruise, she is the expert. They are in the bar in the centre of the ship, and stand looking up and down at the atrium that she already takes for granted. He tries to imagine the three live shows she has performed from the ballroom floor below and then looking at her four bodyguards he feels a little inadequate as he realises how special she is.

"It all seems a bit too wow, right?" Prisha says, very happy on the drinks she has already consumed.

She has caught him in his dizzy day dream.

"Err, yeah."

"Think of me, coming from a big family, all living in a converted shipping container in a slum."

"What? You lived in a shipping container?"

"Yeah, we were lucky. Eleven of us. My income over the years has moved them out, but I wonder sometimes if they are happier. There's a story for you." She toasts Ricky with a confidence she would never have had years ago, even months ago.

Macey comes back.

"Our buzzer's gone off; it means our table is ready," she glees, leading him off. Prisha grabs the wine bottle and follows. Almost all the team are joining them.

The ship's large dining room is awash with mirrors and gold, with waiters and wine, and people. Ricky's jaw is dropping.

"So you eat, and play, then there is another day," Ricky stumbles.

"In a new town," Macey finishes for him.

"I love it. We're sailing down the coast of Florida."

"To Canaveral," she says, enjoying finishing his sentences.

Kieron, Hunter, Billy and Zack have endless military chat to exchange. They have not stopped laughing, but they are watching. The two pairs had never met before and Kieron and Hunter are finding out more about Dwight than he has ever revealed. Billy and Zack were in his company. He definitely commanded a 'behind the lines recovery team' of very hard men. They were there to dig out anyone who got stuck, anyone like him working deep undercover.

Prisha has been chatting to Big Dog most of the evening, who, although he bought new clothes, is loving being a Zulu King for formal night. He may never dress another way, just like Prisha with her white boots. They sit at a table for twelve with four seats still available.

"Who are the other seats for?" Ricky asks, looking at the empty seats.

"Bedriška arrived with me, but has a package she's trying to smuggle on below decks somewhere. She'll be here," Big Dog explains.

"Clément is late, and I guess neither of the other two seats are for Jill?" Prisha says with an alcohol-infused smile.

"Jill? No. Nor her four forgers!" Zack starts.

"They are innocent. They thought she was selling the paintings to passengers," Prisha thinks out loud.

"There's a lot more to her story, or I wouldn't keep her in jail," Zack pitches.

Ricky is concentrating on Macey, but his ears prick up at the word 'jail'.

"The ship has a jail?" He asks her.

"I don't know," she replies, not having seen all the ship. .

His attention is split, as he is spellbound by Bedriška approaching looking like the star of the room in a long silver dress. She is carrying a black case that Big Dog, Kieron and Hunter all recognise as the case of guns she obtained in Russia. Clément eases out a chair for her as the waiter hands them menus.

"Sorry I am late, I was choosing dress in ship's laundry."

"Good choice," Prisha laughs.

"I was at the gallery desk. One of the assistants can do that job from tomorrow," Clément says, sitting.

Prisha toasts but she is too early, no one is ready

so she downs the wine she brought in. The pre-dinner drinks have gone to her head. The wine waiter arrives at Bedi.

"Wine, madam?"

"No, vodka."

"Single or a double?"

"Just one bottle," she says clearly, so there is no confusion. "And glass of ice. I drink vodka from red-wine glass."

Bedriška looks across at Ricky.

"I like. Privet," she says, to greet him in Russian with approval.

Hunter pushes Billy's bottom jaw back up.

"Privet," Billy mis-pronounces.

"I was not speaking to you, but, hello."

Ricky thought the group was already eclectic, but Bedi is an experience he instantly enjoys. He watches her triumphantly open the black attaché case just enough to show what she has retrieved from storage.

"Still full of tools and love letters," Dog smiles, peeping in.

Bedriška nods. The guns and bullets are intact.

"I love pallet wrap," she says." I was tied up with it once. They thought it was start of my torture, but I loved it."

The table goes quiet for a moment.

"Do we all take a gun now?" Big Dog jokes. "Feels like Chicago with these big tables and glass chandeliers. We need a jazz singer sliding between the tables."

"No. That is down in the lower deck, a cabaret dining venue," Prisha slurs. "Maybe they will let you all have your guns out down there."

This is the first time she has drunk too much. They had been in the Atrium Bar for a good hour before dinner. She was feeling a little left out of the lads' conversation, and Macey had Ricky. Neither Clem nor Bedi were there for her to turn to, and Big Dog was being a King and waving at people.

"Are you alright Prisha?" Kieron asks. "You seem a little squiffy."

"Sorry. I have had a few too many. Please don't gang up on me."

"Why would we gang up on you? Who does that?" Bedi asks bluntly.

"Bees."

"Bees?" Clément asks.

"Bees get drunk all the time," she says to defend herself. "Drunk on amber nectar. They have flying accidents because they fly whilst drunk."

"Give her water," Bedi orders.

"When the drunk bees get back home, the other bees gang up on them because they are drunk."

"Good story. It finished. No one gang up on you," Bedi says.

"See what I mean? Just like you. Humans, bees, they are all the same."

Macey stops Prisha from talking any more, and she is lost in the ordering of food as the waiter goes around taking notes. Big Dog is last and has real indecision with the main course.

"I will bring both, sir," the waiter says. His time is tight, but the food supply is not.

The waiter puts the menus back down at his station. One assistant disinfects each menu cover, removes the inlay menu sheet, and puts tomorrow's menu in before returning the folders to tomorrow's pile. The other assistant runs to the kitchen for the soup. They are very close.

"Two meals?" Macey beams at Dog.

"Just in case I get tossed off to take the Greyhound at Canaveral."

"No, you were pretty cool in a difficult situation back there," Hunter says, and he shows him a fist as a no contact appreciation bump..

Dog asks. "I liked that bigger long range piece."

Soup bowls placed down.

"I feel like I've been dropped into a weird dream," Ricky shares with Macey.

"I'm real. You're here, and we're looking for art thieves," Macey says as they finish the soup. Ricky hasn't touched his.

The table goes quiet. Soup bowls are removed, the main course is laid out. Big Dog's second one is left near him with a plastic cover on to retain the heat.

"It's a crazy group," Ricky adds.

"We're a group of private investigators and we each have our own talents. But, sadly for you, we already have a journalist," Macey says, thinking of Izzy in Miami.

"Yeah. I met her. Your sister."

Macey's face goes solid. Not a muscle moves.

"Have I done it again?" Ricky hits quickly with trepidation.

"Izzy is my sister?" Macey asks in horror and a worried look of realisation develops. "And Croc is my brother?"

"I, I said you had siblings."

Ricky is feeling uncomfortable. Macey is stoic. He does not know whether to cuddle her or not.

"Sorry," he whispers.

He dares to put his arm around her.

"It's so obvious. But I was too wrapped up," she

replies. "We must be triplets."

Silence hits the whole table. It is not Macey's situation. Unexpectedly, Mike walks up to the table.

"Ladies and gentlemen I want to introduce you to Mike," Zack says, letting the head of security from the Italian dockyard sit.

"Good evening."

He sits and looks across at Big Dog's spare dinner. Big Dog puts a hand on it. Mike retracts; food is not something to argue over. Dog then offers it to him.

"Enjoy," Dog says, reading the game.

Mike nods in gratitude, the waiter is behind him to take the lid.

"Where's Bentley?" Kieron asks.

"I thought I'd travel up ahead of the art crew. A little R&R. Is this seat for Jill?"

"Is she turns up, she's welcome to it," Zack says. The whole table knows she won't be joining them, and they feel the tension.

"We don't have to talk tonight, we've got all day tomorrow," Mike says in the hard way villains speak politely. He then turns to the table. "Now, can I buy a couple of bottles of wine?"

91 – CANAVERAL

Day 12 - Florida -0830hrs

8.30 in the morning is a time that splits cruisers into distinct groups. Many have been up for a couple of hours, exercising on the deck, waiting for the gym to open at 7am. Some are straight into breakfast, then take up their towel to bag a sunbed before the crowds arrive. As it is a port day, many will be up for excursions. Some will rise later. These include the cabaret artists and musicians; they catch the main breakfast bar before it closes at ten-thirty rather than the limited breakfast that runs until midday when lunch opens.

Whatever the time, someone is doing something on the ship, and it is busy this morning. Many rush to get to the major theme parks. Their return can be late because the ship stays in the dock tonight and will sail to Miami mid-afternoon tomorrow. For those who stay onboard tonight, it will be a fun formal night.

Having walked away from the ship and down past the earthworks where they are building yet another cruise port, Macey and Ricky continue hand in hand through Jetty Park towards the beach.

Once over the little footbridges and past many birds in the small creek that would have enticed many artists to stop and capture, they are in the sun with no cover. The sea is out quite a way, and the beach seems to go forever. Macey has led Ricky down to the sea and the walk along in the lapping waves. It is quixotic; some way behind, Clem carries her art materials, Billy and Zack watch.

"You see them?" Billy asks, flicking water in front of him.

"I see three," Zack confirms. They are back in military talk because they have noticed they are being tailed.

"Copy that. I'll take the rear."

Billy kicks out at the sea loudly but loses his balance and goes down. Zack goes to him, dragging him from the very shallow water. The others turn to help but are waved on. Zack helps him up but every time Billy tries to put weight on his ankle he collapses. Zack acts torn between his mate and staying with Macey. They play out until they know they are being watched, then Zack leaves Billy and hurries to catch his convoy.

"Don't get too close, Billy," Zack tells Billy as he leaves him in the sand.

Billy is left trying to walk but falling down. He watches as his team walk on. Annoyed, he lays back, punching the sand. He feels he should have an award for his acting as he watches the three men continue to follow his team and eventually go out of sight. They didn't leave one watching him, rookie error. Billy is up and running, off the beach to circle around behind the three tails.

In the ship buffet, Kieron watches the three art assistants leave Bentley and rush off excitedly. They are on a day out.

Kieron gets up and goes to join Bentley.

"Mr Double Barrel."

"You try so hard to be funny," Bentley says.

"You're right in the middle of this art scam," Kieron accuses.

The remark takes Bentley back. He was not expecting that.

"How?" He asks.

"Apart from Russia, apart from your dad, where do I stop? You sent four paintings to St Petersburg."

"Yes, two lesser works, a LeRoy and a May.I.see. There is quite a fuss about her. It just needs something special to make it take off."

"And does the artist get paid?"

"Do they ever?" Bentley sighs.

Kieron slows down. Here is where answers start to lead somewhere. "Anoataly is Mr Russia?"

"Yes. My dad's gallery works with Mr Schmeichel. I send the paperwork, all done. They only have to sign it and send it. I never see them after the van leaves, nor the commission; like the artist."

"You're the postman?" Kieron says deliberately down-grading him.

"I can paint. I was selected because I can paint."

"All the assistants can paint," Kieron hits hard. "You're just living off your dad."

"I am actually a much better painter than nearly all the others."

"I don't see any of your paintings being sold."

"I have always gone unnoticed. If only I had Macey's talent," Bentley sighs. "Few do."

"You copy. Why would you want to copy?"

Bentley hesitates. Kieron knows more.

"The mysterious leap from copying to forging, and where the difference lies: Hmm," Bentley sighs. "There's a huge amount of money in being a renown forger constantly in demand. That can be a way of having a name."

"But you're not the best in that warehouse. Not good enough to be painting the forgeries going to Russia."

Bentley realises that Kieron does know it all, well most. He doesn't know that sometimes he does paint and his ego lets more of the story slip.

"Well, some. Sometimes. But no, most are done by a Chinese guy in his garage."

"So where does it all go after Anoataly?"

"Who gives a shit? I don't care about them after they leave me. I check them through, they go, I forget about them."

"The problem is, you're not doing all of them, and they don't all go through your dad, and they're not all for Yonan."

Bentley thought he knew it all, but it appears Kieron knows more than he does.

Kieron watches the poker faced Bentley as he stands to take his empty plate away.

Kieron joins Hunter and Prisha in the forger's room Jill was using in the low crew deck. The two bugs they found in Yonan's dining room during at the very first lunch have been set and he finds his two fellow agents with plastic doctors gloves on. Hunter has an envelope of hair.

"Nice touch." Kieron says, noticing Hunter pulling strands and dropping them on the floor where Jill was tied to the bench, and wedging them into a crack in the table.

"We need Mike to panic enough to make a move."

"I agree. Did Jill just give you handfuls of hair?"

"She was very obliging when she saw the knife. You know she doesn't get many visitors in that cell," Hunter says, standing back to look at his work and holding up an earring. She lent me this as well." He turns to Kieron. "Such a giving young thing."

"Doesn't suit you," Kieron says.

Hunter drops the earring.

"We need some fresh blood to put some urgency to it."

"She didn't offer that?"

"No."

Hunter offers his knife. Kieron slits his forearm and lets the blood drop as Hunter artistically directs the position. Kieron passes the knife back.

"First aid kit." Hunter looks around the room, but Prisha is already taking the crew one from the corner of the room. "I've set the sound up next door, but I don't want to sit there all morning. Do you fancy listening?"

"No, you do it. Mike will be here soon. He didn't fly all this way to go to the Kennedy Space Centre. He's desperate to find Jill. Only three went off to theme parks. We have Rosemary and Bentley to look for the store keys. Rosemary seems a keen young puppet, following him for a promotion."

They leave the room and move next door where Prisha has the listening device and recorder from the service room of Yonan's dining room, is now set up.

"Sharp eyes on Rosemary," Hunter says.

"She just looked pathetic," says Kieron.

"Yeah, and remember she said she couldn't even change a canvas; that seems odd now. I've learnt a lot about art from these kids." Hunter says, sitting down.

"I'm so glad you're becoming cultured," quips Kieron.

It does not take long before they hear Mike enter and start looking at the clues in the art stock room next door. Kieron recognises Rosemary's voice.

"Why is she with him?" Prisha whispers to Hunter.

They scuttle around, all kinds of sounds, but Mike doesn't speak.

"Would they have handed Jill over to the police, dad?"

Now Mike speaks. They are both worried about

her.

"No. They may have taken her off, but no police. She may have needed a medic, that might give me some clues. You go and search the local hospital. She could be under any name."

Mike leaves the room angry and with no answer. Kieron has a moment of fear of Mike storming in on them, being next door. The two outside clear.

"Prisha, you know how to upload that?"

She nods yes.

"Then try and keep Rosemary on the ship?"

Hunter decides that despite the upload, the 'take your daughter to work day' demands an actual call to Dwight.

Hunter has come up to get cell phone service. Prisha may have to in order to send the file, but she knows her way around a ship. The promenade deck on the ship is empty. He is about to call Dwight, but his cell goes. Mike is very direct.

"Where's Jill?" he asks sharply.

"You must have the wrong number buddy," Hunter replies coolly.

"I want her back."

"You came all this way for an assistant?"

"We need to talk, you have no idea what's going on."

"When and where?"

"Get the number 9 bus to the pier, now," is a sharp order. "I'll meet you at the pier bar."

"I'll check my calendar," Hunter says, ending the call.

Hunter immediately reports the call to Dwight. The bus can wait.

CRUISE SHIP ART THEFT

In Miami, Dwight has a huge energised smile. Izzy looks in a panic as her board is becoming crazier, and Croc is still deep-sea trawling his version in layers. They have just fast spooled Kieron's room tape recording.

"Rosemary called Mike 'Dad'?" Izzy asks, looking at the 'Mike chain' of her tree, previously very thin. "Croc, can you search these two and connect them up?"

"No. Sorry. I've just got pictures in from Billy. He's following three 'Ali Babas' carrying long bags. What's an Ali Baba?"

"It's an insurgent, they'll be snipers. Rifles in the long bags. I want names to those faces please," Dwight says with a lot more urgency.

Dwight turns back to his workstation and talks to himself. 'Father, daughter, one certainly has a phoney name.'

"Or both do," Izzy says, now over his shoulder.

A face to face call from Hunter appears on his screen.

"I've been invited to the pier on a no 9 bus. But he desperately wants Jill; for him it's all about Jill. Why does he care about a replaceable worker?"

"Thanks," Izzy says. "Is that what we are?"

"I'll leave you to philosophise on that one Izzy. It kept me awake for nights, for many, many years," Hunter answers on the screen.

"My legs are still at that party," Dwight adds.

"Are Jill and Rosemary sisters?" Hunter asks.

Izzy moves away to her board.

"Mia Murina, Human Resources at Bianchi Ship Builders is all over every appointment. I'll have her dig deeper the family connection. But, is Yonan pulling the strings of every player?"

"You mean the Yonan you don't like because he bought -"

"- he stole my painting," Dwight insists.

The call ends. Dwight is back to work.

"You sure Bentley's not in the middle of this?" Izzy asks Dwight, finding it hard to move him from the middle. "The team in Cuba said they were instructed by Bentley."

"Cubans never saw a Bentley face, just a Bentley name. I'm sure of only one thing; everyone works for Yonan."

92 - UNDER THE BOARDWALK

Day 12 - Florida -1230hrs

Dog and Bedi are enjoying the sun and the shade as they walk through the campsites in the woods set back from the beach. Trailers and tents sit on lots between trees, and there are washroom blocks and facilities every few hundred yards. Dog trails behind her in plain shorts, though his Caribbean shirt is a bit loud. Bedi is getting golden brown in her tiny top and shorts, and the only odd thing is the attaché case she carries. They have found the three suspected snipers but no sign of Billy. She feels his report on the weapons they carry is correct, which means they are useless, if not a hinder in close arm contact. Billy, if he were around, Bedriška, and maybe Dog, could easily hit the three trailing Macey's group, but it would stop whatever is to happen and they would not get to the real answer CSCI as a group might be heading towards. Zack is sure he has Macey safe; or he would not go through with this, they are his explicit orders from Hunter. Whatever it is, it seems to revolve around Mike, or who is employing him. His men will be very dangerous when in position. They stay close. Assuming Billy is around, it is now three on three. The beach goes forever and the pier is still a little way away. Bedi is annoyed she can't see Billy.

Macey and Ricky are kicking sea at each other under the boardwalk amongst the wooden pillars that hold up the 800 foot traditional pier. Pillars that have stood there for over fifty years also give them intermittent cover. The couple have not a care in the world, and Macey loves it. If it was not for Ricky stealing all her attention, her easel and paints would have been out long ago. Clément is exhausted; he has carried the two pads and her easel along the 3.5 miles of sand. Two hours of walking on sand is not easy.

"You could 'ave 'elped me," Clément says to Zack as he crosses to him. But Zack is looking at both sides, not him.

"You're right. But I would have been exhausted and I need to be on my 'A' game. I need to be fit to do my job, sorry. Now, you set her up behind a pillar, this side of the pier."

Shoes off, easel set down, Clément joins in the water kicking, which spoils the intimacy of the two. As soon as he can get near to Ricky's ear, and Macey is turned, he fires his requirement.

"She is 'ere to work, Ricky."

Macey collects the wooden tripod from where Clément left it. She carries it to where she sees the steps.

"Macey. This is a CSCI order," Clément says, moving her back. She has never heard that term before but goes back to the other side of the pier. She is not concerned yet; the sun has an hour or two to set.

As directed by Mike, Hunter rides the number nine bus, sitting two seats from the back where the floor rises for the engine and rear axil. He would sit at the back, as expected, but then he becomes a sniper target through the large glass rear window. He is on the inside of the seat and his right leg flares out to stop anyone going past. Apart from his defence position, he appears to be relaxed, enjoying the journey, scanning through reports from Dwight.

Kieron is in a hire car following the bus. He has the confused Bentley to his side, who ends a call on his cell and turns to Kieron.

"That was my father."

"He had my table delivered yet?"

"He's not in New York. He's with Yonan, sitting in a bar near Westgate Pier."

Kieron speed dials. "Hit speaker," he orders Bentley as he passes him the cell. "Yonan and Crouch are at the pier."

"Roger that. You driving?" Dwight asks from Miami.

"Yes."

"You won't have read my text. Jill Quarrington, otherwise known as Jill Quant, sister of Rosemary Quarrington, otherwise known as Addington. Daughters of Mike Quarrington, otherwise known as Mike Peeke who did time for robbery with violence. He has been accused of murder twice and got off both times. That's prison ink, not navy. You want more?"

"Quarrington?" Bentley jumps in. "There's a gallery chain called Quarrington. They have site in Durham, another one in Alnwick, and others down the A1 in all the old English tourist villages with castles. The main one is a nice gallery in Lincoln. They play to rich tourists, similar to the cruise ship market. Pull them in with a classy expensive piece, sell them a shitty castle."

"Dwight, chase that. How big's this family business."

"We're talking big money already," Bentley says.

"These guys won't mind killing all of you to keep the money train going," Dwight shares. He is worried about them going to a meeting at a location Mike has chosen with his snipers watching. "You're heading to a Bag of Dicks."

93 - BAG OF DICKS

Day 12 - Florida -1605hrs

Hunter had to walk down from the bus stop. He joins Kieron and Bentley who are sitting at the far end of the bar with glasses of rose. He doesn't comment. The wooden wall behind them gives good rear cover and their open front is a view across the bar and out to the beach and sea. They can see the steps up to the left and the walk down the pier to the right.

"Enjoy the ride?" Kieron asks.

"The tourist commentary wasn't working."

"Ask for your money back?"

"Two dollars. Someone's robbing someone," Hunter says, as his pre ordered beer is cracked open and served in a foam sleeve to keep it cool. The barman is wearing a Polo shirt with the rodeo. Hunter nods at the wall behind them.

"Checked it. Stockroom and kitchen. Empty," Kieron says.

Hunter acknowledges two old regulars a few seats along from them at the bar with a nod and raised bottle. Both have full beards, neither in a hurry for life's next step. One wears a white Amasa Vitafelt Stetson with a small feather in the trim. The other an American Rangers hat. But Hunter's politeness is not to be social, it's to notice they are both packing guns on their belts.

"Love your hat, man," Hunter says genuinely at the Stetson.

"Yep," is the slow reply. "I wanted the red one, but, little loud to sit here."

"Too loud to sit next to me," the Ranger says.

"Should have got me a wife, would have been less noise," the Stetson jibes.

"You have to put up with this every day?" Hunter asks the bartender as a joke. Except it isn't a joke; he wants to know if they are locals or plants.

"Yep," the barman says.

Hunter raises a glass, they toast him back.

"We're here every day if you ever wanna come and join us," the Stetson says.

"Don't move till the sun goes down. Then we're the other side watching it dive," the Ranger finishes.

Hunter turns to Kieron having seen past the two customers.

"REMF arriving."

"Think your dad's walking in," Kieron translates.

Surprised, Bentley positions to stand but Hunter stops him. Bentley eases a better position on his stool and raises his glass to acknowledge his father. Yonan and Crouch nod as they sit sheepishly on the bend at the very far end of the bar. It is a confirmation of trouble.

"Remf?" Bentley asks.

"Just a term," Kieron says.

"Rear echelon mother fuckers," Hunter enjoys saying.

"He means Yonan, it means those with cushy jobs who stay out of the combat zones."

"But he's here," Bentley says.

"No, he's up there so he knows there's gonna be trouble at this end," Kieron explains.

Bentley becomes more nervous.

"Yeah. With snipers out there somewhere and I still ain't worked out who they're squaring up. YODO," Hunter says, and swings his bottle at Kieron's. There is anger in his do or die bravery.

"Not today," Kieron says as they crack together. "Zack's down by the wooden coffee shop."

"Yep. Saw him on the way in. Guess everyone else did," Hunter says then swigs from the bottle. "But not our secret weapon."

"Billy?"

"Billy."

They flick the bases of their bottles together again.

"What does that stand for?" Bentley asks.

"Stands for Billy, and no one knows where the fuck he is, or who he'll kill first," Hunter plays loud enough for the crowd around the bar.

"Billy," Bentley cautiously toasts, then swigs. "And YODO?" He asks.

"You only die once, kid," Hunter smiles.

Bentley moves to leave, but both Kieron and Hunter hold him on the stool.

"Enjoy the view, you're on a roulette table," Kieron says holding his thigh firmly there.

"Am I a hostage?"

"With a glass of fucking rose?" Hunter asks him, but that is not an answer.

Bentley understands he has to stay. He toasts them again, trying to be brave.

"We don't die today," he says, more hopeful than banter.

Kieron didn't want to expose their backs to the open sea and sand. Having the forward exposure makes them vulnerable to the front only and places the snipers in one aspect. They watch Mike climb the wooden steps and sit opposite, the sea behind him. He's out of the way of any site line from the land. No one would try a shot from the sea, and he must be perfectly lit for a sniper looking into the bar thus ensuring he can be avoided. They will be lit too, but not as well. The scene is set.

"It's over Mike," Hunter starts. "Now, let's have a beer and split the spoils."

"Beer," Mike signals to the bartender who is already topping a bottle.

"We need to formalise a deal," Mike says.

The bar tender must have seen enough of life to know that these considerably tough men are angry even though their speech is calm. Many a wetlands oil deal has been thrashed out over this bar, and his position appears to ensure he will be no part of any affray. He polishes glasses in the middle by a low display of spirits under a few dangling brass pans hanging from high. The guys in the hats, however, have been retired far too long to miss anything and are set to enjoy the pre-match fight.

"Yeah. You return what you stole, then fuck off," Hunter says.

"Sounds like a mighty fair deal, stranger, if you don't mind me saying," the Stetson chips in, then he shares a post script with his friend. "Ain't had a front row seat for a long time."

The cowboy is ignored. Mike's look focusses on Bentley.

"Glad your knees are better, kid. I never did believe that performance down the line. See, I was in touch with my daughter on her second cell. You dropped the ball not finding that."

"Zack left it with her deliberately. That's why he kept her prisoner; he knew he had a fish on a hook. While your lips still hurting, you don't have one real painting," Kieron reveals.

"Let me tell you a story," Mike starts as he works a big fat cigar.

"Don't spoil a good beer," Hunter says, signalling the barman to bring another round, and include the two old-timers who are now involved. Two more guns might be useful, and might be cheaply bought.

"Is it the one about the guy with prison ink who marries a woman with a chain of art galleries in the UK?" Kieron asks.

Hunter looks at Kieron.

"Now, you're encouraging him," Hunter says, even though he doesn't know that story. "And I wish he'd just shut the fuck up."

Mike ignores him and starts his story.

"A guy bought a box of super-expensive cigars, I mean, the price you don't smoke," Mike starts. "So, he insured them, fully insured them against everything, even against fire. After he had enjoyed smoking each one, he claimed on his insurance because they were all completely damaged by fire. The insurance company did not want to pay out, but in court, they lost and had to pay. Now here's the good part, and listen real good. As the man left the courthouse, smiling that he had won, the police arrested him on twenty counts of arson."

"Nice story," the man in the Stetson said.

"So, maybe Mr Schmeichel would like to join us?" Mike asks.

"Why?" Kieron asks.

"Similar story," Mike says.

After a nod up the bar, Yonan walks down and sits a couple of seats from Mike, not next to him. Crouch follows him down and is joined in, opposite the cowboys. The uneasy shift in power is felt around the bar as neither Kieron nor Hunter were expecting Yonan to move adjacent to Mike.

"I'm confused," Bentley says softly. It is aimed at no one, but shows he is just a foot-soldier, working for the higher power as instructed, not knowing who the deity is.

"Whose your money on?" The guy in the Stetson asks.

"Some poker game. I ain't seen all the cards," the Felt Ranger growls softly. "But I think the kid's being held as ransom."

CRUISE SHIP ART THEFT

94 - SHOW DOWN

Day 12 - Florida -1635hrs

The atmosphere around the open bar is so tense it could be slashed with a sabre; but which way? Where? By whom?

"Who's the crook here? You're having his paintings stolen, very efficiently," Mike says as if continuing his cigar story. "Claiming on the insurance while the originals are tucked away. Theft makes the value of any painting go up; all great works need a history. The value of student copies or official numbered prints also go up; which you sell to Russia. But, you could do time for insurance fraud: not arson. Meanwhile, I'm running away with a few of your lesser paintings."

"I wouldn't call the Kandinsky lesser," Yonan says, entering the game.

"No, I stepped up there," Mike says, his eyes still across the table at his military opponents. "It's why we need a deal. Boundaries."

"Except the Kandinsky too is a copy," Yonan says.

"It still sold," Mike barks, unnerved slightly. "We even documented the theft to add to its provenance."

"Greed, always gets you," the Stetson enjoys saying as if talking to the television.

"Ease it down partner," Mike says, affording them no more than focussed peripheral vision.

The cowboy grunts, eyes to his partner, who grunts back.

"Have we backed the wrong horse?" the Stetson whispers.

"I reckon there's a woman in this somewhere," the Ranger shares quietly.

"Here's the problem," Mike says. "Everyone's happy. So, I suggest you return my daughter, and Mr Crouch's son, and you two child-snatchers 'do one'."

Hunter looks to Yonan, who offers a small agitated shake of his head which means no.

"Our employer says no," Kieron fires.

"I'm already dealt into this card game. You see, we sell to the same Russian dealer. We have a parallel business, but, **Anoataly Istov** now earns more money from us than he does from you. Same dealer, same deal."

"We've been there. He's been told to behave," Kieron says very politely.

"And I told him that I'd deal with you two. Neither of you are in the game."

"It's not us Anoataly has to worry about," Kieron confirms.

"The Russian woman?" Mike laughs. "The one so drunk each day she couldn't wake, couldn't walk, couldn't work. Drunk last night at the table. The one who is so rock bottom as an alcoholic that death is overdue. Come on. He can't fear her," Mike adds.

"We don't want a deal. You're not getting a deal," Kieron says.

"And I never claim on any insurance, but I am an underwriter at quite a few. But I found your cigar story mildly amusing," Yonan says. "There is no deal and no employment left for you at any of my companies."

"I told Anoataly I'd deal with her too, with all of you," Mike ends, "I have a side deal to your sales or…" he pauses, leaning back on his chair. He indicates behind him. "This might help your decision. I got the best sniper in the world. And the second-best sniper, in fact, of anywhere on the planet."

Both Kieron and Hunter can see the gun-sight reflections; they are meant to. One in the window of a white lifeguard's hut with a blue fence railed around it, sitting in the middle of the beach. The other amongst the canoes over on the shipping container planted on the small grassy knoll beyond the beach volleyball area. The deadliest thing that every military agent dreads is a kill shot. A sniper. The one chance they have is to see the reflection of the gun sight and take cover. The crack of the bullet would be heard after the hit as all rifle bullets travel faster than sound. They have seen the gun sight and are still dangerously in plain sight.

The White Stetson leans over to the Felt Ranger.

"It's gonna be a day with stories to tell."

"Yeah," the Ranger agrees. "But who you gonna tell? I'm the only friend you got."

They both look back at the gamble-for-life table to their left.

"Without my paintings, you have nothing," says Yonan.

"And without your daughter, Jill. Who does your dirty work? Not the other fucking idiot, Rosemary; she can't even frame a dish cloth," Hunter says, finding Mike's weakness.

"I don't do deals at gunpoint!" Mike snarls.

Yonan almost interrupts, now the exchanges have got serious. Mike's daughters are his weak spot. Yonan may or may not know this is normally the point at which someone gets killed. But then again he truly is REMF. He does not care, he wins whichever way the party ends. Without him, his money and art deals, Mike has no business. Yonan survives at any outcome, he just survives better being totally in control. When the bodies start to fall, those on either side will ensure he lives.

Hunter stands up shaking his head, no agreement.

"I'm out. This jumping on money is all too much for a poor kid from a mid-west small holding."

It might take most people a while to take in his self-pity. Mike has his hand on his hand gun, as do the two observers at the bar.

Zack is way down the pier close to their third heavy, the one who has one hand down inside his long fishing bag. It is holding his gun with his finger on the trigger. Zack knows Hunter standing is his signal. He raises both hands to scratch his hair then restyle it running his fingers though it before stretching high. Four seconds. That is the unmissable wave to Bedi and Big Dog. In just a few steps he hits the guard shoulder-first, in exactly the spots which null every feeling and potential muscle movement. Eight seconds. The other two henchmen are unable to see any of the action because their eyes are fixed looking down a gun sight. They will have either Kieron or Hunter in their crosshairs and Mike the only focus of the other eye so they can see all his signals. If started, the kill shots would have hit already. Zack's gunman is in an involuntary sleep and being cable tied to the wooden pier. Zack then removes all ammunition and breaks the Barrett M82a1 snipers' rifle down. He cable-ties the gun bag to the wood but keeps the essential bolt carrier, which carries the firing pin, in his hand so the gun cannot be used without him. He can build it as quickly as he broke it. He looks along the beach, less than twenty seconds have past.

Bedi is on the container. She pushes the barely conscious sniper over the edge. His head bounces off the steel container and he dangles by his tied ankle. Both mercenary warriors look to Big Dog, knowing they can't expect the same, but she gestures that he is taking too long and will leap off the container to run across the sand and do what he is not up to.

Big Dog enters the lifesaving hut where the first sniper Mike pointed to lies in wait. The lifeguards are tied up on the floor. Dog doesn't have the talents the others have to take these professionals out. With a brutal kick and a heavy rage of blows, Dog floors him with his street talent. Somewhere in the mess, a knife goes into the gunman's right hand and pins it to the wooden floor. Dog finally pulls a cable tie tight around the gunman's neck. A second tie fastens him to the table. Then he is knocked unconscious. His work is effective but untidy. He breathes, happy, then cuts the lifeguards free.

"Thanks," a lifeguard says.

"Welcome. Look out, check he didn't shoot anyone."

The life guards rush out onto their balcony. Big Dog walks outside a lot slower feeling like a superhero. He leans on the blue rail for a moment, looking back at the pier.

"Have I been shot?" Kieron asks.

"No," Hunter says. "Me?"

"No, who would be shooting at us. Best shooter in the world?"

"He missed. Must be the second best," Hunter says, sitting back down waving and ordering another beer.

Mike looks out and sees Big Dog at the hut waving back, and his other man hanging from by his ankle down the front of the container, swinging and pulling to get free.

"There are others," Mike threatens, looking. "Let's do a deal before it gets bloody."

"Your third guard's strapped to the fence back there," Kieron adds.

"Did you hire from the local AJC?" Mike asks.

"They never gave me a call," the Stetson says to his buddy.

"Me neither."

"Guys, butt out, it's the end," Mike says to them. "Both of you have seen and heard too much to leave here alive."

Both Stetson and Ranger pull their guns and place them on the bar. Very cool, very quietly. They both start on their fresh cold beers bought by Hunter.

Mike concentrates on Yonan.

"We're gonna negotiate," Mike says. "because I'm the best. It's why you employed me."

"You lost your snipers, Mike," Bentley says, deciding to join in. He stands up with a jolt.

"Sit down, Bentley. You always say too much to my men and you know you get slapped for it."

Neither Kieron nor Hunter stop him.

"It's over." Bentley says, moving away from them. He rounds the bottom of the bar past Mike, past Yonan and stands with his father, Crouch senior.

"Sit down kid," the barman says, pulling a short body auto from under the bar and pointing it straight at him.

"As my men are always telling you, don't try and play in the adults game. You see, Bentley, I still hold all the cards."

Bentley sits down with his father.

Mike's focus is back on Yonan, and so is the automatic weapon.

"I told you. I don't do deals at gunpoint."

Mike continues to nod. The short weapon is pushed into Yonan's forehead.

"Man's asked for a deal," the barman said.

"No deal."

95 - WALKING BACK TO HOUSTON

Day 12 - Florida -1641hrs

Both Crouch senior and junior back off, with a deal being demanded next to them at gun point. Bentley has made his last smart remark.

"You're not part of my plans Mike; you never will be," Yonan says standing his ground.

Hunter ignores the action and turns to Kieron, both still seated and calm. "This little town used to be called Indian River City. The postal service is blamed with the change saying it was too long. I reckon it was because it had the word Indian in it."

"Wow, would you like another beer?" Kieron says. "I'd like to hear the rest of that story."

"Barman's busy. We'll go somewhere else in a minute," Hunter says.

Mike knows they are trying to annoy him. It won't work, he remains cool. World class poker players live dangerously on bluff, so do the two investigators;

neither of them has a weapon and their conversation is to ensure each other knows they have both worked out the old timers are also working for Mike. The obvious card was the phoney barman. Being phoney means he can't have seen the old timers here every day. The previous card was Mike's unnecessary telling them it was over and they wouldn't leave alive as they knew too much. It was an order for them to get their guns out ready and they both followed it together. The two CSCI agents expect there might be other local players. Mike is sure he is holding the winning hand but he just can't call it. Yonan has enough money to raise the pot knowing he can't be matched. At the moment the two CSCI agents are the jokers with empty pockets and lots of bluff.

"Yonan, where've you been last few days?" Hunter asks.

"New York. I took in some exhibitions and stayed out of your hair. I felt it would stir a few things."

"Sure did," Hunter says. "Mike has a pretty good double for you."

"I've got someone who can sign your signature, too, so I can completely execute your art deals. I like that word. Maybe I don't need you," Mike suggests. "Though I might keep you finger for prints."

Kieron's phone beeps. He looks at it on the table: Dwight.

"At last. Hey Mike, on the way over, we were discussing you," Kieron says reading the text. He looks up with a grin and slides his cell phone over.

"Press play," Kieron demands.

Mike won't touch it.

"Suggest you press play."

"What have you done to my daughters? You know that's a factor in you living."

Yonan leans down and presses play. He knows he won't get shot and feels they won't.

On the phone is a shaky picture of a woman being dragged down into an art gallery. It is dark, she is gagged and her hands are tied. A torch pans through the dark to the contentious May.I.See picture of Dwight. It is the main feature of the wall.

"Where is this?" Yonan asks.

"Lincoln, England, its evening there. Mike's wife, Mrs Quarrington. Conveniently she lives above her gallery," Kieron explains. "So, we have both of your daughters and your wife. We could report your chain of galleries to the police for forgeries."

"Is this the best hand you got, Mike?" Hunter asks looking around the bar.

Mike grins at all the other players, the CSCI agents still seated, the old timers yet to reveal themselves but they are ready for them.

"You're gonna be 'Walking back to Houston," Hunter says.

"I don't know that one," Kieron says.

"Means he won't even be able to afford to fly, let alone pay his guys," Hunter says looking at the barman.

"Ben!" Mike shouts. "Bring Macey up."

Kieron and Hunter both rise up from their seats. The two local old timers are up like shots, taking one step back and raising their guns.

"Yee-hah," the Felt Ranger says quietly but directly to Hunter to let him know he has played before. "Thanks for the beers, but your man here did do some employing through the local American Job Centre. I got my money up front."

"Hope you'll be leaving it to someone who spends it well," Hunter says.

"You really are an annoying chancer," the Felt Ranger says.

"You really think you can get a shot off before I take that gun off you?" Hunter asks looking straight down his barrel.

"You better have a sling-shot up your sleeve to match that mouth, boy."

The excitement has brought life to the faces of both the White Stetson and the Felt Ranger.

"Vietnam?" Hunter asks.

"You kids'll never understand what that word means."

"Soldier. If you've played poker, let me tell you you're holding the wrong hand," Hunter tells him.

"We draw the line at Macey," Kieron says. "And for you, she's too valuable for this."

She's expendable, and all the best artists are dead ones. Plus, you ain't drawing any lines.

"Oh we are. She's not for sale. Just her," Kieron says still holding it together.

"Weak spot?" Mike gloats, then he shouts again. "Bring her up!"

There is a muffled hustle under the pier but no one is on the stairs. The sound is out of everybody's sight.

"Ben!"

"We don't play with Macey. She's not a card in anyone's deck," Kieron states.

"You've played her since you started," Mike accuses.

"Never. She's never been in danger, I made sure of that," Hunter says.

"Seems you dropped the ball." Mike shouts again, "Ben!"

Bedi walks towards them from behind, able to walk the length of the pier because everyone is looking at the stairs. She has her confident swagger

"Sick man."

Mike turns.

"The drunk who could never make it to work," Mike says as she joins them. "Can you stand up? Are you sober?" He is now looking at her. "Ben! Get up here!"

The noise on the steps, reveals Mike's two daughters, Rosemary and Jill are being hustled up by Prisha, hands tied in front of them.

"Ace, King. The worst hand to hold," Hunter says. "Don't turn another card. Stop now." Whilst that is directed at Mike, Hunter shoots a look at the old timers. "Three snipers. You won't even hear the shot."

The Felt Range shakes his head, no.

"Whatever stupid game is. It over. Anoataly will never work with you again," Bedi tells him.

"Whore killer," Mike says to her past the barman with his gun on Yonan, and past both the Crouches.

"It is badge, not insult," Bedi says, getting close to him and ignoring the barman with the automatic weapon. But as she passes, she spins away from the barman. The whole force of the full 360 degree spin, connects and rams the barman's face into the bar so hard it crashes like a base drum, her right hand slides up his pulling him towards her over the bar, her arm lifting the gun arm which she bends back dislocating it as viciously as if she were eating a chicken. She catches the gun as it drops. Her face portrays death and as she winds the weapon towards the two old timers. They lower their hand guns having seen her ruthless kill-style. Hunter collects them both. The stand-off is over.

A fifty calibre bullet hits the brass pans hanging from the ceiling and goes straight through them. It leaves them chiming like bells.

"I hope that Billy from container because I show Big Dog how to use sniper rifle and he is very keen," Bedi says, rising like a phoenix from her destruction of the barman. She taps Mike on the side of his head which a bullet would hit if he was shot from the beach.

"I not go to work in Italy because he has been to Russia," she says addressing her partners and pushing her hand into Mike's face as if to remould it. The weapon in her left hand, she turns to Mike who is still bent over with her violence. He knows a kill shot means dead, and he knows she is crazy.

"He has visit Anoataly in apartment selling art from ships, and know my table of 'Whore Killer'. Like stupid man he slobber wrong story at me when I get job in Italy."

Bedi slides the gun to Kieron and hits Mike once, twice, three times to leave him breathless face down on the rail. She grabs his balls. If she lifts he goes over the rail, but she won't; that is to the sand and he would survive.

"He just hear word whore and in Italy he insult me and touch me and offer me good promotion." She leans to him bent over the railings and squeezes. "No deal."

Turning back to her partners she explains her anger.

"I should have killed him but it would have ruined job for Yonan." Squeezing hard she continues, "you remind me of worst time. My sister still there, being used, maybe by men like you; but I not whore now…"

As a final destruction, she jumps up, landing her elbow, point down, into his back at the edge of his right shoulder blade breaking it with a crack. Everyone winces.

"…not since child. He make me remember why I make table. Table is my climb out of street with blood of tens of men on me."

She jumps high again, then destroys his left shoulder blade. His cry of pain rises way above mixing with the sound of summer on the beach. Leaving him broken, Bedi vaults the bar and opens a bottle of vodka.

"Salute." She glugs it down. "Table is badge. I wish for more young women to find way out from men like him. Kill them."

His daughters are allowed to go to him but any touch or help is mortal agony. Bedi throws a beer to Hunter and looks for wine.

"It look shit wine, Philips."

"The rose," Kieron says.

She passes him the bottle and looks at the two local guys.

"Let me try hat," she demands.

"It comes in red," the Ranger hesitantly says.

Wearing the hat, she turns to Yonan. She glugs the vodka. "His daughter, her," she points to Jill, "she steal from ships. Him, Mike, have art people stealing from yard. He sell original to Anoataly, and copies, he is crook you know. We find some copy places."

"But not the Chinese man in a garage," Hunter says.

"I can find him," Yonan says.

"His wife sells from her galleries," Kieron adds, pouring the rose.

"But you in art," Bedi breathes into Yonan's face. "You know how bad deals work, yes?"

"I'll buy you that red hat," Yonan offers, then I would like to take you to dinner.

She glugs at the vodka.

"Job finished, now you make Macey famous."

"Macey gets more famous every minute," he tells her.

Oblivious of what has happened on the stairs or above, under the boardwalk, safe where she was told to work from, with the low red sun blistering through the pier's wooden structural supports, Macey paints and Ricky watches, having missed a story he could never write. But, he is not there for the story.

"You're such a natural talent," Ricky says to Macey. "You must be so pleased your work is getting known everywhere, and you can vacation when and where you like, and go home when you have to."

"Yeah, but I have to go home and face two siblings and a mother I never knew I had."

"Your best friends."

"It ain't going to go down like that. Then, I really feel I need to see the mother who brought me up, and maybe get her into some serious rehab."

Ricky looks at her, worried again.

"Macey, your mother died of an overdose. Sorry..."

The air turns cold. Macey is in distress. Ricky moves forward to hug her.

"No. You know all my life."

He lifts her chin and looks at her.

"You're wrong. I want to know all your life, and I want you to know mine."

He kisses away her tears.

POST SCRIPT

Since this book was written, the statue of J C Calhoun has been removed from the column in Marion Square in Charleston. Macey seems to have got her way. However, as the crowd of locals watching and cheering was notably small, maybe she was right in noticing the world has quite some way to go. But with that down I need to find another issue for her to pick on… that won't be hard.

……. And then there was COVID-19, and cruising was different as you will find in the next book.

DISASTROUS COVID-19 CRUISE ROMANCE

THE TEAM

Editor Jean Heard is the main presenter for the cruise port guides YouTube channel www.YouTube.com/DorisVisits and the 'Doris Visits' web site www.DorisVisits.com.

Editor David Withington runs the online cruise resource 'How To Cruise'.

Considering your **FIRST CRUISE**?

Check out my
HOW to CRUISE
Website & Blog   HowToCruise.co.uk

Finally, Thanks to my Laura Aikman, for always reading my drafts and giving honest feedback. As an actress always on your screens, she shocked many playing Sonia in the 2019 Christmas special of Gavin and Stacey.

CRUISE SHIP ART THEFT

OTHER CRUISE MYSTERIES BY THE AUTHOR

Fast paced cruise mystery thrillers

C.S.C.I.

CRUISE SHIP CRIME INVESTIGATORS

Cruise Ship Heist

Cruise Ship Serial Killer

Cruise Ship Laundry

Cruise Ship Art Theft

Disastrous Covid-19 Cruise Romance

(Cruise Ship) Blood Diamonds

They can all be read as stand-alone stories, but the growth of the agency and character development are appreciated by reading in order or going back to see how the story got where it is. Enjoy.

EXCITING CRUISE MYSTERY THRILLERS
ENJOY THE CRUISE ANYWHERE THE BOOK TAKES YOU

CRUISE ACCURATE NOVELS FROM DORIS VISITS
THE PEOPLE WHO KNOW THE SHIP ABOVE AND BELOW DECKS

Other books not in the series, but from the author.

For quizzers and new cruisers or those who always wondered, our compendium of terms is out.

ABC of Cruise Terms

This is also an ICON Pictures movie, FREIGHT.

Human Freight

ALL BOOKS AVAILABLE ON AMAZON

Printed in Great Britain
by Amazon